THE
SEDUCTION
OF SISTER
SKAGUAY

A novel by Bill Miles

Acknowledgements

Sincere thanks go out to readers Jerry Daugherty, Clifford Groh, Esq., Mike Haggerty, Peter Meinke, Margaret Ann Morse, Barbara Milles Robinson, Dr. Jeff Robinson, Julie Rogers, the late Patricia Roppel, Lee Stoops, and Catherine Wallace. Over the years, they have sacrificed much to improve my work.

Ken Erickson and Thomas E. Harvey have battled overwhelming odds to teach me about electronic publishing. I only hope our friendship has remained throughout their efforts.

Sterling Watson, writer, teacher and friend, has been there for me for fifteen years. Without him, none of this would have been possible.

Writers' residencies–the Virginia Center for the Creative Arts, the Jentel Artist Residency Program, and the Kimmel, Harding, Nelson Center for the Arts–have generously provided time, space and freedom to work the craft. Special thanks to The Kerouac Project for honoring me with a three-month residency in College Park, Florida.

Contents

1. A Fair Divvy

The *Al-Ki* chugged into the Skaguay wharf and sounded five short, searing whistles. After five days aboard the steamship, the throng of fortune-hunting stampeders let out with a universal huzzah, but before the gangplank could be lowered, two broke into a mighty brawl. A bloody tooth struck Sister Margaret Mary Angelorum and stuck, momentarily, before trailing a sluglike line of pink slime down the nun's starched, white chestpiece. A second nun bent to retrieve the tooth. Sister Angelorum said, "Leave it be, Sister Bernadette. It's nothing you can cure or convert."

The fighters clutched, toppled over and rolled toward the nuns. Sister Angelorum, a short woman but as stout and sturdy as a sea chest, stepped forward, fearless in the defense of her much younger colleague. The other passengers ignored the nuns and followed the brawling men.

"I got a dollar on John Stewart."

"Covered!"

"Anyone else?"

"I'll take four bits on the Swede."

"Down."

"The jewels, John. Go for the family jewels!"

John Stewart, a clean-shaven youth but for his oiled moustache, freed an arm and jammed a thumb into the Swede's eye. Sister Angelorum winced at the squish. The Swede bellowed like a sow giving birth. Harriet Pullen, a widow lady with the countenance of a wood stove and the only other woman aboard the *Al-Ki*, pushed through the crowd. Angelorum knew the plump dumpling was not one to be trifled with. The mother of four, she was coming north to begin a new life. In time, she planned to send for her children.

"Sisters," the Widow Pullen said, "you shouldn't watch this." She shepherded the nuns toward the steamer's stern.

"But–" Young Sister Bernadette tried to protest. Angelorum tut-tutted her just as John Stewart's boot stomped the Swede's hand, causing a primal scream shriller than the *Al-Ki's* whistle.

The Swede fought back from the stomping and the gouging. One-handed, he gripped John Stewart by the belt and drove his head into Stewart's nose causing an explosion of bloody mist. In a hell-whoop move, he hauled John Stewart to the gunwale and dumped him overboard. The bettors rushed to the rails and laughed as Stewart floundered.

Angelorum made the sign-of-the-cross. "We have arrived at the chosen land."

The ship's bell clanged, officially announcing her arrival in Skaguay. The stampeders loosed another rollicking cheer. So great was their enthusiasm, had they been forced to follow John Stewart into the milky waters of Skaguay Bay, they would have happily chosen to swim to the Klondyke.

*

Never again would Sister Bernadette stand by and allow such an outrage to occur. Not only would she and Sister Angel cleanse Alaska's fallen doves, they would right any other wrongs in their path. Joan of Arc would fight no more fiercely. They were none other than Good Shepherd Sisters of St. Paul, Minnesota, and would make their mark in the hooligan land as much as any stampeder. Their riches would be measured in souls, not nuggets.

The ship's captain stood atop a crate marked FRESH EGGS. He raised a voice enhancer to a beard as unkempt as any of his passengers and croaked, "Gents, you have reached the gates of heaven. A fair divvy awaits you all. This is the end of the line. Good luck and Godspeed to you all. We depart for Seattle in four hours."

Sister Angel smashed a fist into her open palm. "This way, Bernadette." She bee-lined for the captain, shouldering larger men from her path.

Bernadette knew that Skaguay was not the end of the line . . . most certainly not the end of the line. Before leaving Minnesota, Mother Francine had provided thirty-two dollar tickets for steerage passage from Seattle, Washington to Dyea, District of Alaska, not Skaguay. She fished into her satchel for the receipt.

"Captain," Angel said, her considerable frame being jarred by the press of passengers already alighting, "there is some mistake. We've paid for transport to Dyea."

"Dyea ain't not a problem. It's only ten miles up the trail, a trail trodden smooth as a baby's be–"

"Sir!" Sister Bernadette pushed the receipt toward him, her voice flush with chastening. "We are paid-in-full to Dyea and expect this boat to take us there."

He accepted the paper, but didn't so much as glance at it.

Angel patted the young nun's outstretched arm. The pat of caution was one she'd used many times since they'd first met. Sister Angelorum pointed to a line on the receipt. "Sister Bernadette is quite right, Captain. Dyea. It says right there . . . Dyea."

"Well, you can go to Dyea if you choose. The *Al-Ki* ain't. We're way behind schedule with hundreds more passengers waiting back in Seattle."

"Captain, how do you expect us to get our goods up to Dyea?"

"Like I said, Dyea ain't a problem a-tall. Judas Priest, there are packers all over town." The Captain pressed the voice enhancer to his mouth and hollered instructions to shoremen on the wharf. He was clearly anxious to see to his business. Angel rested her hand on the voice enhancer.

"Ladies, ladies," he said, "do those bonnets of yours impede my words? There's a trail to Dyea as beat down as a cobblestone road." He waved the voice enhancer for space. "These stampeders are the ones with problems. Getting themselves out of Skaguay may be a problem, and if they're able to do that, getting over the pass may be a problem, and if they do that, getting up the Yukon River may be a problem. The Klondyke is 600 miles from here. So I say again, Dyea ain't no problem. Now, good day to you."

"Sir!" Even though the man was bereft of manners, Sister Bernadette would not be brushed off like a common housefly. "You mentioned a pass. Is Dyea over a pass?"

He spat on the deck. "No, Ma'am. Just a mild trail."

"And our goods? Our other medicinals?" Sister Bernadette held up her satchel.

"Packers consider a trek to Dyea a walk in the sun. You'll not face any devilment. You a nurse?"

"No, Sir, but I am, nonetheless, a trained medical dispenser."

"No nevermind to me. A cheechacko is a cheechacko."

Angel whispered, "That means *newcomer.*"

The Captain wadded up the travel receipt and tossed it overboard. "Ladies, I got no more time to waste on you. See one of Soapy Smith's boys in camp for packers. Tell him Captain Baker, Captain Harley Baker, sent you and you'll not have a problem."

The Seduction of Sister Skaguay

Sister Bernadette noted his name and would report his impudence at the first opportunity. Apparently, the man had assumed from their religious garb that they were tenderfeet to be easily ignored. He'd soon learn.

*

Skaguay was cradled in the windgap of steep mountains that had been brushed with stands of fir, pine and spruce as luxurious as any in Minnesota or Washington. Above tree line, sharp, bare rock outcrops angled upward to peaks–not especially high peaks, no more than six-thousand feet–with the mountain tips frothed in scud as thick as tapioca. Eagles flew vast circles between the ranges, unconcerned with the hurry-scurry below.

Across the tideland, a single street was rutted with parallel wagon tracks. Workers along walkway boards were bent under loads of lumber on their shoulders or bulging packs strapped to their backs. Hammers pounded out a syncopatic rhythm creating a construction orchestra in full play. A calico cat struck out across the boggy street only to get itself stuck in the quagmire and rolled over by the wheel of a mule-drawn cart. The calico never surfaced. Men cooked on iron stoves, their holstered pistols on hooks next to dangling spatulas, rifles at rest against oven doors.

Wrestling with a Gladstone, Angel was struck by the vagabond army on the tide-flat, hundreds of ne'er-do-wells living in seeming disarray. Fly tents were scattered hither and thither among flimsy lawn tents and larger wedge tents. Grey, brown, dirty white. Cotton, duck, drill, canvas. A few with smokestacks and rain flies. Most so fragile-looking as to be unable to withstand a sneeze. Shanties, shacks and all manner of stands and sheds stood like mismatched boxes among the tents. Horses and mules–she even saw a pair of llamas–were tethered to stakes or roamed at will. Wild dogs from mutt to malamute harassed animals unable to give chase. A muleskinner cussed his span of mules, their hind hooves buried to the hocks in the tideland muck. Not a woman was to be seen.

Shoreward, roped off corrals protected mountains of merchandise, bales of hay and more mules. One puncher tried to move a pair of hitched oxen. He began with the whip. The animals held fast. He cursed, withdrew a rifle from its sock and bludgeoned their hindquarters.

"God in heaven," Angel said, and blessed herself again. "They are savages."

*

On a three-day roister, Sven Lazlo stumbled toward one of the flimsy tide-flat huts, his spine curved into an outhouse moon from three decades stooped over sluiceways. Chew-drool stained his yellowed whiskers. His boots sunk into the muck as if he were wading through porridge. The hut–nothing more than three walls, a tin rain roof and a single counter with neat stacks of maps–bore a hand-scrawled sign:

KLONDYKE MAPPAGE
50c
pay durt garanteed

Over the price, a horseshoe hung in the breeze from a moose hide thong.

Lazlo fell across the shelf, scattering one stack of maps. "Them things is shit paper."

"Scram, you old sot." Portland Pete, the proprietor, was a wizened drunk himself. His bones ground hollow as he bent to retrieve the maps.

"Sotted I am," Lazlo said, "but I got six bits to the pan at Fortymile. Honest prospecting." His frothy spittle sprayed Pete's face. "You wouldn't know a prospect hole from a whore's hole, you chiseling thimble-rigger. You ain't ever been inside nothing but your momma's legs."

Pete wiped his face, drew his thumb-buster and aimed it at Lazlo's chest.

Frank Reid, adjusting his surveyor's compass, heard the dust-up. "Goddammit it all to hell." He smacked his Stetson against his thigh. Every time another boatload of fortune-hunters arrived, Reid thought, the town erupted. As predictable as morning sunrise.

Reid slogged over to the shack and grabbed the barrel of Pete's pistol, forcing it toward the ground. "Pete, lay back, goddammit. The old guy's just whiskeyed up. Don't deserve to get shot."

Pete tried to pull the gun from Reid's hand. "Let go, Frank."

Reid held like a bench vise.

Lazlo swept his arm across the shelf, dooming another stack of maps to the muck.

Reid shouted to Lazlo, "Old man, stop!"

Pete again tried to jerk the pistol from Reid's grip.

Reid said, "Pete, you quit, too. I got work to do."

11

Lazlo reached up to the dangling horseshoe and snatched it from the nail. He swung it down so wildly Reid had to duck. Then buried the calkin in Pete's temple. Pete smiled as if he'd just downed a jawbone drink, released the pistol and toppled over the shelf, eyes wide open. Blood trickled from the gash and ran down his neck. He couldn't have been more dead.

"Jesus Christ!" Reid backhanded Lazlo with the butt of Pete's pistol. The old man crumbled.

Reid knew he'd just bungled things. He had no love for Pete or the rest of the town's shakedown boys, but now he was guilty as sin for messing up a spat between an unarmed drunk and a harmless old swindler. "Son-of-a-bitch!"

"You handled that well, Frank." The voice behind Reid was satin and syrup, as cocky and smug as the whip hand in a poker game. Soapy. Of course it was Soapy. Of all people, it *had* to be him. Here to meet the *Al-Ki* and the stampeders. Goddammit it all to hell. Together, they stared at Portland Pete and the horseshoe sticking from his temple.

Soapy felt Pete's neck for a pulse. With a silk handkerchief, he slowly and deliberately wiped his fingers clean of blood, a smirk on his face. He hooked his hand through Pete's belt and lowered the old-timer to the wet sand. "No sense getting blood on what good maps haven't been soiled."

"Nor on them shiny brogans of yours." Reid pointed to the blood seeping toward Soapy's shoes. Brogans at tideland, Reid thought. What the hell was the man thinking? Reid answered his own question: Soapy was thinking about his standing among the gathering crowd. He'd make prime use of Frank's malapropos. "You're just full of pity."

"Frank, *you* were here, I wasn't."

"Goddamn."

"A body could make a case that you abetted the crime."

"Doubtful," Reid said. "Fact is, I should have shot that flim-flam booster of yours myself."

Soapy said, "There's no place for vigilantism in Skaguay. It won't be tolerated."

"Stow it," Reid said. The man had no end of gall. He was having Reid on. Soapy Smith's tongue was as slick as any gasbag lawyer's.

"Lazlo will stand trial before summer runs it course," Soapy announced. "Don't you agree, Frank?"

What could he say? "No doubt."

Soapy waved to a pair of literers. "Will you boys be so kind as to haul poor Pete to Cat Alley for the time. Lazlo goes to the sheriff. The sheriff," he repeated, "not the marshal. The rest of you can get back to work. This show's over."

"Someone put you in charge?" Reid asked.

"Everyone on the beach saw how well you handled things." Soapy leaned to Reid. "If you make a stink, you'll look poorly in this camp. This is 1897, Skaguay, Alaska District, no longer your wild west, Frank. We won't abide lawlessness."

Reid knew that Soapy cared about lawlessness as much as a barkeep cared about beer slops. The literers dragged Pete's body up the beach, his boots leaving perfect furrows in the tidal mud.

*

Sister Angel's job, explained so carefully by Mother Francine back in Minnesota, was to guide the young dynamo. *Dynamo.* Reverend Mother's own choice of words. The vigor of Bernadette's youth combined with Angel's experience would make a formidable combination. They would purify the demimondes of the Alaska District or die trying.

Angel had been the spiritual advisor to Bernadette since she'd arrived as a novice six years back. Over the years, Angel counseled Bernadette that, 'The Lord will provide, and if He doesn't, you're quite capable.' When Mother Francine announced their appointment to the Alaska mission, Bernadette said there could be no greater manifestation of their faith–nor a more glorious one–than saving the Lord's abandoned damsels in such a remote region. Angel might be the guide along the spiritual path, but it would be Sister Bernadette who would bear the weight of the mission.

Before the two set off for the mission, Mother Francine had confided a doubt to Angel about Bernadette. Did Sister Bernadette have the true calling . . . true enough to some day lead the Good Shepherd Sisters? She was intelligent, devout, steadfast and one to whom the Good Lord had graced with natural beauty. There was no questioning her zeal–she had publicly vowed to aid anyone in distress at any time–but so many of the young sisters felt the calling only to learn they'd misheard the message. Angel had been asked to answer these questions, and, if answered in the positive, go on to mold Bernadette into one of the Lord's true gems.

*

13

The Seduction of Sister Skaguay

The stampeders made their way down the gangplank like boys set free from school for summer vacation. Sister Bernadette said, "Angel, do you feel strong enough to begin our new life?"

During the voyage, Angel's seasickness had kept her below deck in their sleeping space, lying across stowed steamer trunks snuggled into Bernadette's great cloak. She saw neither eagles nor orcas; she never inhaled the crisp air with its deep pine scents. Prone to the vomits as she was, she ate nothing. With a wan smile, she even refused tea.

The deck over their sleeping space had been crammed to the scuppers with livestock: thirty horses, a dozen head of cattle and as many sheep. When a crate of turkeys burst, the gobblers scampered about the deck under the bellies of the horses, pecking at their hocks. The horses stomped, and relieved themselves. Their odoriferous gifts ran down the *Al-Ki's* planking and into stowage. "God's will," Angel would say, casting her eyes heavenward, smiling weakly.

Throughout the voyage, they never shed their habits. Privately called Iron Maidens, the garb was fashioned from coarse brown sackcloth knotted at their waists with a rosary of sisal rope. Starched, white wimples covered their heads. Snug linen bands ran across their foreheads, over their ears and under their chins. Tight, stiff collars ringed their necks. Sackcloth capes draped their shoulders. Bernadette longed to give Angel relief from the constrictions of the habit, but public discourse in steerage prevented such. She knew her mentor's discomfort had to have been fierce.

Truly, Angel possessed the will of a Trappist Monk. She fretted about her ample body and claimed it took after her blacksmith father. Bernadette tried to extol the virtues of short arms and a solid torso.

"They exist solely to serve the Lord," Angel said.

During most of the five-day voyage, Bernadette had sat at Angel's side, cooling her brow and grooming her fingernails. Bernadette's mother had been convinced that a girl was first judged by the condition of her nails and a boy by the shine of his boots. Toward those ends, at the appropriate age, each brother received a shoe polisher and blackening. The girls had been given a nail chamois, scissors and file.

"Angel," she now whispered, "if you prefer to alight later, we can rest a spell longer. The rude captain can hardly set sail with us still aboard."

Angel wrapped an arm around the young nun. "It's time." From one of the many folds of her habit, she produced a gilded crucifix.

14

She waited until the last stampeder had cleared the gangplank, then stepped out and elevated the crucifix. Bernadette fell in step behind her, her black satchel in one hand and rifle case in the other. Angel sang, "*Tantum ergo, sacramentum* . . . " They raised their chins heavenward and stepped cautiously down the gangplank, soldiers marching into battle.

As if it were Jesus Christ himself descending, every miner, merchant, carpenter, drover and shoreman, paused to take in the short procession. Then snorted, and returned to work.

*

A deckhand from the *Al-Ki* dragged John Stewart ashore. Two-Chew Calderone, one arm flung over a stobbing post, the other hand scratching an Adam's Apple as pointed as an arrow, said to himself, "The sun is shining on me today." He knew a rube when he saw one. This one was so beaten, it was a double blessing. He spit in his hand and clapped once. "I'll take him from here, pard," he said, and pushed away the deckhand. To Stewart, he said, "You and me is going to be close as two toes in a sock." He hauled the stampeder toward the Reliable Packers' uptide shack. Stewart, his head lolling left and right, did little more than grunt.

Calderone figured the man to be senseless for another two or three minutes. Plenty of time. He knelt, and fumbled into his vest pocket for a vial. "What's your name, pilgrim?"

"John. John Stewart."

"Stick out your tongue, John Stewart. I got something to bring you around."

Stewart obliged. Calderone dabbed his tongue with a potion; Stewart winced like he just tasted kerosene. Calderone set a dip of snuff behind his own lip and waited. When Stewart's eyes went glossy, Calderone rolled the man to his back and slipped his billbook from its pocket.

"Hold there!"

Two-Chew muttered, "By dog!" He braced. "Jesus Christ in hell!" A woman, some kind of religious woman, stalked toward him carrying a rifle case! Even wrapped in all the religious garb, he saw that she had no equal in Skaguay. In her wake was a second religious plug as wide as John L. Sullivan who looked able to snap logs with her bare hands.

"Stop," the beauty said. "Hold, I say."

Two-Chew raised his arms as if he were about to be arrested. Where the hell did they come from? The steamer, of course. Jesus Christ! Time for

15

the switch. "Help me out here," he cried. "This man's been wailed so mightily he's barely within reason."

"I can see that," Sister Bernadette said.

"You one of them holy people?"

"Sister Bernadette of the Good Shepherd Sisters of St. Paul, Minnesota. My companion is Sister Margaret Mary Angelorum. We saw what you did."

"What I did?" He stood to face the nuns, arms akimbo, a teacher berating a class of curmudgeons. "All I did was tote his pounded ass out of the water. Saved his life, I did."

"And pilfered his billbook."

Calderone had been quick as a blink. How could anyone have spotted the move? "Shame on you," he said, and added, "one of God's women, no less. Spouting preachments and barely off the boat. Maybe you're not what you're made up to be . . . maybe you're ladies of ill repute."

"Sir!"

A pair of muleskinners paused, something Two-Chew didn't need. Why the hell were these women foisting themselves into his business?

The beauty said, "Return the man's billbook this instant."

"I didn't cop nothing." He removed the billbook from his pocket, made a show of dusting it off. "It fell when I was hauling him from the water."

"It did no such thing. You deliberately filched it. In broad daylight, I might add."

"Well, goddamn to you, pilgrim. Who the hell–"

"Sir!"

John Stewart rolled onto his stomach, gagged.

"I'm Two-Chew Calderone. Ask anyone in camp about me."

"You robbed this man."

"Not on your life. I saved his niggardly self."

"How did his billbook come to be in the back of your britches? Larceny is larceny, Mister Calderone."

"Not his billbook at all. It's my very own. Besides, your tone is right unfriendly, lady." He snarled at the muleskinners and they moved off, only to be replaced by a handful of curious stampeders from the *Al-Ki*.

"I so meant it that way."

"You need friends in this land. All you can get."

"The Lord is my friend." Angel nudged Bernadette.

Calderone said, "Your fat pard doesn't think so."

"Mind your foul tongue, Mister Two-Chew Calderone."

*

Soapy angled across the tide flat toward the kerfuffle, shaking his head at the constant dose of distress that was his life. Some days, he longed to have a trusty dog by his side rather than his band of merry men. Such was not his lot. "Good day, Sisters. What seems to be the problem?" He tipped his parson's hat and brushed a strand of red hair from his lapel. For a moment, he studied his fingernails. This time, the problem was Two-Chew and a pair of nuns, of all people! He could have almost predicted it would be Two-Chew. The man didn't have the sense God gave a clump of dirt.

The young nun had been talking and he'd not been attentive. ". . . Mister Calderone reached into this unfortunate's pocket and lifted his billbook."

"Hold on, lady," Calderone said. "I lifted nothing. It fell out and I picked it up."

"Let her finish, Two." To the nuns, he said, "Excuse my poor manners. I'm Colonel Jefferson Smith. I believe I can resolve this matter." He knelt to John Stewart, shook the man's shoulders, spoke to the onlookers. "He's had a bad go of things. Take him up and have Lank look him over. Put it on my pad." To the nuns, "Sisters, on behalf of Skaguay and the entire District of Alaska, welcome to our camp. Sadly, this is not a proper greeting." To Two-Chew, he said, "Be on your way. I'll take care of this."

"But, Boss–"

Soapy raised an index finger. "We'll talk later."

"But–"

"Later."

*

The Colonel was quite dapper in waistcoat, vest and creased woolen britches. He wore a starched linen collar over a fresh-pressed chambray shirt and an olive-hued four-in-hand. His brogans had been shined before he came upon the tideland and his black beard had been freshly razored. His pronunciation marked him as a southern gentleman. Alert, but non-plussed by Calderone's indecencies.

Sister Bernadette tumbled out their story: their orders to Dyea, the rude Captain, the fisticuffs. The Colonel listened, mannerly and without interruption.

17

The Seduction of Sister Skaguay

When she'd concluded, he said, "At times, if a steamer captain has little or no cargo and only a few passengers, he simply cancels the Dyea stop. This is August, sisters. Very little traffic going south. Now, if I may be so bold as to inquire, I'm curious to understand your reason for coming into the Alaska District?"

Angel stepped forward. "We are here to cleanse the soiled doves. Such is just one of the missionary callings of the Good Shepherd Sisters."

"Good Shepherd Sisters." He took in Sister Bernadette's black satchel and rifle case. "You're nurses?" Then lightly added, "Or bank robbers?"

"We are specially-trained medical instruments of the Lord. Fully competent to dispense education and certain medicinals to the fallen."

"Education and medicinals? Wonderful. Skaguay now welcomes you with open arms."

"We need to get to Dyea first. That's the charge from Mother Francine, our Abbess."

The Colonel scanned the tideland. "A man of the cloth, one Reverend Charles Bowers, is supervising a shipment to Dyea as we speak. " He waved a finger at a boy. The boy scampered off. "He'll be able to direct you to a trustworthy transit operation."

"A *reverend*?"

"In Alaska, we all wear many hats." He pointed to Bernadette's rifle case. "A long gun?"

"My father's," she said. "It's an 1892 Winchester .44-40. Lever action, twenty-inch barrel. Six pounds. Quite ample for anything up to a buck. Father fully trained me in the use of rifle, shotgun and pistol, as well as all farming implements."

"He sounds to be a dedicated and thorough parent."

"*May he rest in peace*," Bernadette said. The nuns blessed themselves. "I trust in the Lord that I should not encounter anything larger."

"Sisters, permit me to give you a brief topography lesson. You'll likely opt to make your headquarters in Skaguay, not Dyea. It's a much friendlier camp. Both vie for the stampeders' business. In time, far more people will come through Skaguay. The Chilkoot Trail out of Dyea is much higher, barely passable by man, certainly not conducive to the sled. The White Pass, from Skaguay, is lower and allows access for horse, sled, wagon, and pack train. Without a doubt, this camp will be the commercial center of the Alaska District," he said. "However, I must warn you, we have a small share of charlatans. Earlier today, I had a dust-up with that one." He pointed to Frank Reid who'd recommenced his surveying. "Take care with whom you associate. Watch your belongings at all times."

"We've been told this is a difficult land."

"It is that, Sister. It seems, however, you've come prepared. Ammunition in the satchel?"

"Medicinals for the doves."

"Excellent," he said. "I have to excuse myself now. Reverend Bowers will be here shortly." He reached to shake Angel's gloved hand, brushed his lips courtly to it. He took Bernadette's hand and repeated the gesture. When he released her hand, she found shining like a tiny star in the center of her black mitten a gold nugget.

"Heavenly days," Angel said, staring into Bernadette's palm. "Is that . . . ?"

The Colonel ignored Angelorum. "Gold for a goddess," he said to Bernadette. "And since you are the first of your kind to visit our fair camp and have not deigned to give me your name, I'll call you Sister Skaguay."

Bernadette's throat blocked as surely as if a noose had been tied around it. No air in or out. She tried to swallow. She'd only seen pictures of nuggets. This one was so much more brilliant, as if it had been polished with a nail chamois. Almost crystalline. Sparkling slashes of light flashed as she turned it round and round. Good Lord in heaven, a nugget! She slipped it into a tiny pocket within the inner folds of her Iron Maiden alongside her most prized relic of St. Jude. She placed a hand over her heart. A nugget!

2. Of Gum Boots and Snow Excluders

"Reverend Charles Bowers at your service, Sisters. I am pleased to assist fellow laborers of the Lord." He extended a hand to help Sister Bernadette from the tide flat onto the boardwalk. A kindly man if ever there was one, she thought. A man of genuine beneficence. His face exuded piety, even though his gray jacket marked him as a member of a faith other than the true one. His religious collar, yellowed and frayed, was an embarrassment to the calling. His bushy gray muttonchops were so wooly, they appeared as if still attached to the lamb. Bernadette's guard was up, but certainly a fellow missionary was a welcomed encounter.

The center of town was being constructed in front of the nun's eyes. Carpenters' banging echoed so loudly that her ears throbbed, even through the armor of her wimple. In the street, horses drew carts piled high with stampeders' gear, lumber, and household furnishings. All the while, a team of malamutes slept in the mud, deaf to the noise, tails curled around their twitching noses.

The Pack Train Beanery and three saloons, The Mint, The Bank and The Mascotte, lined one side of the street. Clancy's Music Hall, Skaguay's lone single two-story building, dominated the other. The Klondyke Mercantile and a telegraph office were the only other fully-completed wooden structures.

"The street is called Broadway?" asked Bernadette.

"Named with a firm tongue in cheek, I presume," Bowers replied.

Bernadette nodded agreement. "To what faith are you called, Reverend?"

"Are you familiar with the Maritime Provinces in Canada, Sister?"

"I fear not."

"Then you probably do not know of the Newfoundland Calvinists."

A follower of John Calvin! Almost pagan! "No, Sir. I fear not."

He gave her a pleased smile and said, "We're a small band of northeastern missionaries. Terribly understaffed."

"Such is the Achilles heel of the Lord's forces."

Humbly, he bowed again. "I'm afraid you're right."

Even though the man was barely a Christian, Bernadette was warmed to have made a friend. "My companion and I desperately need to secure assistance in getting some of our goods to Dyea. Our orders are to establish an outpost in Dyea first, then return to Skaguay for a more permanent mission."

"You've got to be careful in this town. It's infested with vermin who'd just as soon skin you as speak to you."

Bernadette explained the encounter with Two-Chew Calderone and his lack of Christian comportment. "The man should be reported to the authorities."

"Calderone," he repeated, and fondled a brown chin mole the size and shape of kidney bean. "I regularly attempt to bring him into the fold. Alas! Seeds sown on barren ground. Insofar as transporting your goods, however, you'd do best to take your trade to Reliable Packers." He pointed to a tent erected adjacent to the telegraph office.

"I can't thank you enough."

"Just a prayer, Sister. Just a prayer." Reverend Bowers bowed and offered a helpful arm. Together, they stepped into the quagmire.

At Reliable, the reverend introduced the sisters to a gartered clerk and left them to strike an accord. The clerk charged the outrageous sum of seventy-five cents per pound to move their goods, full payment in advance. Bernadette was shocked but possessed of few options. Angel remained strangely quiet during the negotiations. The difficulties of the voyage still plagued her.

On the boardwalk, Reverend Bowers appeared again. "Sisters, did your transaction go well?"

"Yes, Reverend, they did. We concluded our business cordially. We leave in the morning on a mule train with a portion of our goods. Some of our belongings will be placed in storage and await our return. A packer will find us this evening to help us in separating our goods. The arrangements were amicable, but it's clear the Lord does not spare the coffers in the Alaska District."

"I presume you travel on a limited budget."

"We have some money, but Sister Angel and I plan to beg alms when they run out. I'm sure you're familiar with that part of the calling." She made him blush, bless his heart. Likely he, too, was not heeled well. Even though he was not of the true church, he seemed a decent sort. She would heed Colonel Smith's advice and stand her guard relentlessly.

Reverend Bowers led them to the telegraph office, a shack of bright new pine boards. There was something pure and honest about newly-cut lumber. Its scent alone was heavenly. The shack must have been built within the past month; the wood still retained its forest sap. At that moment, Colonel Smith happened from the office.

Sister Angelorum explained the arrangements to the Colonel.

Colonel Smith said, "A mule train? The Dyea trail is not difficult, but a mule train is no way for two women of God to travel."

He stared into Bernadette's eyes with a gaze as penetrating as a beam of sunshine. Unnerved somewhat, she said, "I assure you, Colonel, Sister Margaret Mary and I are quite capable. I am from stout Midwest stock. I can plant a field, prune an orchard, take down game and handle a team of horses. Sister Angel is the lone female from a family of eight siblings. We were carefully chosen for this assignment."

He took her hand in his again. For a man in a gruff frontier town, his fingers felt like silk. She sensed tracings of skin balm or pomatum. In a polished way, the Colonel reminded her of her father, an upright man, strong of character and unflinching in his beliefs. It had often been said she received her directness from him.

The Colonel said, "Sister, I meant no disrespect. Would it not ease your burden to travel with a group of dry-goods' drummers? I know of a caravan leaving tomorrow, men traveling with a sourdough teamster and an ox cart. Far more accommodating to fine ladies of your stature."

How could they say no? Why would they want to? "And you could arrange this, Colonel, at no additional cost?"

He bowed. "The pleasure would be mine."

The *Al-Ki* sounded three short blasts. The Colonel said, "She sails within hours."

*

As the sun started to sink, another side to the camp awoke. Music rang out from the saloons into the crisp air. A hussy, the first woman to appear to the nuns, danced along a hitching rail in front of The Mascotte. Raucous laughter bounced into the street from the Pack Train and The Bank. An occasional gunshot echoed between the mountain ranges. The nuns ignored the revelry and joined other travelers on the wharf, unrolled their sleep bags and knelt for the evening rosary. The headwaters of Lynn Canal lapped easily against the wharf's pilings, a gentle backsound to their prayerful intonations.

During the Sorrowful Mysteries, a boy with golden locks to his shoulders and skin whiter than milk from a teat, came to call. He introduced himself as Jimmy Fresh, a packer, and bid them down to the tidelands where he paced off their cache. "For the trek up to Dyea, k-k-keep only w-w-what you c-c-carry in a packsack. No m-m-more than a quarter of your own weight. Be b-b-back in an hour." The guttersnipe, sixteen at best, no more belonged in these wild parts than did any other child. Bernadette thought to reprimand him, but feared Angel's admonition.

After repacking their belongings, Angel and Bernadette had their first set-to since leaving Minnesota. Angel thought it best to wear their shiny new rubber boots–called Yukon gum boots at their Seattle outfitters–because the sisters had seen little more than tidal mud since their arrival. Bernadette argued that they were setting forth on a ten-mile trek, that they should dress more for warmth and rugged terrain. Their snow excluders would give them the best footing. "Sister," Bernadette said rather sternly, "this is the Alaska District."

"Yes, Sister," Angel said, not relenting, "I know. But see the men on the beach, the men walking up to town. Most are shod in gum boots."

Their spat waxed and waned like a tug-of-war. In time, Bernadette prevailed. They packed away the gum boots and slid into the snow excluders.

For her personal packsack, Angel chose a small pouch of privacy goods and the Holy Bible. Bernadette carried her treasured books, *Quo Vadis* and *Joan of Arc,* plus her Winchester. She would not allow her father's gift from her sight.

The blond-haired boy returned with three scrawny cohorts. None appeared able to carry anything bigger than a highback chair. However, they made no waste as they piled the nuns' goods onto two wooden sledges and necked off. One sledge for the local storage, a smaller one for the trail.

"S-s-see you in Dyea," the boy said.

Bernadette waved, and paused to wonder what the ten miles to Dyea would hold. They might be in the remote North country and that much closer to heaven, but their missionary road could be strewn with rocks. As they recommenced the rosary, adjacent men fingered their pipe bowls and twisted their handlebars, most appearing as if they had never seen sisters at prayer.

Bernadette spoke sharply to them. "Gentlemen, I hope we aren't disturbing you."

"Sorry, ladies," one said. "We're a long way from home. I guess we lost our ear for prayer words." Without further ado, the speaker shooed the men back to their own business. "You might say one for us wayfarers," he said. "Lord knows we need it."

After their prayers, they settled into their sleep bags. Bernadette was in that twilight space, not sure if she was awake or dreaming. Angel touched her hand and said, "Sister Bernadette, our lot in life is not as difficult as that of Widow Pullen."

"What makes you think of that now?"

"She is completely alone, her four babies back in Washington. We have each other, and the hand of the Lord to guide us."

"The woman is starting to make a place for her children in this new land."

"Nevertheless, she is quite alone." Her voice thrummed with concern.

"Yes, Sister," Bernadette said, wondering what could possibly be going through her mentor's thoughts.

As if she were reading Bernadette's mind, Angel said, "You've never told me how you came to the convent."

Curious, Bernadette thought.

"Do you wish to speak of it?" she asked.

"Some day, perhaps."

"By all that's holy, I'd take it to my grave."

*

"Here comes the one Colonel Smith warned us about," Bernadette said. Her hand went inside her habit to the relic of St. Jude and the gold nugget. Frank Reid stepped over and around the prone bodies of the argonauts, most burrowed into their sleep bags and paying him no mind.

"'Evening, Sisters."

"Sir," Angel said, neither cordially nor coldly.

Bernadette's choice would have been to greet him with silence. There was simply no reason to risk dialog with a charlatan. He did not so much as remove his Stetson, a beaten down old sog of a hat as full as a pin cushion with fishing flies.

"My name's Frank Reid. I heard on the flats you were out here."

Bernadette felt obliged to speak. The man needed to know point blank that they were onto him and would brook no foolishness. "And what are your intentions?"

Mister Reid recoiled, the tone of Bernadette's voice signaling her alertness.

"Well . . . Ma'ams . . . I . . . "

"We are aware of your reputation, Mister Reid. We'd hardly touched ground when we were warned away from you. Let me tell you, we are single-minded of purpose and will not be easily misled." Bernadette felt Angel's jab and decided to be still. The message had been delivered.

Mister Reid hitched up his denims, britches patched and repatched like a common hobo. A pistol drooped lazily in its flap-holster. He stank of day old–week old?–fish. His gum boots were punctured with holes and he was badly in need of a razor, his face streaked in beach muck and axle grease. His handlebar moustache had been waxed so stiffly, it would support Christmas tree ornaments.

He said, "My reputation?"

"Mister Reid," Angel said, her tone kindly, "we wish to go forward with our mission without incident. Perhaps you could state your business . . . ?" She left the question hanging.

Mister Reid was clearly flummoxed. He coughed, shuffled his feet. He knew he'd met his match.

"I . . . I have a cabin. Up from the water's edge. Dry land, as much as it ever dries out here. It would be more comfortable–and private–than this wharf."

Bernadette could not hold back. "What are you suggesting, Sir?"

The nudge.

"Just for you to get shut of the elements. No telling if it will rain or snow, but you can bet on one or t'other."

Bernadette scowled. "And our goods?"

Angel looked askance at the young nun. They both knew their goods were off and safe with the packers. "Mister Reid, thank you, but we decline. We've been told to keep close watch on our belongings. Such is what we shall do."

"I'll look after your gear, Ma'am. You could rest easy and warm under a roof."

"Thank you, but you have my final word."

Angel set her jaw. If the man caused a ruckus, she was sure some of their fellow travelers would come to their aid.

"Yes, Ma'am," he said. "In that case, I'll say good night and wish you luck on your Dyea nursing venture."

Somehow, he'd received faulty information about them. "We are not nurses, Sir. We are, however, trained medicinal dispensers. We are going to Dyea only temporarily. We will be back in Skaguay to establish a permanent mission."

"Be safer in Dyea. Soldiers there. Some honest law. The Commissioner. No one here to keep order but a local sheriff who's crooked as a switchback, and one over-matched federal deputy still raw as July corn."

"We'll be fine," Angel said, her tone dismissing him.

"Yes, Ma'am," he said, touching the brim of his hat. "I see." And walked off.

Bernadette felt that they'd handled the situation with grit and backbone. If he put notice out in the camp that they were not to be trifled with, so much the better.

Angel fell quickly to sleep. Bernadette said a silent *Memorare* and closed her eyes, her hand covering the St. Jude relic and the nugget. A sudden uprush of air swept over the wharf sending a chill through her. She whispered to herself, "No matter what travails we face, neither slacker nor bounder shall blunt our mettle."

3. Cat Alley

"To Portland Pete." Soapy nodded his beer glass toward the shot glasses of Two-Chew Calderone and Charlie Bowers. It came to mind that he hadn't had anything stronger than beer in months, wistfully recalling the hell-come-all days in Creede and Denver, back when drink had turned night into day, when his soap game made him king of the plungers and when there was no tomorrow. Not any more. Too many pots aboil. He was at the apex of his life; an opportunity like Skaguay would never come again.

"An aces hand," Two-Chew said. Nervously, he tapped time on the table with his glass until Soapy glared him to silence. The table, stretched with green felt, was the largest in Clancy's, and belonged to Soapy and his boys any time they arrived. It was set in a nook in the rear of the saloon, closest to the free lunch. The back door led to Cat Alley. There, an old wooden crate, long and wide enough for a pair of grandfather's clocks–or the grandfathers–rested under a stairwell to the second-floor jailhouse. When Clancy's patrons were too drunk to walk, they used the crate for sleep. When reasonably sober, they used it as a bench to await their turn in one of the crib tents across the alley.

Bowers kissed his fingertips and bowed. "Well, he's fetching up to the Lord now."

Soapy asked, "Any kin?"

"Wife once. I don't know where."

"See to a decent burial and a marker, Charlie."

"Which account?"

Soapy paused, thought. "Oh, hell. My own."

Bowers made a note.

When Clancy appeared with a bottle, Soapy covered his glass and said, "Leave it for the boys." He had to deal with the Lazlo business, and needed Bowers to handle it just right. In business as in life, some violence was necessary, some incidental. Both demanded appropriate handling and at least appear to abide the conventions of legality. He pronounced his judgment as if announcing the weather. "Lazlo has to hang." Then added, "But not right away."

Bowers said, "Miners won't like it. He was a rounder."

"They'll learn, just like the citizens. Especially the citizens. It's for their own good. Skaguay cannot run amok. Murderers pay."

Bowers rubbed his mole as if the act would give him the answer to a complex question. "He had a lot of friends, Boss, old timers, boys who've been over the pass a dozen times before the strike."

"Good," Soapy said. "Can they argue against a fair and speedy trial? I hope they do. We'll encourage it. That's real news, and a plus for us. At the trial, Van Horn will convict, but no hanging straightaway. More time makes more newspaper articles. Makes the stories grow before the world's eyes. Lazlo will become the symbol of law and order in Skaguay. The skirt-wearing newspapermen in San Francisco and Seattle are commencing to speak of our rowdiness. Charlie, I want you to create a history of thievery and mayhem for Lazlo. Even murder. Make him a wild west outlaw who'd hied out to the Alaska district where he met his just deserts. Talk to Sherpy at the NEWS; tell him to spread the story. Our judicial reputation will be, if not polished, at least seen as intrinsically apropos."

"What's that mean?" Two-Chew asked.

"In the eyes of the world," Soapy said, "it'll mean that Skaguay has done the right thing. We have dealt properly with a scoundrel. And here, unlike Dyea, the rubes can have a good time. You see, Two, stampeders are not accountants, doctors, lawyers, college professors–or ministers." Soapy tipped his hat to Bowers. "They're workingmen with dirty hands and grizzled faces, but they carry a stake in their pocket on their way to the promised land, nuggets and dust on their return. Our job is to excise a goodly share of those pokes each way." He could go off on an explanation for Two-Chew, but he'd cede that to Charlie. "Speaking of our share, Two . . . . " Soapy opened his hand. He didn't reach out, didn't ask.

"What?" Two-Chew said.

Soapy looked to Bowers; Bowers bowed solemnly. "Two," Soapy said, "the billbook."

"I had to–"

With a single index finger, Soapy pointed to the green felt. "Now."

Calderone produced John Stewart's billbook and slid it across the table as if it were his last two bits. Soapy tucked it inside his jacket. "You were clumsy today, Two."

"How the goddamn hell could I know they was watching?"

"It's part of the job. Of all people, you know that."

Calderone slunk down in his chair. "Goddamn bitches. I'll square it with them."

28

"No, you won't. You'll let them be."

Two-Chew said, "You going to put the looker in the cribs? I'd stand in line to give her a tumble."

Somewhere, Soapy figured, Two-Chew had been clubbed on the noggin. In battle, the man would be decorated time and again. He'd loyally follow his officer's orders until he followed the one that ran him frontside to an eight-pound cannonball. To Two-Chew, thinking was a foreign language. Still and all, the stakes were too high to let miscues like this go unmentioned. Skaguay would be a boomer, Soapy knew. Bigger than Creede, maybe bigger than Denver, if the color were as rich as last year's cleanups. Bigger than Deadwood, Bodie, Leadville, Tombstone, Cripple Creek. Two-Chew would atone; one person could not endanger the payload.

No one revered history's open secrets as much as Colonel Jefferson Randolph Smith. No one learned from them as much as he did. Back in '48, San Francisco had eight-hundred souls. A total of eight merchant ships had sailed into its Bay. Within eighteen months of the gold strike, 750 ships sailed into a town that had grown to twenty thousand! In '90, Creede added two-hundred people a day after a silver strike. Shipped out a million dollars in ore every month. If Soapy could keep Skaguay as the main gateway to the Klondyke, it would eclipse them all. If . . . .

The Klondyke gold strike would guarantee a steady stream of stampeders as long as a July 4th parade. Soapy's job was to keep them coming through Skaguay, and that meant keeping them happy. All they ever wanted was a decent square, a drink, a woman and some gambling. The so-called honest townspeople would require some coddling. In time, Soapy knew he'd have to build them a school, a firehouse and a theater. Maybe a hospital. He was already working on the church; his own saloon was nearing completion. He was on top, but had to keep everyone happy . . . a balance as delicate as an assay scale.

Now, though, he was out of patience. "Charlie, I'm going to chat with Clancy. Fill Two-Chew in."

*

Bowers produced three walnut shells from his pocket and positioned them in the center of the table. He didn't relish the idea of trying to explain anything to Two-Chew Calderone. The man was uneducable and totally lacking in self-control. He could go off on a toot and run his mouth like a breakaway locomotive on a downhill scream.

Calderone said, "I ain't playing monte with you, Charlie Bowers. I ain't from yesterday."

"We're not playing, Two. I'm going to use them to explain our situation." Bowers pushed one of the shells across the table in front of Calderone. "That one is us, up here at the top of the world. Think of the North Pole where Santa Claus lives." He pulled the second shell to his own side of the table. "This one is Cuba, way down by Florida and the Equator." Bowers palmed the third shell. "America is set to go to war in Cuba any day. Ships, troops, food, guns, ammo . . . all being staged down south, ready to be deployed."

"What's deployed?"

"Ready to be sent into battle."

"Why?"

"The *why* isn't important. Believe me when I say we are. When a country goes into war, it needs doctors and nurses and, importantly in our case, medicines. The threat of a war has cut off the normal supply of medicines to Alaska. We need them for the crib gals. Big Bo says she's scraping bottom right now. These sisters–"

"Fuck them sisters."

Bowers hand went to his mole. "The good Lord dropped those women into the boss's lap and he needs them. At least for right now. They have access to medicine."

"They skinned me out."

"Two, you rolled the rube in broad daylight right on the beach. A hundred people could have seen you." Bowers placed the third shell in the center of the table. "This shell is the nuns' supply of medicine. Down in Minnesota somewhere. We need it up here." He slid the shell up to Alaska. "If Bo keeps the girls clean, they keep working. If they catch a dose, word spreads faster than the clap they dish out. They're off their backs and the rubes quit knocking."

"I ain't looking for no dose."

"Likewise, I'm sure. No one else is either." Bowers beckoned Calderone closer. "Now, never mention what I'm about to tell you. Cross your heart."

Calderone obliged.

"The girls are twenty per cent of our business up here. We've got to protect that. The nuns might be the key. Until we know for sure, we have to look out for them. Got it?"

"I got it," Calderone said. "But I get the first shot on the looker when you turn her out."

"I guarantee it." Bowers loosened his clerical collar. Didn't the bible speak to casting pearls before swine? "One other thing. Soapy says to stay things at the wharf until this boils over and Reid gets his jaw back in line. Just a day or two. Go spell Syd at the telegraph office. Send him to the bath tent."

Calderone looked as if he'd received a public slap. "I hate them sisters."

"Two!"

"Okay, okay, I get it."

Bowers lifted his hat twice. Soapy caught the signal and broke off the conversation with Clancy. He rejoined Calderone and Bowers. Bowers said, "Two'll spell Syd at the telegraph office."

Calderone jumped from his chair. "You ain't mad, are you, Boss?"

"No." Soapy smiled. "Just keep low for a trice."

"Can I have one more drink?"

Soapy poured. Two-Chew downed the shot. Soapy clapped him on the back and, with a smile, thumbed him out of the saloon.

"Boss," Bowers said, "you are a patient man. Your reward will be in the hereafter."

Soapy said, "I want you to send Missy to Dyea."

"Missy?" Bowers asked. "I figured Old Man Tripp."

"Both. I don't want the nuns back switching and deciding to open shop in Dyea because it has more law. Besides, the sooner they get back here, the sooner they discover what they left in storage has been heisted, and the sooner they send for more. Tripp guides and Missy keeps him sober. She can scout some new territory in Dyea."

"Lots of law there," Bowers said.

Soapy said, "Think of it as untapped potential. A soldier or a marshal has the same yens as any stampeder. And, he gets regular paychecks. I don't really think there's much of a future in Dyea, but things may change."

*

The Seduction of Sister Skaguay

Frank Reid joined a circle of merchants on the boardwalk listening to Soapy's discourse. He'd heard such drivel before. The words rang as true as a slack-jawed politician on the stump. Even less.

Soapy noticed Reid on the fringe. "We were talking about Lazlo, Frank. I allowed as how I hope he swings until his tongue turns black. But of course, it's up to the judge." He made it sound like the trial would be held in an unbiased court.

Reid said, "Lazlo was drunk. Your boy pulled a shooter. Lazlo shouldn't die for defending himself." Slowly, the merchants dispersed.

"Lady justice is blind. She'll decide."

"She ain't blind with you feeding her."

"Frank, Frank, Frank." Soapy placed a paternal hand on Reid's shoulder. "Do you not believe in the code of law?"

"Every day."

"And do you not believe murderers should pay?"

"Smith, that ain't the point and you know it. Lazlo was drunk, unarmed. Portland Pete was peddling them phony maps. No secret. You had 'em printed in Seattle."

"San Francisco, but you have no proof of that."

The man had an answer for every question. Now, an old miner–drunken fool that he was–would be hung. "The law-abiding citizens know Pete was just one more of your lackeys."

"Frank, I'm surprised at you." Soapy drew his sideknife and began to clean his nails.

Reid's hand eased to the scarified grip of his Frontier .45. "Nothing about you surprises me."

"Did you get up on the far side of the bed this morning?"

"Lazlo was drunk. He's no killer."

Soapy blew on his fingernails, then studied Broadway's muddy ruts. "Area's going to explode with people, Frank. Absolutely explode. We need law and order, then we'll all get rich. You have a problem with money? We both want the same things, Dyea be damned."

"No problem with money. My problem is the slant reputation you're building for us."

"Slant reputation? You and me are for law and order. Lazlo's trial will prove that in every newspaper in the country."

"Hanging one helpless drunk won't prove scat." Smith had a way of hiding the truth under a layer of well-sounding locution. A penny for every lie he'd ever told would have made him a wealthy man by now. A body couldn't tell where one left off and the next commenced.

"You got things wrong, Frank. Lazlo's trial is exactly the type of law and order we need to display. No renegade hangings; none of your vigilance committee shenanigans. Good, solid, law-abiding justice."

"It'll just be another killing, a sully on our reputation. Along with all your crooked games, general thuggery and everything else."

"We offer civilized pastimes and general entertainment, things not found in Dyea. Why two nuns showed up just yesterday."

"Met them."

"Good for the camp. Religious influences soothe an upheaved heart. You'd do well to spend time with them, maybe start a school. You were a teacher once, no?"

"I was," Reid said. "That has nothing to do with the affairs of Skaguay."

Soapy slid the knife into its sheath. "Today, more than most, you seem intent on riling me."

"The good people around here won't tolerate your shenanigans forever."

"They have a local sheriff, a federal deputy and a judge to remedy their discontent."

"Your sheriff. Your judge."

"Frank, I read you like an eight-pager. Hear me true. This town won't abide any of your old west lawlessness."

Reid spat on the boardwalk. He'd been holding his temper in check. Goddammit, he was the one who'd been in Skaguay since its startup. Drew up the original plat for the town site, he did. Soapy Smith was nothing more than a duded up devil who listened only to the jingling eagle. Goddammit to hell. And the town was going along with him.

4. One Slick Operator

The kerfuffle with Frank Reid gnawed at Soapy and put him out of sorts. The man was a thorn that had to be removed. First, though, he had to deal with Missy. Not a dot taller than five feet with fiery red hair, she had hips that could stop a runaway convict. Pert enough to grace the cover of dream books and dress magazines. Yet, everything about her seemed designed to get her into trouble. Him, too. Now, she dabbed at a corner of her eye with a blue taffeta hair ribbon. "I don't fashion it, Jeff."

"Start."

"There's bugs and slippery rocks. What if I fall?"

"You'll get a nice bonus."

She reached out and let her hand dance along the front of his trousers. "How nice?"

Soapy backed away. "Look, I need someone to make sure they get there and back in jig time."

"Can I at least take Julie-Julie with me? I need someone to talk to."

"You can talk to Tripp."

"He pumps the jug."

"That's another reason you're going. See that he doesn't. With you gone, Bo is short one gal. She can't spare Julie-Julie. If you don't want to talk to Tripp, get to know the nuns. They might do you some good, give you some spirituality."

"You're a stinker. I might as well baby-sit the whole damn camp."

To Soapy, Missy was treading on the soft side of usefulness. Her judgment was turning askew. She was a top earner, but insolent beyond patience. She wasn't the only filly in the stable. "You're going . . . one way or another."

She hung her head, dabbed a final time at her eyes and stuffed the ribbon into her sleeve. When she looked up, she was as dry-eyed as a desert at noon. Her wide smile, the one that had first caught his fancy, beamed. Just part of her magic.

He'd first spotted her at a rodeo in Creede, her face lathered in fetching elfish freckles and graced with dimples deep enough to hold water. She was sassing school boys, turning their faces red, then sauntering off, her skirts held just high enough to show her ankles. They ran after her and circled her. She showed no fear. Soapy broke the circle. She put her finger to her lips in bemused wonderment. He tipped his hat and exposed his pearl-handled Bisley. "Scoot," he said to the boys. They did. He told her that she'd have nothing to fear when he was around. She told *him* she had nothing to fear when he wasn't around, and slipped her arm through his. In time, she became expert at pushing house hooch, then coaxing miners to buy her champagne. She'd taunt them with more than a bare ankle. They'd follow like puppies and, as the night wore on, buy the rest of the package.

"Jeff," she said, pulling his face to hers, "I was just teasing."

"You had me fooled."

"Why don't you come by the crib? I'll prove it."

In her tent, she could prove north was south, fat was skinny, and cold was hot . . . so hot that a body'd never shiver again.

*

Missy stroked the spindly, stubby cactus that was Old Man Tripp's beard. "You and me is doing this because Soapy says us to." On the trail, she knew the old man would carp from sunup to sunset, but in the end, he always did what Soapy said to do. "Don't mean we have to like it, or them religious heifers," she added. "If I had my rathers, I'd be in the bathhouse."

Tripp hooked his thumbs under the two pairs of galluses that criss-crossed his mighty girth, a trunk that challenged a redwood. "I don't rightly mind the duty. Good for a man my age to get out and knock the rust off."

They hadn't covered a mile of trail when Missy called a halt to the procession, sat on a rock and took a stick to the mud caking her gum boots. "More muck on this trail than all our tidelands clumped together. Look at these ugly boots. Look at my dress!"

They traveled with four drummers, two mangy oxen, a covered cart and a drover named Mahoney. The animals pulled without a balk. It was the drummers who needed the whip. They whined worse than old widows about the trail. It stabbed them with berry brambles and prickly devil's club. Weblike tree roots grew right out of scree and trapped their feet like nature's clamps. Two drummers approached Missy. "Everything hunky-dory, Miss Bonteiller?"

"Fine, boys, except my feet are twice as heavy as normal. Glad I don't stand on them when drumming my wares."

"We might have to find out about that come Dyea."

"We surely might." Missy shushed them back to the front of the caravan and whispered to Tripp, "Soapy said to scout business. He should give me the bonus for starting early."

"You say it, I'll swear it."

"Tripp, tell me true. What's so goddamned important about them two religious ones? Why do I have to keep an eye on them? If I have to watch them, then I got no time to do my scouting so's I might not as well come along at all."

Tripp whistled up to the heavens.

"I know one appears to be a looker, and pretty counts a peck with all you organ grinders, but we don't know a lick about what's under all them sacks she wears. Besides, she ain't no prettier than me."

Tripp continued staring at the sky.

"She ain't, is she?"

No answer.

"Say she ain't or I'll tell the girls you got a dose of the leaky dick."

"No, she ain't as pretty as you, Missy. No one is as pretty as you."

The young nun was a beauty, no doubt. Probably the reason Soapy wanted her back in Skaguay so fast. Keep her in his sights. If he took a shine to her–And why wouldn't he?–he'd land her, sister duds or not. He was a swinging peckerwood like the rest of the boys. Unlike the rest of the boys, he always got what he set his trap for. That would make her own self unnecessary. And she knew well how Jeff Smith got shut of unnecessary people. "Tripp, what's that hussy's name?"

"Don't rightly know. She's just one of them *Sister* people."

"Well, me and Sister gonna get a few things straight before this trip is done and gone, I'll tell you that."

*

"Calm yourself, child." Angel had seen the concern in Bernadette's eyes since they'd departed Skaguay. Perhaps it was the remote trail, perhaps the dearth of people. Both had wondered why the painted lady was tagging along? Clearly she was not a tenderfoot to the area. Angel studied Bernadette's right hand, gripped so tightly around her rosary that her knuckles were as white as boiled bones. "My dear," Angel said, "shall we pray?"

Bernadette shook her head, her lips moving lightly, but her burden weighing her down like a water-soaked blanket. It would pass; it always passed with the young nun, but it always returned at the most unexpected times. "Sister Bernadette, look at this as a new territory we will be conquering for the Lord. If you take that approach, no harm can come to you, to us."

Bernadette loosened her grip on the rosary and smoothed the folds of her sackcloth skirt. "Of course, my Angel. And you *are* my Angel. I'd be adrift without your counsel."

"Posh."

*

Bernadette said, "This trek is our Way of the Cross." Although a sunny day, little sunshine made it through the dense canopy of fir boughs. Aspen and cottonwood leant their branches to the overhang. The nuns' skirts became soaked crossing numerous creeks. Their snow excluders did nothing to keep their feet dry. Perhaps the Angel was right about their choice of footwear. Yet they persevered, pushing on well into the afternoon. Once, Angel sunk to her ankles in a mossy bog, then slid off a carpet of shale and skinned her shin right through her leggings. They fell behind the caravan. The men and the ox cart did not slow, but the sisters refused to ask for a respite. When unrelenting roots tore at the toes of their snow excluders, they bore on as silently as a cold night. When they felt particularly wearied, they prayed the *Credo* and asked–begged!–for the Lord's fortitude. He would not let them down!

Ahead, the drummers continued to curse the roughness of the trail. When they finally paused, they collapsed against the closest trees, almost too weak to light their pipes. Even though the nuns were exhausted and lagged behind, they would have continued. Bernadette vowed to speak to the sin of pride at her next confession.

A drummer approached them. "Where's the grub?"

"Grub?" Bernadette said.

"Food," he said.

"I know the meaning of the word. Why ask us?"

The drummer barely was able to subdue a snarl. His accusatory eyes convicted the nuns of a crime. With all the warmth of a witness to an execution, he said, "Your end of the accommodation."

"You might inquire of Mister Mahoney for any accommodation. We hired packers in Skaguay to portage our goods and Colonel Smith indicated you would provide us an escort to Dyea. That is the extent of our agreement."

The drummer looked into the roiling white water a hundred feet below. "Ma'am, it looks like Smith has had a good laugh at our expense."

"Meaning . . . ?"

"He came to me yesterday and asked if we'd mind being joined on the trail by a couple of top-notch ladies. He didn't say you were women of the cloth, only that cooking came naturally to your ilk."

The Colonel had said nothing to them about cooking. Bernadette's surprise showed. "He said we were cooks?"

"Not in that many words. Something's aslant here. Dickens take all! If I had to guess, I'd say you ain't got so much as a hoe cake in them packs."

Bernadette stood to face him. "No, Sir, we do not. I believe you've been hornswaggled. We're neither cooks nor scullery maids. Our mission, the Lord's work, is to see to the cleansing of–" She checked to see that the child was out of earshot.–"of the strumpets. And we shall, mark my words." Angel tugged her skirt. *Ite missa est.*

The drummer heeled around and returned to his compatriots. He took a knee and whispered loud enough for the nuns to hear, "I say we leave them." To which there was general disagreement.

Mister Mahoney overheard the conversation. He uttered clear, concise invective against the nuns. Apparently the drummers were not the only ones promised a fine meal. Mahoney produced a slab of bacon, sheared off a chunk and tossed it into a coffee pot.

Angel said, "The Way of the Cross, my child, is one station at a time."

*

Tripp sucked at the beard bristles on his lower lip. Finally, he said to the nuns, "After this little rest up, we come onto the Devil's Slide. Take care to heed your steps. You might need both hands to keep your balance. I'd strap that long gun across your back."

The young one said, "We're capable of seeing to ourselves, Mister Tripp."

"I can tell that, Ma'am. Nevertheless, you're stuck with the sorry likes of me giving out with advice. The Colonel's orders. I always kow-tow to his orders."

Tripp spread a duck cloth tarp on the ground and covered it with a quilt. Without a word, Missy took a seat in its center.

The older nun extended her hand to the girl. "I'm Sister Margaret Mary Angelorum."

"Pleased, I'm sure," Missy said.

The young nun and Missy glared at each other, their eyes crossing in a swordfight, their cheeks as flamed as blood. The Colonel had asked Tripp to do some strange things, but escorting two religious ladies and one hooker was a first. And a last. He felt two volcanoes about to boil up and spew hot coals. Anyone in the vicinity would get a scalding. The only sound was the rush of the river. The chill silence between the women was hard to bear. He said, "You know, the Colonel give up most drink years ago."

Angel gave an agreeable nod. Missy and the young nun had not unlocked their gaze.

"When he was a drinking man, he was a hellion. Useless to try to stop him. He loved spending money. I was a steerer and gripper for him for years–Leadville, St. Louis, New Orleans, Cheyenne. I tell you–"

"Tripp!" Missy clapped her hands. "Stuff it, you old stager. Downwind of you is turning to sour air."

"Oh, sorry, ladies." The gal was right. And it was him supposed to be watching out for her. Well, he hadn't spit out too much. He removed a flask from inside his shirt. Time to say them a good afternoon. Get something into his mouth rather than any more out of it.

*

The trail began an infuriating series of twists, turns and dips, climbing all the while. Roots scraped bare of bark continued to snag the nuns' snow excluders. Angel thought they'd never reach Dyea. They crossed and recrossed a roiling creek, its moss- and lichen-covered rocks slippery as ice. Their feet turned numb, and this was only August.

Angel judged them only halfway to Dyea when they came onto a ledge barely wide enough for the ox cart. It was bordered on one side by a sheer rock wall, on the other by a gorge a hundred feet down. Leah, the lead ox, had been following Mister Mahoney all day. She pulled up at the sight of the canyon and cried like a lamb. The trailing ox, Amanda, stopped in her traces. Mister Mahoney cursed them and swatted Leah with a razor strop. She locked her legs stiff as four-bys and refused a further step. The teamster doubled the punishment.

Sister Bernadette took to the front of the procession. She said, "Mister Mahoney, perhaps you could blindfold the animal to allay its natural fear of heights." She was from farming stock and knew well her way around animals.

"Like this?" Mister Mahoney said, and laid the strop across the animal's head. "I get six bits a pound with these critters. Problem is that this one works like a two-bit whore." Leah bellowed, but would not budge. Who could blame the animal? Looking down into the boiling water, Angel's stomach rumbled. At the bottom of the gorge, one could actually see bones!

Angel heard the impatience in the drummers as they discussed various methods the drover might use to move forward. Clearly, Mister Mahoney was ignoring them. He might do well to abide Bernadette's advice.

Ever the bold one, Sister Bernadette said, "Sir, perhaps what the animal needs is a good example."

"Stuff it, lady, or you'll be leading the way."

Angel moved past Amanda, toward Bernadette. "Sister, perhaps—"

Bernadette had taken hold of Leah's bridle. The ox wailed, threw up her head and kicked out her hind legs.

*

Sister Bernadette saw the animal knock Angel into the side of the mountain. She bounced off the wall of rock and crashed into the trailing ox. The ox reared, causing Angel to lose purchase on a patch of loose gravel. She tried to catch herself, but only succeeded in letting out a scream piercing enough to split rocks. "Sister!" She stretched her arm toward Bernadette who had clamped her hand on a root growing from the rock wall. Their fingers missed by inches. *Lord have mercy*! Angel fell past Bernadette down into the gorge. Her body thudded onto the river bank below.

The Lord's fury did not abate. Angel's screams seemed to loosen gravel from a ridge above. Rock poured down. Bernadette reached to the saving root with her free hand and clutched it with all her strength. She heard shouts of "Back! Back!" from the drummers. Those were the last words she recalled.

She regained consciousness still clinging to the root, her rifle and case still strapped to her back. Falling rock had built itself up around her and buried her to the waist. After prying her hands from the life-saving root, the drummers dug her out, calling her struggle heroic, a miracle.

Never before had she endured such knife-edge pain. Her leg screamed, but she fought all temptation to do likewise. She prayed quietly for relief. Old Man Tripp produced a bottle labeled Doctor Hammond's Internal

Catarrh Cure. She gratefully accepted. The medicine clouded her head. Alas, Angel, Mister Mahoney, Leah and Amanda had been lost.

Tripp and Miss Bonteiller tried to comfort her, Tripp warning her not to look at the leg. Of course, she disobeyed and came to a faint when she saw a grotesque, bloody bone shunted through the skin between ankle and knee, her swaddling habit darkening with blood.

The drummers were less concerned about her leg than the trail. They worked through the night while Miss Bonteiller and Mister Tripp fed her spoons of the Catarrh Cure. It was stronger than any medicine she'd ever been given. So long as she received regular dosages, she remained fairly well in a daze. In the morning, the drummers were prepared to continue to Dyea. Miss Bonteiller and Tripp would help her back to Skaguay.

"Gentlemen," Bernadette said, "I will not leave this spot until we have a service for Sister Margaret Mary and Mister Mahoney, no matter how brief it may be."

It was times like these that made being a woman of substance–and one who knew right from wrong without equivocation–worthwhile. In this moment, a person reached the heavens and touched the Lord. No one dared offer a challenge.

In due course, one of the men spoke. "A hundred yards back, there was a stand of black cottonwood. I could make a cross."

In unison, the men read Bernadette for a reaction. Concurrence would, of course, minimize their problem. "That will do," she said, "so long as the cross is stout and bears her full clerical name: Sister Margaret Mary Angelorum, Order of the Good Shepherd Sisters." She'd been Bernadette's religious counselor and spiritual intimate; her spirit would live forever.

The men began issuing orders, each acting like nothing less than a general officer commanding a huge army. The moment held a touch of humor. Here they were, six miles out of Skaguay on an isolated trail of terror, Sister Angelorum and Mister Mahoney gone and a brace of oxen lost with all their possessions, and the ninnies were tripping over each other trying to break camp.

"Please help me up," Bernadette said. Only when Miss Bonteiller and Tripp lifted her did she cry out, then vowed anew to offer up the pain for the pour souls in purgatory and the repose of Angel's soul. The drummers came to attention, shifting from one foot to the other, fidgeting like they needed a nature stop.

41

The Seduction of Sister Skaguay

"Gentlemen, calm yourselves for prayers." They stilled.

"*Heavenly father . . . .*" Bernadette raised her hand and recited a brief history of Angel's life and her many contributions to the Lord, lauding her zest for life and her devotion to her community of sisters, concluding with a promise to provide a proper service back in Skaguay complete with a permanent headstone. Bernadette knew full well her corporal remains would rest forever as she lay. "I am comfortable that her soul is joyfully at the right hand of the Lord as we speak. Nothing else matters. Now you gentlemen go about your business. I shall not be the cause of any further delay to you."

She asked the tart and Tripp to give her a moment alone with her Angel. Using the Winchester as a crutch, she hobbled to the edge of the slide and saw below the mangled form of her Angel and Mister Mahoney, the smashed oxen and the detritus from the wagon. She eased herself to the ground. "Oh, my Angel . . . ." Tears washed away her words, flooding down her collar and onto her cape. Bernadette simply could not imagine life without Angel. She had attended many funerals in her religious capacity, but only now realized what it must have felt like for mourners to have lost a spouse, a parent or sibling . . . void as an empty church. She might have sobbed for days but the Winchester fell across her leg. She could not hold back her scream. Tripp came charging up the trail.

Bernadette assured him all was as well as it could be and advised him that they should be getting on their way. He unrolled his sleep bag, spread it flat on the trail and carried her to it, then expertly hacked down two saplings and explained that he would fashion a travois. He splinted the Winchester to her leg and lifted her onto the litter. She bit her lip to stifle a cry. The hussy tucked in her Iron Maiden and wrapped her in the sleep bag, tut-tutting her as a little child. Then, to Bernadette's astonishment, Tripp stood up and removed his suspenders. "Sir!"

"Easy, Ma'am." He knelt beside her and lashed her to the litter, one band around her shoulders and one around her waist. He said, "The going won't be any easier on the way back. I don't want to dump you." He looped a cord around the sapling frame and stepped into the makeshift harness. "Hang on."

She felt like she was bounced over rock and root with more impact than if she'd been walking. With each collision, she bit down on her lips. This was the suffering of the condemned, the agony of the damned. Miss Bonteiller looked to her with genuine concern, dabbed blood from her chin but said nothing. Tripp dragged her through streams, that, outbound, had seemed like barely flowing trickles. Now, their frigid waters splashed up into her face, keeping all of her agonized senses alert. Her leg thrummed like a band of base drums. Once, after a signal from Miss Bonteiller, Mister Tripp stopped, uncorked the Catarrh Cure and put the bottle to Bernadette's lips. She drank so eagerly that he pulled it away and helped himself to a sizeable swallow. With the powerful medicine, she faded in and out of consciousness.

After coming around from a sleep just shy of sunset, she found not only Mister Tripp standing overhead but a second man, a powerful man with a tripod over one shoulder, a haversack over the other. From the grand handlebar moustache, she recognized Mister Reid. He'd been out surveying a homestead.

Mister Tripp said to him, "If you're headed to town, Frank, I could stand some help."

Mister Reid inspected the nun's leg, and wiped his lips on the back of his hand. "Okay," was all he said. Missy rearranged the sleep bag and tightened the gallusses.

"Thank you," Bernadette said, "Miss . . . Miss . . . "

"Bonteiller. Pronounced BON-TEE-YEA. We ain't yet been properly introduced because no one around here has the manners God give a goat. Melissa Bonteiller. It's French, don't you know."

Darkness had come on by the time they neared Skaguay. They heard the town before they saw it–a gunshot, a whoop of elation, ungodly music. The men hauled her to the boardwalk in front of Clancy's Music Hall. Mister Reid said, "Got no sawbones in town lest one come in the last two days. Our friend Lank is the closest to a vet–"

"Not on your life! I will not be attended to by a veterinarian."

Mister Tripp said, "He ain't no vet, Ma'am." He tap-tap-tapped his boot toe in a rut, scratched his chin whiskers. "In truelife, he's a blacksmith. Up here, he helps out with critters, including human ones, who are poorly."

Bernadette was almost speechless. "Never." She looked directly at Tripp.

"For a fact," Tripp said, "I ain't heard anything close to a 'Thank you, kindly,' but that don't matter. What matters is that I aim to be inside Clancy's taking my drink short of two minutes. Now I'll go and fetch Lank to help, drag you around to Cat Alley, or just leave you two ladies here with Frank. Makes no nevermind to me. Just tell me your druthers."

By the light from inside the saloon, Bernadette saw a smirk on Mister Reid's face. She demanded to know precisely what he was smiling about. In jig time, his comportment changed to that of a solemn pall-bearer.

"Nothing, Sister."

A man wobbled up the boardwalk. "Hiya, Frank," he said. He studied the nun, bound under the sleep bag and stretched on the travois. "You got to hogtie 'em these days, eh?"

Mister Reid ignored the man.

Mister Tripp said, "You got about one more minute until I head through that door."

"Thank you, Mister Tripp," Bernadette said. "You clearly saved my life."

"Pleased, I'm sure. Now where would you be off to?"

Mister Reid turned his back.

Mister Tripp said, "For the time, we'll set you in Cat Alley. I know it well. Slept off a couple of powerful headaches there myself."

Mister Reid said, "Sister, are you sure you don't want to see Lank? You got a bad break."

"Please, let me sleep the night. I'll be able to think better. Take me to this Cat Alley."

Reid and Tripp dragged the travois into the alley behind Clancy's. Mister Reid pulled open the hinged panel to a crate. Then maneuvered her inside as gently as if they were handling a baby. Reid covered her with the sleep bag and his mackinaw.

She said, "You've been kind."

"I'll be back for my coat in the morning."

"Is there more medicine?"

"No, but I'll get you something." He disappeared into the blackness. When he returned, he put a bottle to her lips. It was certainly not Catarrh Cure, but she hardly cared. Anything to ease the pain. "What is it?"

"Never you mind. Take another big gulp and sleep."

She drank deeply, thinking of nothing but the frothy luxury of a soapy bath, her true weakness in life.

*

Missy watched Frank disappear into Clancy's, then peered into the crate wondering what was to become of the nun. "You'll be give up to the dead's sleep pronto." She wiped Bernadette's face with a hemstitched handkerchief.

The nun rolled her head from side to side, her eyes closed, her mouth agape.

"Right on the trail, you made them randy old boys have a funeral. You're one slick operator, lady. One slick operator, no doubt."

5. The Importance of Pharmaceuticals

Soapy's patience with Missy had worn as thin as hand-me-down socks. "Missy," he said, "what about the pharmaceuticals?" Little could be gained by listening to clatter, let alone a whore's clatter.

"Over the ledge with the oxes, Mahoney and the fat nun." She curled a ringlet around her index finger as unconcerned with Soapy's sharp tone as if she were killing time with a beau over a two-straw sarsaparilla.

"Everything?"

"Everything but that old rifle strapped to her back. What's a gal like her doing with a rifle anyway?"

Soapy ignored the question. A nun outside the cribs? That would help business as much as an outbreak of the clap. "Why'd you put her there?" He immediately regretted the question.

"Tripp's call. In case you haven't noticed, there's a boatload of fresh meat in camp that ain't had the time to move up to the pass. All the rooms are taken two and three times over. Same with tents and shacks. Where'd you expect her to go? Our house? You got a half-dozen of the boys there already. That lady's bad hurt. A ball of filth, too. Maybe I should have stashed her in the cribs. She could have mine. Big Bo–"

Soapy raised his hand. "You did right, I guess."

"You guess? Just tell me where–"

Soapy cut her off again, and thought of his wife and children back in St. Louis. In Denver, he'd tried–unsuccessfully–to keep his family apart from business interests. It didn't work. They were better off back east. He'd have to remember to have Bowers send gifts. A nettlesome task. Missy was the second person to mention the cribs for the sister. The nun had the appeal. It could be an interesting challenge. He'd give himself even odds at best. "Get over to the bathhouse. You look decrepit."

"Decrepit? I just come off that hell-for-spit trail with Old Man Tripp and a busted up sister . . . no place to wash . . . all on your orders . . . of course I look decrepit! You don't have to rub my nose in it."

"Stop!" he said. "I thank you for all that. Under the circumstances–" He produced a handful of folding money. Without counting it, he passed it to Missy. "Tell Bo I said for you to take the night off. Go get yourself cleaned up now. In the morning, give the nun a rinse, too. If she's as bad off as you say, she'll need it. Some new duds, too."

"She's buck tough, Jefferson. Howled a couple of times on the trail and once when we got her to the Alley. Other than that, she chewed wood. Of course, Tripp gave her regular doses of juice."

"It never fails."

"She's in a lot of pain, though. Her leg bone punched right through the skin." Missy rolled the money into a tube and pushed it up her sleeve. "What's so all-fired important about her? Except for the fact she's a beauty, that is."

"Medicine. She's been sent here to clean up you girls and put you on the train to salvation."

"That train don't have so much as a whistle-stop in Skaguay. Them holy-rollers ain't should be here."

"Don't be too hasty about manna that falls from heaven. Religious folks live off sinners, the same sinners who support us. Churchgoers tolerate sin, though they outwardly claim to shun it. No sinner, no church; no church, some folks move on. So long as people know they're able to make a fair living, everything will be fine. Churches are important."

"I seem to recall you were on a church committee back in Creede."

"Here, too, as you know. A church takes up an hour a week of a man's time. It clears his conscience to spend his money in other ways. What we discourage are those damnable lodges—the Elks, Moose, Odd Fellows. They take whole nights and entire weekends of time. And far too much money. No, we definitely favor churches."

"Colonel Jeff Smith, the saint."

"At times, I do perform miracles."

*

The pell-mell activity in Cat Alley betrayed comings and goings of the sort that kept Bernadette in a fitful sleep. The heavy clomp of men's boots was usually followed by a high-pitched squeal of laughter and the whoosh of a tent flap. Other times, the men plopped down atop her crate, but always were summoned in short order by a woman's call.

Notwithstanding the cool night temperature, the air in the crate went as fetid as a sty on a summer afternoon. Air holes allowed for freshness, yet circulation was limited. But as night wore on, the alley quieted and jostlings became less frequent.

A rap came on the crate. Bernadette dared not answer.

"Lady, you in there?"

It was Miss Bonteiller. "Yes, child."

"You still alive?"

"Quite," she answered.

Miss Bonteiller pried open the door and shook out a thick flannel blanket covered with hearts.

"That's kind of you."

"Shhhhh. Don't stir the dogs."

"Dogs?"

"Just a saying I have," she said. "How's tricks?"

Bernadette was unable to tell if Missy was trying to be friendly or sassy. Perhaps both. "Fine," she said.

The child set about plumping the sleep bag and, in general, tried to make Bernadette comfortable. When she had worked her way to the nun's leg, Bernadette stifled a moan.

"You might have screamed a few hours back. The oil must be working."

"Oil?"

"Medicine," she said. "Laudanum with a jolt of chloral hydrate." She lifted the bottle to the moonlight. "You're about empty. Watch yourself. Too much and you'll be conked for days." She disappeared into the saloon.

With the lid to the crate open, Bernadette viewed her situation. Across the alley, four tiny tents stood in a neat row, each one small enough to be an ice-fishing tent back in Iowa, each with a lantern hung on a pole outside the flap.

Miss Bonteiller returned and poured a shot glass of a dark liquid into the nun's medicine bottle. "This will help. Take a tiny sip."

Bernadette did as ordered. "Bitter. It tickles my tongue."

"That means it's working." Missy eased the nun back down. "I got to get myself out the road. I'll check on you when I get back."

"Traveling at this time of night? The sun isn't up."

"I got Soapy put down. Most of the boys are asleep. They won't miss me."

"I don't understand."

"It's no matter to you."

"What's out the road?"

"Just the cemetery and the trail to the pass. If anyone asks, I'm going on business. Got it?"

She'd turned curt, almost official. What could Bernadette say? She was at the strumpet's mercy.

"Business. Don't forget." Missy held up the mackinaw that had been covering the nun. "Frank Reid's," she said, clutched it to herself, threw it back across the nun and was off.

Bernadette pulled the mackinaw tightly around herself and burrowed into the blanket as deeply as possible. On more than one occasion, men from the saloon sloshed past her to use the side of the building for their nature call. Each time, she sucked in her breath.

She dearly wanted to sleep, but her leg continued to pound. At times, her head seemed to float right out of the crate. The leg swelled. She fretted the future. There was no attractive picture. And she was without her Angel, yet Angel would expect Bernadette to fulfill their assignment. Bernadette would not relent without a direct order. Advising Mother Francine of Angel's demise would be the first order of the day, although she wasn't sure how she might accomplish that chore considering her condition. She consoled herself with the thought that if the Lord had wanted her to break a leg in front of a hospital, He would have deemed it so. For certain, though, she could certainly not endure the pain much longer. *May Jesus have mercy on the poor souls in purgatory.* She would get herself to the telegraph office the moment the leg was tended.

A scratching raked the crate. A dog snarled. At least she hoped it was nothing more than a dog. The animal sniffed, then clawed at the lid. It dawned on her that the gash in her leg might be scented as fresh meat. The animal prized its snout under the lid. Bernadette gave it a rap with the medicine bottle, the glass shattering over herself and Mister Reid's mackinaw, the liquid drenching into her Iron Maiden. The dog yelped and bolted off. She was saturated. The odor would surely attract other beasts of the night. What would she do then?

*

Pissing to the center of a rock in back of his cabin, Frank Reid was not of a mind to start his workday tending a cheechacko, a disagreeable one at that. He argued himself all the way to Cat Alley that he was just going by to pick up his mackinaw. Deep down, he worried what might happen to the nun. Left to Soapy's boys, she might meet a fate worse than her partner. "Lady, you still alive in there?"

"Barely."

He pulled open the door.

"You might have given me a moment to collect myself."

He should have, he knew. She was a mess: her habit filthy, her remaining snow excluder caked in mud, her face sprayed with dirt. Wasn't much she could do, stretched out as she was on her back. "Apologies," he said.

"I should think so."

The night had not improved her manners. "Sister, if you want me to go away, I'll just take my mackinaw and oblige."

"No, no, I need your help."

He lifted the hem of her Iron Maiden to examine her leg and noticed the shards of glass sprinkled over her. "Where'd that come from?"

"I broke the bottle scaring off a dog."

He touched the leg.

Her face contorted in agony. *"My Mother, My Confidence. My Mother, My Confidence."*

He touched her cheek. Hotter than a branding iron. She gripped her rope rosary.

"You're on fire. Your leg's puffed up like a pillow. We got to get it washed and set lest you go to gangrene. You'll wind up losing it."

"Are you certain there's no physician about?"

"We're advertising in the Seattle papers. For a tooth puller, too. You said you knew some nursing?"

"Hygiene. Women's personal problems. Specialized medical training. Nothing to contend with the likes of this."

"Lank does a decent job with animal or man."

"The smithy?" Her face went from fever red to death gray.

The leg snap had been tough on her. Alaska was always tough on split-tails. "Sister, you got no choice. It's for your own good. I'll tote you over to his tent, then get you some more medicine."

"You've been very kind, Mister Reid."

"You're raw here, but, all in all, you'll be good for the District."

"I'll take that as a compliment."

"So given," he said. "Now let's get you mended up. You're looking blanched as a full moon." Come the day, no telling what shape she'd be in.

Reid strapped her Winchester over his shoulder. He lifted her from the crate; she grimaced almost as if trying to scream. No sound came out. Her eyes went white and her lids closed.

6. Doubting Thomas

Bernadette found herself in a tent stall on her back, her feet and calves raised up onto a hay bale. Mister Reid fed her from a nippled medicine bottle. She gulped greedily. In adjacent stalls, horses snuffled hay and pawed the ground.

The bloomer on her broken leg had been completely torn away, her bare flesh exposed. The leg was set with four white slats bound with hide strips. She felt like the leg had been removed–no pain whatsoever.

She tried to rise, but Mister Reid held her down. A second man stood behind him as if hiding from her. He was a gaunt scarecrow of a man with wild, frightened eyes and lips as thin as meat slices. His cheeks glistened with perspiration and were streaked with soot. A half dozen horseshoe capewells stuck out from his mouth like so many dried up tree twigs.

"Are these like normal gals, Frank?"

"The same. You worked on women before. The difference with these is in the head."

"She scares me. I bet she's one of them voodoo gals. I don't take to that."

"Nothing voodoo about her."

Mister Reid whispered to Bernadette. "You coming around, Sister? You passed out. Probably for the best. The leg is set. This is Lank, the smithy. He doubles as the town vet, sometimes the saw bones."

Bernadette searched for words, but her mouth failed to form them. In time, she managed, "Fence."

Mister Reid chuckled. "Yes. He set your leg with leftover pickets from the graveyard fence. Only thing he had handy. Never to mind. Says it's a clean break and will heal quickly."

As her vision focused, she was horrified to know that two strangers were taking in her bared leg, broken or not. Indignity heaped atop injury. The filthy blacksmith continued to peek over Mister Reid's shoulder staring at her as if she were a two-headed snake. She met his eyes, and his hands flew to his face, a child hiding from a demon.

Lank said, "What you gone do with her, Frank?"

"Leave her be. I'll check on her tonight."

"Here? With me? Not all alone. I had to move Mike Haggerty's sick goat from this stall. I need the space. He's a paying customer."

"Lank . . . . "

"Gentlemen . . . please." The nun reached to Mister Reid, an infant reaching to its parent. He helped her sit up on the hay bale, her head whirring like a hummingbird. She tottered left; Mister Reid caught her. The motion threatened to upheave her stomach. To steady herself, she fastened her hands around the bale wires and took a deep mouthful of air that tasted like damp silage and smelled of farm animals.

Mister Reid dug at his ear, clearly at a loss.

*

The man of my dreams, Missy thought, entering the tent and seeing Frank Reid with a finger in his ear. If he'd just make an honest woman of her, she'd return his heart's desire a hundred times over and teach him proper socializing. Then again, if dreams were nuggets, she'd be sitting in a mansion on Nob Hill with a houseful of service gals making her more famous than Calamity Jane. As it was, the ends of the earth were right in front of her: one ugly blacksmith so scairt of women he pissed like a skittish racehorse when one walked by, and Frank Reid, the man whose boots any woman would like tucked under her bed. "Howdy, boys," she said.

Reid nodded an acknowledgement. Lank backed into the stall.

"Lank, no need to hide," Missy said. "If you'd just pay me a call some night, I'd coax that shyness right out of you."

"Yes'm." Lank wiped his hands on his leather apron. "I gotta go swamp me the corral."

"Frank Reid, do you have anything to say to a girl?" She'd flirted with him since lighting in Skaguay. Never got so much as a tumble. Sure, he'd visited the cribs like any normal man, hers more than the others. It was all business. He gave her so many dreams: now, a big cottage with young 'uns gamboling about, a fine pair of Lipizzaners to pull their carriage, closets over-flowing with ball gowns. Soapy might have been a smooth-talking man of the world, but Frank Reid had that quiet swagger that turned every gal's head.

Reid tipped his hat. "Missy."

"That's all you have to say?"

"Lank here did a fine job on the sister's leg."

"How about me? You like my new day frock?" She pirouetted. She'd tend to the sister in time, but wouldn't pass the chance to turn an ankle to Frank Reid. Something in him brought out her wanton shamelessness. If

53

The Seduction of Sister Skaguay

Soapy knew she was so openly brazen with him–over and above the flirty way all the gals used on all the boys–he'd put the strap to her like she was an orphan mule. It was a good thing she was so quick of thought.

"Very pretty."

"You just jolt a gal over with compliments, don't you?"

Reid said, "I'm flummoxed what to do with this nun."

"What else would a gal expect from an old Indian fighter? You got the two most beautiful women in town right in front of you and you're flummoxed."

The nun said, "Miss Bonteiller, I resent that implication."

"No resenting truth, lady."

"I'm Sister Bernadette of the Good Shepherd Sisters and would appreciate it if you would respect the community I represent, even if you choose to scorn me."

"No scorn to it. I'm just speaking my piece because I have to take care of seven-eleven people's problems. Lord knows what would happen if I weren't around. 'Sides, what you wish don't count snot right now, at least not in your current condition. The bathhouse is what you need. I'd take you to a good spruce steam bath if Frank Reid here or some of the other boys would get to building one. It would fix up everyone's rheumatism. Consumption as well. Probably the grippe, too."

"Missy–" Reid said.

"Soapy sent me by to get her into the bathhouse and see that she takes a wash. She looks like hell."

The nun said, "Did Colonel Smith inquire as to *my* wishes?"

"No, he did not. He never does. So for now, I'll hold my tongue." She turned to Frank Reid. "Unless you want to hold it."

Reid ignored the come-on. "The bathhouse?"

"You got something more ample in mind?"

Reid threw up his hands in self-defense. "No, Ma'am."

The nun cut in and spoke to Missy. "Your name? On the trail, you said it was French. *Parlais vous Francais?*"

"I never use them French words up here. Folks think you're a Canuck."

Frank Reid bowed courtly. A show bow, for sure. He'd been freed from his charge and backed out of the tent, continuing to bow.

*

Bernadette wondered if this soubrette were an actress practicing a character or just uncontrollably saucy? Most young ladies would earn a paddling for such impertinence. From Miss Bonteiller, however, it seemed almost piquant.

Missy whispered, "How long since you had a bath?"

"Miss Bonteiller!" Her effrontery continued to shock the nun. Bernadette realized the child was likely not asking out of ill intent. She softened her tone. "Seattle," she said. "I must be offensive."

"First off, no more of that *Miss Bonteiller* handle. Call me Melissa. I gave myself that name and am partial to it. Some folks just use *Missy*." She swatted at a mosquito the size of a hornet. "What do you think of that Frank Reid? He's the secret beau of most of the gals in town, what few of us there are. The story goes that he was a fierce Indian fighter and killed a thousand braves. He heads up a pack of local vigilantes, too."

"Vigilantes in the Alaska District?"

"The honest men. Them who ain't with Soapy. A month back, he busted the jaw of one of Soapy's boys so bad, Lank had to take the pieces of bone out of the side of his mouth with a pincers. Soapy just shipped the galoot off to Seattle to get fixed up proper. Soapy don't take kindly to folks crossing him. He'd have evened the score inside an hour with most men but he walks a tight trail around Frank Reid. He'll pick his time, when the stars and tides are lined up just right so he can't miss . . . then Katy-bar-the-door."

"They both sound vile." Bernadette was thinking about how gently Mister Reid had helped her into the crate. Yet she'd been warned away from him. "I've been led to believe that he's as troublesome as that Mister Calderone."

Miss Bonteiller faced Bernadette squarely. "Hogwash. Frank's the choice bull in the pen."

The nun said, "Miss Bonteiller, how old are you?"

"Plenty enough," she said. "Not important. What's important is to get you on your feet and over to the bathhouse."

With no further ado, she wove her tiny fingers through the shoulders of Bernadette's sackcloth and snatched her upright. She may have been a mite, but it was clear how she survived in his hardy land. "You *are* a strong one."

"I've been told that," she said. "How does the leg feel?"

To Bernadette's amazement, she hardly felt the injury. Of course, she was standing on her one good leg. She didn't dare put down the bad one.

Miss Bonteiller found Bernadette's Winchester and tucked the stock under the nun's arm. "I'll get you some padding for this once we get to the bathhouse. Maybe a real crutch."

Each step seemed to take minutes. The nun had to let the crutch settle into the bog before proceeding onward. Together, the women made their way to an oversized square tent stretched over a scantling frame. Miss Bonteiller held open the flap.

The tent had been divided into four quarters. An entry held a desk and a captain's chair. Pinned to the canvas wall behind the desk was a sign scratched out in childlike scrawl.

BATH....................$1.00
NEW WATER...........$2.00

"Sister, this is Syd Dixon."

At the introduction, the man never moved his muddy boots from the desk. Rather, he swiveled his head toward Bernadette, exposing a drowsy countenance to his face and nothing but the black pit of a hole where his right ear had been. He looked like he should be a customer at the bathhouse, not its proprietor.

Missy said, "Don't mind him, Sister, he's a drug head. Soapy lets him run the bathhouse because he's able at pinching pokes. Foul of temperament, though."

Dixon said, "Missy, where the hell you been?"

"Errands that are none of your nevermind."

"Look, you little twist, you're in for a whipping one of these days."

Bernadette felt that she had to come to Miss Bonteiller's defense. Syd Dixon was not going to threaten the child in her presence. "She was helping me out, Mister Syd Dixon."

Dixon wiped his nose on the sleeve of his underwear shirt, ignored the nun and spoke to Miss Bonteiller. "How the hell did you end up with a nun? Soapy ain't going to like it."

Miss Bonteiller gave him some of his own thumping. "Not that it's any of your business," she said, "but Soapy himself sent me to fetch her here."

"Just a damn minute." Dixon rose from his chair. Missy turned full on him, didn't shy away a step. Rather, she stood on her tiptoes to speak to his ear. Bernadette concentrated on their conversation—one with by much gesturing–but could not make it out. Other sounds of men and women came from one of the curtained-off sections toward the rear of the tent, sounds of laughter and devilment and splashing water. Mister Dixon and Miss Bonteiller seemed not to hear the fracas.

Bernadette hobbled outside. Four goats were tied to an aspen, ribs as pronounced as if they were about to slice through their saggy hides. Gray and splotched with dried muck, they still had packsaddles attached to their backs. Some drover had been sorely negligent in his duties. She would have unburdened them but Miss Bonteiller appeared. "Sister, it's all right now. You can come back in."

"Saints preserve us, not on your life, child. I may be in need of a good scouring, but I'll not endanger my immortal soul by entering such an establishment again. Especially with that horrible proprietor."

"Sister, you're a cheechacko. It'll take you some time to get used to Alaskan ways. Up here, you do what you must. Last night, you slept in a privy and felt–"

"What?"

"A privy. An outhouse. That crate you slept in? It was Clancy's johnny pot until he moved his business into his new high-fancy wood building. He put his own crapper inside and dumped yours into the alley. Ever since, the boys been using it to sleep off the hooch, or just wait for us gals across the Alley."

"Miss Bonteiller, I think–"

"Don't matter what you think. It's been home to finer folks than you. What I need to know is, do you want this bath or not? I got Syd out of there and fresh water on its way."

Was there no end to the guttersnipe's insolence? Yet, she had a point. If Bernadette wanted to bathe, she had few choices. In the face of adversity, the Lord looks for personal strength. "You say Mister Dixon is gone?"

"You won't see him and I'll stand right outside your room."

"You call these canvas compartments rooms?"

"Sister, bathing a holy woman in this camp ain't no every day event, I can't argue that, but why are you so contrary? Do you want the bath or not? Yes or no?"

Her skin fairly crawled with itchiness. "Yes, child. Yes."

Once back inside the tent, a woman joined them who had been dandied to the nines for some child's party or a stage play. She was twice

The Seduction of Sister Skaguay

Bernadette's age and several sizes stouter than her Angel, the woman wore her hair in an updo, festooned with a gigantic red bow and carried, of all things, a bishop's crozier. Her light blue taffeta dress was plumped up by what must have been a dozen crinolines. She dropped herself into Mister Dixon's chair. It wobbled under her weight. With barely a flicker of her wrist, she reached the crozier across the desk, hooked it around Bernadette's neck, and pulled the nun's head forward. Inches from Bernadette's face, she squiggled up her nose. "I don't see too swell."

"Madam!" Bernadette protested.

"I am one, for a fact. So, strip down. Let's see the goods."

The gall! Did she for one moment–Bernadette could not so much as *think* the words.

Miss Bonteiller said, "Sister, this is my boss, Big Bo Peep. To the woman, Missy said, "Big Bo, you won't believe this. I just learned that this gal is my cousin twice removed. You be nice to her. Soapy hisself said to get her cleaned up."

The nun had no idea why Miss Bonteiller told that whopper. It didn't seem to make the large woman the least bit pleasant.

While they tiffed, Bernadette began to see a side of Colonel Smith that had escaped her earlier meetings with him. His hand touched every enterprise in Skaguay as if it were the Hand of God. He held most answers, and when he did not, he told the flock to have faith. Now, if what Miss Bonteiller said about Frank Reid were true, he was in conflict with the Colonel. Yet, Colonel Smith had been so kind, generous and helpful; Mister Reid was helpful as well, but so rough, cut from a coarser bolt. If the strumpet were to be believed, he was a nonpareil gent. Bernadette had grave doubts about her judgment.

" . . . so get her out of them holy clothes and into a soaker pronto," Big Bo Peep said. "Or I bounce her out into the street." The large woman stormed out before Miss Bonteiller could reply.

"Never you mind about her." Miss Bonteiller led Bernadette to a side cubicle. "Get shed of them duds; I'll take care of the rest."

The water in the plunge tub was clean and steaming. It drew Bernadette like a Miller Moth to a candle, yet she couldn't disrobe with the strumpet looking on. "Miss Bonteiller, I'm afraid I'll decline the bath. Modesty demands–"

"Hooey! I'll just step outside. You peel 'em off and climb in. I'll see that no one bothers you."

The temptation was too strong. Bernadette quickly disrobed and stepped into the bath. She inhaled the aromatic scent–buttermilk soap, she thought–and let the vapors engulf her. Not until she'd sunk herself so deeply into the water that only her head and game leg were above the soaker's rim did it dawn on her that she was completely naked and defenseless in what amounted to a foreign land. She allowed the pleasure of the wash to push the horrible truth from her mind.

"Boo!" Miss Bonteiller poked her head around the canvas curtain, scurried in and gathered the nun's Iron Maiden, and every other bit of her habit and underthings. "I'll get them to the laundry. Back in two shakes of a lamb's tail." She was gone before Bernadette could collect her wits to protest. She was now not only in a foreign place naked and defenseless, her Iron Maiden was gone. *Saints preserve us.*

7. Shams

Careful to keep her picketed leg up on the soaker's rim, Bernadette soon found herself as near to heaven's gate as she had been since sailing from Seattle. The water washed not only her flesh but her soul. And never was a lavage more necessary, nor appreciated. Her wicked weakness for the bath stemmed from being raised in farm country. As often as not, the cistern was low so she was unable to wash properly. Life next to the earth had been pure, yet it included an eternal coating of soil and sweat, as thick as if she'd been dipped in warm molasses and hung up in a sandstorm. A bath, when Saturday rolled around, was a treasure. Had she been able to bathe every night, she would have.

She fell soundly to sleep and awoke to find her habit folded neatly beside the tub, wet but clean right down to her bloomers. She dried herself until she was pink, struggled into the wet clothing–everything was accounted for except her cape–and hobbled outside to face not Miss Bonteiller but Reverend Bowers.

"Missy was called away and sent me to see to your needs," he said. "Sister, with the loss of your traveling companion, I assume you'll be returning home?"

"Not on your life," was her immediate response. Then she couched her reply, "That is, not if I have a choice in the matter. My mission was determined long ago: cleanse the women, body and soul. It's not changed."

"Surely you won't go on alone?"

"I admit, it would be rare for a sister to travel alone. However, I'll take advantage of the telegraph office, wire Mother Francine of my plight and ask her guidance."

"Allow me to escort you."

"Reverend Bowers, my cape has not been returned from the laundry. Might I impose on you to seek it out? I must look a fright in these wet furnishings. Someone made an effort to iron my wimple, but it needs starch." Her nugget and relic were safe, among the few possessions she'd retained after the accident.

"I'll try to track it down just as soon as I get you over to the telegraph office."

"You're so kind."

Like a true gentleman, Reverend Bowers held open the telegraph office door. Much to her amazement, who was behind the counter? Mister Two-Chew Calderone.

He said, "I told you we'd meet again." His Adam's Apple danced its wicked dance.

"Ahem." Reverend Bowers wished to speak. "The good Sister would like to send off a wire."

Mister Calderone pushed a Western Union pad across the counter. "Fill it out," he said, a little too smugly.

Mother Francine:

Al-Ki dumped us in Skaguay. Rock slide between Skaguay and Dyea took Sister Margaret Mary's life. Gave me broken leg. Lost half our supplies, all our money. I'm back in Skaguay mending. Do I continue original plan? Return Minnesota? Will you send second Sister? I await your in-structions.

Yours in Christ,

Sister Bernadette

"Five bucks," Mister Calderone said.

"Five dollars!"

Reverend Bowers said, "So many things in the District come with outrageous prices. This is just one, but it's what everyone pays."

"I'm afraid I have no money. I'll pay you when Mother Francine wires me, or I will go out and beg alms. I am quite competent to do that. Being hobbled may aid my cause." She lowered her eyes–the affected look of the humbled–then asked Reverend Bowers for any suggestion he might offer.

"Have you no money at all, Sister? Nothing of value?"

Mister Calderone said, "No one goes on the jawbone here, lady. Cash on the bar or no telegram."

She produced the nugget Colonel Smith had given her. It would be akin to giving away a first born, but she had little choice.

Reverend Bowers examined it, placed it on the counter. "Mister Calderone, weigh this up. Looks to be a quarter ounce."

Calderone dropped the nugget onto the scale, adjusted the slide. "Almost exactly." He placed it on the counter, seeming to dare Bernadette to take it back.

"You're in luck, Sister," Bowers said. "That'll not only get your message sent, it will cover the return wire."

"Oh, I don't have to pay for a return. Mother Francine will pay for that."

"Receiving charge up here, Sister. We're so far away from the next telegraph station–Juneau–and the line is so long, he has to charge a fee both coming and going." Reverend Bowers shook his head. "Mister Calderone, what do you think? About three hours for a return?"

Mister Calderone nodded.

Bernadette apologized to the Reverend for being so naïve to the ways of the North. "I'm lucky to have you around." She took a last look at the nugget, kissed it as she would a relic of the true cross and pushed it to Mister Calderone. "The Lord provides somehow."

Back on the boardwalk, he asked, "What will you do now, Sister?"

"I have no place to go. Perhaps I'll seek temporary housing. Where does a person of the cloth such as yourself stay?"

"Among Alaska's scoundrels and ne'er-do-wells, the deprived and decadent. I live on a cot in the corner of an unwholesome flop house among men so fallen that even when they cast their eyes heavenward, they see the fires of hell. But, they are my cause in life."

"Do they have rooms for women?"

"None of any kind. A single room with a dry bunk would cost you dearly, far too much for us ministers of the Lord."

"I could always stay in the crate."

"If you have a roof, Sister, lay claim to it.

Broken leg or not, Bernadette needed to be about her mission without malingering. She would make the crate her home for the present and beg alms to improve her lot. No shirking or self-pity. This time when she begged, *she* would be the needy and homeless, the poor. Carry on for Christ! "I will do just that Reverend Bowers, and set about immediately to remedy my financial misfortune."

"Meaning . . . ?"

"We Good Shepherd Sisters are a hardy bunch. Inventive and industrious. I will beg alms, a task I have performed often over the years."

"Beg alms," he repeated, his voice as lifeless as a grave marker.

"There." She pointed across the muddy street to Clancy's Music Hall. "Men spending money on drink and debauchery can well afford to show charity to the needy. The Lord will smile on me."

"Clancy's," he said. "Ah . . . yes. Of course." He tipped his hat to take his leave. Abruptly, she thought. "Good fortune to you," he said. "I must hurry along."

"Thank you for your kindnesses, Reverend. I feel certain our paths will cross again."

"Clancy's" he repeated, this time with an ominous tone to his voice.

"For the Lord," she said. But the Reverend was already down the boardwalk. Bernadette thought, Truly he is a fine, humble man of God, if ever there was one.

*

In Clancy's, noxious cigar and pipe smoke combined with smoke from a ring of brass wall lamps to create a suffocating layer of barely-breathable smudge. The malodorous smell of the devil's own brew made Bernadette feel as if she'd made a terrible mistake. A painted woman in flowing silks sat just inside the door at a window piano, her fingers arched yet motionless over the yellowed keys. She did nothing more than listen to the scratchings of the fiddle player at her side. Along one wall, a mahogany bar was filled with malingerers hunched over their potions like vultures over carrion. Along the other, a dozen round tables with seated men. In the rear, if the huzzahs and cursing were any indication, some form of gaming was in full flavor.

Everyone noticed her. Though her resolve was strong, she shook as she approached the line of men at the bar. She needed to trust in the Lord. These were, after all, his creatures. Good resided in each. Perhaps there were Christian men among them pursuing honorable trades. They were honest working men pursuing an honest dream. She produced her coin purse from her secret pocket and unfastened its clasp. "Alms for the poor?" She leaned against her Winchester crutch, displaying the empty purse.

"Hell, lady, I'm as poor as they come," one man said. "You earn up a stake for me, I'll get you some alms."

A second said, "Got a hitch in your get-along? That's some walking stick. I won't give you no dole, but I might buy that fancy Winchester of yours. I could use me a shooter like that what with all the bushwhacking I do."

63

"Gentlemen." She had to assume the righteousness of the Lord. She knew the lines well. "Children of God the world over die hungry this very day because they do not command the wherewithal for a crust of bread. They have no roof above them, no bed below them. And you good people hold the key to their lives. True, I am destitute at this moment, but I pledge to you any financial token you share with me will be repaid in heaven . . . if not here on earth."

The men tipped their drinks; some rudely showed her their backs. Others shifted uncomfortably. Perhaps this breed of men needed a stern hand to guide them. She'd begin anew, with a stronger tact. "Gentlemen, I promise you, I will not leave the premises until you have done your share. Surely you can swap the price of one . . . concoction . . . for eternal salvation." Now, the entire crowed had stilled. She was their sole focus, a leading lady alone on stage. "Will no one be the first?"

As surely as if she were in a stage play, she felt a curtain drop. A half dozen men, too timid to hold her scathing stare, gathered their pokes and made for the door.

"I'll be the first, Ma'am. I truly will." The men at the door stopped.

The voice came from the back . . . Colonel Smith. "You boys making hellwhoop for the street? Rein it in." He plopped a poke onto the bar and untied its drawstring. "This is the sister lady who was caught in the rock slide over toward Dyea." He pinched together his thumb and forefinger, dipped them into the poke and displayed a nugget the size of a pea. "That's pushing a half ounce, so, Sister, you got your poor folks almost a ten-spot. Good enough for a hundred pounds of beans or twenty pounds of coffee." To the silenced crowd, he said, "Boys, this is one fine lady. We'll stand no cussing or spitting in her presence. She's fallen on hard circumstances, like we all have in our lives from time to time. I would take it kindly for you to help her. All of you." He waved to the barback for an empty shot glass and dropped in the nugget.

*

Soapy thought, Anything to get her out of there and get the argonauts back to their spending money where and how it should be spent. This was one brave woman. She just didn't belong in a saloon. Not yet. Next thing she'll be knocking on the crib doors for donations. It's one thing to work an honest trade to earn an honest wage, quite another to ask for handouts without lifting hand or skirt.

64

*

"I'm afraid I used your first nugget for a telegram to Mother Francine. I'm now awaiting a reply."

Colonel Smith twisted to a frown. "What a pity. That means you'll be working the . . . you'll be soliciting alms all the time?"

"I have no choice."

"Sister, I don't mean to alarm you, but this is no place for a woman of your culture. Henceforth, you should steer yourself away from Skaguay's saloons. You don't wish to discover the many reasons."

"Colonel Smith, I thank you for your concern, but I have begged alms for years. I put my trust in the Lord."

The shot glass was passed down the bar, each man making a deposit, a funereal solemnity to each face. At the end of the bar, the barback reached under his apron and topped the glass with a silver dollar. "A good lode," he said.

Colonel Smith said, "Sister, in these parts, the word *lode* is synonymous with the word *Lord*. Trust in that and you'll stay alive."

Then, as if escorting her from a cotillion, he led her through the door, all the while holding her arm tightly. A great huzzah escaped the men at the bar. She ignored it to examine the shot glass. Nuggets nested in gold-dust flakes like gilded pearls.

"What about the remainder of your possessions?" the Colonel asked.

"Gone, except for what we stored before our departure."

"Your medicines?"

"We have some stored, Colonel. The rest went . . . down Devil's Slide."

"I see," he said. "What will you do?"

"Prior to leaving Minnesota, Mother Francine had made careful arrangements to replenish all of our supplies on a pre-arranged schedule."

On the boardwalk, he said, "Perhaps I can help."

"Who are you, Colonel, to command such respect from the townsmen?"

Colonel Smith tipped his hat. "A compliment of sorts, Sister. Your tone, however, bespeaks another feeling."

Of course, the man was right. She was perplexed. On one hand, he'd provided help and guidance. On the other, he assumed to lead her life, as if it were his to lead. And did so with no concern for her feelings. "You confuse me, Colonel Smith. In this frontier town, you're impeccably dressed

65

with the manners of a Southern gentleman, a charmer to friend and stranger alike. You seem to be lord and master over a world to which you don't belong."

"Sister, I am a simple merchant and an expediter, and about to open my own a saloon shortly. I'd surmise you wouldn't approve of that, either."

"No, Colonel, I would not."

"Sister, you and I seem to have struck out on the wrong foot in spite of my efforts to help."

He was right again. He *had* helped. Perhaps she was being impetuous in her judgment. She was being pulled 'twixt and 'tween. "I've been overwrought by the loss of my beloved companion. I have no reason to challenge you."

"Had you two been together long?"

"She was my spiritual advisor from the time I entered the novitiate. I loved her dearly."

"Let me suggest a memorial for her. Right here in Skaguay. Perhaps a statue. Fully sponsored."

"I was planning such, but had no money. She is most deserving."

"I presume you'd provide details for a suitable inscription?"

"Of course." Once again, he took her breath away. First the nuggets. Now this. How could she continue to doubt him?

"Thank you." He bowed. "Leave the other details to me."

"How can I repay you?"

"There is a way, now that you ask."

Her guard raised like a flag climbing its pole. Then she chided herself for being so foolish without hearing him out. "That being?"

"I've been laboring to build a church. You've seen enough of our infant town to realize none exists. Mine would be a first, and the finished product would be a praise house for four denominations, Catholics included. Yet there is no one of the Catholic faith who has stepped forward to assist, perhaps because we have no priest. Would you consider lending a hand until you leave?"

How could he suggest such? Work with heathens, pagans and falsifiers? Clearly he didn't realize there was but one true church. None other could be recognized. They're all pretenders.

With her hesitation, he said, "The Catholic bishop in Seattle has given his blessing to the effort."

Did Bishop Parker realize to what he was agreeing? She doubted, but would never question any of his directives. Still, she could hardly speak her mind in light of the Colonel's gracious offer regarding Sister Margaret Mary.

"It's to be called the Union Church."

"Of course I would need permission from Mother Francine."

"Even with the Bishop's prior approval?"

"Church hierarchy, Colonel. Let me see what new orders I receive in response to my telegram."

Miss Bonteiller happened along. At a perfect moment, no less. Before the Colonel could wheedle more from her.

The Colonel said, "Missy, I was just asking for the good Sister's help on the Union Church project."

Bernadette said, "And he's offered to hold a memorial for Sister Margaret Mary."

Missy twirled the parasol resting on her shoulder. "Well, ain't you two kindred souls all of a sudden."

"Missy," the Colonel said, his tone notched with pique, "why don't you take the Sister to the Klondyke and get her properly outfitted. Her habit's in shambles. And find her a decent crutch. She can hardly go around using a good Winchester as a hobble-help. Tell Piedmont to put it on my account."

Missy snapped shut the parasol. She pinched his cheek until he winced. "On account of you're so cute."

8. Truths

This nun, Missy thought crossing Broadway, has worn out her guest towel. And Soapy's even worse with his gall asking me to dress her up. What if she decks out in chaps and a duster? That'd fix his pump handle.

By the time the nun reached the mercantile, Missy was inside haranguing the clerk, cross beyond words. "How can the women of Skaguay keep up with the latest fashions if this store carries nothing but gingham and calico? No style goods nor the wherewithal to create them? How can the men of Skaguay be kept happy if the women don't look their finest?"

A single narrow aisle ran down the center of the store. On one side, an assortment of candles, spicy teas, dried fruit, moccasins, mittens, snow excluders, weaponry. Kegs of sweet pickles and crocks of eggs in brine. Flour and pinto beans in sacks tied with thongs. On the other, tins of canned goods, coffee beans and cheese wheels. Lanterns, pots, pans and packsacks hung from ceiling beams alongside cured meats and hides too awful-smelling to touch. A deerskin robe for three dollars. Duck cloth and waxed canvas. Bolts of gingham. Hoes, adzes, froes. Kettles and tack and horse blankets.

"By the way," Missy said to the nun when she'd finished with the clerk, "I already talked to Lank about some hay for your mattress. He's going to bring by some spruce boughs, too. We'll line that bunk of yours and you'll sleep like a baby. Right through the night business." She held up a towel and a pair of red balbriggans. "We'll put you in men's britches for now."

"*Saint Christopher, guide me.*"

Missy figured the nun was put off some, but it made no matter. "You're missing your cape." She displayed a bright red poncho.

"I could never–"

"'Course you could, Sister. We'll size it down same as the original. In a month, no one will know the difference."

"But . . . red?"

"You don't want it?" Missy said. "Okay. I ain't going to force you. Go jump the moon for all I care."

"I'll take it, child. I apologize."

"Ain't no child, either. How many times I have to say that?"

"Are you unsettled with me? I wish you wouldn't be. I can't help the position I find myself in."

"Me, neither." Missy said, and thought, The nun ain't a bad egg, just different. "Maybe it's just me, Sister. The curse. Do you get the monthlies? You must. You're a gal like all of us before you turned into one of whatever you are now."

"Miss Bonteiller, we should speak on a different matter. The Colonel said he would arrange a memorial for Sister Margaret Mary. I trust it will be in good taste. What do you think he has in mind in that there is no priest around?"

"Oh, it'll be a gut-buster. His boys'll see to it that people go. Then, he'll put on a big feed at Clancy's. That's when the real memorial will take place. Your crate'll catch lots of sitting time." She twirled her fingers through her hair ribbons and winked.

"If he thinks for one moment that I'll stand for–"

"You already flew that cliff. No going back. It's in his hands. If he says the affair will be grand, it will be. If he says contrary, it won't be a thing a dog lifts its leg on."

"I don't understand."

"'Course not. You're not supposed to. You're a cheechacko. Just keep smiling and keep one hand on your wallet."

"I'm afraid I–"

"Yeah, yeah. I know. You got no money."

"He spoke to the men in Clancy's and they suddenly became most generous. As if he were the governor or the pope."

"In this town, he might as well be, but *Colonel* suits him fine. You got no idea about nothing. Why–" She suddenly waved toward the street. Frank Reid passed on the boardwalk. Reid tipped his hat, shifted his tripod from one shoulder to the other and kept walking.

Missy said, "The man is so dreamy." She wondered if the nun was ready for the facts of life in Skaguay. She was greener than any fresh fish. At least the men had a sounding for what they wanted–rock-sized nuggets, hootch and gals. This one had no idea except saving souls. The only way to save souls in Skaguay was to leave them on the boat.

"Heavens," the nun said when she saw the price for the mackinaw. "Two dollars!"

Missy examined a pair of baby moccasins. "If you was a baby, these would be fine. Only four bits. Don't quibble on prices. Time's short. I got to get out the road pronto."

"Out the road? Again?"

"You religious folks seem to choke on the idea of business. If you spend much time in Skaguay, you'll learn."

*

Soapy paused at Clancy's door. He was trying to keep all his boys pulling together, but was woefully lacking a lead dog or two. He needed cappers and a couple of top boosters, boys who understood their jobs and handled problems. A few gals, too. Faro layouts and roulette wheels. He'd give an arm to be able to track down Clubfoot Hall and his lightning hands. Clubfoot could teach the games to any stiff willing to learn. The town needed a doctor and a firehouse, too. More money.

"Colonel Smith! Colonel Smith!" A greenhorn with some years to him, yet with a lively spring to his step, took direct aim at him. The new reporter. Soapy knew that newspapers from New York to Denver to San Francisco and Seattle determined a community's feelings. Skaguay would be no exception. Reporters, however, were as meddlesome as grannies at the gossip fence. Soapy stopped and extended his hand.

The man said, "I'm Elmer John White. Folks call me Stroller, late of Seattle, out of the farm fields of Ohio and fresh to your town."

"The pleasure is mine." Soapy bowed. The man wore a suit that had seen too many seasons: threadbare worsted, shiny at the elbows and knees, likely the behind, too. Reporters always looked like they dressed in their fathers' hand-me-downs.

"I've been interviewing the town's leading citizens to get a feel for my new home. Sheriff Taylor, Judge Van Horn, Frank Reid, Big Bo Peep."

At the mention of the boss whore, the men shared a smile. Soapy said, "I've heard the names."

"Do you have time to answer a few questions? Nothing invasive."

"I'd hardly call myself a leading citizen, more like a struggling merchant and expediter."

" . . . but one of great influence. The SKAGUAY NEWS would be interested in your opinion of the past, present and future of the camp."

"A broad subject, Mister White."

"Stroller," the reporter said. He pulled out his pad. "How has the town changed in the year you've been here? I understand you arrived last August."

"It's doubled in size already. Grown by a thousand souls. Look around you. Building, building, building. Now, this very street has but a handful of stick shanties. Mostly tents as far as you can see. In a few more months, the opposite will be true. We'll have completed the growth from canvas to clapboard. There's your answer."

White scribbled in his notebook. "Where's it going?"

"No telling. If we can maintain law and order, we'll have ourselves a miniature San Francisco without the misdeeds."

"Do you consider Sven Lazlo a misdeed? The story goes that he bludgeoned to death one of your associates."

"A half-dozen men saw him do it. If I have anything to say about things, we'll not tolerate such lawlessness. Lazlo will stand trial, as he should."

"Any prediction?"

The newsie was getting close to an edge Soapy didn't like, asking questions whose answers could be turned athwart. "How long have you been in town, Mister White?" He knew the answer, and knew Editor Sherpy's fledgling newspaper could affect his fortunes. He just wanted the reporter to admit outwardly that he was a cheechacko.

"Long enough to know I shouldn't call you Soapy."

"An appellation of unfortunate origin."

"'Unfortunate origin.' I like it." The reporter made another note.

"The town has an unlimited future," Soapy said. "We need a school, a hospital, a firehouse. Presently, we're building its first church. Considering our country's troubles with Spain, there's a war cloud on the horizon that has already re-routed some badly needed supplies and manpower. These are problems to overcome. But this is all obvious." He was talking down to the reporter. As wise as betting against weighted dice. He'd be far better off giving the man something of interest. "You're a drinking man?"

"With a squirt of lemon, I surely am. But back to Lazlo. Any prediction?"

"I certainly won't try to outthink the judicial process, but if I were the judge, he'd hang. You can print those words if you like. Now, what say you to adjourning this chat inside? I'll give you the first-ever public airing of my own plans for a new club."

"You're venturing into the libation business?"

"A man can't have too many interests in a growing town. Perhaps you'd be interested in a new line of work?"

*

Two-Chew Calderone ignored Miss Bonteiller and aimed for Sister Bernadette, his gap-toothed grin and leering eyes most unsettling. "This just come back," he said. He slapped a telegram into the nun's hand.

Remain Skaguay until I find suitable
substitute to join you. Tend the ladies
as planned. Stay the course of
Christianity in all ways. You are doing
a splendid job!

Mother Francine

Miss Bonteiller seemed to sink deep in thought. She watched Calderone head back to the telegraph office. "It's all rot, you know. A sham. Ain't you figured it out yet?"

Bernadette waved the telegram. "The Lord acts in mysterious ways. We may not understand His actions, but He provides nonetheless."

Miss Bonteiller said, "It's time you come of age. The Lord may provide where you come from but he don't provide here in the Alaska District. He don't even visit."

*

Miss Bonteiller dragged Bernadette to a lot behind the telegraph office, checking over her shoulder, the look on her reddened face clearly one of fear. "Child," Bernadette said, "what in heavens name . . . ?"

Missy clamped her hand over the nun's mouth. "Sister, listen." She spoke in hushed tones. "If I get caught telling you this, you can look for me splattered next to your pard. They'll kill me deader than . . . . " She pointed to the crucifix at the end of Bernadette's rosary. "I work for Soapy. He holds paper on half the town and runs most all of it. He and me came up here last summer with a band of gunsels he gathered up from Denver, Creede and Seattle. They been the boss bears since. They're a confidence mob, a bunkum bunch, for sure. A meaner hoard ain't never been formed. Half already on the dodge. Remember that Sven Lazlow?"

"His capture was the first thing I saw when I landed on the beach."

"The old guy he clobbered was one of Soapy's boys. Soapy don't abide anyone crossing his action."

"Really, Miss Bonteiller, Colonel Smith is a gent of the first order. He gave me nuggets twice. Does that seem like something an outlaw would do?"

"Lady, he's a bunco artist and a killer, the best sure-thing grifter Denver ever saw. Sworn friend to Bat Masterson and Bob Ford, the plug who back-shot Jesse James himself. He owns Two-Chew Calderone, Old Man Tripp, your friend Reverend Bowers, John Fay, and fifty other fellows like poor Portland Pete. All the crib gals, including Big Bo Peep herself, are on his pad. He's the one and only town nabob. You're best off to lay clear."

"Crib girls? Working for the Colonel?"

"I'm Soapy's spread-leg fancy piece. Believe me, I know what's what. That's why I can get away with so much." Her face flushed again. "If you haven't summed it up yet, I work the fleshpot, too."

"Piffle. You're just a sassy young tart who should be in school." That this very girl could be a harlot was preposterous. Her skin was covered with more childhood freckles than a tree had leaves.

She said, "I been standing my own porch going on three years. I'd already taken up with a freebooting cracksman in Creede when Soapy found me. I fell for his slick ways. He talks the gilded words a gal loves to hear. Then he turned me to the hog ranch."

Bernadette could hardly believe what this–this baby!–was saying. Colonel Smith? Reverend Bowers?

Missy peeked around the side of the telegraph office as nervous as a mom cat. "His gun sharks don't trouble the town folk much so long as they pay him a cut. For it, his boys keep the wild miners in line. His main aim is for the stakes brought up by the stampeders going into the fields and the pokes they carry out. He sure don't want no religious gal raising a ruckus."

"But he's been so generous."

"You got what he wants."

"Miss Bonteiller!" Bernadette would never tolerate such talk.

"No, no, no. Not that. Maybe, in time, not just now. You got the fix for us what catch a dose."

"Not as much as before the slide. What remains is safely stored with Reliable Packers."

The Seduction of Sister Skaguay

"Sister, have you got a cow pie for a brain or are you just deaf as deadwood? You ain't heard a word I said." She took Bernadette's shoulders in her tiny hands again. "You ain't got no supplies any more. They're gone and no one can get them back. Not even the vigilance committee. Take yourself a visit to Reliable; see for yourself. They'll give some tut-tut about why they're gone. You'll not see them again, I assure you. Bowers took you to Reliable. That's one of Soapy's fronts. He'll keep them medicines and whatever else what he needs. Ship the rest south to some crooks in Seattle along with tons of other stolen goods. He gets folks coming and going."

The child was, by now, pleading. Bernadette felt for her coin purse and squeezed. Could it be that this was her sole defense against total poverty? The Lord would not let that happen. Weakly, she said, "I have my orders. You read the telegram."

Miss Bonteiller pointed to a wire that ran from the telegraph office to a series of three tall poles thirty yards apart, all cleanly barked and standing shiny. They followed the line from pole to pole. Missy stood at the final pole and stared up. Then she pointed to a boulder where the line went underground. "It ends right there. Under that rock. Give it a jerk."

Bernadette gave the line a little tug and ended up with two frayed copper ends in her hand.

"Another one of his confidence games."

"But I paid Mister Calderone. I received a telegram in return. You read it!"

"Calderone's nothing but a boot-licking dry-gulcher. Period. All outgoing telegrams are read by Soapy, by Bowers if he's standing in for Soapy. They personally write every reply. You should see all the wires the stampeders receive after they send one out—wires speaking to sick young 'uns back home needing emergency surgery, a roof needing replacement, a terrible accident—all with specific directions how to wire home the money from this very office. The dumb rube always gives us the money and always gets a telegram back, thankful for the funds." She snatched the copper telegraph cable from Bernadette and tucked it back under the rock like she was tucking in a baby. "All written by Soapy or Bowers."

Bernadette asked, "How does he get away with it? Where's the law?"

"The law in Skaguay is decided at miners' meetings. Soapy runs those by paying off a handful of pretend gold-seekers, and enforces it with his strong-arm boys."

"I don't understand."

Miss Bonteiller chewed her lip. "The town's like a triangle. At its wide bottom are citizens, boosters and swampers, folks that don't have a thought in their noggin. Next up are lookouts and bouncers, then maybe the dance callers and case-keepers. The top of the heap is the faro dealers. Somewhere along the line is the commercials, but it's hard to tell where. Us demimondes and dance-hall janes are all up and down the ladder. Mostly down. Real law can't hardly be seen. That's why Soapy is so successful. His head-bangers keep the wild miners under control. Bowers, Big Bo and Ed Fay keep a constant eye on things. Folks get caught knocking down, they get a pasting. Get caught again, they're lucky to get blue-ticketed to Seattle. More likely, they wake up dead at the bottom of the Devil's Slide."

"But the decent folks . . . ?"

"We got Deputy Marshal Rowan, a federal who's honest, but he's only one man and his wife's in a maternal way. He sees to her closely. We got Sheriff Taylor, a lying skunk. Soapy buys his every bullet and bean. Frank Reid has his vigilance boys, but they're mostly lily-livered merchants. Don't know fighting from farting, excuse my talk. They all get strong-armed by Calderone and the other cutthroats. Sometimes Soapy makes the merchants partners, like he did with John Clancy. Men here just want to run their businesses and climb the money mountain. They're not fighting men. Except for Frank Reid."

Bernadette still didn't understand everything Miss Bonteiller was saying, but had a sudden chill, like being alone in church late at night when a cold wind gusts through. Over her life, her total consecration to the Lord had been her strength. She took seriously her perpetual vows of Poverty, Chastity and Obedience, and accepted the great comfort they afforded. The little strumpet's warnings put her terribly on edge. She hardly knew what to think about the Colonel. He'd been kindly and generous, and rakishly charming. A second chill prickled her. This one was not from fear. She blessed herself. "I will call on Mister Two-Chew Calderone and then visit Reliable Packers. If I don't receive satisfaction, I intend to confront Colonel Smith himself."

Miss Bonteiller grabbed her sleeve. "I can't go with you. I'd be digging my own hole."

"I understand. Do you counsel me against going?"

The Seduction of Sister Skaguay

"Yes and No. Yes, because you'll create another rile. Calderone don't need much of a reason for an ambush. No, because up here, you have to stand your ground or they'll chop you up like kindling. You got to be careful, though. I get by with lots of shenanigans because everyone knows I'm Soapy's gal. At least till he takes another." She paused to wink at me. "The citizens treat me fine, too, because I do them favors with Soapy's boys. He once said he was going to make me mayor of Skaguay because I was a natural-born liar. Truth is, I only use what God gave any beautiful gal." She bounded off, almost pranced away, her skirt rustling.

Considering Miss Bonteiller's youth, Bernadette found it difficult to understand how men sought her favors. Truly, the child's spirit was that of a young mare, sprightly and lively. For certain, she was a slick talker. Given a proper upbringing, she may have gone on to make some lucky gent a fine wife and devoted mother to his children. Marrying her now would be like bringing home a mare with a stomach full of scours.

Bernadette thought about taking a lesson from the feisty child. She'd proven herself in the face of adversity and survived like an animal in the wild. Along the way, she exuded a goodness not seen in most people of any calling. Bernadette wished for her fortitude.

At the telegraph office, Calderone glared. Bernadette would not be deterred. "Mister Calderone, I shall not mince words with you. Earlier today, I paid you to send a telegram, paid you with a nugget. I also paid for a return message. However, I have traced the wire to its end and I find Skaguay has no real telegraph. I demand my nugget back."

The pink of his tongue showed through his missing front teeth. "You'll be damned first."

Bernadette steadied herself on the counter and pondered leveling her Winchester at him. She could never do such. Nevertheless, that nugget was rightly hers and she'd not be bilked. "If you don't see fit to return my property, I shall find Colonel Smith and have him fix your clock."

"Look, lady, you sent a message and got one back. That was the deal."

"But no message ever went out!"

"So you say."

Mister Calderone sneered, making it clear she was to gain no satisfaction. She pushed back from his counter. "You underestimate the might of the Lord, Mister Calderone."

How foolish! Was she going simple of mind? Did she not hear what Miss Bonteiller said? Of course Calderone would not refund the nugget. It made no sense for her to appeal to the sheriff. If Miss Bonteiller were to be believed, he was in the gang. Perhaps that Marshal Rowan?

"Maybe I do," he said, "but I like that new poncho of yours. Red. The color of the night gals."

Jesus, Mary and Joseph! Does the man have no couth! Bernadette set to shaking, dearly wishing for her Angel's counsel.

"Lady, you remind me of my late wife. She'd go all red in the face like you just done."

"You should treat all women as you treated her. My condolences on her death."

"None needed. Died doing what she wanted to do—having a baby. Baby died, too. Probably for the best."

"Mister Calderone!"

"Save it, lady. You ain't getting no refund. You sent a wire, got one back. A deal's a deal."

The effort had been for naught. In spite of young Miss Bonteiller's warning, Bernadette marched herself straightaway to Reliable.

As predicted, her goods had been lost. Bernadette wasted no more time and immediately sought out the Colonel. At Clancy's, she banged her crutch on the puncheon floor. The impact rattled the walls. The ploy was successful. The tinkling of the piano ceased, laughter stopped and a hush rolled over the saloon like a night fog silencing a roiling river. In her most severe voice, she said, "Where is Colonel Smith to be found?"

*

"Here, Sister." Soapy held his parson's hat over his heart as the nun serpentined through the saloon's tables. He rose and bowed, the hat remaining over his heart. What could the woman want now, he wondered. She was beginning to fester like a bad snake-bite.

She said, "I need to talk with you immediately."

He motioned her to a chair. "How can I help?" He didn't want the answer, but her public fearlessness told him he'd be wise to listen.

She related her tale. This time, it was Two-Chew's sorry luck to be working the telegraph office. Soapy'd have to figure a way to keep the pair apart. "Charlatans abound in Skaguay," he said, shaking his head. "I believe I can make inquiries and have your nugget returned."

The answer must have come too easily. She didn't draw a breath. "And what about my supplies stored with Reliable Packers? I'm told they were lost. Just disappeared."

"Sister, I'm no magician."

"Colonel Smith, what if I went outside and began a public discourse about how Reliable Packers cheated me and that you hold a financial interest in that enterprise? Do you not think I'd gain a certain amount of sympathy?"

She had him. He nodded in recognition of her point. "Of course you would, Sister. And I'd be embarrassed. I also believe that the reasonable people of this town would merely ask if you'd been through every tent, storage bin and meat locker in Skaguay? Had you been up the trail to see if they had, perhaps, been shipped elsewhere in error? Had you checked in Dyea?"

She shook her head.

"Nowhere will you find my name written in association with Reliable Packers. You would do yourself a grave disservice by bearing false witness against me. It would be a fool's errand . . . and I know you're no fool." That seemed to give her pause. "Will that be all?"

"No," she said. "I would like to know the details of the memorial you have planned for Sister Margaret Mary."

Clearly, the nun had no intention of ceding an inch of her ground. He withdrew a pack of playing cards from his vest and shuffled repeatedly. Finally, he said, "Do you have a favorite card, Sister?"

"Colonel Smith, I do not gamble in any fashion."

"We have that in common. Sitting at a card table or standing behind my tripe and keister, I'm not gambling. I'm making wages. I never lose, so humor me for a moment. Is there one card of the pack that tickles your fancy? Choose it and tell me."

"I told you—"

"Humor me."

"The Lord is the King of our hearts. I choose the King of Hearts."

"A fine choice." He spread the cards face up across the table. "Do you see your card?"

She pointed to it.

He removed the King of Hearts, slid it to her. "Touch it."

"Colonel–"

"Touch it." He wasn't asking.

She touched the card as if touching a leper.

He slid the King of Hearts into the pack's center. After shuffling slowly, he fisted the pack, cracked it once on the table and flipped it almost to the ceiling. The cards hung together. On the pack's descent, he caught it cleanly and placed the cards, face up, on the table covering. "Find your King."

She sorted through the cards once, twice, three times. No King. She searched again, this time arranging the cards by suit. The King of Hearts had disappeared. She counted the pack–fifty-one cards.

He said, "I am not without resources in this town, Sister. As a gesture of Christian good will, I will see to your friend's memorial tomorrow morning at nine. Leave the details to me. Sister Margaret Mary will be well remembered. Further, I'll have your nugget returned. However, I take unkindly to malicious accusations."

As an adult might pretend to remove a penny from a child's ear, he leaned across the table and drew the King of Hearts from the side of her wimple.

*

Frank Reid turned into Clancy's to slake his thirst. At the back table, he saw the nun and Soapy. Was the fox trying to wile his way into that henhouse? He was an able one, amazingly able. Considering that the man was only thirty-seven, Soapy had come a far pace. He must have started his outlaw ways while still in the cradle. Reid was no saint, but his life was that of a padre when set beside Smith's. At least Frank had his honest-man trade and could hold his head up on Sunday morning, if not exactly being a regular to the church meetings.

He ordered a Belmont, made it a double, and wondered if Soapy knew that he'd stood trial for murder in Oregon near on twenty years back . . . that he'd been a school teacher . . . that, after seeing some of his pards with Piute arrows in them, he'd scalped Indians and had enjoyed the scalping. Frank might not take the same tack today. Back then, he was a young buck pissing nails. He belonged in the saddle or on the trail, not in a classroom. He laughed as the whiskey brought its warmth. The nun noticed him at the bar, pushed back from the table and left through the back door. Smith grimaced, and beckoned Reid to the round table.

"What are we going to do with her, Frank?"

"No problem to me."

"That's good to learn. I'd like your help on her behalf." Soapy explained his commitment to the memorial service.

"Help you put on a memorial for a nun?" Reid asked.

"I gave my word." Smith said. "I can have Bowers round up most of the townfolks. I'd be obliged if you could talk to the new postmaster–I haven't had the pleasure yet–and the marshal. You get on with the federal boys better than me."

"I don't know–"

"Talk to your vigilance boys and the NEWS. I don't know how that Stroller White favors me yet."

"They're the only ones not on your pad."

"Frank, a memorial like this will be good for the town. We both want positive publicity. It'll give us all a chance to pull in one direction."

True, Soapy was openly generous to every town charity. Jumped in front of any new social effort. No denying it. He started shuffling the cards. Reid said, "You gonna have a game at the burying ground?"

"Frank, please. Have a drink. Relax. Sit."

Reid thought, He's got more angles than a geometry book. Yet, a memorial for the nun couldn't hurt. "I guess I can talk to them." He refused to sit.

"The nun is a fine woman. I had conflicting opinions of her at first. Now I see how she can be good for the town."

"You let her stay that way."

Soapy said, "You have no faith."

If the good folks in Skaguay ever grew balls, they'd rise up and run Smith and his cutthroats off a buffalo jump. Frank'd be leading the charge.

*

Soapy found Bowers. "Charlie, you have a new job. The nun has been pestering me to hold a memorial for the one who died. Nine tomorrow. At the cemetery. Spread the word. Get all the boys ready. Reid will handle the federals and the NEWS, if he's to be believed. Charlie, I want the nun's eyes to pop out. Make the show as big as you can. Tell the merchants to shut down for an hour. Hootch on the house before and after. Gather everyone in front of Clancy's ready to march to the cemetery, but don't take a step until I give the signal."

"Food?"

"After the funeral. Have that Widow Pullen prepare it. Tell Bo to have the gals decked out. Put the dealers on notice. We'll make a boodle."

"Trail boys, too?"

"Everyone! I mean to make an impression on this woman. We need her medicines, but she has to learn that we write the Skaguay bible and every book in it."

"Got it."

"And find Two-Chew. Tell him to return a fair-sized nugget to her. From his own pocket. Now."

Bowers made a note.

"Be sure you put in that book of yours that nothing moves tomorrow until my signal."

9. Burying Air

Sister Bernadette paid a second visit to Reliable Packers. Her goods were still as gone as if carted off by the devil himself. She left the office and paused on the boardwalk, noticing the sunset. It carried a gray warning of the coming winter with occasional winds as sharp as lightning bolts. Early snows were on the horizon. She was struck by the intensity of the men at their labors. The drovers worked with renewed vigor, driving the animals with relentless whip and curse. They strained toward invisible destinations with set teeth, the hooves of their horses and mules plodding the ruts of Broadway, heedless of merchants and stampeders.

She noted the paucity of women. In the convent, they'd been taught that men needed the softening and the grooming that women brought. Not ladies of Miss Bonteiller's ilk, no. Women of biblically-strong character like the Widow Pullen. Women who could work behind their men and prepare meals and bear healthy children. As hard as Skaguay was, a shipful of women would make a difference that no amount of Christian doctrine might yield.

Her thoughts drifted to Angel's wonderful humor and her beatific presence. Truly no one was closer to the Lord than she. Bernadette wondered about the memorial. Truth be told, she had no idea what Colonel Smith meant when he volunteered to handle the details. He surely owned the manners of a gentleman, but what kind of service would he put on? Was he as bad as Miss Bonteiller said? Bernadette was at his mercy–in his debt somewhat–and in no position to interfere.

She gathered her Iron Maiden about her and slogged across the mucky street. "You!" she heard. The evil rasp of Mister Two-Chew Calderone. Would she ever be rid of the man?

"Sir?" She turned to face him, putting a slight upturn to her chin. Clearly, he was furious. Tobacco spittle ran down his chin, the glistening brown stream trailing through his whisker stubble. His mouth curved down and his eyes squinted.

"Here." He thrust a grimy hand at her. In the center of his palm, a nugget gleamed like a bright star in a black night.

"I expect to see you at Sister Margaret Mary's memorial tomorrow. Nine a.m."

"When fish breathe sand."

"We'll see about that."

The nugget was half the size of her original. She reached for it nonetheless. Calderone closed his fingers around hers. "You and me is going to have a real dust-up one of these days. Mark my word, ain't no one gonna save you." He spat into the mud. "Not your little whore friend nor Frank Reid neither."

He didn't see Reid walking toward them. Bernadette said, "Isn't that Mister Reid now?"

Calderone scurried off like a flushed whitetail, his displeasure giving her some sinful satisfaction.

"Good day to you," Mister Reid said. He doffed his Stetson and held it behind his back. With his free hand, he nervously stroked his handlebar moustache.

"And good day to you, Sir."

"Can I help you along?"

"I'm doing quite well, thank you. Mending will be slow, but I shall prevail."

"I expect you're a prevailing woman."

The arch to her eyes must have told him that she didn't understand.

He said, "I mean, I expect you know your own mind."

"And I expect to see you at Sister Margaret Mary's memorial."

"I'll be there, for a fact."

Right then–so few words spoken–she knew he'd been taken with her. Even though she'd had no experience with men, she felt his interest as sure as night follows day. It was her turn to blush. "Mister Reid, I am a Good Shepherd Sister and not a woman of this place. Do you understand me?"

*

"You're not going to be happy, Boss." Bowers fingered the mole on his chin, then pointed to three newspapers spread across the bar. "Portland, Seattle and San Francisco."

Soapy already knew the problem but couldn't help taking himself back to the Denver fracas with newspaper editor John Arkins. Arkins had publicly slandered Soapy and refused to apologize. The man continued to rail in his ROCKY MOUNTAIN NEWS, making the mistake in one editorial of mentioning Soapy's wife. Soapy assaulted Arkins and beat him within an inch of his life. The editor did not relent, eventually forcing Soapy and his boys out of Denver. Thus began a series of short stops: Creede,

The Seduction of Sister Skaguay

Cheyenne, Salt Lake City, Ogden, Pocatello. Nothing the size and profitability of Denver. He wouldn't again make that mistake with a newsie.

"This is what happens when we let the miners get out of camp with their pokes full," Soapy said. "If we'd picked them clean like we should have, they wouldn't be so quick to strut their stories to the newspapers. Their embarrassment would have kept their mouths as stoppered as fresh whiskey bottles."

Bowers read from the CHRONICLE. "'From Moore's Wharf where ships dock in sinful Skaguay, Alaska District, to the river banks of Bonanza Creek in the Klondyke, not a mile lies barren of the Colorado strong-arm thugs who cheat, rob and murder those who dare to pass through.'"

Soapy said, "If only we had enough boys to cover that distance properly. Charlie, we need more help on the trail. When weather stops the suckers at Sheep Creek or The Scales or the pass, there's money to be made. They get thirsty, lonesome, frisky. We need our boys to work right up to the divide. Set Bo to thinking about gals, too."

"We're short on many fronts."

"That sin rests on my shoulders. For a month, I've been jabbering about a trip south, yet haven't made a move. No more. I'll get down there anon and round up a crop of new boys. Some gals, too. If we're going to take a pasting in the newspapers, we might as well earn it foursquare." He tapped his finger on an article. "Here's our real problem. 'A far safer point of embarkation to the Klondyke has proven to be Dyea, a point not ten miles from sinful Skaguay. In Dyea, a small outpost of federal troops abetted by honest local government keeps the peace.' *That's* our problem. If the argonauts think there's a safer option, they may take it." Soapy pushed one newspaper from the bar. "History teaches us that big strikes–silver, lead, coal, you-name-it–create hell-on-wheels meccas close to the find. Both Skaguay and Dyea are hundreds of miles from the workings, but with the good water access we share, we're the best West Coast option. Right now, the publicity paints us sorrowfully. We need some admirable hoopla. What do you know of this cheechacko newsie at the paper? I've only met him once."

"Folks call him Stroller. He's not likely to hurt us."

"Why do you say that?"

"He enjoys his drink. 'With a squirt of lemon' as he puts it. He's a citizen, but takes in the games from time to time. Maybe we need to work on his boss."

"Good idea. Toss Sherpy some bones. Get our friends to advertise. Start beating the drum for our new place. Let him know that we'll all spend plenty with him. Make sure he understands exactly who's behind the largesse."

"He's a civic-minded citizen."

"As are we. Get him on the Union Church committee. Handle it personally, Charlie. Tell me how I can help along the way."

"As good as done."

"If we keep getting sour apples, the do-gooders will rise up. Get the Judge over here. That Lazlo character is sitting upstairs. I'm paying to feed and guard him. It's time to spread the word about his trial."

"Maybe you should start your own paper."

"First let's see if Sherpy can be dealt with. Once he knows we're foursquare for law and order, he'll likely come over. If he doesn't, he might have a fire. In the meantime, we'll consider other strategies. Step cautious. Snoopy newsies are dangerous, even if they're on the pad. They're just boys who can't find real jobs."

*

So that Bernadette might have a moment of quiet reflection before the memorial, she left her privy promptly at eight. Her leg screamed at each step, yet the snow-capped mountains, the aspen and cottonwood . . . a more serene setting for Angel's eternal rest could not be found in a poet's book. The cemetery was a mile out the wagon road along the Skaguay River.

Along the way, she questioned herself about the Lord's motives for Angel's accident. Why did He will it? Was Bernadette at fault? It was she who had insisted on wearing the snow excluders. Angel could have insisted on the gum boots. She was the senior, the steel chain with no weak links. She could have worn her gum boots over Bernadette's objection. Still, Bernadette repeated the questions, Why did the Lord permit the death of this vibrant sister? How much blame rightfully belonged on her?

She had no answers.

Toward nine, she reached the wrought-iron gate that served as entryway to the cemetery. Scattered among the tree stumps, rocks, boulders and deadfall were, perhaps, fifty graves. The deceased were marked by plain pine headboards. At the river side of the cemetery, a dozen long boxes with peaked roofs were painted in bright reds and yellows and greens, a Russian cross adorning each. Native burials, she'd heard. Nine graves with white-washed fences and pickets matching those around her leg were clustered at the top of a slight knoll.

In the far corner of the cemetery under a massive spruce, four men in simple black uniforms were smoothing the berm around a grave hole. Bernadette took it for Angel's final home on earth. Three lines of heavily manila rope were strung across the opening. The gravediggers spotted her, laid down their shovels and crossed their hands reverently.

She approached and was caught short. Each gravedigger wore a black uniform with a high-standing collar and a stiff-billed hat monogrammed with the letter "S." *Lord, have mercy on us sinners!* The uniform of the Salvation Army!

To them, she quickly realized that she must have been quite a sight: her hobbled gait that of a true cripple, her white wimple smeared and soiled, the bottom half of her Iron Maiden caked with mud, her new cape a bright red. How her Angel would have bellowed a great laugh at the irony: heathen Salvationists digging her grave, yet no remains to inter. Why then, Bernadette wondered, were they digging a grave? She wondered if her future could hold a stranger event?

She didn't speak to them, nor they to her. They may have arrived in the Alaska District before her, but it remained to be seen who would be snuffing out the last candle. She didn't trust the people at all, and finally said, "This will be a Catholic service. None other will be tolerated." They seemed to realize they were unwanted. Wordlessly, they hoisted their shovels and marched off, shoulders bent and heads cowed like oft-beaten dogs.

At the edge of the grave, Bernadette peered down into eternity. Nothing could substitute for belief in the immortality of the soul. Without immortality, what? The proof was in the question itself.

When she bent her good knee to kneel, the broken leg, unused to carrying any weight, collapsed. She went down like a shoulder-shot buck, yet unhurt except for her pride. As no one was around to aid her, she clambered to her feet, clutching fistfuls of the fresh-turned earth.

It was now past nine. Could it be that Colonel Smith was having a grand joke at her expense? She shifted uncomfortably on her crutch. If she stood too long in one spot, the barrel of the Winchester sunk into the muck and she'd begin to list. She started the rosary, commencing with the Sorrowful Mysteries. With each *Hail, Mary*, she checked the trail. Her crutch and her spirit sunk with every prayer. By the time she'd reached the Joyful Mysteries, the sun was high. She gave up hope. Colonel Smith had made a fool of her.

She felt a faint shudder in the ground, as if, far off, an avalanche was sliding down a mountainside. When she turned, Colonel Smith sat like a cavalry officer high astride a fine dapple stallion. He'd replaced his parson's hat with a gold-piped G.A.R. A gray feather rose proudly from the piping. Angled across his chest was a black silk sash. His mount side-stepped smartly is if he knew he was the head of a parade. Directly behind him, arms linked, Reverend Bowers, Miss Bonteiller and Frank Reid. Following them, a dark-skinned Native, face as wizened as a bowl of dried prunes, hand-led a team of malamutes. A rough-hewn casket rode smartly on a dogsled bedecked in black bunting, three pall-bearers along each side. Had someone climbed down into the gorge to retrieve Angel's remains? It couldn't be. Her body had been too badly–no, it couldn't be.

An army of townsfolk swelled eight-wide across the wagon trail. Bernadette couldn't see the end of the procession. There had to be four-hundred souls. At the cemetery gate, the Colonel reined in the dapple. He dismounted, crossed the cemetery and bowed courtly to her, then bid the casket-bearers forward. When she saw that one of the bearers was none other than sneering Mister Two-Chew Calderone, she almost refused the Colonel's gallantry.

She whispered to the Colonel. "The casket?"

"Symbolic, Sister. We're burying an empty box." The Colonel cleared his throat and turned to the assembly.

He removed his G.A.R. and stared at the crowd until every man had bared his head. In a voice that rang of practiced preachment, he said, "Good people of Skaguay, Alaska has lost another pioneer. She was a woman of the cloth known as Sister Margaret Mary. Some of you know that I once studied for the Baptist ministry, but I'll not be the one to pray today. We're here to pay our solemn respects to Sister Margaret Mary and to share the sadness with her friend, known to us as Sister Bernadette." He stepped back and virtually abandoned Bernadette to the mourners. They appeared to be awaiting loaves and fishes.

The Seduction of Sister Skaguay

"Our Father, who art in heaven . . . " She expected voices to join in, but not a single one was raised. She could do nothing but soldier on alone. She concluded the Lord's Prayer, then added, *"Eternal rest grant unto her, O Lord, and may Your perpetual light shine upon her. May her soul and all the souls of the faithfully departed through the mercy of God rest in peace. Amen."*

The Colonel raised his arms and the citizenry chorused, "Amen."

He must have recognized that her remaining strength had been played out. He waved his hat at the bearers. They lowered Angel's casket into the ground. He took Bernadette's arm and led her from the cemetery, the townspeople filling in behind them as a solid phalanx.

She noticed her fingernails still retained dirt from Angel's grave. Her mother would be shamed. For now, she limped along the path to town, her leg feeling as if it were dragging the full weight of the true cross. She leaned heavily on the Colonel's arm, her grief camouflaged behind a wooden façade as strong as a fortress wall.

*

Holding open Clancy's door, Colonel Smith announced that he would stand a drink for each and every man who'd been to the cemetery. They tumbled pell-mell into the saloon. Clancy's was soon crammed to the guards.

Bernadette stood back so as not to be trampled by the gluttonous stampeders. Imagine, demon drink before noon! She hobbled to the side of the building, thinking of the man being held prisoner upstairs. How lonesome he must be. She would call on him in Angel's memory.

Each stair was as painful as a station of the cross. If only she had some of Mister Reid's elixir. An outer storm entrance at the top of the stairwell allowed her access to a narrow inner hallway and the pent up smell of tobacco, beer slops and vile stenches of unknown origins. Mister Tripp sat under a candle, reading a dime novel. When he saw Bernadette, he almost fell off the chair. He stuffed the book in his shirt and jumped to his feet. "What are *you* doing here?"

"I've come to visit the prisoner."

"Says who?" The book dropped from the opening in his shirt. He scrambled to hide it.

She refused to idle away time with him. Taking a page from Miss Bonteiller's book, she said, "I've just buried my best friend and have been on the arm of Colonel Smith all the while. Now, either you let me in or I shall personally bring the Colonel here and you can answer to him."

"No, Ma'am. Don't do that. You can go in, if you're sure you want to."

"I am."

He took an oversized iron latchkey from a wall hook. "The old geezer is meaner than he seems. You holler if he gives you any cause for concern."

"He shan't." She couldn't resist a question. "Mister Tripp, under what auspices do you guard the prisoner? Aren't you employed by Reliable Packers as a trail guide?"

"At times, yes, Ma'am. Other times, I'm a deputy sheriff. Sometimes I work the telegraph office or keep the boys in line in Cat Alley, if they get too frisky. I work where I'm needed."

She didn't know what to make of this information. Curious, the ways of the north.

Lazlo's cell stank of sauerkraut gone bad. One corner had been turned into a cesspool of chewing tobacco spittle. A brass spittoon sat atop a lantern crate, not a drop of the inky slaver on it. The prisoner was sleeping on his stomach under a pile of quite comfortable-looking skins.

The iron-barred door clanged shut behind her. Mister Lazlo rolled to his back. His full beard of yellowed whiskers grew up his neck from the collar of his flannel shirt. Rather than the coarse facial hair of most men, his seemed to be flaxen, almost silky. He was far older than her paternal grandfather, at least eighty. And, he was barefooted.

"An angel of the Lord," he said, taking in her sackcloth. Thin pink lips shone through the beard. Matching healthy cheeks glowed under his blue eyes. "You're a welcome sight to this old man."

"I am far from an angel," she said. "I am Sister Bernadette of the Good Shepherd Sisters."

"You was on the tideflat."

"I was," she said. "Where are your shoes?"

"Prisoners never get to keep them. Cuts down on runaways." He sat up, rubbed his eyes and extended a knotty hand, its backside dotted in scabrous sores. "Sven Lazlow. Been working the Klondyke since time started . . . Fortymile to the Yukon River. In-law to George Carmacks hisself."

Her look of ignorance must have urged him to continue. "Carmacks and Skookum Jim found the big lode. Started this whole darn mess."

She'd heard a similar story aboard the *Al-Ki*.

89

"Now I'm to swing because some old pusbrain was stupid as a sinker and pulled a gun on me. Me–who's been in these parts thirty-nine year!" The old man ran his hand through his yellowed beard. "In that I'm the one to swing, I guess I'm a stupid one, too."

He slumped back against the wall.

"You haven't had a trial."

"Oh, I'll get one. Then the sheriff'll hang me. He's on Soapy's payroll like most around here. And Soapy got him to do the arresting."

She didn't know what to make of this incestuous lot. It was Sodom and Gomorrah. On one hand, she found the stories about the Colonel almost unfathomable. On the other, the evidence was mounting. She hardly knew what to say. "Will you pray with me?"

"These hoosegow walls would come down."

"But your soul might be salvaged."

"Ain't no prayer can save me, Sister."

Was he right? He had killed a man, but was he a killer? It was hard to believe of the old timer. "I'll take your case up with Colonel Smith. Personally."

*

Unable to locate him, she returned to her privy. It had been rifled. Her poke was gone!

*

Frank Reid figured that if he had a hair left on his ass, he would walk into Clancy's and shoot Soapy Smith right through the heart. Like as not, a half dozen of Smith's henchmen would cut him down before he cleared leather. Frank wasn't looking to be a martyr, but he wouldn't stand to be hectored. He just wanted a decent town to call home. He was fifty-six and tired of roving. If commerce survived, he'd get his share. He'd already staked a homestead parcel overlooking the Bay. Of course, he'd done that a year back. Since, he'd tacked together a flimsy one-room shack, but hadn't dropped the first tree to commence building a real home. The spot was one step from heaven. Someday . . . .

Maybe he was jealous of Smith–what he owned, what he'd done, the goddamn attention he could grab. The man had honed his talents well in other bonanza towns. Now, he was the boss here. "Goddammit," Reid said, "I laid out this town!" His own voice startled him. He looked up to see if anyone had heard, only to find the nun hobbling toward him. Why did a woman like her join the convent? She and Soapy likely had the same problem: Soapy couldn't help himself from being an outlaw and the nun couldn't help herself from being a nun.

"Good day, Mister Reid," she said. "You have a curious look to your face."

"Sister." He touched the brim of his Stetson.

"Colonel Smith tells me you were instrumental in gathering support among some of the townspeople for Sister Margaret Mary's memorial. I've come to thank you."

"My pleasure." He'd only spoken to Marshall Rowan and the new postmaster. Smith did it all, goddammit to hell. And then rubbed Reid's face in it by leading the procession on the big stallion.

"Mister Reid, I am curious to know about Sven Lazlo. I just spoke with him. He's convinced he's going to hang and that no one can save him."

"Probably so."

"The man drew a gun on him."

"Sister, I ain't saying it's right, but it's the law. 'Sides, your friend owns the judge lock, stock and barrel. "

"That's not right."

"Makes no difference." If she kept stirring the stew, she'd find herself inside the pot.

"Doesn't anyone care?"

"Sister, a word of advice. One man, two men, can't alone right all the wrongs in camp. If you start raising hell–excuse my language–you'll get yourself in big trouble. You'd best to walk small."

She gave no answer. Maybe he'd struck bone. "If you don't," he said, "you'll die inside of two months. They won't care that you're a holy roller. My advice is for you to get yourself out of this town now. Take the next steamer south. You got no cause to join your friend."

10. Barrooms and Boomtowns

Soapy hated candied flummery. He swallowed it like a dose of Castor Oil because it came with the job. "Sister Bernadette, you are a rose among weeds, and today, among a very chosen few." Proud as a first-time father, he stood on Holly Street in front of a narrow wooden building no more than five paces wide. "Soon to be *Jeff Smith's Parlor*. My own place."

"For debauchery?" the nun asked.

The woman was unrelenting, a posse of one who never backed off. Under that wimple rested . . . what? He wasn't sure. "Come in," he said, opening the door. "The place is unlighted just now, but you can make out its first-class design."

A long bar was covered with piles of red, white and blue bunting, recently unpacked, ready to be hung. Across from the bar, small tables lined the wall, each table draped with an American flag, also ready to be hung. In the saloon's rear nook, a green felt-covered table sat surrounded by eight captain's chairs. The nook was easily secluded from the main saloon by a drawstring curtain.

"Sister, look here. Right behind the window, I'll have a banjo piano, presently enroute from San Francisco. The latest in ragtime music. Behind the bar, a replica of 'Custer's Last Fight' directly from Anheuser-Busch in St. Louis."

"A saloon, Colonel? I do not approve."

"Set your rigorous standards aside for a minute. I aim to be an honest merchant–no rigged scales or shaved dice–for the honest miner. This will be a place where he won't get skinned. You should thank me."

"Honesty is the best policy, Colonel." She ran her hand along the gleaming mahogany bar, then stumbled over a spittoon.

"No boodle-making here," he said. "Ten cents for fresh Culmbacher. A bit for imported Rainer."

"And whiskey? I imagine you'll sell the devil's potion?"

"Of necessity, Sister, but in extreme moderation. At two bits a shot, I'll limit consumption." At times, Soapy was amazed at the words that dripped from his mouth with no more thought than a horse gave to swishing flies off its ass. He was especially amazed at what people would swallow. "Free nuts to absorb the spirits."

"I should hope so."

"The grand opening will be tomorrow night. Of course, you're invited as my personal guest."

"Not on your life, Colonel. How dare you think I would indicate the church's support for the devil's disease? Do not for one minute think because you seduced me–Yes, seduced!–in here without telling me of its specific future that I'd still my staunch opposition to the evils of drink."

"Never, Sister, never. However, if you would be somewhat less outspoken in your disapproval, it *might* become a place you could very successfully beg alms. If given approval, that is."

"By yourself, I presume?"

"I *am* the proprietor."

She drummed her fingernails on the mahogany. "This would be fine wood for a church."

" . . . which is what I should like to speak with you about." He made a point of closing the door. The nun stepped back. "Sister, you have nothing to fear from me. However, I want to share an intimacy. Shortly after the grand opening, I'll be going to Seattle for a spell. I'd like to leave the church in your hands for a time."

"Are you ill?"

"No, no. Routine business." He mentally reviewed his shopping list: a new faro layout, roulette table, cards and chips; a dozen girls and a half-dozen strong-arm boys; a couple of top cappers and more steerers. The money they'd earn was better than ninety-nine out of a hundred stampeders. "And some items for the new church." Then added, "I'd be pleased to fetch you a gift. Name it."

"Saints preserve us! What would people think?"

"People don't have to know." Damn it all to hell, he'd pushed too hard, too soon. "People always think the worst. I know people who feel that you're the essence of evil merely because you wear the Lord's garb."

"A few," she said. "Nevertheless, I strongly refuse your gift."

"I understand." If he ever told Bowers of the offer, Charlie'd shoot him. Two-Chew would shoot the nun. Sometimes he tired of trying to keep the straying herd on the right trail.

The door swung open. A dapper man in a close-fitting gray cutaway looked into the dim interior. The outside light showed him holding a Colt, a cut-down, double-action Thunderer. A man could draw, thumb and fire the .41 in a trice. Only one man in Skaguay owned such a pistol.

"Ed! Ed, it's me," Soapy said.

The man stuffed the pistol into his belt. "I saw shapes through the window. No candles. I didn't know who–"

"Thanks for your concern," Soapy said. Then to Sister Bernadette, he said, "Sister, this Ed Fay."

Fay bobbed his head.

"Ed will run the place. His word will be law here." To Fay, he said, "You watch out for the Sister while I'm gone."

"My pleasure, Jeff. Certainly my pleasure." He winked at Bernadette.

*

The grand opening crowd swelled into the street. Jumbo Joe Palmer and Yea Mow Hopkins, strong-arm boys easily distinguished from the minions by the tall stovepipes they wore, stood shoulder to shoulder blocking the door. They kept the street's sober hoard from entering. For entertainment, they'd catch a stumbling-out sot and swing him by the hands and boots. The crowd would chant, "ONE! TWO!" On "THREE," the bouncemen would hurl the drunk onto the men's outstretched arms where he would be stripped naked.

Inside, a thin layer of smoke, gray as a morning mist, hung undisturbed just over the heads of the partiers. Frank Reid stood in a corner surveying the chaos. Half of the bunting had already been torn from the walls, although the untouched American flags remained suspended from the ceiling. Centered on the wall along the tables was a photo of President McKinley. It was flanked by a pair of brass bracket lamps. Photos of all the American presidents extended outward. Behind the bar, a gleaming mirror reflected Ed Fay and three barbacks laboring to keep the beer and whiskey flowing. They were sweated through and had long-abandoned their stovepipes. Their overshirts were open to the waist. Ed Fay's neckerchief dripped perspiration. He made no attempt to conceal his belt pistol.

Amid the celebration, Deputy Marshal Rowan held a quiet conversation with the new postmaster, Bill Sampson. Reid knew that the two federal men were good and true, men who would not be taken over by the likes of Soapy Smith. A few more like them and the town would be back on track.

Soapy palavered a cluster of merchants, weasels without a single spine among them. Their eyes were glued to Smith as if he were the Lord Almighty. They weren't a bad bunch, just greedy. The first coin to cross their palm won their devotion. When Soapy moved off to another gaggle, it opened to him as if he were descending from Heaven.

Reid started through the mob toward the marshal. A miner about to conclude an animated story swung his hand backward. His Virginia cheroot struck Reid on the cheek.

"Goddamn!" Reid slapped the cigar from the man's hand.

"Sorry, Frank. Didn't see you coming. Here, take my beer."

"No need." He'd seen the man about town, didn't have an inkling of his name. Just another face biding time before taking the trail. Frank brushed the burned patch on his face. An anthill blister would rise by morning.

He reached the marshal. Rowan was a perpetually sad-looking youth with a forgetful face and brown Beagle eyes always seeming to be on the verge of crying . . . the look of one who'd never been out of the rain. "What are you doing in here?"

Rowan said, "Thought I'd ask the same of you."

A fair question, Frank thought. He turned from the men in a sort of shame. The three of them didn't belong there, but, like a salmon drawn upstream, they came. Curiosity? Loneliness? Frank and the postmaster were unmarried. Rowan had a young wife swelled with child. Skaguay could be a fine place to start a family. The deputy's job was a good one for a young man like Rowan early in a career of constabulary. If the boy survived a couple of years, he'd be able to call his choice of federal jobs. "Guess I'm here scouting the enemy," Reid finally said.

Rowan said, "I'm here for the eats, plain and simple."

Reid grinned. "Your wife not feeding you?"

Rowan caught the gist. "She feeds me fine, Frank. And soon she'll be delivering for me a baby. You should be so lucky."

A wife? Babies? The last things Reid thought much about. Still, he'd burnish the deputy's knob. "I should, indeed, my friend. So should just about every man in this saloon."

Sampson nodded agreement.

Reid said, "This place is destined to become the city hall of Skaguay misdeeds. We should burn it tonight."

"Simmer yourself, Frank," Rowan said. "Here comes the man of the hour."

The crowd parted as Soapy made his way through the bodies. "Greetings, gents. Welcome to my parlor."

95

"Ain't staying long," Reid said.

"In that case . . . " Soapy let the sentence hang like a corpse on a tree branch. He lifted his parson's hat. Ed Fay and the three other bartenders stood back from their stations, placed their hands on their heads. The flow of spirits was cut off; the crowd moaned. In a pulpit voice, Soapy said, "My friends, we're honored to have here tonight our new postmaster, Mister Bill Sampson."

The crowd gave a polite cheer. Then, Bowers, from his post at the far end of the bar, yelled, "Hip-hip . . . "

"Hoo-ray!"

"Now," Soapy said, "you're officially welcomed, Postmaster Sampson."

Sampson nodded shyly, studied his boots then doffed his hat exposing a thick head of kinky red-orange hair to match his few red-orange whiskers that looked like withered prairie grass. "Thank you, Colonel Smith."

Reid saw his chance. He climbed atop a chair and raised his hands. "In honor of our new Postmaster, I'm standing every man here a drink." The crowd cheered, banged glasses on the bar. Two men clapped Frank on the back.

Soapy raised his hat again. "Now that's the way to gin up a party." The crowd hushed. "Ed. Ed Fay! Is that gutgun of yours loaded, and if so, how many loads is it holding?"

Fay made a show of drawing the Thunderer and inspecting the cylinder. As if in surprise, he announced, "Why, Colonel, the gun is almost full. I have five cartridges at the ready."

Soapy stood away from Reid, Rowan and Sampson, made a theatrical circle until the crowd was absolutely still. "In that case, Ed, give every man here five drinks on me."

The crowd erupted and surged to the bar. Soapy bowed to Frank and backed away from the trio.

Frank should have known better. No topping a man in the man's own saloon. Folks would follow Soapy to hell. Pay double for the pleasure. Frank began to work himself toward the door, felt a hand on his back and braced for . . . he didn't know what.

"Where're you headed, Mister Surveyor?"

Missy turned a full circle in front of him, begging for a compliment on her looks, her hair, her dress. The dress, in fact, did her wonders. She bent forward as if to whisper to him, generously displaying more than just the top swells of her breasts. Breasts, Reid thought, that he'd bought a few times, until he realized they were flesh fuses to a dynamite keg.

He chose her hair for the awaited compliment. It cascaded over her shoulders in tight, bouncy ringlets. "New do-up for the party? Them blue ribbons suit you."

"Done it myself. What do think of the dress? Special from Seattle this very week."

"Pretty," Reid said, and continued toward the door.

"Where you going so fast?"

"Stuffy in here."

Missy took his wrist and wrapped his arm around her waist. "Am I really pretty tonight?"

"More'n ever."

She looked down to her breasts, nuzzled them against him. "Yours for the asking." She fluttered her eyes.

Reid sighed. She had the wherewithal to stir his innards, for sure. He felt like Adam facing an apple-bearing Eve. "Not tonight."

"Frank Reid!" She spoke so loudly, several revelers halted their conversations. "You are one contrary man. Any buck in the building would give up their whole poke for what I'm offering you."

She was right. He liked Missy. Truth be told, he liked just about any whore. Easy to walk out of their stalls when the breeding was done. Man did just fine with a visit now and again. Pay for his natural urgings and ride on.

Missy said, "Soapy got your gall, didn't he? He took your best bet and raised you right out of the game."

Frank didn't see Soapy draw up. Immediately, Missy took Soapy's hand and rubbed it around her stomach. "Colonel Smith," she said, "your hoedown is a fine success."

Soapy grinned. "And you continue to beguile every man in the district."

"Stop." She whispered something in his ear that widened his grin.

Reid thought, She is a vixen of the first order. Shameless. It was common knowledge that she shared a cabin with Soapy and Bowers, with Billy Saportas and Yea Mow as guards staged outside in a tent. Reid had heard of a stampeder who'd become so taken with her after one roll, he followed her home. Report was that Missy had cheered as Yea Mow shot the drunken fool in the knee. Such was her effect, and her reaction.

Soapy said, "Get to the paying customers. I didn't buy that dress for you to pose in front of a focus camera."

"–unless the price is right," she said and chucked Reid under the chin.

Soapy signaled her to climb onto the bar. Four revelers quickly lifted her up. She held her arms wide until the men stilled. "Boys, we got Colonel Jeff Smith to thank for this shebang. Let's give him the business."

The crowd obeyed and loosed a rousing cheer.

"Now," she said, cupping her breasts to hoots and whistles, "don't get lost on the way home. Just follow our trusty shepherd, Big Bo Peep." Big Bo raised her crozier. The men laughed, then watched as Missy bravely let herself fall from the bar, arms still outstretched, into the hands of a dozen happy miners.

"She's incorrigible," Soapy said, as if confiding to Frank friend to friend. "What's a fellow to do?"

Reid wanted the evening behind him. He'd been burned by a stampeder, one-upped by Soapy and taunted by a vixen. Thrice embarrassed.

Soapy held open the door, the grin on his face wider than Skaguay Bay. "Frank, you come back any time."

Reid thought again about pulling on him. Put a hole in his black heart. End it once and forever. Of course, he'd be dead before the smoke blew off his barrel. Still, the urge was tough to stifle. "Soapy, one of these days–"

Smith's grin deadened. "No one calls me Soapy to my face."

"You heard me proper."

*

Charlie Bowers was concerned about his boss. Jeff had started drinking at the onset of the grand opening and was still going at a riotous pace. Timbering the house three times over was a bad omen. He'd had generally gone straight sober since the Creede shooting. Bowers figured he'd have cut back, too, if some lousy dry-gulcher had shot off half his moustache. Jeff had knocked off the faro, too. He was now showing the business skills Bowers had seen so many years back. The rough edges had been sanded off. He was full in charge and Bowers was the adjutant. Money came in beer buckets.

Bowers was slick with numbers. Better than Eddie Fay, better than most, but Jeff was a wizard. Soapy's mind was like a machine made to add and subtract, calculate odds. He could figure costs and profits without pencil or paper, so long as he stayed sober. Not tonight. *Bless you, my son.* Bowers unfastened his clerical collar.

"Reverend?"

It was the Widow Pullen. She'd been the party's cook, and had hauled in pan after pan of roast venison, barbecued beef, spuds, dishes of nuts, pastries and cakes for the revelers–all on the jawbone, of course. Pay for the drinks, eat free. The boss wouldn't have it any other way. "Ma'am?"

She said, "This is the last of it." She held up a pot filled with chicken parts.

"You've done splendidly, my dear."

"I cooked up everything you gave me. I'm sorry we've run out."

"Perfect timing." He dismissed her and caught Ed Fay's eye. Fay paused. Bowers pinched his Adam's apple. For hours, excepting the jawbone drinks, the revelers had paid for uncut whiskey and enjoyed free food. Time to milk the cows. Fay nodded, whispered to the other barbacks. They returned to their stations and brought from under the bar fresh bottles of watered hooch.

*

"I declare this evening a huge success." Soapy told Ed Fay to break out a couple of new jugs for the boys. He tossed Bowers' clerical collar into the air as Fay arrived with bottles of Mount Vernon and Old Belmont.

"Where's Two?" Old Man Tripp asked.

Fay pointed to a corner. Two-Chew was draped like a wet towel over a chair-back. A circle of vomit covered the chair's seat. The boys laughed.

Soapy raised a glass. "To you, boys: Charlie, Ed, Tripp, Syd, Sheriff, Joe and Yea Mow–together you brought us great success."

Bowers added, "And Bo is out back reaping the spoils."

"We'll all reap the rewards, Reverend," Soapy said. He placed his parson's hat in the center of the round table. "I am whiskey-ripe."

"Hear-hear," the boys chimed together.

"Boys," Soapy said, "this is the first night of a long run for all of us." He saluted each of the men and downed his shot. Fay refilled it with Old Belmont. "In 1879, Tombstone was laid out on a paltry 320 acres. By '83, after the strike, it had six-thousand souls. Creede grew by three-hundred souls a day after its lode came in. It shipped out a million dollars in ore every month–every blessed month!

The Seduction of Sister Skaguay

"The bounty from those strikes lasted for years. Cripple Creek? Color was discovered in 1890. The next year, twenty-five hundred souls arrived. Five years later–five most profitable years, I'm sure–there were ten thousand people, seventy-three saloons, six churches. They had it all–and we will, too. Whatever your dream, boys, you'll have it."

They downed their shots and drummed their glasses in salute. They were off on a merry upreach to financial heaven. They'd make more money than any miner could hope for. Nothing could stop the color from coming out of the ground, and nothing could stop them from getting their share. Whatever bad luck they'd had in the past was just last year's nightmare. Whatever success they'd enjoyed thus far was nothing compared to what was to come. This time, their ships had come in. "An Oregon farm for you, Charlie, fenced in its entirety with whitewashed pine pickets. For you, Ed Fay, your own Denver bistro with a gilt-edged mirror behind the bar, and you in front in a suit and collar, passing out dollar cigars. Tripp gets his San Francisco hotel suite with a tub of constantly-hot water to soak his sore old bones."

As one, they looked to the unconscious Two-Chew Calderone and silently lifted their glasses.

*

Missy strolled the mercantile's main aisle consoling herself with the notion that shopping in Skaguay was little more than a way to get her out of the crib and off her back. So long as she didn't go to extremes, she could put anything on Soapy's tab. Of course, the general store couldn't stand up to Madam Estelle's Toggery in Denver or the milliners of Seattle and San Francisco.

In one hand, she held up a bolt of medium blue sateen. In the other a swatch of an aqua marine cotton. "Sister, is this a match?"

Sister Bernadette looked from the bolt of gingham she was examining. "A match for what?"

"The fabric of my new dress. I send samples to Seattle to have them made."

"Another new one?"

"Yes," Missy said. "Three this month. Soapy likes his gal gussied."

Sister Bernadette replaced the yardage and tested another bolt. "This blue is much better, but child, why three?"

"Two's what Jeff allots me in a normal month. This month three. We got the hanging."

"Mister Lazlo?"

Missy nodded.

"He hasn't had a trial."

"Don't matter a hoot. Soapy says he'll hang so–he'll hang." Missy couldn't understand the nun. At times, she was as book smart as anyone. Elsewise, she didn't have the brain God gave a peepan. "Ain't you divined it yet?"

The nun turned private, looking dead-willow droopy.

Missy said, "Just think, Sister, Soapy'll be gone two whole weeks. No one to boss me but Big Bo and Bowers. So long as I'm Soapy's main snuggler, they can't get too far out on a limb with me. Bowers don't much care, but Big Bo wants me to rack up as many notches as the other gals *and* be a walking billboard for her. Cripes, I can't do everything!"

Bernadette took her arm. "Did you ever think about changing jobs?"

Missy pulled back. Of course she had. Especially since going soft on Frank Reid. But she stood as much chance of changing her life as a frog did turning itself into a butterfly. "No, Ma'am, I haven't. Nor do I intend to. I been what I am since fourteen."

"You don't have to–"

"Stop! You run around hiding yourself under all that sackcloth and that ugly bonnet–"

"It's a wimple."

"Wimple–pimple. Besides, it's half gone as is your original cape. Point is, you try to cover everything up. Are you ever gonna let your true self show?"

"I don't wish to continue this discussion."

"Okay, don't," Missy said. "You can't talk a civil tongue anyway, so don't talk at all."

They walked the aisles, picking up a notion here and there, a belt buckle, furry mittens, wool socks.

The nun broke the silence. "I have a favor to ask."

"Ask away, if you do it in a tolerable tone."

From under her red cape, Bernadette produced a sealed envelope. "I have no one else I can count on. I need to make certain this letter gets posted to Mother Francine. It repeats what my unfortunate telegram said."

Missy fought off a smirk. "Well snatch my britches. You *are* learning. When you got off the boat, well, you couldn't find an egg in the hen's nest. Now at least you know where to look."

"You're my friend, Miss Bonteiller. Misguided, but my friend. And I *do* trust you. Can you see that this gets down to the next steamer with some honest person? My leg's some better, but I'd be marked crossing the tideflat. No telling who'd be watching."

Missy grabbed the letter, folded it three times and tucked it in the chasm of her bosom. "As good as done."

"Do you swear?"

"I do, I do," Missy said, happy their spat was over.

Two town women entered the mercantile. They regarded Missy and Bernadette, then puffed out their chests, ignored Missy and spoke to the nun. "Sister, you should keep better company. What would your superiors think?"

Missy la-de-dahed at a jar of pickled eggs, wondering what the nun would say.

"And you, you hussy," the other said to Missy, "had ought not to be allowed to shop in a store with the decent people of Skaguay. Don't think we're blind to your calling."

Missy scowled back. "And what's my calling got to do with so much as a plug of chew?"

The women looked to Bernadette for concurrence. When none came, the first said, "Young lady, you debase the good men of Skaguay and spread diseases."

Missy faced the pair, her tiny hands folded into fists, arms akimbo. "And how might you know that, you hag? Did your old man bring you a treat from Cat Alley?" Missy looked to the nun. She could step in, help out. Prevent a fracas. Soapy wouldn't like Missy rippling the water with the town women, but the two witches wouldn't get off insulting her. Why didn't the nun defend her?

"We know who you are, you hussy, and we know where you work and exactly what you do."

"So do your husbands." Missy grinned. "Whyn't you come by some time and I'll teach you how to keep them at home."

"Sister, you should be ashamed. Consorting with a soiled dove the likes of this one in broad daylight. Where did you get your training? I thought you Catholics had better judgment."

Missy waited for the nun to come to her defense.

11. Sucklings, Strumpets and the Syph

In the time since Bernadette's arrival, Miss Bonteiller, who should have been the pupil, had become the teacher. She willingly answered most questions although Bernadette could never devine for certain the veracity of the girl's statements. Often when speaking to the Colonel in the nun's presence, she was as guarded as a bank vault. Other times, she chattered on like a popinjay.

As Bernadette understood her explanation, the Colonel was like a bishop in his realm. He had a multitude of endeavors in place, much as a bishop had many parishes to oversee. He had his pastors upon whom he relied: Messrs. Ed Fay, Syd Dixon, Two-Chew Calderone, John Clancy, Big Bo Peep. She was ashamed to include Reverend Bowers as his intimate, as well. He was as much of a sharper as any of the gang and more wretched than any wolf in a sheep's cloak. In Bernadette's original naiveté, she'd taken him to be a God-fearing man.

New stampeders brought with them stories from Seattle, Portland and San Francisco about the Colonel: hold-ups, shootings, beatings, crooked card games, violent train robberies. Many were chaff. So far as Bernadette knew, the closest train was back in Seattle. Some of the other stories were true.

Miss Bonteiller said he regularly gospeled his strong-arm boys that they weren't to touch a hair on the head of any Skaguay resident. He had other ways of dealing with the citizens. Only the stampeders were lambs to be sheared. Bernadette chastised him severely. He bowed wordlessly, but he never changed a lick. Miss Bonteiller reported that he wanted Bernadette out of town in a most serious way, yet whenever the nun happened upon him, he was as polite as could be. Even deferential.

On the morning he was to leave on his trip, Bernadette awoke in the privy knowing full well that she'd have to find permanent quarters. Her leg was healing at a miraculous rate–*Thanks be to God and Lank*–but her throat pained her as if she were coming down with the croup. Her teeth had ached all night. When she nudged open the privy door, she found the muck of the alley had turned to chocolate ice. Already there had been reports of snow at the pass. The Yukon was in the first stage of its seasonal freeze. The reality of impending winter glistened all about her. Even the pine needles had a thin coating of rime creating a delicate fantasy effect. And it was only mid-

September. True, the ice melted with the first dash of sunlight, but the freeze was an omen, one neither her Iowa farming family nor Alaska's stampeders would ignore.

Tucked into the air hole of the privy was a note rolled up like a cigar. It asked her to track down Colonel Smith as soon as she'd risen. She found him with Reverend Bowers and Sheriff Taylor at the Pack Train. Clancy's may have been a center of commerce in Skaguay, but the Pack Train was the first choice for anything from sinkers to steaks and halibut cheeks. The Colonel joined her at an empty table. Immediately, he ordered for her a stack of hots and a double side of ham. He hooked his parson's hat on a chair post and laid his hands, palms down, on the oilcloth table covering. His slender fingers, always with cuticles pushed back and nails manicured, more appropriately belonged to a lady pianist than an Alaskan. "Sister, winter is at our doorstep. Skaguay will be no place for a solitary woman of the cloth."

"Am I hurting your profits?" A bold comment, she knew, but she was unable to resist.

The Colonel took a long draught of his coffee. "No–and I intend to see that you don't."

"Are you trying to bully me?"

"No, Sister, you're far too close to the Lord for that. Remember, I'm a Baptist. We're as God-fearing as they come."

Her skin was prickly with curiosity to know why he had summoned her, but she was barely half-finished with breakfast. She certainly did not want to be sent away yet. "So?"

"As you know, I'm headed to Seattle. You should go as well. The snow will soon be closing in on sea level, woman, and you're still living in a privy!"

Those were the first words of emotion she'd ever heard from him. His tone had always been steady and controlled with no more feeling to it than there was joy in his smile. Never an invective, never a moment of temper. She said, "You could improve my living arrangements with a single word."

"Then I'd never get a moment's rest from you."

"I only intend to be the salvation of souls. Nothing else."

"Not if you freeze first. In a week's time, only the toughest men will be getting over the pass, let alone up the Yukon. They'll be stuck at Bennett or Lindeman till break-up. Or, they'll stampede back here and try to hunker down for the winter. The soft ones will retreat stateside. Today, we have a few thousand souls, this time next year as many as ten thousand."

Bernadette said, "All the more reason to begin my work promptly. The Lord will provide." Truth be told, however, she was beginning to wonder. If she were living in a privy solely on the indulgence of the Colonel, where would she land if she fell from that grace?

He said, "What are your plans?"

"It seems to me that depends in measure on what you allow me to do."

"You won't go south?"

"Colonel Smith, this may be your town and you may have an army of . . . of . . . boosters and grifters working for you, but I'm surely not one of them. I answer to Almighty God through Mother Francine. I have taken vows of Poverty, Chastity and Obedience and intend to live up to them. You know the terms?"

Embarrassed, he squeezed out a sliver of a smile. "You leave me no choice." He plopped a plain skin poke on the table. It could have come from any miner in the district. "Loosen the drawstring," he said.

She rolled the contents onto the table. Five glorious twenty-dollar double eagles glistened like stars against the oil cloth.

"Far more than enough to get you out of Alaska to anywhere you'd choose to go. First class. Plenty to spare."

By now, she was familiar enough with the Colonel to know his largesse would have a pope's price. His generosity in the past had only been means to soft soap her into his bidding. Of course, she'd accepted his alms for Christian purposes–there was no commandment against such–but now, she felt that this was her watershed. She adjusted her wimple and lifted her chin slightly. Then crossed her arms and buried her hands in her tuba sleeves. "I'm not leaving."

He rocked back in his chair and gripped his chin. "I thought not. Take the money anyway. But know that from this day forward, you'll not be able to beg a sou in Skaguay.

"Do you want me gone so badly?"

"Quite the opposite, but I have my interests to protect. Women preachers have a strange effect on frontier men. I've seen it in the south from the great state of Georgia to St. Louis and west from Leadville to Denver. In Creede, a corner soap-boxing lady railed so, she shut down my saloon for three days and nights. Men preachers, no matter how much zeal, will listen to reason. Women have the faith so strong it blinds clear vision and, at times, rational thought. You have more than most. You honestly believe God provides. If that's true, he's just provided you the last hundred dollars you'll jigger in Skaguay." He slid the money toward her and strode from the Pack Train.

She scooped the coins into the poke before the proprietor could come by and collect for the breakfast. If the Colonel had spread the word she was no longer to be allowed to beg alms, what else had he done? She felt no physical peril, but recognized her vulnerability. With him. Without him.

She pressed the poke to her chest and hobbled after him. She would hurl the Judas money at his feet.

*

Once Colonel Smith had set out on his journey, Miss Bonteiller found the Christian charity to forgive Bernadette's cowardly action–or lack of action–in the face of the rude town ladies at the mercantile. In time, they began to walk the streets together, arm in arm, the child's blue hair ribbons blowing freely. She might toe the line when the Colonel was around, she said, because he insisted on proper ceremonial deportment in public. But when uncaged, she could turn herself into the veritable whippoorwill of Skaguay. If any of the Colonel's minions dared cast her a sideways glance, she'd snap at them. If they bit back, she'd allow as how she'd report the fellow's transgression to the Colonel himself, and report it in her own special way. With the phrase, her 'own special way,' she'd suggestively swing her hips. The first time Bernadette saw it, she was shocked. Ever after, she found it amusing. The men blushed and stammered and retreated like routed soldiers. The child was bold and brazen, fearless of anyone. The only person she did not truck with was Big Bo. "I got my wiles for Soapy and the boys. Big Bo would knock me on the nose if I even winked askance."

According to a front-page newspaper estimate in late October, Skaguay held almost four thousand people. With Miss Bonteiller's temporary freedom, she took long walks out of camp to "get away from the crowds." Merchants were building cabins right around tents they had pitched a month earlier. As the Colonel had predicted, few stampeders were getting over the pass. The successful ones found themselves iced in at Lindeman or Bennett. They laid up for the winter building boats to get themselves down the Yukon come spring.

The Seduction of Sister Skaguay

Bernadette needed to discuss with Miss Bonteiller the possibility of speaking to all the demimondes about the dangers of their profession. Feeling her leg to be strong, she trailed Miss Bonteiller during a walk, the Winchester strapped to her back, her store-bought crutch just grazing the surface of the trail.

At the cemetery, Bernadette paused for a prayer at Angel's grave and mused over how much had transpired since her passing. She wondered what would come next. Past the cemetery, she spied a lightly trodden bypath that led down to the river. She quit the main trail and found a partially-completed log cabin. As she drew near, she could tell the log craftsmanship was superb. On the farm, she'd helped her father build more than one out-building. This cabin-builder, whoever he was, had carved tightly-fitted corner notches, snugging the logs like masons' bricks. Joints were tight. Tenons fit mortises like fingers in a glove. The chinking was generous yet neat. The logs were stacked seven high. Bernadette figured one or two more before the roof would go on. Two duck-cloth camp tents were staked beside the cabin like twins.

Pulling her great cloak tightly around her, she approached. She didn't wish to appear intrusive, yet hoped to get close enough to ascertain the goings-on inside. In the front cabin wall, the builder had carved out a light-providing Yukon window, the glass being none other than a series of clear whiskey bottles. The wall did not yet have a door in place; a duck-cloth flap was strapped shut from the inside. The window was also shaded from the inside.

A sound sharper than the *Al-Ki's* whistle and foreign to Bernadette's ears pierced the chill afternoon. A baby's wail!

She was frozen in her steps. The baby continued to screech. A second baby took up the cry! From the outside, there was no telling what abuse the children might be suffering. She clubbed the doorframe with her crutch.

"Who is it?"

"This is Sister Bernadette of the Good Shepherd Sisters of St. Paul, Minnesota. I demand to know what abuse is being suffered on those holy innocents."

The flap opened. Miss Bonteiller, as red from embarrassment as a full-ripe apple, peeked out. "Sister, goddamn it all. You followed me."

"The wagon road goes right past this path. I took it and happened upon the fuss. I had no idea that you—or any babies—were here."

Miss Bonteiller pulled back the tent flap. "Get in here before someone sees you."

The cabin could not have measured more than twelve feet square, yet its furnishings were as precisely placed as if set out by a Nob Hill butler. A two-burner stove, its tin exhaust rising through an oil can in the duck-cloth ceiling, sat in the middle of the floor. A pot of fermented sourdough hung from a crossbeam. Except for the stove's wooden pad, the floor was nothing more than dirt pressed hard enough to sweep. A sleep bag across a board platform covered with pine boughs filled half of one wall. Three cribs, wooden boxes stamped PORTLAND KEROSENE CO., were placed end to end along another. Around a plank table, six tree stumps served as seats. The table held a dozen whiskey bottles end-capped with rubber health nipples; they were aligned militarily in four rows of three. Flour sacks and tins of foodstuffs were stored on open shelves. Two of the tins had been filled with congealed bacon grease and plugged with burning wicks for light. They ate up the air, making the room close and murky. A sardine tin served as a soap dish; a night jar rested under a shelf by the door flap.

Bernadette faced not only Miss Bonteiller holding a baby, but, to her disbelief, the four grave-digging Salvationists plus a woman cradling two infants. If the Virgin Mary had appeared before her, Bernadette could not have been more shocked. Of course she had no notion that there was a single baby in sinful Skaguay much less three. None appeared to be more than three months old. "I demand an explanation."

True to form, Miss Bonteiller barked back. "You don't demand nothing here. You're a guest. Sister or no, you keep a civil tongue."

Seldom did she find herself without the capacity for speech, but faced with this surprising situation, she could only repeat her question, this time in a more subdued manner. "An explanation . . . please?"

Her presence had no effect on the two squalling infants. The third soon joined the cacophony. So loudly did they wail that the lady Salvationist, without so much as a howdydo, faced Bernadette and placed one in the crook of her arm. What could she do? She let her crutch fall to the dirt floor and began humming the *Panis Angelicus*. Miss Bonteiller's baby and Bernadette's baby soon hushed their cries. The one held by the Salvationist did not. In a quiet voice with a British accent fresh from a jar, she said, "I'll take him outside."

Miss Bonteiller introduced the Salvationists. "These gents are Brothers John, Charles, Robert and Henry." To them, she said, "This here is Sister Bernadette. She has a tart tongue, but she's a good egg under that Paris gown of hers."

The men nodded, but offered no comment. Bernadette thought it odd the pagans carried Christian names.

"Oh, and yes," Miss Bonteiller said, "The lady who just left is Miss Evangeline Booth, head of the outfit. She plays a wicked concertina."

Slowly Bernadette was regaining control of herself. "The babies? How? Whose?"

"I won't go into the *how* part of the question, Sister. As a farm gal, you know about the cows and the bulls. As to the *whose* part, I suppose you could call most of them orphans." She jiggled the child she held. It had long forgotten its fit and slept peacefully, its thumb lost between its pink lips. "This here is Poteet Bleu, the prettiest little thing in the Alaska District, including Seattle. You're holding Annabelle Daugherty and Evangeline has the boy, Tucker Jennings."

Once again, Miss Bonteiller proved to be misguided. Without doubt, Annabelle was the prettier. Poteet Bleu had over-sized ears that stood away from her skull like an elephant. Bernadette thought Poteet Bleu an odd name, but she bit her tongue. The infant seemed healthy enough, as did the others. She asked, "How do they–do you–come to be here? Why haven't I seen the children in town? Miss Bonteiller, I fear you and your friends have a mighty secret."

"No big secret, just three babies, each a wondrous gift."

After Miss Bonteiller and Bernadette had taken their seats, the men joined them. Each carried an anxious, almost tense look. For a certainty, they were not pleased that a nun had happened along, but spoke not a word. Little Annabelle reached for the once-starched corner of Bernadette's wimple and grabbed it in her tiny fist. She took great delight in shaking it for all it was worth. Bernadette allowed her head to be pulled this way and that causing the child to squeal in laughter. This brought smiles to the men. They seemed genuinely delighted with the child's happiness.

"Months back," Miss Bonteiller said, "one of the girls from the line turned up in a family way. She'd been hiding the fact from everyone and doing a mighty fine job at it. Big Bo tossed her out on her ear. She went up to Sheep Camp and delivered the baby, then lit for Seattle. Left us precious Annabelle."

Bernadette clutched the child closer.

Miss Bonteiller said, "Next comes Tucker Jennings, the product of an unknown father and a cook's helper. The gal delivered near the pass, stayed around to nurse him for a week and then abandoned him with the Mounties at the summit.

"God have mercy on us sinners."

"He tries, Sister."

Miss Bonteiller raised the third baby like a priest elevating the host. "Last we have darling Poteet Bleu. She's the pride of the orphanage. Daughter of another one of the gals from the line." She lowered the baby, lavishing her with kisses. "A few of us from the house plus Evangeline and the men take turns looking after them. Only Sister Evangeline really lives in the cabin. The men stay in the tents."

Bernadette could not imagine entrusting the care of holy infants to the likes of Salvationists. There was no telling what type of heathen witchery might be levied on the infants. Turn them into pagan babies is what, never to see heaven's gate. They must be rescued from such a fate!

"I will baptize them at once."

"Sister, you keep your rump on that stump. You'll do no such thing."

The one called Evangeline rejoined them, little Tucker Jennings now calmed. The slight woman, about thirty, wore the Salvationist's uniform with its stiff collar and "S" insignia. The men rose as if on cue from a choir director. Wordlessly, they donned their mackinaws, gathered their axes and departed. Evangeline said, "The men believe they will have a roof over our heads by Sunday dark. The wood will be green, but it will keep the floor dry and the air tolerable." Not for a moment did she look Bernadette's way, speaking solely to Miss Bonteiller. Bernadette could only think of how small this cabin would be, even when completed. Far too small to hold three babies and a caretaker.

Miss Bonteiller replied, "Sister here is in a pickle. She's just getting over a broke up leg and is all alone. Living in town in an outhouse."

The Salvationist said, "I heard about your friend, Sister. My condolences."

Miss Bonteiller said, "Sister Bernadette not only doesn't have a pard any more, she can't talk to her boss. Least mine is right down the trail.

Usually." Miss Bonteiller laughed. Neither the Salvationist nor Bernadette shared the humor.

"Get a load of you two sour pusses," Missy said. "I'm supposed to be on my back making wages and here I sit with two holy grails, three babies and four mutes." She stood up and placed Poteet Bleu in the end crib. "Somehow, this wasn't how my mama had my life planned." She slapped open the cabin flap and disappeared. The sound roused baby Annabelle.

Cradling Annabelle under her great cloak, Bernadette followed Miss Bonteiller from the cabin. The child took the path up to the trail; Bernadette walked down to the river and stood watching the last of the summer thaw head to sea. Snow had worked its way well below tree line. Bernadette wiped a tear from the baby's cheek. The infant burrowed closer to her chest. She breathed in the baby's freshness. The infant's skirts and socks were threadbare, but immaculate. As was her homemade bonnet. The poor thing had not a hair on her head.

Annabelle turned her face toward Bernadette. Could Almighty God have created a more perfect mystery? Could He make anything more beautiful than the child she held? Neither the most magnificent sunset, a Mozart symphony nor a Rembrandt masterpiece could compare. Momentarily, Miss Bonteiller, the other babies, the Salvationists no longer existed. Annabelle had taken Bernadette whole.

*

Missy often tried to calculate the number of men she'd accommodated. Always lost count. She'd been a whore since fourteen and had worked herself up to being a top fancy piece by age twenty-three. Clucked her tongue when she thought of the three women she'd sold herself to, those disgustingly rich women in San Francisco who were of that other inclination and who paid more for her company than any man. Were nuns like that? Is that what made them hide under those rags? The nun seemed like a normal woman–Didn't she enjoy shopping?–but now this new perplexion. As she and Bernadette trekked back to camp, Missy said, "So, you want to talk to the gals about the . . . ." She leaned toward Bernadette. " . . . the syph?"

"Miss Bonteiller, please. They need to learn about all aspects of feminine hygiene, prevention of all diseases and available cures. I'm sure the Colonel would approve. We've discussed the subject."

"You and him talked about the syph?"

"Well, somewhat less specifically."

112

"You talk about leaky-dick, too?"

"Miss Bonteiller!"

"That your way of saying, No, you haven't really talked to him?"

"Not specifically."

"You're speaking cloud talk. Did you ask him or not?"

The nun shook her head.

"Sister, Big Bo gives us a check to be sure we ain't . . . runny. Usually right after the curse goes. She has a calendar on all of us."

"It's not a curse. It's the Lord's way.

"Of what?"

"Of . . ."

"Of giving us working gals a few days off, that's what. Elsewise they'd have us on our backs thirty days a month."

"Nevertheless, it's not a curse. It's called menstruation. Use the proper term."

"You use the proper term." Missy turned away. She found it hard to believe the nun could talk about these things. Hellfire, nuns didn't know tinkle about men; that's why they were nuns.

Bernadette said, "When one of you comes down with syphilis or a gonorrheal infection, you're out of work."

Missy clamped her hands over her ears. "When you say them words out loud, you make it sound like you're talking recipes or dress patterns. Cripes!"

"You might be out for months. What do you do then? You're not well, you can't . . . ply your trade."

"No mama or boss jake is gonna stand a crib going unused for any length of time. They want us–Big Bo is no exception–to be showing our–"

"Missy!"

"–call it advertising then. They want us hanging it out day and night. In some houses, if a gal comes down with the rot, she gets dumped in the street. 'Come back when you're clean. Maybe you get your spot back, maybe not,' the boss bitch says."

"Missy, your language."

"I ain't so polite, I guess," Missy said. "By the way, how do you know so much about–about what goes on down there?" Missy pointed below her waist. "You don't use it for nothing but watering the flowers."

The nun swallowed a smile. "I've had special training."

"I thought you said you ain't a nurse."

"I'm not. My training is very specific. Limited. One of the stated missions of the Good Shepherd Sisters is to eliminate unhealthy conditions in women–wherever we find them."

"How do you learn about such stuff? Don't sound like any training I ever had."

"A variety of ways," Bernadette said. "Books. Classes taught by medically-knowledgeable women."

"Ain't no lady doctors."

"They're not doctors, but they've been trained by doctors. In turn, they teach us. Most are fully-approved nurses. They give us lectures in all aspects of the . . . situation, from penetration to cure. They teach us which medicine to use and how to apply it."

Missy squirmed. "Yuck. I remember once I got a dose and had to get that smeared all over me forever. Tasted awful."

"Mercury," Bernadette said. "And you weren't supposed to take it internally. It's a balm, a lotion."

"I had to try. I was curious."

"Where did you contract it?"

"Silly," Missy said. "Down there." She pointed to her loins again.

"That's not what I meant, you little vixen. Tell me where."

"What business is it of yours? It's personal, don't you think?"

"Not necessarily. A clean body leads to a clean soul, one that pleases the Lord."

"I ain't letting the Lord look at nothing I got, leastways not without cash or a nugget." Missy laughed. Bernadette fought to maintain her stern face. The poor nun couldn't even laugh at a joke.

Bernadette said, "So, can I talk to the girls? It's for their own good."

"My ma said that about Cod Liver Oil and Witch Hazel."

"She was right."

"But you're a nun, for hell sakes!"

"So?"

"I can't rightly say Yes or No. It ain't up to me."

"The Colonel wouldn't mind. I'm sure of that."

"Then why'd you wait to ask me until he was gone?"

12. Enter Christopher

If Bernadette were regularly to make the two-mile trek to the orphanage, she couldn't count on her game leg to hold up. She headed down to the waterfront for help. Just above the tide line, fully five-hundred animals were gathered, hardly one showing decent flesh. She had no idea where she might keep an animal or how she might feed one, but she knew she'd do a sight better than their current owners. She'd been told that the lucky critters were those that perished on the trail. Those that lived clearly suffered continuous mistreatment through starvation, beating or overwork. Horses, mules and oxen were staked out, their bone-pokey ribs like barrel staves and their scrawny legs as skinny as spindles. The unfortunate swaybacks were scarred with lash marks from heinous beatings. Their flesh hung from their necks like mudslides. Many were without ears or tails. If she could find a solid young dobbin, she might be able to nurse it back to health. The Lord would, somehow, provide her with feed. If not He, perhaps a good, God-fearing man.

The men on the beach were as down-trodden as their stock. Only two months back when she'd first arrived, the waterfront was combed with hopeful stampeders, fresh with the excitement of the hunt. This first gust of winter at the summit had transformed the beach into a battle camp of men who'd failed to cross. She'd heard that many had arrived at The Scales–the foot of the pass–looked up and broke down into tears at the severity of the climb. Some tried it and collapsed. Some died. She'd not seen the brutal pass, but the stories defiled the senses. The men who struggled back to town remained subdued, their belongings abandoned, their spirits gone the way of their stakes, their ragged clothes draped on skeletal frames. Their vacuous, disturbed eyes saw little, remembered all.

In quick time, she found a comely young mare, a chestnut, half asleep. Her sign claimed she was two years old; Bernadette guessed four. Still plenty of good years left. Her coat, mangy and unkempt, had not seen a curry comb since God-knew-when. However, her teeth were healthy–perhaps because she'd had nothing to chew–and three of four hooves were well shod, the shoes held firmly in place with solid number sixes.

The seller took no notice of Bernadette. His head rested on a decent Morgan saddle, much like the stock saddle on which her father had trained her. She assumed the man was asleep, and nudged his moccasin with her gum boot. "Sir?"

He pushed back his hat, exposing a wizened face. He didn't speak.

She said, "Sir, what price are you asking for the mare?"

"For you, nothing."

"I beg your pardon?"

He closed one eye, then the other and pulled the hat over his face. "I ain't near enough conked to do business with you. Good day."

"Your sign says she's for sale."

The man jumped up. "I don't give a goddamn what the sign says! Soapy's boys said you wouldn't listen. Guess they was right. She ain't for sale to you. Not ever."

Snatching the sign from the mare's back, he wadded it up and stuffed it in his hat. Then he resumed his place on the beach, his head on the Morgan.

So the Colonel had been true to his promise. He'd put the hex on her. She could only presume that his word would be law when she set out for alms. Nevertheless, she couldn't give up. She needed a horse.

Down at the tide line and away from the encampment, a mule half the size of the mare stood motionless and untethered. His mossy grey hair had fallen out in splotches; bared patches of skin attracted all manner of sand flies. Dead mosquitoes clogged his nostrils. His ears hung flat and scrawny like rotted cabbage leaves. The short bristles of his mane were hopelessly matted yet one look at his teeth and eyes and it was clear that this animal had years of good packing left. He favored a hind hoof–spavin. He'd been worked to the bone, but with some rest, regular feedings and grooming, he'd make for fine transportation. Considering the harshness of the trail, a mule might be superior to a horse.

His owner, a stout man barely taller than the animal, wore a kerchief over his face. When Bernadette completed her inspection, he said, "Five dollars." She scoffed, knowing full well never to take the first offering in a trade. Her father had taught her well.

She said, "He doesn't have a saddle or bridle."

The man pointed to Bernadette's rope rosary. "That'll do."

"Sir!" She was hardly outraged, but thought it best to set a stern tone in the negotiations. "One dollar in coin," she said. "And that's overpayment."

"Sister, I'm flat, but I got me a ticket on next week's steamer south. I need to eat till then. He's worth every penny of five dollars."

"One dollar," she said. She wouldn't budge. Not yet.

"That gets me but two days' eats. I ain't had a morsel since I can't remember 'cause I got nothing left to sell or trade. I'll starve before the boat gets here."

He had little room to bargain. She pressed her case. "You've not had a single offer on this wretched animal. A dollar is generous, and only offered because I am a Christian woman. What I want is a horse. You should take my offer before I decide to shop further." Of course she had him. He did not understand that he was dealing with one who had wheedled alms for the poor as shamelessly as the Cat Alley gals plied their trade.

"Four dollars."

"Why do you have the kerchief about your face? What are you hiding? Am I dealing with a desperado?"

No reply.

"Sir?"

Muttering indistinguishable sounds, he turned away.

"I didn't understand you. Why the kerchief?"

"I can't lie to a woman of the cloth. The critter bit my nose off."

"Maybe I should reconsider–"

"Three dollars."

The give and take was over. They both knew it, but Christian charity could be overwhelming at times. "Two dollars is my last offer."

Meekly, he extended his hand.

She quickly uncinched her rosary belt, fashioned a makeshift halter and slipped it over the mule's head. Later, if she'd need him for packing, she'd throw a pair of diamond hitches and he'd be able to carry hundreds of pounds. Just now, he pulled away from her, strong as Samson. She cooed to him as she had to Annabelle and he settled right down.

The man said, "His name is Utah. I called him after the new state."

"Utah no longer," I said. "He'll be ferrying me to whatever destiny holds. His name will be Christopher."

Unsure as to where she might care for him, she tied him to her privy door and sat down for a think. Mister Reid came by for the expressed purpose, he said, of congratulating her on the purchase. Privately, she thought he might be calling on one of the line girls and became too embarrassed upon seeing her and Christopher. Before inquiring where she might board the animal, she drafted him to build a tiny shelf inside the privy, a place for her tooth powder, brush and fingernail chamois. She also asked him to install a lock-and-screw-eye that she could manage from inside.

He said, "Why don't I walk you to the livery? See if Lank has a spot for that ass."

"Mule, Mister Reid."

"Either way, you can't have him stuck between Clancy's and the cribs. Soapy'll have his boys slit its throat and sell him for beefsteak. C'mon."

Sweat rolled off Lank like hot oil. He was no cleaner than the day he'd set her leg. Mister Reid tied Christopher to a hitching ring. Lank refused to look at her. "Lank," Mister Reid said, "we need a spot for this mule."

Lank sneered at Christopher. He looked to Bernadette and stepped behind Reid. "Not here." He made a motion as if to shoo a fly. "No, not here, Frank. Not either one of 'em. You gone bereft of reason?"

"Lank, we need some help. Please . . . ?" Bernadette said.

"No, no, no." Lank cowered behind Mister Reid, his sooty face turning gray. The man was truly terrified of her.

"The woman is double cursed. She's got her own voodoo and Soapy nixed her. Two-Chew himself came by and set me straight."

Mister Reid put his hand on the butt of his pistol. "Maybe I should set you straight."

"I ain't feared a you."

"Maybe you should be."

Lank retreated into a stall. "No, Sir. If you're to give me a whipping, I must have one coming."

"Lank," Reid said, "you rent out stalls. In your rope corral, you got plugs, clubbers and three-and-a-halfs. One more won't make a difference. You bring 'em all back to life. That's your business."

"Won't have no business at all if I get cotched helping her."

It was time for Bernadette to act. She'd seen how Miss Bonteiller could alter a man's thinking with a simple wag of her forefinger. "Mister Lank?" she said over the stall wall.

He threw his hands against his face.

"Mister Lank," she repeated, and gently prodded his fingers free. The man shook. He looked as if he'd wet himself. She said, "Help me, please. Just until I get situated. I promise not to be a bother."

Mister Reid added, "Just put the mule in the corral. Stuff his muzzle in a feed bag. No one will be the wiser. The sister will come and go through the back."

"You tell her not to spell me?"

"Lank, goddammit–"

"Mister Reid!"

"Excuse me, Sister," he said. "Lank, I swear to you, she won't put a spell on you. No one will know it's her critter. I'll cover the cost."

"Critter appears sickle-hocked."

Bernadette said, "Mister Lank, I believe you'll find he's bone-spavined. Some proper trimming and shoeing will cure the ailment. You *are* a blacksmith, are you not?"

Lank bent to the hind leg. "By God–" He cut himself short. "Frank, she knows her beast."

Mister Reid said, "If you take this one on, I'll toss in my lucky button." He produced a button shaped like a four-leaf clover. "Had it since I survived the siege of Atlanta in '64. Nothing bad has struck me ever since. It's foolproof. You take it."

"You mean it?"

The fear was leaving Lank as clearly as if he were being exorcised. In the simple button he saw protection against all the horrors Bernadette might wreak on him. Poor man. Such idolatry.

He accepted the button and Christopher's harness and led the mule to the pen out back.

In her confessional voice, Bernadette said to Mister Reid, "A lucky button from 1864?"

"Might have stretched history a bit. I found it on the Dyea Trail two weeks back."

*

The following morning, she awoke in the privy, her surroundings as quiet as a cemetery, her underthings as damp as if she'd been plowing on a summer's afternoon. Breathing was difficult; her left bicuspid ached horribly. When she poked her finger through the air hole, she discovered snow. It had finally worked its way down the mountains.

She was anxious to see the great Alaska District in its cloak of pure white, yet she was also mulling the words of the sourdoughs. They said once the dust made it down the mountains, it would be six or seven months before they'd again see sod. Being from farm country, the thought didn't sit well. She unclasped the lock and pushed at the privy door. It refused to budge. She pushed with both hands. The lid held as if chained. In the closeness of the chamber, she quickly became exhausted. If this was meant to test her, she'd blanch not a whit.

"Someone help me, please. This is Sister Bernadette and I'm trapped."

"Thought you could hide from me, did you?" The voice belonged to Two-Chew Calderone. It frightened her more than the entombment.

He said, "I can see there's no tracks so you ain't been up all night. Too bad. Mighty pretty out here. About a foot of fresh white and no sign of stoppage. The snow on your crapper door probably weighs a ton."

"Mister Calderone, release me immediately."

"When I'm ready. Soapy left town not too happy you're still around. The other preacher lady rarely shows in camp no more. We don't even speak about her."

"Release me this instant!" She was in a fit and the devil himself was twisting her tooth.

To her relief, she heard the sound of a broom sweeping across the privy. She could visualize the pink of Mister Calderone's tongue swelling through his two teeth. She gave the door a mighty push. It sprang halfway open, then slammed back down.

"I just thought I'd take me a snooze, Ma'am, now that I got your house all shoveled clean."

She imagined him stretching full out atop the privy. She pushed and pushed, but was unable to dislodge him. He brayed like Christopher and said, "I can almost see you in there, pretty as a picture. Want me to climb down there with you? I'd keep you warm."

She kicked the door with all the might her good leg could summon and received a crude guffaw in return.

"I bet you were a pistol before you got all holy. I can see it on you. Kept all the boys happy."

"I assure you that you will regret this immeasurably."

"Can't threaten me no more. Soapy may be gone, but he's short-handed as it is. I may get to be the new deputy sheriff. Think about that." He hopped off the privy; his laughter abated. "You're free . . . for now."

She pushed open the door and sat straight up to see him scooting around the corner. Then she was buffeted by a wind so strong, it nearly tore the poke bonnet from her head. She pulled on her wimple. Using her hand as a shield, she scoped the mountainside as if on a hunt. From the crowns of the mountains down to Clancy's second story roof and the tent tops of Broadway, everything was as white as fresh frosting on a sheet cake.

Winter had arrived. She had to confront her resolve and admit what everyone had been saying: she needed living arrangements other than a privy. If the Lord were whispering in her ear to assume leadership of the orphanage–He surely could not mean to entrust the babies to the care of the pagan Salvationists–the cabin might solve her lodging quandary. Perhaps she should call on them.

She bundled up her sleep bag–henceforth she'd do little traveling without it–both to wrap around her great cloak and to serve as a riding blanket for Christopher.

Lank greeted her from behind a stall wall. "I checked your mule. How'd you come to pick him?"

"Not by the mange of his coat. No, I chose him because of his age, his teeth and the stoutness of his legs. No windgalls or rain rot. If his internals are healthy, he's redeemable."

"You got a good eye," Lank said.

He approved of her choice. She no longer seemed to be that frightening voodoo woman who took up his precious space. She was a person who could speak with authority about livestock.

He said, "Frank's right. You keep him here. Out in the pen."

Yesterday, hardly a word from him and when he spoke, his words had been terror-filled. Today, he was practically a jabberwocky. "I won't impose for long."

Lank said, "I'll feed him once a day. You groom him as you can. Help yourself to a curry brush from the shed out back. He'll be fine."

"Precisely why I chose him," she replied, accepting his generosity with a curtsy. "You've been very kind."

"Good eye," he repeated. He fondled the four-leaf clover hanging around his neck and disappeared into his tent.

She'd begin Christopher's rehabilitation after returning from the orphanage. Now, she fitted the sleep bag over his back and her packsack over his neck. The Winchester went over her shoulder. She took his long ears and gave them a brisk pulling. He liked the attention. "You take care of me," she said, "and I'll see to you. Lucky I came along lest you dry up and die on the beach." He jostled his head up and down, seeming to understand.

They headed out of town, not breaking trail through the snow, but not far behind those who had. If mules were ever reincarnated as people, she wanted them for her apostles. Although they had a reputation for their contrary ways, in truth, if treated with decency, they'd be as steadfast as the most loyal dog. And they'd work until their last breath.

She rode modestly with her legs to one side, not in accord with her father's teaching. He'd put all his children, boys and girls, into denims as soon as they walked. Mounted them on horses without delay, figuring horse riding was needed as a second nature to all farm folk. By age five, they were experts. Not only riding, but with the curry comb, brush and wool sponge. Upon her profession, Mother Francine forbade Bernadette from "riding like a man." If she were to ride, her legs would have to be properly draped to one side of the saddle. No exceptions.

Bernadette endured the side-saddle riding until the town's last tent fell from sight. She tied her Iron Maiden into pantaloons, pulled the great cloak around her, laid her sleep bag over her lap and rode astride, blaming her disobedience on the harshness of the weather. Another order violated to add to her growing encyclopedia of sins.

The sun, now up over the peaks, twinkled on the pine branches and snow-laden boulders and showed the creeks running crisp and clear. Yes, this was the Lord's blissful Alaska. The scene was nature as the Almighty intended. She lifted her chin to allow the sun to bathe her face in its warmth.

At the cemetery, she hitched Christopher to the wrought-iron gate. She could hardly pass her Angel without a prayer. The cemetery had taken on the serene look of a hill-and-dale quilt, slight rises and dips in a blanket of snow that reached halfway to the tips on the picket-fence enclosures. Markers poked through the carpet like flagpoles. Angel had no marker yet. Months ago, Bernadette had felt a marker so important. Now, it seemed no more than a token, hardly worth the effort in such an unforgiving land.

As she brushed the snow from Angel's grave, she reflected on her novitiate year when they'd first met. She was lost in the memory when a hoarse *haw* from Christopher broke her dreaminess. She wasn't alone. A trio of stampeders had gathered around the mule, staring at Bernadette. Black rims circled eyes that betrayed hell's own torments. Spittle clumped in icy wads through their beards. Rags bound their feet and hands; strips of towels were tied around their necks. Their packs drooped, provisions long gone. She immediately confronted them. "Are you gentlemen headed to town or up to the pass?"

She received a one-word reply. "Out."

Nothing she said could help them now. *"The Lord be with you."* These men had challenged the summit and had been defeated.

They nodded thanks and shuffled off.

She boarded Christopher and urged him toward the orphanage.

Since her first visit, the mutes had built up the cabin walls to nine logs and had affixed a pitched roof frame rising to a ridgepole. Two of the mutes bucked logs on the ground while the pair on the roof joists hammered saplings into place. The work appeared square and plumb, as if St. Joseph the Carpenter himself had trained the men.

With the incessant hammering, the infants were a choir of wailers. Evangeline did not hear Bernadette approach. Inside, the Salvationist held one infant and scooted from number two to three trying to ease their howls. Wordlessly, Evangeline handed Annabelle to Bernadette. She took a seat on a tree block, but knew straightaway that she would not be able to calm the baby within the sound of the hammering. She bundled the baby and carried her to the river. Once away from the pounding, Annabelle took to her bottle and suckled quietly. Evangeline followed, her arms filled with Poteet Bleu and Tucker Jennings.

Bernadette said, "Madam, may I ask your intentions as to the future of these children?"

Evangeline didn't know. Her superiors were unaware that the Yukon was frozen for months on end. Thus, she faced a crucial decision: stay put until spring and then sprint over the pass, attempt the pass now, or retreat to town and steam to Seattle. Bernadette allowed as how she would be staying, at least until definitive orders from her Mother Abbess. She didn't say how convenient it would be for her to move into the cabin, with or without the babies. When completed, it would be uncomfortably small, but the best accommodation Bernadette might find in Skaguay. It was far enough from town so as to offer pleasant seclusion, yet little more than a brief ride.

"Sister Bernadette, you would be welcome here with us. The cabin is tiny, but it should provide protection against the winter. The mutes live in the tents. They'd be no bother."

The Seduction of Sister Skaguay

Almighty God would strike her to stone if she entertained the notion of sharing quarters with pagans. In the novitiate, they'd learned the atrocities performed by the heathen demons. If the worst occurred, she would make do in her privy.

Evangeline stood before Bernadette, the wind having abated and the snow falling as if in a heavenly shower. "No," Bernadette said, "I think not. But should you decide to move on, I could assume the orphanage duties, at least until my assignment is clarified. Of course, I have no money and, I fear, the Colonel has seen to it that I shan't be able to beg. I'm not quite sure what I will do for sustenance."

Evangeline said, "The Colonel is single-handedly responsible for our survival. He has provided the funds for the orphanage. The only requirement he made was that we remain out of camp. He's been most generous, so long as we keep to our place."

Evangeline then tilted her head. "Sister Bernadette, have you breakfasted?"

"Well, no, dear. No, I haven't."

"Let's take ourselves and the babies inside. Maybe I can get the men to pause from their pounding. I'll fry you up some bacon and beans. Humble, but filling."

"If you insist." To Bernadette, it sounded like a Thanksgiving feast.

*

As Christopher plodded toward town, Bernadette pondered her current fix. She could never share quarters with the heathens even though she was now being forced to live her Vow of Poverty. Good Shepherd Sisters counted on Mother Francine for staples, an occasional extra pair of stockings, a chance book, a hearty dessert once a month. In Bernadette's current circumstance, she had not so much as a stable or a manger. No food on the table–no table! She had to make do for herself. She repeated the adage: *The Lord helps those who help themselves.* This was precisely the type of obstacle she would need to overcome to build the strength of character which would enable her to–some day–become Mother Abbess.

She would find a commercial situation.

13. Card Tricksters

Mrs. G.I. Lowe operated a laundry in a wood-floored tent beyond the end of Broadway's boardwalk. Water barrels and washtubs stood sentry along one side of the tent. On the other, all manner of clothing hung from a spider's web of crisscrossing lines. In front, the sign read:

LAUNDRY
BOILED SHIRT...25c
MENDING FREE OF CHARGE
FORTUNES TOLD
"WE DON'T DICKER A LICK"

On a square of cardboard, a hand-scratched addition to the sign read, **HELP WANTED**. Bernadette reined Christopher to a halt. A tin pail of murky water was heaved through the tent flap splashing poor Christopher's legs. Mrs. Lowe followed, giving the pail a good shake. Her sleeves were held above her elbows by gambler's garters, her bared arms as pink as a baby's bottom. Her dress was pulled up and tied into leggings just below her knees so that she resembled a Cossack dancer. When she saw Bernadette, she shouted, "Don't sit there gawking. Come on in and I'll get those filthy duds of yours cleaned like store-bought new."

Bernadette led Christopher to the side of the tent and tethered him to a wash tub.

"You're a mess." Mrs. Lowe looked Bernadette up and down. "And a woman of God, no less."

She was right, of course. Bernadette's Iron Maiden had not been washed since her visit to the bathhouse. She now regretted her decision to return the Colonel's poke of money and cast her eyes to the ground.

"Never mind about payment," Mrs. Lowe said. "You can earn your keep. Nothing on the jawbone at Mrs. Lowe's. Get inside and get yourself shed of them duds. I'll have you scrubbed and starched inside of two hours. I'll use nothing on your rags but genuine Bross Brothers Mottled German soap. What you can't pay for, you work for. You *do* work, eh?"

An absurd question, Bernadette thought. Of course she worked. She just never worked for material wages. She told herself that her Vow of

Poverty did not include starvation. The laundry could be an ideal situation. "May we speak in private?"

Inside the tent, more clotheslines zigged and zagged with all manner of long johns, shirts, trousers and under apparel. In a corner, two kerosene crates sat on end. Between them, a pack of cards rested on a wooden case marked NO. 4 NEWHOUSE TRAPS. Next to the case, a curtained off dressing enclosure. Kerosene lamps smoked the entirety of the tent fabric. Atop a semi-circle of sheet-iron stoves, pots of water hissed like hollows of enraged snakes. Flat irons and polishing irons ringed the stovetops, miniature Conestogas circled up for the night. Steam rose to the top of the tent and dripped back down to the floor. Four identical Anthony Wayne washers, a pair of table mangles and two dolly tubs completed the equipage.

Mrs. Lowe reached for Bernadette's wimple. Bernadette pulled back.

"Relax, dear," she said. "Just testing its coarseness. We'll scrub that dirty thing till next month. Use some turpentine or chalk on it if needed, then starch it up like new with Borax."

Having never asked for a job before, Bernadette was uncertain as to the protocol. She stammered, "I should like to apply for the job you have posted."

Mrs. Lowe wiped a line of perspiration from her upper lip and swept a wayward curl of hair under her bonnet. Then she walked around Bernadette fully five times, inspecting her as Bernadette had inspected Christopher.

She asked, "You strong? You'll need a back strong as a redwood."

Bernadette detailed her farm upbringing and the physical labors she'd performed as a member of the Good Shepherd Sisters.

Mrs. Lowe told her that part of the job would be hauling wood for the stoves and collecting ash to make the lye, not the most pleasant chores. She continued to circle Bernadette and began a lecture about the seven steps to professional laundering: carrying water, stoking the stoves, scrubbing, rinsing, hanging, mangling, and finish-ironing. Once in a while, she had to leach dye from alders. "We take extra care with boiled shirts for the dandies. Charge some, too. Some likes 'em stiff so we use the Borax. Others like 'em lightly starched so we soak them with chopped up potatoes. We always aim to please. Brick hard, or soft and furry. Iron in the creases with sealing wax." With the toe of her gum boot, Mrs. Lowe tapped Bernadette's crutch. "I'm trying to overlook the hitch you got in your get-along. You'd be a one-armed worker."

"Not for long," Bernadette said.

"We got all sorts of men coming to town. Women starting in, too. Within a year, Skaguay will have folks with young families and genuine hotels and a hospital and a school. Soapy's already building a church. You'll do soiled diapers?"

Bernadette hadn't thought much about the town's growth insofar as families were concerned. She couldn't envision sinful Skaguay as the respectable town Mrs. Lowe painted, but she held her tongue. This shrewd businesswoman was tackling the present head on while planning for the future.

Mrs. Lowe sidled up to her. "Do you tell fortunes?"

"I certainly do not."

"If you go to work here, you will learn. Does that fret you?"

Bernadette didn't know how to answer and still retain hopes for employment. Fortune telling was gypsy work, and the gypsies were the devil's hand-chosen tools.

Mrs. Lowe didn't suffer her silence long. "Sister, the boys come here, strip down to the altogether behind the curtain and toss their duds over to me. I throw them back a horse blanket. They pull up a kerosene case and start on their jug. I do the laundry and entertain them by turning over a fortune card every now and then, and charge them a damn site to do it. It don't mean hooey. Nothing evil about it. I tried storing up dime novels. After a week, those books sucked up so much dampness, the pages were as thick as shirt collars. I couldn't make money on them. Besides, most of the boys read about as much as blind men. Fortunes are my bonanza. Good tippers get good fortunes. Good fortunes make good tippers. Pikers get the spades. I've husbanded away a pretty penny and earned every bit of it by sweat."

"You can't predict the future."

"Sister, I can give them hope of the rainbow's pot. Like you do when you sermonize on the grandeur of eternal life hereafter. I just put it in words they take to."

"It sounds as if you make it all up."

"Pretty much," she said. "Every card has a basic meaning–I'll tell you those–and the rest is like, well, gospel stories. You just say what needs to be said to make your point and go on from there. We charge two bits for a boiled shirt, the same for a fortune reading."

While Bernadette's Iron Maiden dried, she sat inside the dressing enclosure wrapped in layers of yellowed sheets destined for the cribs. Mrs. Lowe prattled on. " . . . hearts, clubs and diamonds are usually good, except for the pikers. Spades is bad, except the Ace is wonderful. Remember, the Queen of Spades. She's awful. Defeat. Ruin. Death. End of the world."

*

A job? A by-gosh paying job? The nun was learning what made the sun come up each morning. Missy treated her to a bath. Through the privacy curtain, she said, "Soapy tells me he cut you off from the saloons."

"It's my lot in life. The Lord will provide."

"If you say so," she said. "On his trek, he worked the trail all the way to the pass but bumped into the Mounties. Ran him right off. In Dyea, he found more federals than a pillow has feathers. They ran him out in a day flat. But back to them Mounties. They're a tough lot. Handsome in their red uniforms. I once had me–"

"Stop!"

Missy filled a lamb's-wool sponge with the fresh hot water and squeezed it over her head. It cascaded down her face and onto her freckled shoulders. The nun's heaven could never feel this fine. "He only spent a couple of days in Seattle. Came back with some top cappers, a new gal and a new pistolman. Lots more on the way."

"None of your ilk, I hope."

Missy flew out of her tub and exploded through the privacy curtain. She stood before the nun, her skin glaciering suds to the floorboards, not the least bit concerned about her total nakedness.

"Miss Bonteiller!"

Missy grabbed the nun's sackcloth and wrapped it around herself like a Turkish tidy.

The nun shrieked. "Leave! Leave at once!"

Missy merely turned her back.

The nun scooted low into the soaker. "Have you no shame, child? No modesty?"

"Shame? Why be shamed? We got the same workings. Naked's the way we came into the world." She threw the sackcloth on a stump. "It itches." She scooted to her cubicle and returned, pulling a chemise over her head. "You got no right to talk that way to me. *My ilk*, indeed. I know what that means, what *you* mean. I know that haughty tone."

128

"I merely mean to infer that a young, attractive woman such as yourself could find gainful employment in another profession. Look at me, I'm now a laundress. You don't need the Colonel to dictate your life."

"He looks after me, whole and wholesome. Tends to us all, but me especially. He wouldn't take kindly to me quitting. How would I get out of Skaguay? I'd walk five paces down the wharf and Two-Chew would have me in an arm lock and up in the clinker with old Lazlow. Then what would happen to . . . ?" She paused, chopped off her thought, began again. "Don't be sore at *me* because he shut off your begging. And if you tell me that God will provide one more time, I'll toss your duds onto Broadway."

Missy reached over the rim of the soaker and pushed the nun's head under water. Bernadette surfaced, laughing. "Is there no other career you could pursue?"

"Once a whore, always a whore, they think. You saw how them citizen women treated me at the mercantile. I ain't someone's regular wife." She pushed a stump to the side of the nun's soaker and draped her legs into the water.

Missy began rocking herself, tears swelling in her eyes like rain clouds.
"No need to cry, child," she said. "Do you wish to hear a secret?"
Missy wrapped her soggy head in a towel.
Bernadette said, "You look like you're wearing a novitiate bonnet."
"Fat chance." She knew her skin was bared of all her rouges and powders. She must look a fright. Under the water, she wriggled her toes against the nun's leg, then quietly said, "Yes, I'd like to hear your secret." Missy surely carried plenty. It seemed like every gal on the line had a hat full of secrets they told only to her. Maybe, she thought, it came with being the top gal. She had her secret, too. One more in the pack couldn't hurt. "Go on, tell me."

"I didn't enter the convent out of choice."

Missy jerked her feet from the nun's soaker so quickly, she thought she'd fall right off her stump. "What?" She flung away the towel and shook her head. Her red hair whirligigged out in thin, straight lines. "Tell me!"

"My father was a stern man. Usually a fair one, too. Mamma was a fine wife who'd given him three sons and two daughters. My twin sister, whose name I chose as my religious name, and I were the youngest of the brood and the end to her baby-making. An incident occurred one Sunday at a barn-raising bee. The afternoon was sweltering. Bernadette and I snuck off to the quarry for a swim. We'd done so in past years but we never told.

"After the swim, Bernie spread out a blanket and bid me sit beside her, only to produce a dime novel. I'll never forget the title: *Eve's Garden*. We lay across that blanket in rapt reading, giggling like the schoolgirls we were. I was both drawn to and repelled by the prurient matter in the book. I never stopped reading. Of course we lost all track of time until our father found us. When he saw the book title, he tore off his suspenders on the spot and gave us both a licking, claiming that we'd shamed him forever.

"Bernie and I were banished to a Minnesota convent school. Three weeks later, Bernie climbed into a horse trough and cut her wrists with a grain sickle. The good father at the school said I caused her death and should enter the convent to atone for it. I did so, never questioning his advice, figuring my ultimate martyrdom would be the only way to fully make up for my sister's suicide. When I returned to Iowa five years later, I was the professed Good Shepherd, Sister Bernadette.

"Did the book have pictures?" Missy tried to envision the sisters sprawled out on a blanket reading an eight-pager.

"No, Melissa Bonteiller, it did not. Shame on you for asking such a question. My sin was bad enough without pictures."

"By the way, I got more bad news for you," she said. "Big Bo said you can't talk to the girls."

"Why not?"

"I think she's afraid you'd turn us all into your Jesus people."

The nun slapped the water sending out a starburst of droplets.

"Don't be mad. You can tell me the business and I'll sneak it to the gals when Big Bo ain't looking. It'd be good for us to know the latest."

The nun couldn't hide her disappointment. Missy knew the feeling. The woman, nun or not, had just been denied the whole reason she'd come to the Alaska District. Nothing Missy could do about that. Curious how a nun could get the blahs like normal gals. It was Missy's turn to do the cheering up. "You gave me your story. Want to hear mine?"

"Not now, child."

"Yes, now. You got a big hoop-de-do somewhere else?"

"No."

"Okay."

Missy had been a schoolgirl in New Orleans, the youngest of a band of nine and the only gal. She fell in love with a Cajun crawdad fisherman who seeded her straightaway. "I'd hardly come of age and trusted him to do right. The Cajun refused to marry me, so my no-account brother, Graven, lopped off his fingers with a filleting knife and ran him out of the parish, threatening to do far worse if the rascal ever showed up again. I visited a voodoo queen who took out the baby. A shame on me. Real shame. I vowed then and there to have the next one fully birthed no matter what came on.

"To get out of New Orleans, I signed onto a riverboat as a chambermaid. By the time the boat reached the northern stretches of the Mississippi, I'd lied myself into table tending. I got fired for sassiness and took residence with a boy just to get out of the cold. From then on, I sold myself for room rent. Turned sixteen during my first Yankee winter then wandered south and west. I stopped in Colorado. Met Soapy. That's it. I'm an ignorant night gal not fit to share the floor with a slop jar nor walk the street you're on. But I'm blessed with–" She cut herself off again. "When you say the Lord provides, you're right on the applejack. He's provided for me like a stampeder standing treat for the whole town."

"Is Melissa Bonteiller your real name?"

"'Course not," she said. "It's Eunice Culpepper Blanton. Yours?"

"Sister Bernadette–"

"No. Before that. When you were a real girl."

"I haven't thought of my family name in some time. After ten years wearing the Iron Maiden, I think of it only when I think of my sister."

"Your name," Missy said.

"Mary Kathleen," she said. "It feels odd to say the words. I can't remember the last time I said them aloud. Mary . . . Kathleen . . . Morley."

*

"Big change is on the horizon," Soapy said. Bowers, Ed Fay and Big Bo Peep inched their chairs closer to the round table. "First thing to say, your wages are all going up. Ten per cent across the board, plus new come-ons for each of you according to your own specialty."

Bowers, Fay and Big Bo tapped the table with their glasses.

That was the easy part, Soapy thought. They might not like the rest. "For it," he said, "you'll have to work harder. Use your heads more. Ed, you get your barkeeps pouring more sauce. No more jawboning. From now on, no one buys drinks save for you, me, Charlie and Bo. Second, I brought back a case of soporifics and a fresh supply of Deadly Nightshade. I saw a few drops of the new brand take all of sixty seconds to make a two-hundred pound merchant marine look like he'd been hit with a log maul. Use it on any fat poke you see, but be sure the boys are around to steer the mark out back. Bo, get your gals in the saloon rubbing shoulders when they're not toes-to-the-ceiling. No more knitting in the cribs waiting for business to come knocking. Missy's the only one chasing business right now."

Big Bo said, "You going to spring for fancy duds for all of them, too?"

Soapy felt like giving her a crack on the jaw. Of course, that wouldn't improve profits. He'd just visited the Bell Street houses in Seattle. Things were different. The big cities always led the way. "I brought one new gal with me, six more by month's end. Get them all plenty of hours. The time is ripe."

"Where the hell do I put them?"

"Charlie will get new tents set up until we can land some adequate housing. Maybe build a decent house."

Big Bo said, "Do the new cunnies realize they'll be bunking in canvas for a winter?"

"Better than a privy," Soapy said, and sapped Big Bo's harsh tone. She did her share of carping, but always came through. And, she didn't steal. "You got two gals down right now. You need the help."

"You been talking to Missy again."

Soapy understood the jab. Bo hadn't yet told him of the two doves out with the clap. "She don't keep too much to herself."

Like feed to chickens, Soapy tossed a handful of round metal tokens on the table. "We also have these coming. Pure brass. Each one stamped with the likeness of hands folded in prayer. Especially made for us. None other like them in the world."

Big Bo inspected a token, rubbing the shiny disk in her hand. She bit down. "Praying hands? Colonel, your humor ain't suffering."

Soapy said, "You three are the only ones who will have these. From now on, no cash or nuggets to the girls at all. You carry the tokens at all times. When the boys want a slice, they buy a token from you and give the token to the gal once inside the crib. We all know the gals knock down when cash is involved. These tokens take the cash out of their hands, except for their tips. Bo, you'll be working nights, six to six. Charlie, you never sleep anyway. I want you around for the collections at both sixes too, then work day operations in between. I'll help out in the evenings."

"Raising prices?" Ed Fay asked.

"Not yet. Let everyone get used to the new system first. We'll bump up prices come the holidays."

"The new gals?" Big Bo said. "What are they like?"

"Run of the mill save the one I brought with me. Stella. She's a bright light. Like Missy."

Big Bo, Fay and Bowers groaned. Not unexpected, Soapy thought. Missy was a man pleaser–one of the best working gals he'd ever come onto– but her ways were turning nettlesome. Give her a half hour, she could have any man thinking he was in love with her, willing to open his poke as soon as she opened her legs. But she had a mouth, and a snippy way that was appreciated about as much as skunk soup.

Soapy always liked just one gal to see to his needs. He didn't like to spread his seed indiscriminately. He had his health to think about. Plus, it just wasn't good business to be fraternizing at random. He'd have to deal with the Missy situation in due time. Even the most fetching whore could be vexing.

"Two other items," he said. "First, Thanksgiving and Christmas. The Seattle steamships are booked to the gunnels through spring. The argonauts don't really understand that crossing the pass in winter challenges the measure of any man. They'll be coming in hoards, and stack up here like cordwood. Some broke, some with cash. We'll be jumping. Ed, I'll want your advice about new pricing in the Parlor."

Fay nodded.

"Second, we're going to have a huge turkey shoot the day before Thanksgiving. We'll open up the bar for a bit. Bo, the new gals should be here by then. You be ready. I've also got a hundred live chickens on the way to give away as prizes."

Bo scowled.

"Something wrong?"

Bowers said, "The chickens are nice, but if you hope to set a free-spending tone for the holidays, put up some cash prizes. We'll get it all back at the bar, the games and the line."

Soapy said, "You're right, Charlie. Figure out what works and we'll do it."

"What's left to this meeting?" Bowers pocketed the tokens. "I have collections to make."

"An idea for you all to ponder." Soapy twirled his hat on the tip of his finger. "I want you to start thinking about a grand opera house."

Fay and Big Bo looked to each other, stifling their reactions.

Soapy said, "We'll just *call* it an opera house. Bring in some vaudeville shows–they've been the rage for five years–singers and dancers and actors. The can-can. Tombstone alone has the Crystal Mansion and the Bird Cage. We'll convince the town about the benefits of an opera house, then build a magnificent palace with curtained sections for private entertaining, a casino, bar, a first-class dining room."

"In Skaguay?" Fay asked. "We got nothing but mud for streets and you're talking about an opera house?"

"Ed, if the color keeps coming, the stampeders will pay their eye teeth for such entertainment. And it'll curry favor with the citizens. Right now, I'm just asking you each to think about it. Think what your place in such an operation would be. Think how much money you'll all make."

Big Bo said, "It'd put Skaguay right up there with Denver."

*

Soapy was ashamed of himself for being so anxious to see the nun. "I see you've stayed on in spite of my urgings." He dumped a satchel of laundry into an empty boiling tub. He doffed his hat, nodded to Mrs. Lowe and held the tent flap open as she departed. Unlike the nun, he thought, Mrs. Lowe knew her place.

Arms akimbo, the nun faced him square on, modestly turning down the tuba sleeves of her habit. "My mission is to save souls in Skaguay, Colonel, and that I will do."

He held up his hands, palms toward her, asking for peace. "You are more stubborn than your mule."

"You know about Christopher?"

"I caught the wind."

"He is a symbol of my strength. Stubbornness, as you see it, without reason is a vice. Following the orders of Holy Mother the Church is a virtue. I do not intend to be cowed."

"I believe that now," he said, "and I'm not totally disappointed. Last night, Missy claimed that you're the most beautiful woman she's ever seen. I believe the girl is jealous."

The nun backed away. Soapy tried to soften his gaze. He knew that he had eyes that bore through people like diamond drills. He once stared at a man so intently, the man pissed himself. "I brought you this from the Seattle cathedral." He held a rosary in front of her, the dangling crucifix reflecting the tent's candlelight. "The padre said it had been blessed by the pope. I notice you lost yours. I'd be pleased to provide you with store-bought tack for your mule."

"Not lost. Put to another use."

Soapy shrugged and urged her to accept the rosary. She reached, withdrew her hand, and then accepted the gift. "It's lovely. These stones are . . . ?"

"Zircons."

"My."

At the fortune-telling crate, Soapy fanned the cards and displayed their faces. He bundled the cards back together and cut them, leaving two stacks on top of the crate. "Have you taken up cards?"

"Harmless, frivolous fortune-telling to pass the time. Not gambling."

"Not so harmless to believers." He turned his attention to the cards, cut them again and again, stacked the pack face down in the center of the crate. The woman intrigued him to an embarrassing degree. He said, "Touch the top card."

She did.

"Now turn it over."

She revealed the King of Hearts, then retreated to the space between the boiler stoves.

"Before we continue, I need to speak to you about the partially-built cabin two miles out the road."

"I hear the Salvationists have the roof on," he said. The nun needed to realize the breadth of his knowledge, that like one of her confessors, he heard everything. Odds were slim he could supplant her religion; a card player had to know when to go for the inside straight. She didn't seem to be surprised that he knew of the roof.

She said, "Being the Christian that you claim to be, would it not be better for you to have me reside in the cabin? The infants would at the least have a Christian inclination later in life. In the end, it would save you the problem of the children."

He asked, "Do you know who the children belong to?"

"I've heard one belongs to a woman who traveled through Skaguay and is long gone."

"The others?"

"Perhaps from Big Bo's flock."

So she doesn't know, Soapy thought, or else is playing the game. She's either learning the way of the world quickly, or is not as sheltered as she makes herself to be. "Flock, indeed." He turned the King of Hearts face down on the top of the deck and folded his hands in his lap. "You'd have me run the Salvationists out of town and give you that fine-looking cabin?"

"The cabin is not designed for three babies. That can be corrected with an expansion."

"This from a woman who sleeps in a privy?" He smiled, then quickly reined in the warmth. "Do you realize how lonely it would be out there?"

"I would be out of your hair, doing Christian good for the babies and have more time for meditation."

"You've raised how many children?"

She blushed.

"Winter's on the way. The weather will be awful. That's good for town business, bad if you're stranded out the road. Evangeline Booth has a crew of able bodies to see to her needs."

"I am of hardy stock, Colonel."

He tapped the pack of cards three times, then rose and departed without a further word, thinking, Let her ruminate on what she's asked. He could give her an immediate answer, but that would serve no purpose. The dangling cross, he said to himself.

Bernadette looked after him, then stepped to the table and peeked at the top card. The Queen of Spades.

14. Soapy, the Supreme

Soapy told Missy to grab the new gal and double up on the first tenderfoot they found. See how the newcomer handled herself. Introduce her to the ways of the north.

Missy knew right off that Stella LaStarr needed no introduction to the game or to the north. She was ten years older than Missy, a head taller and so conformed as to bust open any bodice not hand-made to order. The stampeders would love her. She had a lusty country vogue that said she was long-lost kin, the kind who was always itching to show any cousin the hay loft. Missy's own game was that of a flirt. No competition. So long as Stella didn't sight in on Soapy, they'd get on fine. Maybe Stella would be a good one to put a smile on Charlie Bowers face. Of late, he'd been grumpy.

The two women took a table in Jeff's Parlor and spotted a returning miner, Andy McGrath. Stella showed enough of her swells to make the whole camp gasp, the chasm between them deep, dark and beckoning. McGrath dropped his saddlebags on the bar and eyed the gals like seeing females for the first time. Missy lifted her index finger from her chin. Andy was at the table in a trice . . . Andy, Andy's saddlebags and Andy's store-bought fluted shirt. His clean-shaved chin showed a dried-over razor nick as fresh as a recent stop at the tonsorial tent; he smelled sweet as lilacs. Missy's guess: he'd hit it big and was on his way south. Andy took in Stella's offerings and agreed to a ten-dollar bottle of champagne.

"What about me?" Missy whined, eyelids fluttering, head flouncing her ever-present blue hair ribbons.

"Give 'em each one, goddammit," McGrath told Eddie Fay, then bent to Stella's inviting left breast and sucked out a bright red flower.

Stella let out a lusty roar. "You best give me a matched set." She offered her right breast. "I wouldn't want to topple sideways from the weight." This time, she and McGrath roared together.

McGrath hollered to Fay, "A bottle of Belmont for me, too."

Stella hiked her assets onto the table.

"What size are them udders?" McGrath asked.

"Big enough for you. And I know how to use them."

Missy, one hand under the table, found the miner's coveralls and ran her fingers up to his crotch. She felt his firmness. With the two of them working the poor sap, he'd be a pushover inside a quarter hour. Missy gave him a squeeze and watched his eyes whiten. Yep, he was ripe. She'd pass him off to Stella and report to Soapy that the new spread knew more about temptation than Eve.

Ed Fay delivered glasses, the Belmont, two bottles of champagne. McGrath downed a shot and filled the champagne glasses.

Missy asked, "What boat you catching, Andy?" The new gal had to learn to get the dope's dope. When was he headed south? How had his claim paid out? Was his cache in the saddlebags? Anything to get a leg up. If the gal didn't get the dough outright, the strong-arm boys would. Then they'd have to split the take. No need for the boys or the knockout drops with Andy McGrath. Stella was solid enough to handle him alone. Missy gave him another squeeze, but he was off between Stella's breasts.

Stella sucked McGrath's forefinger up to the big knuckle. She wasn't subtle. Didn't have to be. He couldn't budge his eyes from Stella's gap as she worked the finger. He downed two more shots. His eyes teared up. The lids slid halfway down.

Goddammit! The dope drops! Missy recognized the effects. Goddamn Eddie Fay. McGrath was Stella's rube and now Eddie would claim a cut. Maybe Missy could get him to the crib first. "C'mon, Andy, lets go out back. Have some fun. You be nice and give Eddie a big nugget for a token."

McGrath shook his head, trying to focus his thoughts. The fog wasn't clearing. He rubbed his eyes. "–the fuck?"

McGrath collapsed. His head slumped onto his arms, knocking over the bottle of Belmont. Instinctively, Missy and Stella snatched to safety their champagne bottles.

"Goddamn you, Eddie!" Now, neither Missy nor Stella would get a full share. They'd have to cut Fay in.

Fay hollered, "I'll call the boys."

Missy told Stella, "This was our rube. We had him dead to rights. You and me was to split but I was going to give him to you whole and wholesome as a welcome-to-Skaguay present. Now, Fay'll horn in. We didn't need him. Goddamn it! Stay here."

Missy strode to the bar, eyes afire. "You fish brain. We didn't need your oil. We nabbed him fair and square. Now we both know he's no good to trick. Couldn't raise it with a noose."

Stella was running her hand through McGrath's hair. He wouldn't come around for an hour.

Fay said, "Just giving the new twist some help."

"And cutting her out of a full share, you bastard."

"Watch your tongue, little girl."

This wasn't the first time Fay had knocked down. Missy couldn't figure why Soapy gave him so much badge. He'd screwed the gals over plenty. It was only a matter of time when he'd try his chiseling way on the boss. Katy-bar-the-door. Fay was quick with the gun, but if crossed, Soapy'd finish him pronto. He'd drop anybody who crossed him. Herself included. Fay was nothing but a gun-toting barback. "I'll watch nothing, you chiseling son-of-a-bitch."

Fay said, "Two-Chew and a couple of the other boys is laying for you so don't splash that red-haired snatch of yours around here. This is my claim. Yours is across the alley, on your back with your heels on the ceiling."

"I had his snoogle in my hand. Harder than you ever got."

"G'wan," Fay said. "He had eyes for the big chest. Didn't shine to your scrawny self. I'll get the boys to shag him out and dump him in the privy, unless your friend has it all curtains and lace by now."

"You don't know shit from sawdust, Ed Fay, but you can bet Soapy will know about this. He won't cotton much more."

"Fuck you and the big slit, too."

"Not with that soft little pinkie of yours."

Fay brought his hand around and cuffed Missy, then pulled his belt pistol. "Get out. Go cool down somewheres."

Stella jumped up. "C'mon, Missy."

Missy stared at Fay. "Gun don't scare me, Ed Fay. Shoot me and Soapy will have your family jewels nailed over the bar. I'm the last gal you'll whack around. Count on that."

*

McGrath howled. His thinking had been slowed, as if his head had been dipped in honey. When he realized what happened, he shook out the privy sleep bag like it was a dishtowel. Nothing. He dropped to his knees and pawed the crate head to foot, tossing the nun's tooth powder and trinkets into the snow. He dumped out a small war bag of fingernail do-dads. Failing to find his poke or saddlebags, his fury flew. With his boot, he stove in the side of the privy. He reached to his side. No gun or holster. He uprooted the privy. Nothing. His boil frothed. He tore at his overshirt, popping the buttons, his rage out of control. Passers-by paused as he reeled into the center of Broadway.

A mule cart bearing lumber from the wharf drew to a halt. The teamster hollered, "Git the hell out of the way!"

"Fuck you!" McGrath swung at the mule's head, hitting the animal in the neck. It brayed, kicked, jerked to the side and dumped the top boards from the cart. The teamster jumped from the wagon and charged. The men collided in the mud.

Marshal Rowan, in front of the livery with Lank, ran to the fracas and jerked the teamster off McGrath. Rowan calmly listened to his story, then ordered McGrath to reload the lumber. McGrath went for the teamster a second time. Rowan barrel-tapped him on the side of the head, enough to renew McGrath's befogment, but not enough to put him out. Rowan said, "You clobbered the mule, you went after the driver–what the hell were you thinking?"

"I'll kill them fucks," was all McGrath said.

"Who? And why?"

"Them cunnies, the barkeep. All of 'em. I dunno. Someone laced my whiskey."

"Where?"

McGrath hitched his thumb toward Jeff Smith's Parlor. "Got my poke, saddlebags and gun. Forty pounds of color I was carrying. A year's work. I'll kill all three of the sons-a-bitches."

"No one gets killed here, partner," Rowan said. "Right now, I got a wife in labor. Soon's I see to that, I'll come back and we'll look for your goods."

"Fuck you, badge. No looking needed. I know where the stuff is." He crossed Broadway and pushed through Jeff's door. McGrath found Ed Fay behind the bar. "Hey, shitkeep, where's the cunnies what oiled my drink?"

Rowan followed McGrath and put himself beside the miner.

"Marshal," Fay said, "get this stumblebum out of my saloon. This is the second time today he's caused a ruckus and I'm tired of it. Emptied the joint out the last time. He won't do it twice. I got me a full house and aim to keep it."

McGrath roared, lurched over the bar and caught Fay clean with a roundhouse. The marshal pulled the miner back. Fay drew the Thunderer from his belt.

"No!" Rowan yelled.

Fay fired into McGrath's head, the force of the impact at such short range hurling the miner back into Rowan. Both went down to the sawdust. Rowan came up with his own gun drawn. Before he could get aimed, Fay fanned the Thunderer twice. Rowan was dead before hitting the floor.

*

"The man was so roistered up," Bowers told Soapy, "he never got a shot off. Rowan neither."

Never a moment's peace for the wicked, Soapy thought. He knew the long-term blackness an incident like this might bring on Skaguay. More federal lawmen. Maybe the troops from Dyea. The town was already short-fused what with winter coming on.

Bowers said, "I got Eddie stashed in the cell with old man Lazlo. Tripp and Sheriff Taylor are standing guard, but the mob knows he's up there. They're clamoring for his neck."

Soapy, still in his under drawers, razored his neck below the beardline. "We got to get him out of town."

Missy came in, out of breath. "You heard?"

Soapy said, "Missy go to the bedroom and don't budge. Lock the door." With blood in the air and the righteous on the rise, all he needed was for the babbling whore to be loose. "Charlie, get one of the boys over here to sit on Missy."

Dressing quickly, Soapy adjusted his four-in-hand and settled a Bisley into the specially-tailored holster built into his suit jacket. He stuffed a two-shot into a trousers' pocket. Bowers checked his own revolver and readied a pair of shotguns.

"No," Soapy said. "Long guns will give the hot heads an excuse to start shooting. That's the last thing we need. Our worry is the vigilantes. Something like this is exactly what Frank Reid has been waiting for."

Soapy couldn't figure Ed Fay's play. Why in blazes would he gun down a rube *and* the deputy? "Charlie, are you certain he did it?"

"He's always spoiling, Boss. Fay tells it that Missy and the new spread were working McGrath and the man went loco. He needed cooling lest he tear the place up."

"Missy, get out here!"

She jerked open the bedroom door. "I heard that, Charlie Bowers. It ain't true." Then added quickly, "Stella and me had him set up, buying

141

champagne and Belmont. He was already half piped. We was ready to spring him. I was going to give him to Stella, her being new and all, and then goddamn Eddie Fay goes and loads his whiskey. The rube folded like a bad poker hand."

Who to believe, Soapy wondered. Charlie didn't have a horse in the race. Never lied anyway. No telling what might come from Missy. She didn't know the difference between the truth and a tea kettle. "Makes no matter now. Fay's the one at risk. We'll sort out the details later."

Missy said, "Nothing to sort. The rube didn't go loco, goddammit."

"Okay, Missy, back to the bedroom. You know where the gun is stashed."

"I got my own muff gun, but don't let me near Eddie Fay. I'll blow his balls off."

Soapy couldn't hide the grin.

Bowers said, "Townfolk and miners have packed the street outside Clancy's. They're bellowing up at the jail. Let's go the back way and arrive from inside Clancy's. At least we'll be facing them."

"Good." Soapy buttoned his suit jacket, thought about wearing his duster and decided against it. He had nothing to hide.

"Missy, on second thought, you get up the back stairs to Tripp and Taylor. Pronto like yesterday. Tell them to get Eddie over to Dyea and on the first ship south. I'll stall the mob."

When Bowers and Soapy ducked into the alley, they saw the torches and felt the buzz, a hive of angered bees. Bowers slipped on his clerical collar. Soapy saw the kicked-in privy, wondered about the nun. No time for her now, though he paused to make certain she wasn't about. He warned the line gals back to their cribs. "Stay put. This'll be over shortly. You'll be getting some extra business tonight because the folks have their blood aboil."

Soapy emerged through Clancy's front door, and the mob howled. Pistols were fired into the air. McGrath had been a kindred miner. He deserved revenging. Rowan had been on his way to help his wife through childbirth. The mob knew Eddie Fay's reputation as a bully and had heard that neither man had got off a shot. That's all the evidence they needed.

More guns fired and Soapy just watched, thinking, Let them calm themselves down. He scanned the crowd. The men would follow the first horse out of the barn. He was surprised to see Hal Howard, the new clothier he'd helped set up. Hal was about ready to expand his tent into a full-line store rivaling the Klondyke Mercantile. If Soapy lost the merchants, he'd be in trouble. The one who might give them unity, Frank Reid, was nowhere to be seen. A good omen, Soapy thought.

Bowers raised his hands. The seasoned miners, those who'd been around longer than a week, knew Bowers was no more a preacher than they were, but the collar had a gentling effect. The men quieted. One voice sounded out: "We knows he's up there, Colonel. We're taking him. Andy McGrath wouldn't hurt a fly what landed on his pecker. We're taking Ed Fay."

The crowd took up a chant. "Ed Fay! Ed Fay! Ed Fay!"

Soapy stepped forward, crossed his arms.

"He's ours, Colonel."

"We're taking him."

Soapy pulled out his pocket watch and made a show of snapping it open. He studied the time piece far longer than necessary. In no way would he try to out-shout the mob. He knew better. The men were down there in the mud of Broadway, he was up on the boardwalk, dry. He recalled his days as a preacher student, how he'd been taught that a timely stillness generated attention. Finally, he snapped closed the watch and pocketed it. "I got all night." He shrugged, plain-faced as a bowl of pudding.

The men shuffled from one boot to the other, examining their hands, chewing their lips. They hushed.

"Boys," he said, "our town has suffered mightily this day. We've lost one of our own in Andy McGrath and one fine and noble lawman in Marshal Rowan. Both were taken in the prime of life, the Widow Rowan at this moment giving birth to a child the marshal will never set eyes upon."

"Don't make a hoot what you say, Colonel. Fay's hanging!"

"Who said that?" Soapy scoured the crowd. "If someone has something to say to me, be man enough to come up here and stand at my face."

No one budged. He had them. His thought shifted to Sheriff Taylor and Old Man Tripp, hoping they had Fay on his way to Dyea. Another minute or two and they should be well clear of town.

"Fine," he said. "If there's no one else to speak up, I'll finish my piece. Then you boys can do what you must. But I'm telling you one thing: there will be no lawlessness–no lynching–so long as I'm around Skaguay. You boys know me, know that I stand foursquare behind my words. I'm saying again, there will be no lynching. What there will be," he said, removing his hat and handing it to Bowers, "is a collection for the Widow Rowan." He reached into his pocket, removed a banded roll of paper money and made a show of plopping it into the hat. "Reverend Bowers here will go among you. I hope you will find it in your heart to share mightily of what you have."

"What about Eddie Fay?"

"The law will take its course."

"We can save time."

Soapy leaned forward. "Only through me," he said, daring anyone to challenge him. No one moved. "Be generous to the hat, boys. Then I'll stand every manjack to a drink at my place."

A huzzah erupted. He'd turned the herd. Bowers went down to the crowd, saying at each donation, "Amen, brother." And bobbing his head toward Soapy's parlor.

Soapy stepped down into the mud and accepted congratulations from a half-dozen miners. Hal Howard said, "Thought for a moment we'd have us a dust-up."

"I was surprised to see you with the mob, Hal."

"Just keeping an eye out," he said, walking backwards away from Soapy. "Just keeping an eye out."

At home, Soapy poured himself three fingers of Belmont, his first drink since the grand opening. He pulled off his boots. Missy was already asleep. Bowers would keep watch at the saloon. Tripp and Taylor were on their way to Dyea, and Fay was out of trouble. All he wanted was one day when he could nap with both eyes closed. He'd earned that much, and the drink, but he had to do something to quell the underlying unrest the shootings would bring. The sainted ones would get to stirring the coals. Reid would stoke the fire.

The town needed a public showing akin to a pick-pocket's diversion. It was time to get on with Lazlo's hanging. The publicity from a legal hanging, all proper and judicial, would make good headlines in the coast papers. He'd have Bowers write it up. Get it done between Thanksgiving and Christmas so everyone could enjoy a peaceful holiday.

*

On the trail back from Dyea, Reid ran into Sheriff Taylor, Old Man Tripp and Eddie Fay. He sawed back on his big grullo's reins and sent the mare into an uprear. Something was out of true. Why was this trio of scruff headed to Dyea? Why this time of night?

Tripp and the sheriff edged their horses down the trail. Fay lingered, his fingers drumming his belt buckle next to the Thunderer.

Reid thought, This guy's worse than Two-Chew Calderone. He's smart. Can add up the price of a dozen drinks as fast as they're ordered. Add four bits for his own pocket, and come out with the same cost every time. Now the bastard was taunting him. The other two were clearly itching to move along. If it came to a play, he'd get Fay first.

Fay broke the silence. "How was Dyea, Frank?"

"Peaceful," Reid said.

"You go there on vigilante business?" Fay's salty arrogance was meant to grate.

"Someone has to stand up to you strong-arm boys."

"You, by chance?" Fay covered his gun stock.

Old Man Tripp back-stepped his horse. "Eddie, let's git. We got orders."

So they were being sent to Dyea? No doubt on Soapy's orders. Why? If Soapy were going to expand, he'd send Bowers. Maybe with Big Bo to line up a decent crib. Not his lackey sheriff and the old man. The federals would tell them to pound salt.

Reid unbuttoned his duster and let his .45 show. "Now's as good a time as any." He was playing a bluff hand, hoping he wouldn't be called. He'd get Fay, maybe Tripp. By then, the sheriff would have him. When Frank and his brother had been schoolteachers, they'd often spoke about how school boys pushed teachers until the teacher dropped a hammer. His brother counseled Frank never to crack a smile in front of a new class for the first month. Elsewise, the kids'd run the schoolhouse. Like as not, the lesson was one more reason why Reid left the classroom and took up Indian fighting and surveying.

Tripp slipped himself between Reid and Fay, hands held over his head. "Eddie, goddammit, if I take this move back to Soapy, he'll–"

"Stow it, old man. I'm just jobbing my friend, Frank, here." Fay jerked his horse toward Dyea.

Frank double-timed back to Skaguay. At the livery, Lank told him everything about the double shooting. Goddammit! The town let Fay get away. He, himself, had let Fay get away.

He gave Lank a list of names. "Tell them to be at Rowan's office tonight. Ten o'clock. You, too."

"Frank, I ain't in this fight."

"You're in, Lank. You're a decent man and want to see a decent community. You're in, all right. Ten o'clock. Tonight."

At the meeting, Reid didn't couch his words. "The federals won't help without a say-so from the higher-ups."

"Ever?"

Reid studied the faces. They were men of substance, but most, like himself, long in the tooth, a year and day past prime. Citizen Tom Whitten, California vigilante Bill Fonda, straight-shooting Cap Tanner, Major Strong, others. "They won't come without orders from the War Department. We can make a stronger case, what with these recent killings." He'd already stormed the men about letting Fay get away. Tanner had told him to simmer, that none of them knew what had been going on. Frank had made the mistake of asking if Soapy was the only man in town with a thinking cap. Then took a rug whip to himself for the rudeness. He'd never get over their stupidity, but he'd squash those feelings for the time.

Bill Fonda spoke up. "I say we arm up and treat Smith the way his henchmen treated Rowan and McGrath. Soapy ain't the only one who can shoot."

"Bill, you got no store," Tom Whitten said. "You got no tent that can be burned down, no stock he can poison. Easy for you to say. Not so simple for boys like me." Tom owned one of the few good wood buildings in Skaguay. Honest as a spring day. Frank figured he'd make a good mayor, if they ever got around to electing one. But Tom had a point. Soapy and his boys used fire as fear. Folks knew it.

"Tom's right," Cap Tanner said. "Thems who got investments can't risk them–not without some protection. Rowan was the one man stood his ground and look what it got him."

"Hold on," Frank said. "No sense arguing among ourselves. Is there anyone here don't think we need to do something?" Maybe an easy nudge would move them. His ranting hadn't.

"No gun play," Tom Whitten said. "We'd lose."

"Guns is all they savvy."

Goddamn, Frank thought. They're going to sit on the crapper until it rots from under their asses. A stick of dynamite in the hole wouldn't budge them.

"Let's go back to what the federals told Frank. They need orders to move. Let's write the War Department. Send the letter to newspapers in Seattle and San Francisco."

"And tip our hand? We'd be dead as soon as the paper landed at the dock."

Jesus Christ! Frank had used all his words. More talk, more wasted time. He was ready for a showdown, but knew he couldn't go it alone.

"How about we just write the War Department? Not a word to the newspapers."

"Maybe a petition?"

"I'll sign."

"I'm not willing to sign anything until we've set a plan."

Frank thought, Not a stiff dick among them.

"Okay," Major Strong said. "How about this? Tom, Bob and I can meet at my place. Draft up a petition and bring it back to the group. If we agree, we'll write it up all formal and name someone to quietly hand carry it down to the War Department office in Seattle. Do nothing else without the group's nod."

A compromise had been reached.

Except in Frank's eyes. The wilted lilies would wait until Soapy's boys picked them off one by one. Frank wasn't waiting around.

Not him.

Not him at all.

15. No Price Too Dear

Bernadette needed to tell Miss Bonteiller of her decision. She rattled two crib lanterns before learning that Missy was in the third. Dressed in a white corset and muslin drawers, Missy jerked her inside and snatched closed the tent flaps. Missy wrapped a cashmere shawl around her shoulders and tied it at the neck. "Imagine this," she said. "A nun of God in a crib house. Don't that beat all."

The tent was no larger than Mister Lazlo's cell, barely wide enough for a single bed. An oil cloth covered the bed's bottom half. A washstand held a salver with ewer and basin. On the floor, a slop jar. A hall tree with an outfit of street clothes on its pegs stood to the side of a narrow pier glass. Not a hint of frippery. Not so much as a chair.

Missy motioned Bernadette to the bed. Enjoying the luxury of a real mattress and spring, Bernadette bounced up and down, the bed screeching like a funeral keener.

Missy said, "Soapy claims I wore it out. That's a compliment in my line of work."

"Yes, well–"

"Don't never come knocking here again. You'll get in Dutch like nobody's business. I mean it."

"I have news."

Missy retrieved a war bag from the windowsill and drew out a fingernail file and a nail chamois. "Go ahead," she said.

"I know how I can make enough money to get you out of here and get myself a decent place to live."

"I ain't worried about getting out, just yet. If I were to try, I'd worry about being able to walk. Besides, I ain't worried about money. I ain't made the poor-boy promise you made."

"It's called a vow."

"Vow, then. I don't fashion a lady such as myself living how you do. Not to be offensive, Sister, but you live in a privy."

"I'm going to fix that." Bernadette let Missy examine her fingernails.

"Almost shameful, they are."

"I've neglected them something fierce. My mother would boil me in oil."

Missy set to work on Bernadette's left hand. "Go on," she said.

Bernadette closed her eyes. She'd seen rich ladies in fancy parlors having their nails polished, never dreaming of the luxurious feeling it could bring. Missy filed smooth her rough edges. Bernadette began dreaming of Mary Magdalene doing her nails, then massaging them with fine oils and drying them with her hair. She barely heard Missy humming contentedly.

"Hey, you," Missy said, tugging on Bernadette's thumb. "Wake up. You said you got news."

"I'm going to enter the Turkey Shoot."

"Are you kidding? Every gun in town will be shooting. Probably some boys from Dyea and some from up the trail and The Scales, as well. Maybe even some of those cute Mounties. This'll be bigger than Christmas!"

Bernadette pulled back her hand. If the tart didn't think she could shoot, she was sadly mistaken. She didn't know daddy's lessons. "I was raised on a farm. We hunted every year–rifles and shotguns. I turned out to be the best shot in all of Sheldon, Iowa."

"And just how big is this Sheldon, Iowa?"

"Maybe two-hundred. But I could outshoot all the men, outshoot most in Sioux Center and Hospers, too."

"Maybe Soapy won't let gals enter. Ever think of that?"

"Do you think he'd keep out the likes of Annie Oakley or Calamity Jane?"

"They ain't . . . your type of gal." Missy picked at the sleeve of Bernadette's habit. "Phew!"

"What does the habit have to do with it, you hussy?"

"Nothing, I guess," Missy said. "It's the men."

"Well, I intend to enter. The Colonel is welcome to try to stop me." Bernadette held out her right hand.

Missy said, "Is her highness ready now?"

"Miss Bonteiller, I didn't mean to imply anything. It was you who started the filing."

"Sometimes you got a way about you."

"Meaning?"

"Meaning nothing. You just do. I ain't no one's servant and you ain't a princess at a king's ball."

"I agree. You could be anything you want. You don't have to be a–"

"Stop! You go ahead and enter your old Turkey Shoot. You'll be sorry. They'd shoot *you* rather than let you win."

149

"I can do it. Don't you think I got all sorts of cross-eyed stares carrying a Winchester from Minnesota to Seattle and then on the boat? A nun with a gun? Mighty strange looks, indeed. But I persevered. And I'll continue until I hear differently from Mother Francine. I'll win us money and get a decent roof over my head and you a ticket south."

"I told you, I ain't ready to tie my tent flaps once and forever."

"When will you be?"

"When Frank Reid gets smart enough to sweep me off my feet."

"If you're in love with him, why do you live in Soapy's house and do what you do?"

"'Cause I can't go anywhere. I got ties. Folks are watching me all the time. And if you ain't figured it out, you're dumb as sow snot." She gave the back of Bernadette's hand a pinch. "Now go on home, wherever that is." She turned away and began to cry.

*

Bernadette returned to the laundry to find Mrs. Lowe bent over a rinse basin and the Salvationist woman dressed in what appeared to be every garment she owned, even though the temperature was barely below freezing. She eyed Bernadette like a shop-window curio. "Your habit changes frequently, Sister Bernadette."

Her obvious reference was to Bernadette's missing rosary and cape, and the new ties around her skirt to keep it up and out of the tent's mud. "No, Madam, the habit of the Good Shepherd Sisters never changes. One must, however, make accommodation for one's station in life." It was clear that they'd continue to be incompatible.

"As you'd have it, Sister." She extended a gloved hand. "I've come to say good-bye and wish you well in your new undertaking."

At that, Mrs. Lowe pulled up from her rinse bin, wiped her hands and sidled slow as a maple drip to the rear of the tent. The Salvationist continued without a skipped beat. She explained that Two-Chew Calderone had visited the orphanage and announced that the Salvationists' work in Skaguay had been completed. She, along with her four minions–dummies, Mister Calderone had called them–were to move on up the trail. By the Colonel's own order. Be gone by today. Bernadette was to take over the orphanage.

"Me?" she asked.

"Sister Bernadette, you sound as if you know nothing about this turn of events."

"Not on your life."

"You never spoke to the Colonel about the possibility?"

She'd never asked him to put the Salvationists out of their home. She had merely suggested that the children might be better off with a Christian influence in their lives.

The Salvationist said, "Well?"

"I never asked the Colonel to oust you." She was under no obligation to go into the details of a private conversation. The Lord knew the truth. His judgment would prevail.

The Salvationist handed Bernadette a sheaf of written notes about the babies: clothing, food preferences, illnesses, sleeping habits. She'd just spoken to Widow Rowan and two other women. They had agreed to spell Bernadette when the nun needed to be in camp. The Salvationists were off to Dawson.

Bernadette said, "But the pass is covered in snow."

"The men will roll me up in a rug like a bacon-wrapped frankfurter and strap me to a sled. The Lord will provide the rest. Isn't that what you preach?"

"He provides–yes. But He has given us the power to reason. It's this gift that separates us from the birds of the air."

She said, "We leave at noon."

When she departed, Mrs. Lowe rushed through the flap, pausing only to cast on Bernadette a condemnatory glare. She yoo-hooed to the Salvationist. Judging by Mrs. Lowe's somber scowl, Bernadette's days as a laundress were numbered.

Had she been completely truthful with the Salvationist? The question vexed her. True, she'd said that a Christian influence should be paramount in the babies' lives. True, also, she never specifically asked the Colonel to evict them. Did it have to do with the Colonel's Christian background? Or her? She satisfied herself by answering *both* to the questions, while realizing a touch of Miss Bonteiller in her reasoning.

Within hours of the Salvationist's news, Bernadette gathered her few possessions, left word for Miss Bonteiller and headed up the trail for the cabin. In time, Miss Bonteiller followed and went straight for Poteet Bleu. Bernadette said that she was confused about the Colonel's predilections toward women of the cloth.

"He likes the cut of my cloth," Missy piped, and returned Poteet Bleu to her crib. She produced two dream-book dress drawings. "For my new gowns. Soapy said to pick out two: one for the hanging and one for Thanksgiving."

"Mister Lazlow? Mister Fay? Neither has had a trial."

"Oh, Fay's long gone. Tripp put him on the boat out of Dyea. It's Lazlow's hanging. He'll have a trial by the time he's hung. Old Judge Van Horn will find him guilty as sin and sentence him to hang. End of the book. That's how Soapy does it."

"I've never seen the likes–anywhere–of what appears to be accepted activity here in the Alaska District. I'm appalled, stupefied. Can nothing save poor Mister Lazlo?"

"Soapy could. The vigilantes could rise up. The Commissioner might come down from Dyea with the soldiers. All about as much chance as daisies sprouting in December. Don't fret yourself over a hanging. Think about Thanksgiving. Most folks will be celebrating. I don't know why. If they're here, they ain't in happy places like the Klondyke scooping up color or at home with kin."

By Thanksgiving, Bernadette would have been in the district three months and still no closer to fulfilling her assignment than the day the *Al-Ki* deposited her on Moore's Wharf. She had no money, yet now had three babies and a cabin to care for. On reflection, she was, of course, horrified by Skaguay's lawlessness and licentiousness, her feelings made clear to one and all. Her sin was that she was also titillated by the rakish lifestyle. It was the same feeling she had when she'd read the eight-pager with her sister.

"Miss Bonteiller, I–"

While her mind was occupied, Missy had unbuttoned her bodice and begun to feed Poteet Bleu. Bernadette's eyes must have gone the size of carriage lamps. Missy said, "Yes, she's mine."

*

KLONDYKE JUSTICE
by Stroller White

In his day, the Stroller has sat through a number of trials, some of them his own, and that is as much as you will hear about them. However, the Lazlo trial was one of a kind.

Yesterday, at Clancy's, the Stroller lolled near the door to witness Judge Van Horn's trial of Sven Lazlo, a miner who freely admitted to driving a horseshoe into the head of one Portland Pete, local purveyor of gold field maps, three months back. Why it has taken so long for this carriage of justice to be readied is anybody's guess, and only one of the curious aspects associated with this event. Anybody who knew the answer was not talking to the Stroller, and the Stroller asked plenty. The Stroller can speculate, but will not. He prefers dealing in facts, at least occasionally.

Easier to answer is the question: Why was the trial held in Clancy's Saloon? For this, a plethora of answers was available:

1. Clancy's is directly below the Skaguay hoosegow so transportation of the accused is a quick and easy matter.

2. Clancy's is the second-largest wooden structure in all of greater Skaguay. (The proprietors of the Pack Train food emporium, one Anton Stanish and one Louis Ceovich, explained they could not prepare and serve the meals demanded by trial goers and still make their digs suitable for a trial.) (The wonder of the official Skaguay Rumor Mill has it that John Clancy paid a slight tribute to Messrs. Stanish and Ceovich for their abstinence, but this is purely hearsay.)

3. Clancy's had just received a fresh shipment of spirits so as to be able to guarantee trial-goers an unending supply of their favored libation.

Next in the litany of oddities, the Stroller knows well (but not intimately) the identities of the lovely ladies who occupied the chairs in the front row of the courthouse. (The ladies gave new meaning to the terms "court" and "house" and that is enough said on that subject. What the Stroller—and you!—need to know is the reason six of the eight front-row seats were occupied by demimondes.) Before the gavel fell, the trial had all the earmarks of a first-class shivaree.

As to the trial itself, the Stroller would like to know why it was scheduled for ten a.m. but failed to begin until shortly before noon? The suggestion that the time was well-utilized for commercial transactions of the high-proof variety is hereby rejected as a sham. Still, no other reasons have surfaced.

Judge Van Horn proved to be an able courtroom disciplinarian. For a full quarter of an hour, he posed perceptive and probing questions to Sheriff Taylor, who gave the expected and unsurprising answers, to wit:

JUDGE: Do you see the defendant in the courthouse?

SHERIFF: (pointing to Lazlo) Yah, over there.

JUDGE: And why is the defendant on trial today?

The Seduction of Sister Skaguay

SHERIFF: He pounded a horseshoe into Portland Pete's brain pan. Killed him dead out.

JUDGE: Did you personally see him perpetrate said act on the deceased?

SHERIFF: Not on no deceased. He done it on a live Portland Pete.

Lazlo admitted to the episode, claiming the maps were rogue forgeries, that he was only defending himself and that he might have had a drink or two prior to the event . . . rendering him in less than full possession of his faculties. The courtroom, to a man and lady, seemed to stifle its laughter. In truth, eye-witness accounts on Broadway claim that Lazlo was swamp-draining drunk.

Lazlo continued the levity, noting that it had now been three months since he'd wet his whistle and asked the Judge if he might be allowed to sip a cup of kindness if he could find a sponsor, for he held not a sou to his name.

Three miners leapt to their feet and offered to satisfy Lazlo's long-run thirst. "Give him a whole jug. In fact, give everyone in the house a taste."

The Judge gaveled the trial to a recess during which the barbacks earned a mighty penny for John Clancy. The ladies in the front row utilized the time to socialize. Two disappeared and did not return.

Upon resumption of the trial, the Judge opined that he had heard enough testimony and was prepared to rule, unless other pertinent matters needed to be considered. No one spoke until the Judge raised his gavel, at which time Col. Jefferson Randolph Smith, salon proprietor and one of Skaguay's leading citizens and, perhaps, the town's most generous charity donor, rose. He gave an eloquent and impassioned plea for justice, noting how in any society, 'justice' was the balance between civility and chaos. He spoke to the meaning of the American flag under which all jurisprudence operates, even in a faraway district like Alaska, and condemned any lawless acts of vigilantism, past or future. For his efforts, Col. Smith received an ovation. He concluded his remarks with a plug for the Thanksgiving Turkey Shoot, noting that he had imported prizes for the top shooters, and a special prize for the team shoot.

(ASIDE. He received the standing ovation either for the speech, OR for offering every man in the house a drink at his parlor on adjournment of the trial.)

Oh, and yes. Lazlo was found guilty and sentenced to hang.

*

By mid-morning on the day before Thanksgiving, those not shooting warmed up in Jeff's Parlor, Clancy's Music Hall and the other hospitality houses. Throughout the Skaguay Valley, gunfire reports bounced between the mountains as sharpshooters and tinhorns alike honed their skills for the one o'clock shoot.

At first, the contest committee—none other than Colonel Smith and Frank Reid—had planned to use as targets the scraggly dogs that had found their way back to town from the pass. Bernadette protested loudly against the use of any live targets. She told Mister Reid that she intended to enter the contest and would no more shoot the most useless cur than she would shoot him, but that she'd think twice about shooting him if he let a single person murder a helpless dog. In a customary terse reply, he said he'd see what he could do. In no time flat, wooden cutouts shaped like sled dogs had sprung up all over town, and were quickly riddled with holes by anxious shooters.

Bernadette mused about the contest and found it more and more curious that the Colonel and Mister Reid should act in consort as contest committee chairmen. Over the months since she'd arrived, and certainly during conversations with Miss Bonteiller, it had become clear that these two were the most bitter of enemies. That they could come together in harmony for the Turkey Shoot only showed the mysterious ways the Lord uses to secure his ends. What evils—or good—such an arrangement might portend were, to Bernadette, completely befogged.

For the shoot, the Colonel and the merchants put up prizes: nuggets valued at $25, $50 and $100 . . . with a grand prize of $250. The Colonel announced a special team prize of $100. Bernadette dearly needed the money to expand the orphanage to a livable size. Since she'd taken over, Miss Bonteiller had secreted her cash on occasion, but it was never enough. The Colonel was most generous to his consort in all material ways, but since the new system of tokens had come on, the child had less cash than a down-and-outer. Bernadette told her that such resembled her own Vow of Poverty. Missy didn't see the similarity. On the plus side of the ledger, Poteet Bleu now had a Godmother who would care for her and the other babies as true Christians. Miss Bonteiller had no reason to quit her illicit labors.

The Seduction of Sister Skaguay

In Iowa, Bernadette's father had taught all his children the rights and wrongs of shooting. He'd made them work first with his old Marlin octagon repeater, then a shotgun and finally a revolver and rifle just as he made them work horses behind a plow. He felt strongly that man and woman alike should know how to hunt and fish and trap and farm. Her father's training included hours in the back quarter at target practice. Every roasting ear cob that didn't go into the sty served as a target. Bernadette could hit them in the air almost as well as Annie Oakley. True, she might now be a little rusty, but it would all come back.

She'd explained to Miss Bonteiller how she was going to win the grand prize, but that she needed to hone her skills. Much to the unhappiness of the babies, she'd spent several afternoons near the cabin at target practice. To sight in the Winchester with precise accuracy, she had gone so far as to remove her wimple. Its starchiness forced her head up and away from a clean sight along the barrel. She wouldn't be able to afford this luxury in public. Nevertheless, she'd regained her previous sharp-shooter's eye. She'd win this contest not only for the babies, but for the memory of her beloved father.

On the day of the shoot, over two-hundred contestants gathered outside Clancy's. Mister Reid shouted out the rules. Just as he was completing his message, Colonel Smith and Reverend Bowers emerged onto the boardwalk from within the saloon, Bowers holding a burlap bag. The boys whooped. The Colonel raised his hands for silence. "After you shoot, boys, go on down to my place. I'm standing each of you to a drink." The town gave him a cheer followed by a volley of gunfire that would have loosed an avalanche had they been up in the mountains. Bowers bag began quivering like it held the original palsy. Once opened, Colonel Smith withdrew a flapping chicken. "Boys, one more thing," he said, grandly displaying the chicken, "I have one hundred of these fine Oregon layers and I'm donating them to the top one-hundred shooters of Skaguay!" Another round of cheers exploded. The Colonel casually snapped the chicken's neck and flipped the quivering carcass down to Mister Reid. Mister Reid caught the chicken one-handed, a none-too-pleased frown on his face.

"Frank," he said, "that's what my boys will do to your vigilantes in the team shoot."

At the far end of the wharf, three wooden cutouts painted up as snarling gray sled dogs had been set up. A rope line had been laid across the wharf fifty yards from the targets, a distance even a poor shot should be able to handle. Shooters toed the line in sets of three, each taking a single shot at the dog in their lane. Bernadette took no end of jobbing while awaiting her turn. The men generally guffawed that she had God on her side, and such was not considered sporting. She couldn't help but smile when her turn came. At fifty yards, she could have hit the cutout blindfolded. No windage, no elevation, no lead. Amazingly enough, half the shooters, most wavy as corn tassels, missed. The Alaskan men were not as crack as one would think. More likely it was the demon drink.

The line for the second round was moved back to one-hundred yards. This was not a sure-thing distance, especially considering the slight breeze that kicked up from the mountains, and the gentle motion of the dock as it groaned against an incoming tide. Because Bernadette had laid back to the end of the pack, she was able to watch for any edge. By the time her turn came around, only thirty-eight men remained in the competition. She admitted to a spot of pride; she wanted badly to best those who had tried to make her life a purgatory on earth. She went on and shot through the new target as if she'd been close enough to touch it.

For the third round, fourteen shooters remained. The line was moved back to one-hundred twenty-five yards. The men teased her relentlessly, Two-Chew Calderone the only one who did not engage in the light-hearted banter. He was bent on winning the top prize, or at least seeing that Bernadette didn't win it. Most of the on-lookers gave her huzzahs as the round began. Mister Calderone did not.

Bernadette smoothed her cape and nestled the Winchester's stock to her shoulder. Aiming slightly left to allow for the windage, she steadied the bead on the chest of the sled dog. *My Mother, My Confidence.* The starched cotton of her wimple pressed into her ear, but she shut out the distraction and closed one eye. As she squeezed, a gust of wind reached the inlet. She knew she'd missed.

She made her way down the wharf to polite clapping, as cool as Saturday bathwater on a Sunday morning. She nodded, her wimple bobbing in perpetual motion, her tongue pressing the roof of her mouth behind sealed lips. She completely forgot about Christopher and started up the trail, the Winchester over her shoulder. She hardly cared that she stumbled and fell twice before reaching the cemetery. She'd lost to poorer shooters than herself. Lost!

She did not stop to give Angel the news. She waved, and only then realized that tears were dripping off her chin.

Was she more tight-jawed over her humiliation in the contest or over her dread about the babies' necessities? She couldn't tell. The babies were desperate for diapers, booties and sleep sacks. Her pride was sorely scorched, but her responsibilities took precedence. She had no more than reached sight of the cabin than she heeled about and headed back to town.

She had to think first of the babies. They were in a precarious position. The Colonel's generosity was legendary, yet he continued to prohibit her begging. What manner of man was he? He had the effect of confounding her.

In town, the celebration was in full bacchanalia. Men danced together in the mud. Women, two as bare-bosomed as statues, cavorted openly and shamelessly. To her sorrow, she learned that Two-Chew Calderone had won the individual competition and that the Colonel's shooters had easily bested Mister Reid's. She pushed into the Colonel's parlor and found him and his henchmen admiring the soon-to-be-erected sign, JEFF SMITH'S PARLOR. She announced, "Gentlemen, please excuse the Colonel and I." He nodded them down the bar.

She said, "You must end the curse you've put on me."

"Curse?"

"You forbade me to beg alms in your camp." He stepped around a pair of arm-wrestling miners and walked toward the rear of the saloon. Like a connected twin, she followed. "Don't you dare walk away from me."

He turned, his hand raised as if in blessing. "First, I didn't forbid you from anything. I merely said your efforts would come to no avail. Secondly, this is not my camp. It belongs to the good citizens."

He was having her on. She was determined not to tolerate the charade. "Colonel, your word is bible here. Everyone knows it. Insofar as your linguistic niggling is concerned, the result is the same. I am penniless. My needs are few, but the babies need much. Either you provide for them or I shall haul them into town and place them in the middle of Broadway with a sign decrying your stinginess."

"People know of my generosity."

She showed him her back, but would not step away. Not until he agreed to help.

He began talking, almost rambling, about his poor childhood in Georgia, his brother, Bascomb, and his father, a lawyer controlled by the demon rum. His mother had been a southern beauty and bible-righteous Baptist who'd convinced him to undertake ministry studies. His story rolled on, not a word of it emotionally spilt. He talked in a toneless soliloquy that was borne from a strange and distanced soul.

When Bernadette turned to face him, he barely knew she was present. He was reciting history as he knew it. He'd taken his story to Creede and Denver, to all his acquaintances: Bat Masterson, Bob Ford, Ruby Bob Fitzsimmons. "Good men all," he said, "except for that back-shooter Bob Ford."

She let him continue his odyssey until she could bear it no more. "Colonel, this is all interesting, but I have the babies to concern myself about. I need bottles and blankets. Yesterday, I used newspapers for diapers."

In his same toneless voice, he said, "I want you to stop nagging Missy about her circumstance."

"I don't see where that's any business of yours."

From inside his vest, he produced a square of paper and a pencil. "Give me your list of needs."

She scribbled furiously and held the paper out to him. He didn't reach for it. Her hand remained in front of his chest, the white paper against his black suit seeming as large as his storefront sign.

"You don't have to save every soul you meet."

"Colonel, I can't–"

With a vicious swipe, he snatched the paper from her hand, crushed it and threw it to the sawdust. His fists balled up and his face reddened. He was going to strike her!

Almost as quickly as he lost control, he relaxed. "I believe the babies will have all their needs provided to them if you stop preaching to Missy." He retrieved the paper and made a show of brushing it off.

Her wimple bobbed up and down.

16. Puberty

Reid surveyed the dead nun's grave. He wondered about religious people. How could they daydream their lives away? They were decent folks, that much he knew. What he couldn't understand was how any person could give up an entire life. They didn't clerk a store, teach school, raise a family. Didn't do things normal people did. Sister Bernadette allowed the burial of an empty coffin and called it her friend. Made as much sense as curling up in a tree hollow and calling it a home. No, he didn't savvy the woman at all. Maybe that's what drew him to her. She was a curio, a magnetized one, a woman he could take seriously.

Missy was another breed. In her tent, she'd make a man moan. He recollected the time–not so long ago–she pulled up her skirts right at the orphanage. Gave him a whirl on the jawbone, standing up, and laughing at him because he first made her turn the cribs front side backward so as not to disconcert the babies.

"Shit." He looked around to see if he was being watched. Then admitted it. He found the nun fetching. A feeling that came naturally, and strong.

He trod through the cemetery, forgetting his graveside admission. Got sore as hell at himself all over again for losing the Turkey Shoot to Soapy's boys. "Goddammit!" Hindsight being clear as a spring day told him it had been a bad a idea to toss out the challenge to a gang of hired gunmen. They were professionals. Like the Earp brothers. Would have lost to them, too. "Shit, howdy, it was dumb." Now, the vigilantes, even though good of heart, would think twice and three times about facing down Soapy's boys. Pure good and pure bad were getting mixed like whiskey and branch water. Soon, it'd be impossible to separate them.

At the orphanage, Frank drew rein and dismounted the grullo. He talked low to the mare. "Why the hell did I ride all the way out here? Makes no goddamn sense. A passel of babies and a goddamn nun." He rapped lightly on a log–the door still nothing but duck-cloth–not wanting to hail her lest he wake a sleeping baby. She peeked out, motioned him to silence and slipped outside. Wordlessly, she took him toward the river.

"Mister Reid, how nice of you to drop by."

He lied. "Got to measure a homestead a mile out. Thought I'd see if you needed anything."

"The list is endless: booties, blankets, sleep sacks, diapers. A bigger cabin; I have less room here than I did in the privy."

"Whoa. Can't do much about that. I could probably manage to hang a proper door for you, though."

"Such would be most appreciated," she said. "Have you been well?"

"Well enough, after last night," he said. "A handful of the vigilence boys got together again. Showed some gumption. Don't say nothing, especially to Missy."

"Please be careful." She touched his arm with her finger.

"Missy touches folks like that."

"Mister Reid, I have a favor to ask."

"Well, right now, I'm–"

"No, no. Nothing now," she said. "As you know, Christmas is not far off. Could I impose on you to be our Santa Claus. I'll put up some makeshift trimmings inside. It will be the first Christmas for all the babies. I'd like to do it up fine."

"If you can't find someone more suitable, I guess I can," he said. "I got to go now."

"Thank you, Sir." She gave him a hug that kept him warm all the way into town.

A hug!

*

By Christmas Eve, Miss Bonteiller and Bernadette had the cabin splendidly bedecked in holiday cheer. They'd pushed the cribs together for more space. They cut a small Sitka spruce for a holiday tree. The other line gals sent so many trinkets for the babies, Bernadette cut two more trees, suspended them from the rafters and hung the gifts on tree branches. They strung the cabin with garlands and pine boughs. Miss Bonteiller even made Bernadette a red-plaid band for her wimple to match a snowsuit she'd made for Poteet Bleu. Bernadette made three new diapers from her linen veil. Heaven forbid that Mother Francine see her now: her rosary and cape gone, her sackcloth skirt turned into pantaloons, her wimple stained beyond hope, and her veil used for diapers. Bernadette would be drummed from the Sisters in a trice!

Miss Bonteiller had collected from the doves enough money for a sparse celebration. Bernadette had loaned her the use of Christopher, but could never understand how the child made time for her twice-daily trek out

161

to feed her daughter. Watching Poteet Bleu nurse–each time it was like experiencing the miracle of birth–gave Bernadette rise to new questions about her faith. How did Mary nourish the Infant Jesus? Did St. Joseph watch? How did he feel about the Virgin Birth? Clearly, some of these questions were mysteries central to Catholic faith.

On Christmas morning, Bernadette bathed the babies. They seemed to know it was the Lord's birthday. They giggled and squirmed and playfully pulled at her wimple. Once they were powdered and dressed, she tended to herself only to find a slight pink stain on her towel. A cracked corner from a crib mirror showed traces of red along her gum lines. Her teeth had pained her at night. Now, several had turned wobbly. True, she'd not had but one or two helpings of fresh vegetables since her arrival in the district, but she did maintain absolute cleanliness whenever possible. She vowed not to let such a trivial matter dull the Christmas glow a whit.

Mister Reid arrived with a cluster of elves, Julie-Julie and the girls from the cribs. They shook snow everywhere, jabbering all at once about how no one visits the cribs on Christmas and covering one corner of the cabin with more brightly-colored packages. It was such fun! On a plank table, the girls heaped comestibles: a Christmas goose, figgy pudding, cookies and candies and cakes galore. They said that Big Bo Peep knew their plan, but so long as they shared the pastries with her, she was content to give the girls free rein. And free rein they took, even with Mister Reid, decking him in a white beard and red plaid hat that matched Bernadette's wimple trim. On his gun belt hung four sleigh bells so that he jingled whenever he took a step.

During the revelry, Bernadette took him aside. "I have heard that you were an Indian fighter. It's not true, is it, that you deliberately killed women?"

"Not the very young or the old."

"Sir?"

"Those of breeding age, yes. Each could make four or five braves who'd be after my scalp."

Abruptly, she turned to the caroling. On the second turn through the carols–Bernadette, of course, had become the choir mistress–a strong hail from outside surprised the singers. Colonel Smith and Reverend Bowers stepped through the doorway. Mister Reid backed to a corner of the cabin, his thumbs hooked over his gun belt, a sourness to his face. The girls looked from the Colonel to Mister Reid to Miss Bonteiller. Even the babies knew to be mum at this time, turning so quiet Bernadette thought she heard the snow landing on the roof. Colonel Smith slapped his hands together in a piercing clap and broke into a smile. "It's Christmas! Why are you all so prune-faced?"

The collective sigh must have expanded the cabin by a foot. Bernadette extended her hand. "Colonel, a Christmas welcome to you." The Colonel gave her hand a cursory pump, but his eyes remained fixed on Frank Reid. Bernadette said, "I apologize for our cramped quarters. Truly we need an addition, but you're welcome to what space we have on this, the birthday of our Savior."

The Colonel winked so one and all could see. "If everyone's so welcome, maybe I should have brought along Two-Chew?"

Bernadette's dust-ups with Mister Calderone had been no secret. The Colonel's joke brought a flush to her cheeks, but he'd said it in good humor. All enjoyed the quip at her expense. She said, "On this day, he, too, would be welcome."

"Wonderful," the Colonel said. "He's outside."

The look that crossed her face tensed the relaxed faces. It was only when Reverend Bowers exploded with laughter that they realized they'd been jobbed. The Colonel stepped around Miss Bonteiller to Mister Reid and said, "Merry Christmas, Frank."

"Likewise."

There was neither smiling nor hostility between the men. Theirs was such a peculiar relationship. Bernadette could have read the Old Testament for as long as they held their eyes and their handshake.

In time, the Colonel said to her, "I've brought a few things." He took the pillowcase from Reverend Bowers and delivered to each girl a gift with her name written on it. He had packages for the babies and even a handsome new deer-foot hunting knife, sheath and sharpening steel for Mister Reid. Of course, there were no gifts for him.

He finished his largesse and said, "I have one gift left." From inside his vest pocket, he produced a silver puff box. He beckoned Bernadette to him. "Turn around and close your eyes." She should have protested then and there, but followed his order unflinchingly. When she felt his arms reach around her shoulders, she stood stiff, trembling inside and out. She felt something fall lightly onto her chestplate before his hands snapped closed a clasp. "Open your eyes."

He'd given her a nugget cross, every stone precisely the same size, shape and hue as the next. To match them so perfectly must have taken an eternity. The girls flocked to it, inspecting, stroking, touching the stunning cross. They agreed that there was no finer piece of jewelry in all of the Alaska District. Missy stood away, cradling Poteet Bleu.

At the door, the Colonel gave out with a hearty, "Ho! Ho! Ho! Santa has other stops to make." He followed Bowers into the brisk afternoon. Mister Reid waited ten minutes and, without so much as a good-bye, followed. When the girls left–as jolly as when they'd arrived–Miss Bonteiller and Bernadette slumped onto the cot, Missy feeding Poteet Bleu and Bernadette holding bottles for Tucker Jennings and precious Annabelle. Neither were able to draw their attention from the cross.

Bernadette slept fitfully Christmas night, repeatedly waking to the dream of some indistinct figure dancing on her Angel's grave. She pressed the nugget cross to her chest, shivering each time she recalled Colonel Smith putting it around her neck. She couldn't tell if the Colonel's touch or the nuggets caused the shivers. The man was unlike any other she'd ever encountered.

The cross, she knew, was not an alm for the church. It was a gift for her, and, if accepted, should be sent directly to Mother Francine lest Bernadette break her Vow of Poverty. However, she reasoned that, when necessary, she could use the nuggets in furtherance of the Lord's work. For now, she'd defer the decision.

*

The nun would learn, and learn this day, that he, Colonel Jeff Smith, not her God, was lord in Skaguay. All things came from him and went his way. She would hornswoggle him no more.

Before sun-up on the day after Christmas, he was saddled and out of town, alone. By the time first light had danced its way into the valley, he was at the orphanage turnoff. From outside the cabin, he heard a baby squawk. The nun cooed. A second baby cried, almost sounding like one of his own babies in Creede.

In his mind's eye, his own children had seemed to have arrived quickly, almost one after the other, like he had been part of a baby-making parade. One gave way to the next and the next. He sent money, plenty of money.

Although he had no feeling left for their mother, she had given him a family. He'd proven he was not a settling down man, but he was a settled one. Settled in what he wanted. If he'd remained in the ministry studies, he'd be a church tower today. Maybe he should have taken up the law like his father. He realized he could have caught the whiskey plague himself as far back as the early Denver days. Only his steel will had made him turn away from it and beat it back.

He drew his Bisley and rapped on a log.

"Come," the nun said.

He slipped through the duck cloth door. The nun faced him, standing, a babe in her arms. The Winchester stood beside the entryway. He said, "I'll shoot that beauty some day. I've admired it since I set eyes on it that day on the beach. A .44-40 as I recall?"

"Yes, Sir."

"In a way, I was hoping you'd win the Turkey Shoot. It would have given me hours of joy hanging it over the boys."

"Why did you not shoot?"

"I don't particularly care for guns. I can use them, and do. Seldom with any pleasure. I don't even hunt, now that I can afford to purchase meat."

"Colonel, why are you here?"

The woman didn't realize she was in a poker game. Masterson had told him to watch the eyes. Watch for confidence or fear, guile or strength. Often they were better guides than a bet. "Your cabin is twelve by twelve?"

"Of all people, you should know it is."

"I do." He removed from his vest the scrap of paper. "To double the cabin's size, you'll need sixty twelve footers plus roof stock."

"I beg your pardon?"

"The expansion you'd like."

"Colonel, are you–"

She would never make a poker player or a gun fighter. Her eyes had the sallow cast of a titless pup. He passed her the calculations, but had to cradle a baby before she accepted it.

She said, "They seem accurate. Mister Reid has promised a real door."

"Bowers planned this cabin. We can expand it," he said. "But to the reason I'm here. Missy and I would like you to join us for the church grand opening. It will be a gala affair."

"Colonel, I–"

She was waiting, unsure. Her eyes shied from him. If he could double the bet, he would. She'd accept the offer. In time.

She waved the paper square.

"As good as done." He reached out to pluck the paper from her hand. "Yes or no?"

"Will you permit me to speak to the girls about health and safety? I can teach them how to be clean, how to care for themselves if they fall to a disease. They will be so much better off."

"Have you mentioned this to Big Bo?"

"I used Miss Bonteiller as an intermediary when you were in Seattle. I was rebuffed."

"And you'll attend the church opening with us?"

The nun nodded.

He lifted the nugget cross off her chestplate and held it toward a candle. "The Lord will provide." He thought, She has learned the bamboozle and she is smart. She is very dangerous.

17. Nothing But the Truth

Missy unfastened the top three buttons of her new gown. "That's better," she said, more to herself than to the nun. She bent low to see the effect–as tempting as a fresh-baked pie. She'd brought the gown to the orphanage–still in its shipping box–along with a mirror the size of a sheet of letter-writing paper. She explained that she had to try on the dress to make any necessary tailorings and didn't want Soapy or the girls to see it before the hanging. "Bad luck, you know," then added, "I think I'll leave this mirror here."

"I have little use for one," the nun said.

"That's true on a bet. Maybe you should. Wouldn't hurt anything." Missy swirled around to give the nun the full effect of the billowy ball gown. She loved to swirl about in a new frock. She especially liked to embarrass men trying to sneak a peak at her bloomers.

The nun turned Annabelle toward Missy and said, "Annabelle approves."

"Even the –" Missy stuck a finger into her French corset.

"Of course not. You're incorrigible."

"Just trying to do my best with what God gave me." She lifted up her breasts. "He almost left me flat as a barn door up top. Stella likes my red hair. I offered to swap for her come-ons."

"Shame, child!"

"It slipped out. Happens some times." The nun's blank stare said she'd missed the joke. Not surprising. Missy said, "You going to the shindig?" She hoped the nun's answer was No. Bernadette was just too damn pretty, even without a war bag of beauty potions. All the men saw it. Goddamn her, she glowed! Lit up a whole room when she walked in, even in her ratty old rags.

"I did make a promise."

"What promise? To who?"

"The Colonel."

"He told me you was going to the church opening with us, but said nothing about the hanging." This was Soapy Smith being slippery as a fresh-caught trout. He was trying to make the nun another notch on his gun butt. Goddamn her. Goddamn *him*! What's a gal to do? Missy freed up two more buttons. "How's this?" She hiked up her now almost fully-exposed breasts.

"Child, cover up!" The nun put Annabelle in her crib and picked up Tucker Jennings. The baby wailed. "Even this boy-child doesn't appreciate such a display."

"Given time, he will." Missy whirled. "I think it makes me fetching."

"Sinful is the word."

"Did Soapy ask you to go to the hanging or not? I know for damn sure he don't want you causing a commotion. If you raise a ruckus, he'll be mightily put out. He's looking for a perfect hanging, quiet and peaceful. All legal and proper, so the reporter can write that Skaguay is as law-abiding as your convent school."

"To answer your question," the nun said, Tucker Jennings now riding her maternal hip, "he didn't ask me either way. I feel my position demands I show up and told him so. Mister Lazlo needs comforting in his final hours."

"Ain't nothing comforting about stretching a rope. Ever see a hanging?"

"No."

"I been to three." Missy unbuttoned the entire gown and stepped out of it, enjoying the nun's discomfort as seeing her in pantaloons and chemise. "Always a little upchucky in the gut, but they bring out the crowds, and the quaffing. Business is ding-dong right after. I guess the boys get to thinking it could be them dangling so they'd best be enjoying life's finest while they're still ahoof."

"I wish I could stop it. Mister Lazlo doesn't deserve to die."

"He got judged to die. He stove in a man's coconut with a goddamn horseshoe!"

The nun raised her eyebrows at the language.

"Sorry." Missy had been curbing her cusses around Bernadette. Around the cribs, too, and Soapy. The nun had convinced her it wasn't something proper ladies did. "Soapy hisself ain't going."

"That's surprising."

"Not so much. He'll be close enough to pull the rope if need be, but you won't see him. Feelings are running high about now. He don't want to be the cause of any set to. You can bet your sweet britches–sorry–he'll be around if that reporter fellow wants him."

Truth was, it was surprising to Missy, too. Sometimes she didn't understand Soapy's thinking. If Missy had her druthers, neither Soapy nor the nun, Big Bo or Bowers, would be there. She could frolic more. Fun the fellows. But Bowers would be on guard to see that it all came off without a hitch and Big Bo would be standing by to peddle poke tokens. A hanging was a bigger bust-out than the 4th of July picnic.

*

On hanging day, Missy arrived at the orphanage with Julie-Julie. "Soapy says for me to remind you that Lazlo was convicted in a court of law duly supported by a miners meeting. Under no circumstances are you to disrupt the doings. He said if you so much as raise an eyebrow, you'd regret it."

Bernadette was perplexed. It seemed that the Colonel had taken a shine to her even though he continued to withhold privileges from her. It was almost as if she were back on the farm under her father's strict tutelage. "What more could he do?"

"Maybe burn down the orphanage, with or without you and the kidlets in it." She listed a number of monstrosities that his henchmen might enjoy and seemed genuinely frightened. Bernadette, on the other hand, while recognizing Missy's fear, was strangely affected by the threat. It was much like her reaction to the hanging. She knew the injustice of it, yet would not, under any circumstance, miss bearing witness. She could no more stop herself than Christ could have stopped his crucifixion.

They left Julie-Julie with the babies and rode Christopher toward town in silence, Missy's arms wrapped around Bernadette like a child clinging to her mother. Bernadette was still dwelling on Missy's words about horrors the Colonel might perpetrate.

Missy asked, "Are you taken with either of them?"

"I beg your pardon?" She gave Christopher a nudge.

"You know, do you think about men? Think about them like us normal gals do?"

Bernadette took her meaning. She was a woman of the Lord, but certainly not one without feelings and emotions. Early in the novitiate, they'd been taught to deal with their concupiscent urgings as adults, not to allow their bodies to conquer their spiritual calling. Of course, that didn't mean they failed to have the same desires as other healthy young ladies. It only meant that they had to defeat them. At each temptation, they needed to put forward their faith. Bernadette hung her head. "Yes."

Missy slid off Christopher's back end and hooted into the air. "You do? Honest?"

169

"Miss Bonteiller, please get back on. We'll be late."

"Old Lazlo won't be any deader."

"Shame, child. How you talk!"

"You really think about boys? Down there?" She pointed below her waist.

Bernadette nodded.

"Soapy or Frank?"

"Miss Bonteiller, please." Her first thought was: Thank the Lord the Angel was not around. On second thought, Bernadette wished she were. She'd be a source of strength.

Bernadette refused to answer the tart. Not out loud. Her words brought back the sin of her past. Her skin went gooseflesh, her silence an admission of guilt.

Miss Bonteiller hopped up and down in the middle of the trail like a spooked jackrabbit. Then she brayed right into Christopher's face. Bernadette urged the mule forward and would not let Miss Bonteiller climb aboard. She didn't seem to mind. She taunted and teased Bernadette, dashing in front of the plodding mule, shouting, "Yes, you do! Yes, you do!" right up to the edge of camp.

Skaguay was cloaked in a funerary pall. Miss Bonteiller and Bernadette hunkered between Clancy's and the bathhouse, keeping a close hold on each other, their trail discussion forgotten. A single, stout lodgepole pine had been attached to the roof of the hoosegow. Directly under the pole, Bernadette's privy, now patched up, rested on the bed of a flatwagon. Atop the privy sat a piano-player's stool. Hitched to the wagon, two mules waited, unmoving, in Broadway's muck. Miss Bonteiller explained that Lazlo would be stood on the stool. On command, the mules would pull the wagon from under the stool and Mister Lazlo would be left dangling. Sheriff Taylor had been experimenting with sandbags to be sure that the fall wouldn't tear off Lazlo's head.

By the appointed hour, as many people had gathered on Broadway as had invaded the cemetery for Angel's funeral. Mister Lazlo was led from behind Clancy's by none other than Two-Chew Calderone bearing a bayonet, and followed by Sheriff Taylor. The procession was painfully slowed due to the sandbags tied to Mister Lazlo's bared ankles. Bernadette's eyes touched him, but he showed no recognition. She gripped Miss Bonteiller's skinny arm like a lifeline. Now that Bernadette was present, she wished desperately to be any place else. She thought of Mother Francine and said to Miss Bonteiller, "Have you received a reply to my letter?"

Missy shook her head from side to side.

Lazlo approached the wagon seemingly as unconcerned as if he were on a Sunday afternoon stroll. He was lifted onto the wagon and, prodded by the evil Calderone's bayonet point, used the privy to step onto the piano stool.

The Sheriff said, "Any final words, old timer?"

Lazlo cleared his throat. "Skaguay got a damned crooked judge so I'm played out. A neck-stretching is what you want and what you'll get. You all know the man I kilt went for his iron. I kilt him fair and square with one swing . . . that's all I got left and that's all I got to say."

Sheriff Taylor slipped the noose in place and jumped from the wagon.

With no warning, he backhanded a mule's flank. Neither animal budged. He swatted the other mule. It merely yawned. The townspeople shifted in their traces as if unable to scratch an itch. Taylor drew his pistol, placed it beside the near mule's ear and fired skyward. The wagon lurched forward and the piano stool flew into the air. They all heard a crack. Mister Lazlo awked. His body jerked. Spasmed. Bernadette buried her head in Miss Bonteiller's red hair and found herself biting down on a hair ribbon. Missy snatched herself away and made Bernadette watch. Lazlo continued to shake in fits–one wave, two waves, three–until he'd shaken loose one of the sandbags. The other hung down, not inches from the Broadway mud.

When Lazlo finally stilled, his hands dangled from his sleeves as if his jacket were five sizes too small. His wrists were no more than chicken bones. His eyes bulged big as honey jars. His tongue, white with froth, hung over his lower lip. He swung left, then right, and back to the left. The color drained from his cheeks as slowly as sand through an hourglass until his face was white. A wet spot spread in his coveralls. Bernadette turned shaky in the knees and leaned against Clancy's hitching post.

Even the strongest of the onlookers covered their mouths and held their breath, their eyes glued to the lifeless form as if Lazlo would somehow make a miraculous awakening.

The Sheriff called out, "Who's to claim the body?"

Somehow, Bernadette expected the Colonel to appear and respond. No one spoke.

"Come on, boys," the Sheriff said. "He must be pard to someone."

The crowd edged back, the men toeing the street's mud, muttering to themselves. They dispersed into the saloons up and down Broadway.

The Sheriff stood beside the dangling man, seemingly embarrassed and at a loss for words. "Anyone?"

Bernadette stepped from between the buildings and said, "Colonel Smith will claim the body. If you'll be kind enough to lay him down in the privy, I will see to him on the Colonel's behalf."

*

Missy, her chin cupped in her hand, a winsome smile on her face, watched the stragglers drift off. One looked her way. Without moving her hand from her chin, she tilted her head coquettishly and lifted her index finger. The straggler approached.

*

Frank Reid looked out from the Mascotte Saloon. "What the hell's she doing now–mumbling prayers?" The nun had been sitting atop the privy for an hour, the Winchester across her lap as if she were a guard. The privy still rested on the wagon, a wheel buried to the axle in mud. Every rider, ox cart and dray driver was forced to squeeze around her.

Missy said, "Waiting for Soapy. Skinner came by and pulled off his span of mules so she tried necking that craphouse. Of course, she couldn't budge it. Been there since."

"For a whole hour? Hasn't she figured it out?"

Missy said, "Ask her and she'll tell you about faith."

In unison, Frank and Missy turned from the window. Frank said, "Have a sup of whiskey?"

"Sure. Already it's been a long day."

"Customers?"

"Only one. Right after Lazlo breathed his last. You interested? You ain't been by in a long while, Frank. A gal could get the wrong notion."

"Can't. Got to finish a layout up the trail. Been putting it off."

"Another hour won't hurt. Job won't blow away." She touched her lips with her forefinger, gave him the slightest beckon. "I might, if you treat me right."

"Not today." He fancied Missy well enough. Always had. For sure he'd enjoyed being down her well. And he liked her attitude toward being a night gal. She made the whore business seem like going off to a gay sociable.

She said, "The nun don't know it, but Soapy ain't coming."

"Shit," he said. "Someone's got to move that body. Guess it's up to me."

"Double shit, Frank Reid. You go on then." She downed the whiskey and made for the door.

For the best, he thought, and tossed a haversack over his shoulder, then hoisted his tripod and transit. He could at least help the nun out to the cemetery. Death is a goddamn lonely business, regardless of which end you look from. Why the nun took Lazlo's hanging so personal was beyond him. Maybe that's what made her a nun. She sure didn't lack for balls. He blushed at his choice of words.

"Mister Reid, good day to you." Bernadette sat cross-legged atop the privy looking like a Buddha, not minding the inconvenience she was causing folks.

"And to you. You enjoying your new position up there?" He immediately regretted his tone.

"My bum leg gave out sometime back. Look at my Iron Maiden."

"Iron Maiden?"

"My habit. When my leg collapsed, I plopped into the mud."

"The habit will wash. What about your leg?"

"It's healed, but still weak," she said. "I need someone to find me a mule team so I can get Mister Lazlo to the cemetery. Anyone you know who might help? I fear the Colonel's shun continues."

"Probably so. Where's your own mule?"

"At Lank's."

Reid tied his grullo to the back of the wagon. He tossed up his haversack, a satchel of tools and then slid his tripod onto the wagonbed alongside the privy. He excused himself, only to return with Christopher and a second mule. Quickly, he hitched them to the wagon and pulled himself up to the spring bench. "Hup!" He snapped the mules' traces.

The mules turned, empty-eyed. Didn't budge.

"Git up, you mangy goats." He spit a wad of chew into his hand, hurled it at the animals. "Git!"

Christopher brayed.

Reid turned to the nun. "What do you do to get this critter moving? He's as stubborn as you."

"Ask him mannerly. Animals are like people. They like to be treated with gentleness."

"I forgot." He set to thrashing the mule's back with the loose ends of the reins. "Move, you sad sumbitch or I'll come down there and cut your goddamn ears off!" He waited for the nun's reprimand. When none came, he figured her leg troubled her more than she let on.

She said, "Mister Reid, I find he likes to be coddled. Cajole him some, then he works well."

"I'll cajole him with the points of my tripod."

"Now, now," she said, patting his arm. She clambered down and set to cooing into the mule's ear. He'd seen her do it with the babies. She caressed the mule's head. Christopher inclined an ear toward her. She whispered, "Go," and the mule took a step, tightening the traces. The second mule stepped off, not smoothly, but they were moving.

Two packers hooted. "Good going, Frank."

"You got 'em now, Frank."

"Next stop, Seattle, eh, Frank?"

*

There is a serene silence to a land covered in snow. The outlines of the trees, hills and mountains seem more muted, the white blanket smothering any sharp crag. After Mr. Reid rode off, the stillness moved Bernadette's thoughts to her Angel. She still husbanded guilt for her friends' demise much as she did her sister's. Without her, these fugitives from her soul would be alive today. Why did it seem that the women closest to her met their final fate at her hand? Bernadette didn't feel herself to be a terrible sinner, yet her many flaws were so evident. One held a peculiar curiosity: the wantonness of Skaguay was akin to the excitement she felt when she'd stood in the midway of Iowa's traveling circus. Blinking electric lights and cart rides. Games of chance. Painted women. The shills with their snappy patter, and the wayward looks they gave girls. She'd always thought that her faith was as strong as the mightiest mountain, that her spiritual convictions could defend her against any occasion of sin. Now, she doubted. Thievery, cheating, debauchery, lying were the daily fare. Yet somehow, it was all exhilarating. Her Angel had no answer.

Outside the cemetery, she managed to slide the privy from the wagon, knowing full well the sacrilege she would commit by bringing Christopher onto the cemetery grounds. She wrapped the privy line around her waist, but was unable to budge it. Whoever was responsible for digging graves in

January could take over with her blessing. For the time, Mister Lazlo and his privy would remain at the cemetery gate.

Throughout the New Year's festivities, Lazlo lay in the privy outside the cemetery, unburied. Stampeders came and went. Not one had the Christian decency to bury the old man. Each time the town ladies spelled Bernadette from the orphanage, she'd pass him on her way to town and quietly say a prayer for the repose of his soul. In time, she could no longer abide the disregard. She charged into town and stopped Miss Bonteiller in mid-street to speak of her outrage with the Colonel. Miss Bonteiller patiently told her to save her breath because he'd do nothing to help, nor would any other man in Skaguay. If she wanted Lazlo buried, she could tote a shovel out there and burn him a hole just like a miner working a winter claim. For all Soapy cared, Missy said, the nun could dig it with a teaspoon. She said those were the Colonel's exact words.

The man had rules Bernadette failed to understand. On one hand, he'd asked her to work toward the opening of the Union Church and went so far as to invite her to attend the opening with him. He'd given her money and gold. On the other, he didn't allow her the opportunity to beg alms, to do for herself, the babies or the church. He refused her the opportunity to earn. The man was a paradox.

Being the Christian she was, she vowed to fulfill her duty and bury Mister Lazlo. She went to Lank and borrowed a box of sulfur matches. He allowed her free rein of his tool shed. She selected a shovel and a pickaxe and tied them onto Christopher.

The spot adjacent to Angel was as flat as the top of a cook stove and as unused as any in the cemetery. Though the ground was hard as a grindstone, Bernadette chose it for Mister Lazlo's final resting place. After scraping surface snow from Lazlo's plot, she began hacking with the axe. Within minutes, she learned why miners could work in sub-freezing weather wearing little more than shirtsleeves. She picked and dug to remain warm. Her Iron Maiden became soaked as if she'd been caught in the devil's own downpour. After working through the top layer of muskeg, she'd gained no more than six inches before hitting frozen tundra. Mining style, she covered the plot with pine branches and set them to fire. As they burned, she gathered more deadfall and layered more wood onto the fiery heap. She repeated the process until dusk.

The Seduction of Sister Skaguay

"Mister Lazlo," she finally said, "I hope you appreciate this. It's near dark and you're no closer to being buried than you were when you were stretched out at the end of the noose. You'll have to wait until morning." Had the Salvationist mutes been around, she would have begged for their help.

The following day, she dug the ashes from the pit and scraped off the char. She'd made almost a foot, but was furious with the townspeople for leaving her the task. Her ire made her more determined. At the end of the second day's labor, she managed to clear another two feet from the hole. "Angel," she said aloud, "how would you feel about having a man next to you without the propriety of a coffin?" In that Angel's remains were not truly in the grave, Bernadette knew she wouldn't mind. The thought caused her to wonder about the state of Mister Lazlo's remains after his weeks of abandonment outside the cemetery. She pried open the privy door to see an ashen–no, alabaster–Sven Lazlo exactly as he had been last seen: his neck burned raw from the rope, his left ankle still strapped to a sandbag. His trousers hung askew over one hip. He looked to be a perfectly-sculpted statue of a man, frozen, and not the least bit unsightly except for the blanched pallor, pasty gray the color of frozen porridge.

She removed her mittens and reached to his face to make the sign of a cross. A drop of blood spattered onto the middle of his forehead. She jumped back, shocked, her bare hand to her mouth. When she removed her hand, more blood. Not blood from a wound, but from within her mouth. She'd been working so feverishly, she must have bitten her tongue or rubbed a gum bare. Indeed, her teeth had continued to fret her at night, no doubt from the lack of a suitable diet. Two wobbled freely with the slightest pressure from her tongue. She slammed down the privy lid.

Her life in the Alaska District continued to take bizarre turns. Once she was shocked to learn the box in which she'd lived had been a privy. Next, she was happy to have its protection. Now, it had become a coffin, and a decent one at that. Yet the box never changed. What else lay in store for it? For her? Why was she digging a grave when everyone around her was digging for the precious metal? Questions only the good Lord could answer.

As much as it pained her, she returned to her back-wrenching task. She swung the pick wildly. Blue and white sparks flew from the rocks. She struck and struck again. She could tell her mouth was bleeding freely but she was in a fury. She couldn't stop. Until the pick tip cracked off. She collapsed in the hole ready to abandon the chore, yet it was impossible for her not to continue. She knew what the animals would do come spring if Mister Lazlo remained unburied. Throughout the effort, she prayed that Mister Reid, Lank or some honorable men would take this cup from her hands. Missy had said that Mister Reid was in Dyea, Lank far too busy to come out. The tart refused to dirty herself, so Mister Lazlo remained outside the cemetery, awaiting his proper interment. Outside waiting to get inside the cemetery–life's voyage to heaven.

After four days, she'd dug a proper hole. It was then she yielded to temptation. *God forgive me*. She dumped Mister Lazlo from the privy, knotted Christopher's reins around the man's ankles and led the mule into the cemetery. There was no stopping now. At the grave, she urged Christopher to pull Mister Lazlo, feet first, up the berm of freshly-dug earth.

He balked. She cajoled, pulling on his bridle, silently wishing to have Miser Reid's cursing ability for comfort if nothing else. Christopher remained immobile, Mister Lazlo's feet at the top of the berm, his head at the bottom and his body as rigid as a bridge.

"Christopher, please!" She was exhausted from the four-day effort, black from gum boots to wimple. God bless miners and their daily labors.

She stepped behind Christopher. "Move, damn it to hell!" And blessed herself to atone for the curse.

Christopher eyed her as he had Mister Reid in the street. She begged. Nothing. She picked up the shovel and swatted the mutinous mule on the hind end, swinging so fiercely, she fell into the grave. The animal bolted. Bernadette heard a pop, like the report of her Winchester, only to see the mule running toward the cemetery gate, dragging his traces still encumbered of Mister Lazlo's frozen feet. He didn't stop until he reached the privy.

She scrabbled out of the hole. With her last bit of strength, she rolled the footless man into his grave. He ended up on his side, his nose pressed against a frozen wall. No one was watching nor would anyone come out to inspect her work. She retrieved Mister Lazlo' feet and tossed them into the grave, covering it with loose earth. She smoothed the surface of the mound like frosting a cake, then backed against an alder for support. *"Eternal rest grant unto him, O Lord . . . "* She had no strength left to finish the prayer.

She must have fallen into the deepest of sleeps for when she awoke, the sun was low in the west. She was chilled to the bone, almost as immobile as poor Lazlo. Collecting her tools, she noticed a bit of glitter from the top of

Mister Lazlo's mound. She plucked off her mitten and reached to the spot. It was a stone of some sorts, caked with mud. She brushed it against her filthy habit. A nugget! Yes, a nugget!

God in Heaven, pray for us! She rested against the mound and spit on the nugget. Shined it against her wimple. Dirt made no difference in her condition. Her forehead dripped, this time from excitement, not from work. The thrill of the discovery rendered her speechless. It may have been freezing cold, but the discovery of a nugget stoked a raging furnace in her.

For days, when the town ladies spelled her from the orphanage, she was drawn to the cemetery as surely as a compass needle pulls north. She loaded Christopher with two wash buckets of loose dirt from Mister Lazlo's mound. At the river well downstream from the orphanage, she deposited the dirt into a pile. After the pile became a sizeable rise, she visited Lank again, casually asking to borrow another pick, hoping for a wave toward his shed. This time, she selected two picks, a wash pan and a gold rocker. She cached them at the gravel pile.

Under the guise of making a novena for the repose of her Angel's soul, she'd turn the babies over to the town ladies and traipse to the river. If she found one nugget by accident, how many more might she find by working? She even brought along an empty tomato can to carry them home. She hiked up her Iron Maiden and washed a handful of pay dirt in the pan. Nothing. She shoveled a spadeful of dirt into the rocker and shook until her teeth rattled, watching the dirt wash free of gravel through the rocker's screens. No luck again. It was only her first try.

To mask her actions, she made certain to replace the cemetery's dirt and gravel with a like amount from the river bed. She could risk neither discovery of her find nor desecration of the site. Over two weeks, she didn't find a fleck of color. She conjectured that, perhaps, her discovery might have fallen from Mister Lazlo's trousers. Then she opined that a visitor to her Angel's gravesite had dropped it. She even considered the discovery a random act of kindness from the Lord, as if he dropped it onto Mister Lazlo's grave solely for her to find.

Such thoughts were lepers to be shunned. She forced them from her mind, truly believing that she'd discovered color and might, in time, figure out ways to locate a paystreak.

18. The Sinking of the State of Maine

Outside the orphanage, Missy and Julie-Julie wrestled a shipping box the size of a chiffonier from atop a sleigh piled high with logs. Soapy had ordered them not to open the box. It was for the nun. The way Missy saw it, he was using her as a messenger. The nerve of the pisspot!

"I'm in a snit," she told the nun. "Nothing to do with you. Well, yes, it does. No, no it really doesn't." She breast-fed Poteet, the nun, as ever, glued to the process. The goddamn woman couldn't get over a mother feeding an infant. Hell, gals had only been doing it since forever and a few weeks.

The nun said, "Annabelle and Tucker Jennings have already been fed. They'll sleep now."

"You're getting the hang of this job."

"Mothers are blessed by the Lord."

"Not to hear some of them talk."

After the feeding, Missy gripped the nun by the shoulders, looked her up and down, turned her this way and that. Without a further word, she pushed her across the cabin and took her measure like a photographer looking for the ideal angle.

Bernadette said, "What in heavens name are you doing?"

"Sizing you."

"Sizing me? Does this have to do with the froth you're in?"

"Never to mind. It's over. Go stand by the window."

"Am I posing for a portrait?"

Missy opened the box. A stunning black gown. Gold appliquéd collar, embossed braiding. A bolero cape. Missy wondered how it would look and held it up to her slight frame and swirled about. The gown flowed out in a merry-go-round of taffeta.

"You have another new gown?"

"Oh, no," Missy said. "A gal like me couldn't even dream of this elegance. If you get on my track, you'd likely never see the likes of this. This came from San Francisco."

"Then . . . ?"

Missy loved Bernadette, no doubt about it, even though the nun didn't know enough to step under a shingle during sleet. "Sister, this is *yours*."

By the look on Bernadette's face, Missy could have pushed her over with a hand fan. The nun's eyebrows lifted; she clasped her hands to her chest.

Missy said, "Don't look so surprised. This gown has a story."

"Miss Bonteiller–" Bernadette couldn't get her words out.

"The day Soapy got back from Seattle, he bust into my crib with a *Sears, Roebuck and Co. Consumers Guide*. Asked me to pick out its most beautiful gown. I was in no hurry. Shopping from a dream book is almost as good as the real McCoy. 'Sides, I thought I was getting a new frock. Knock me down with a spoon if he didn't ask what I thought *your* size might be."

"Melissa Bonteiller!"

"Hush," Missy said. "Soapy wasn't about to buy you a dress from an old dream book. 'For a proper lady.' His exact words."

"Does he have no respect for the sanctity of the Lord's cloth? What does he take me for?"

"Soapy takes anybody for anything he wants and I'd say he's taken with you. He had Bowers order it from a San Francisco dressmaker."

"The scoundrel!"

"Him? What about me, nun? I'm his fancy piece and here he is asking me to pick out a gown for you." Missy turned her back, thinking, The nun won't ever wear that gown. Not even if her pard rose up whole and wholesome from the bottom of Devil's Slide. Sometimes Soapy didn't know his ass from a dough ball. "Didn't you agree to go to the opening?"

"I never agreed to wear a gown."

"Soapy must think you did. He's like that. He assumes things will go his way. They usually do."

"Not this time."

"At least try it on. It comes with a full-veiled bon-ton and a pair of four-button silk gloves."

"Miss Bonteiller, only with a special dispensation are we allowed to wear secular clothing. In fact, I needed to secure written permission to wear my great cloak. It's out of the question."

"Hold it up. Let me see." She pressed the dress against the nun's habit. "Just pretend."

"And pretend it will be."

"Spin a reel."

"Child–"

"May I have this dance?" Before Bernadette could reply, Missy had her enwrapped and was leading her to a hummed tune.

"Stop!" The nun pushed her away, held out the gown.

Missy said, "Please try it on. Please, please, please. You're sin beautiful."

"What will come out of that mouth next?"

"Won't be nothing compared to what goes in it."

The nun was horrified. Made Missy think of a frothing dog. She'd seen the look from her teachers. When Missy had behaved badly in school, they'd send her home. Until she'd stopped going to school altogether. "You can't go to the grand opening–church or not–in that dirty rag you wear. This is the biggest shindig of the year!"

"Miss Bonteiller, this dress is harlot's garb. I will not wear it!"

Missy said, "There's something I forgot to mention. There's a carriage out front, Cinderella. Real horses, not mangy old mules. Julie-Julie is seeing to them. It's a sleigh Soapy sent to take you to the ball."

"I don't understand."

"Julie-Julie will tend the babies. Soapy's got the whole bathhouse reserved for us all alone for two hours."

"Never."

"Don't jump from that cliff just yet" Missy said. "The sleigh is filled with the first load of logs for your addition."

*

With no one to offload the logs, Bernadette and Miss Bonteiller returned to town on Christopher, the child chattering from one topic to the next. Bernadette stayed quiet, musing in thoughtful silence on right and wrong. She would never wear the dress–never wear anything except her Iron Maiden–but she wondered if she was being complicit in something illicit by accepting the logs in trade for her appearance at the church gala? On the one hand, the orphanage dearly needed expanding. Too, the bishop had sanctioned the opening of the Union Church, or so she'd been told. Would a nun attending a gala be improper? The greater goods–the orphanage expansion and support of the first church in Skaguay–ruled the day. She was stepping over no line, although once she'd thought through the conditions, she was not sure if the line had moved.

Bernadette sunk into the soaker and held her breath for as long as possible, only to burst up with a great splash. She soaped her hair into a

181

meringue of lather and slid under water again. Miss Bonteiller smuggled a bottle of champagne into her cubicle and tried to coax Bernadette into tasting it. Bernadette held fast in her resolve, perhaps doing Miss Bonteiller an injustice. The child drained the bottle in its entirety. Then excused herself saying she'd be back in an hour. Bernadette was to get herself ready. It took no time at all to don her Iron Maiden, thinking the while about the splendid gown back at the orphanage. She chased the sinful idea from her mind.

Outside, townspeople strolled toward the church, much gaiety in their tones. The gala had driven their obsessive strike-it-rich thoughts from their minds. Bernadette began to hear short bursts of applause from the church. Speeches must be the order of the evening. The handbill announcing the dedication had promised theatrical performances and music as well. There was also a promise that adjacent saloons would be open for business as the gala strictly prohibited alcoholic libations.

Next she heard an oom-pah band. Men began to hoot. She was enjoying the strains when Miss Bonteiller came by bedecked in a most daring off-the-shoulder burgundy gown, plain mukluks on her feet. "I got my Julia Marlowes in here." She held up a small valise. "I aim to dance all night. Let's go." She inclined her neck to Bernadette. "Sniff my attar. Essence of gardenia."

Reverend Dickey had overseen a miraculously-fast job of the church's construction, having started and finished within a matter of two months. It was only the second two-story building in Skaguay and, although incomplete inside, clearly more imposing than Clancy's. As yet, it held neither pews nor an altar. In its north alcove, a wooden platform served as a band stage. Chairs collected from the saloons in town were covered in white pillow cases gathered from the cribs. Tables were adorned with centerpieces of paper flowers stuck into empty whiskey bottles. How the Lord makes do!

Two-hundred men–miners and merchants alike–and perhaps fifty women, stood in a ring around a dance area. They shared pleasant party bandiage while a dozen couples enjoyed a schottische. Bernadette was taken at how few people she recognized, but then, Skaguay had blossomed to five-thousand souls since she'd arrived. She wondered if San Francisco had grown as fast during its gold rush? Now, new stores, beaneries and saloons were rising as quickly as the men could pound in tent stakes. Skaguay had as many as forty wooden buildings. Soon it would rival Dyea in size. Never in comportment, however. Dyea had Commissioner Seibert, Marshall Shoup and a phalanx of federal militia to maintain order. Skaguay needed some of that jurisprudence.

Before Miss Bonteiller had moved five paces into the church, a circle of gents formed around her. She was clearly going to be the belle of the evening. With each new admirer, the vixen curtsied and introduced Bernadette as her escort, then howled in laughter as the men hemmed and hawed their embarrassed replies. Merchant or miner, each was clearly taken by the child's charms. Had she been Joan of Arc, she'd have won every battle not with a sword but with her fetching ways.

*

Soapy's hand shielded his mouth. "It's about time the snippet showed."

Bowers said, "There's two of them. Four times the delay."

Soapy smiled courtly across the table at the Widow Rowan, a handsome lady in her own right, motherhood having bestowed on her a pink, serene glow of fulfillment. Her appearance at his table–the largest in the church–was a good sign. The camp could see she bore him no malice over the death of her husband. Nevertheless, she'd be reduced to a spot on the tablecloth when Missy and the nun reached the table.

"Charlie," Soapy said, pointing to the red, white and blue bunting that festooned the walls, "who did the décor? It's more than adequate."

"Mrs. Pullen."

"The woman's a magician. She cooks, sews and plans galas. We should give her a bonus."

"Done." Bowers made a note.

A steady stream of visitors brought Soapy accolades for the church's completion. Before the evening concluded, he figured every guest would stop by for a hat tip. Skaguay had turned into a bonanza and he was the peacock with the brightest feathers. The town was building faster than he'd expected, money coming in from the games, the parlor, the girls, plus the protection business and a dozen enterprises the boys had cooked up or brought from prior locales. He had a good life, the respect of his men, the bodies of women and the acquiescence of the town. The deputy marshal was out of the way. Only the saber rattling from the vigilantes needed to be silenced. In good time.

Missy and the nun neared, a pair of eye-snatchers in comparison to the other dowdy women in attendance. The nun hadn't worn the gown.

Soapy pasted on a wide grin and rose. "Ladies . . . at last." As if no one had ever met, he formally introduced Missy and Sister Bernadette to Reverend Dickey, the sheriff, Widow Rowan, a Seattle banker and Bowers.

Soapy said to the nun, "You look somewhat mis-dressed."

She replied, "I won't be staying. The gown remains at the orphanage."

"I only wished to see beauty regaled in beauty." He would conquer this stubborn beauty or fall on his sword trying. One day, his combination of affection, discipline, money and charm would rule. "Please sit."

Reverend Dickey held a chair for the nun, Bowers a chair for Missy.

Before sitting, the nun said, "This church is made up to look like a gathering of politicians."

"No thanks to you, like I'd hoped."

"I'm a pariah, by your own hand."

"Sister Bernadette, we are off on the wrong foot. I'm here to tell you that you may speak your piece to the girls. I will instruct Big Bo to handle the arrangements."

"Fine, Colonel."

He heard the ice in her words. The woman was not the least bit appreciative. Not so much as a Thank You. Every manjack here would trek to Seattle if he asked. She wouldn't take the first step across Broadway. Women may be God's gift to men, but men fool themselves if they think they understand the inner workings of the gentler gender.

The band struck up a new song. "It's a quadrille," Missy said. "Who's going to dance with me? And where's my champagne? No barroom hootchinoo tonight!"

Regardless of the prohibition, every man had smuggled in a jug. Under Soapy's table, a tub of iced champagne was on hand, two bottles already upside down. Soapy signaled Billy Saportas for two fresh pickling jars and filled them from a towel-wrapped bottle.

"I should leave," the nun said.

"After you accepted my invitation? After I sent out the logs and the sleigh?"

"It's improper for me."

"Woman, you're in a church!" He raised his voice slightly, then controlled it. "Please reconsider. Just wait until I speak." No sense giving her time to be an embarrassment, which she was warming to be. He rose, raised his hand. The band and dancers stopped.

"Tonight, in addition to honoring the warm, giving people who have made this building a reality"–he paused to float his arm first over the head table and then over the entire congregation–"I am announcing that I will donate to the church a bell tower, steeple, brass bell and cross, construction to begin as soon as possible. I anticipate completion to be about the time the altar arrives."

To a man, the revelers pounded their fists on their tables, stomped their boots until the piney scent of fresh sawdust was uplifted from the cracks in the puncheon floor.

*

Bernadette didn't know the depth of the Colonel's displeasure so she remained at the orphanage, out of his line of vision, ordering necessities through Miss Bonteiller, blaming her absence on the heavy snowfalls. By measured count, over five feet had fallen within three days. It came so quickly and heavily, Miss Bonteiller made the trek only once daily. Needless to say, Poteet Bleu became cranky. Bernadette, too, was irritable. She'd been accustomed to remote living on her Sheldon, Iowa farm and had learned the secluded life in the convent. This, though, was isolation as empty as a dry well.

Time and again, she rearranged the cabin's limited furnishings, often to the babies' irritation. It came to be that she almost enjoyed hearing their squalls; the winter stillness frayed the fabric of her being. Each time she moved her cot, she peeked at the boxed gown, going so far as to shake it out and hang it from a rafter to prevent wrinkling.

Missy urged the nun toward town, but, in truth, Bernadette's teeth had begun to give her serious agony, and not just at night. They continued to bleed freely at the gumline. Almost daily, it seemed, Bernadette found a new wobbler. Considering her teeth and the Colonel's continued displeasure, she chose to remain at the orphanage.

In a fit of pique during the third week of her hermitage, Bernadette snatched the gown from its hangar and rubbed its luxurious taffeta against her face . . . as soft as baby's skin. She let her fingers caress its flowery bodice. One night after the babies had gone down, she slipped off her Iron Maiden and pulled the dress over her wimple and her bulky underclothes. She sauntered to the mirror as she'd seen Miss Bonteiller do and let her mind take her off to school days when she had committed her sin. Looking back, the sin was really no more than a young girl's indiscretion. Her sister's suicide was the real sin. Bernadette continued to bear the weight of that guilt.

She wondered how she would appear in the gown with no vestige of her habit. She peeled off the dress, sinfully shed her underthings and wimple and re-donned the gown, the elbow-length gloves and hat. Her décolletage, bared in front of the mirror except for the nugget cross, glowed as white as a wedding dress. Some imp in her had been set loose. She roused sweet Annabelle and took her up. Together, they danced in front of the mirror, the two most beautiful ladies in all of the Alaska District.

For her part, Annabelle cooed and giggled, reveling in each turn and dip. Bernadette held her in front of the mirror and swooped her low, her cries of glee warming Bernadette's heart like never before. With a love she had never known, Bernadette clutched the baby to her bosom, and let her pull on the cross without scolding. Nature must have taken over; Annabelle tried to suckle.

What was Bernadette doing?

She put Annabelle down, stripped off the gown and gloves and donned her Iron Maiden. How dowdy the remains of her habit now appeared, truly the raiment of a beggar. Mother Francine would have her whipped–no rosary, a wimple that was as limp as a linen rag, a red cape–so little that resembled a true Good Shepherd Sister.

She was scolding herself for her display of vanity when Miss Bonteiller's hail came from the trail. The child was a brave one for managing the trek in the dark and snow. In spite of her friend's calling in life, Miss Bonteiller's maternal instincts proved to be a most rewarding virtue.

Inside, Miss Bonteiller shook herself like a puppy, and without a word, opened her dress to begin feeding Poteet Bleu. When she finally talked, she could scarce stop, rattling on about the big news, never saying what it was.

"More huzzahs in town than Thanksgiving or Christmas."

"This big news being . . . ?"

"Soapy is giving a speech about it tomorrow."

"About what, child? Calm yourself."

"I can't be calm. I don't have a gown for the speech."

Bernadette pointed to the box. "Take it." This would remove a proximate occasion of sin from her temptation.

"Could I?"

"Of course," she said, "but only if you tell me the news."

"The townsmen are astir something fierce. Soapy said it was a great opportunity for him to make a pronouncement. He called it an inroad."

"Eunice Culpepper Blanton! What is the news?"

"Soapy said the state of Maine has sunk right into the ocean."

19. Maine and Venereal Disease

The *Al-Ki* arrived on her final February visit with Seattle headlines blaring news about the sinking of the *U.S.S. Maine*. Two-hundred sixty-nine men had died. Feelings against the Spanish ran high. William Randolph Hearst demanded a declaration of war. Joseph Pulitzer agreed. A young assistant-secretary for the Navy, Theodore Roosevelt, shocked the country by proclaiming that if President McKinley failed to declare war, he had "no more backbone than a chocolate éclair."

Skaguay folks were equally riled, freely firing sidearms into the sky as if the Spanish were there. Soapy wouldn't let the opportunity pass. First, he drafted a letter and then set out for the orphanage. He presented Sister Bernadette with a dozen new diapers, but withheld a second parcel, one wrapped in brown paper and tied with white twine. He deliberately teased the nun with the package and his silky words, explaining how the sinking of the *Maine* was going to change the life of every U.S. citizen, even those in the Alaska District. As a country, America ultimately would have to fight– and defeat–the Spanish and thereby establish herself as sole ruler in that part of the globe. The United States could not cotton foreigners killing her men. "That is," he concluded, "unless President McKinley turns tail. I suspect he'll turn to conscription instead."

He predicted that the President would call for volunteers from the Atlantic to the Pacific, the north to the south. As such, Soapy was going to beat the man to the draw and begin plans for a volunteer company of Alaskans. Soapy had lived among fighting men from Leadville to Creede to Denver–man fighters, bear fighters and bar fighters, Indian fighters and Mexican fighters. "Why our friend Frank Reid was a notorious fighting man himself and no mean play with a gun."

"I've heard that rumor," the nun said.

"I'm going to tell the President what I'm doing, in case he'd like to use the idea."

The nun said, "You're going to *tell* the president what to do?"

"He has to hear what his people think. All leaders need that. You're a bright person. I'm here to listen to what you think." He passed her a folded piece of writing paper. "Would you review this and give me your opinion?"

Skaguay, Alaska District
March 1, 1898

The Honorable William McKinley
President of the United States
Washington, D.C.

Sir—

I take pleasure in announcing the formation of the Skaguay Military
Company to be organized for the sole purpose of responding to any
call you may make for volunteers in the event of a war with Spain.
It is my desire to convene the company at once. I wish to know if
the Skaguay Military Company may be furnished with the necessary
arms, accouterments, etc., for that purpose. The company, I hope,
will become a permanent one with cavalry, artillery and medical
units comparable to no other. It will be drilled to respond to your
every order in any time of trouble. I plan to create the toughest
company of military fighting men that this country has ever seen.
They will be at your beck and call at any time. I am,
Very respectfully,
Your obedient servant,
Jefferson Randolph Smith

The nun said, "Is war unavoidable?"

"As unavoidable as a bear shit—"

"Colonel!"

"What I mean is that he can't let those men die in vain."

"An eye for an eye?"

Soapy explained to the nun the need for the country to defend itself, but felt the effort fell on unenlightened ears. Sister Bernadette was naive where lay matters were concerned. "The letter? Is it well drawn?"

She passed it back. "I know nothing of these matters."

"Are there glaring errors?"

"Paragraphing and syntax."

"Will you correct them?"

"I will not."

"Very well." He folded the letter and tucked it into his jacket pocket. "Just know that I already have a one-time military man in mind to lead the corps, with a sergeant and a chaplain foaming to go. I don't have a doctor yet, but aim to collect one from Seattle or San Francisco as soon as I land

189

one for the camp. And, I'm garnisheeing all of Missy's hair ribbons for badges. You'll head up the nursing corps. This will be a first-rate outfit."

The nun declined, pleading ignorance in all areas of medicine save one. He wasn't surprised. He countered that her organizational abilities would overcome her lack of medical training. "A good sawbones will teach you everything you need to know. You've got no experience having babies and look what an expert you are in that arena."

"The Vow of Obedience."

"You haven't been ordered to tend these babies and you haven't been ordered *not* to head up the nurses. It will only take a few hours a week. All sorts of men are coming back from the pass with spirits as shattered as dropped china and pockets as empty as a church poor box. We'll fill them with patriotic fever and give them new life. I'll get the men drilled. You can organize the ladies any way you want. Just roll us lots of bandages."

He handed her the parcel. "You didn't wear the first dress I sent you. Maybe you'll see fit to wear this one." He put his fingers on her sackcloth skirt. "This sorry looking rag would shame a beggar."

*

Once alone with the babies, Bernadette tore open the package: a steel grey tricot wrapper with a golden military braid. The nurse uniform was a most practical and durable garment–not at all fashionable like the gown had been. After making sure the babies were asleep, she could hardly get shed of her Iron Maiden quickly enough.

*

Soapy had been railing for a quarter hour and not a soul had left his saloon, his audience rapt as if frozen and hypnotized. Perhaps he should have remained with his seminary studies. Or gone into politics. Even Frank Reid and the reporter had stayed. Soapy's father, the disbarred, drunken lawyer, would be proud.

Finish with a flurry, he told himself. " . . . so my Alaskan friends, by the week's end, I will have established a recruitment tent right on Broadway. America has been attacked. Her blood has been shed. Her sons have fallen in her defense. Who among us would refuse to ignore such a heinous crime?"

"None," came the reply from Bowers.

"Who among us would cower in the face of the Spanish devil?"

"None," came a dozen voices.

190

"And who among us would not give his all for this great land?"

"None! None! None!" The men rose as one, stomped the floor as if in a march. "None! None! None!"

Soapy raised his hands for quiet. He'd received the response he'd planned. Now to translate it into action. "Sign up with Reverend Bowers." He pointed to the crowd. "Maurice. Billy, Jack Fuller. You, too, Frank Reid. And you there, newsie, Stroller White. You appear to be as able as any. I call on you all to join the Skaguay Military Company."

The reporter waved his pencil.

Men cheered.

Reid wrinkled up his face.

Soapy thought, By God, some day, I'll erase that smirk of Reid's for good. But said, "All of you! For Alaska! For America! For God!"

Another rousing cheer shook President McKinley's likeness from the wall.

"Drinks for every patriot in the house," Soapy shouted, then winked at Frank Reid.

*

Americans were dead, Reid thought. Half of the town's brass–the sheriff, the new reporter and the old editor, among others–continued whooping it up. A war was coming. How could huzzahs come out of that? Exactly why Soapy Smith was so dangerous. He'd turn a palace into a pig pen and not bat an eyelash. He was one shrewd son-of-a-bitch. No slicing the loaf any other way. He'd use the war to tighten his chokehold on Skaguay. Goddammit!

Reid took one of the tree-stump seats outside the saloon, resting against the saloon's front wall and letting the vibrations massage his back.

"Are you not taking up the Colonel's generous offer?" The newsie. The man's face was as rumpled as his tweeds. City dude. He saluted Frank, drink in one hand, tablet in the other. "With a squeeze of lemon," he said.

"I'll never again drink with that man."

"You sound like a person with something to say." Stroller opened the tablet.

"Put it away."

"As you wish." The reporter obeyed. "Off the record? Nothing for attribution. My ears only. I'm no sourdough, as you know. Probably won't

191

stay around long. I am the Stroller, not just in name, but also in spirit. One place to the next."

"And you don't presently have two nickels to rub together."

"Precisely."

Keep moving, Reid thought. Like the stampeders. Pass through and keep going. The rest of us will stay here. Make a decent town. Maybe die trying.

Stroller said, "What grudge do you bear a free drink?"

"I got nothing against a jawbone drink. I'd buy you one any time. I do have something against being yakked about in your papers, so I got nothing to say. No offense intended."

"None taken." The newsie hoisted his glass and drank. "So my tablet is buried and my pencil stowed. Between you and me, what is it you have against the Colonel? As far as I can tell, most folks cotton to him. He's certainly a charming fellow. And very generous."

Frank waved the reporter to a tree stump. "I been here since this town started. Laid out its original plat. It was a diagram for a first-rate town. Name me an area that compares. Fish and game. Water, commerce, a good shipping lane. We got it all. Unless we turn it over to the henchmen and hucksters. I'm not saying I don't partake of a card game, even visit the night gals now and again. But I ain't about to let the hooligans run everything. Piss runs in their veins." Frank paused. "Sorry. You got me on my pet subject. Sometimes I shoot off my mouth when I should stuff it with sawdust."

"What's wrong with a little patriotism?"

Frank checked the boardwalk for eavesdroppers. "If Soapy Smith puts together a volunteer corps, he'll turn it into his own private gang. Legal as hell. Bigger and meaner and less law-abiding than the boys he's got on his pad now. If the corps gets a federal charter–you know, government uniforms or arms, money and whatever else–he'll own the town and everyone in it. He already got rid of the only honest lawman that stood in his way. Got the killer out of town without a scratch. But war is almost a sure thing. Soapy's right about that. No one will give a hoot about Skaguay, Alaska District. If we want real law and order, the merchants got to stand up for themselves. Right now. If we don't–"

A gun shot sounded. The reporter disappeared into the saloon.

Reid couldn't figure the merchants. They lived their lives in chains like slaves and did nothing for themselves except send off that petition to the War Department. Then the *Maine* gets sunk halfway around the world and Soapy has them spoiling to take on all of Spain. Goddammit!

*

Bernadette had given the hygiene lecture seventeen times. She never abided tomfoolery. She'd begin by looking as proper as possible, and go on to conduct her instruction as orderly as mass. She ironed celluloid starch into what was left of her wimple even though its fabric was now as lifeless as a blade of dead grass. Her Iron Maiden had been patched and laundered.

The first page in her copybook listed the lecture topics in alphabetical order:

. Aborticide

. Birthing Limitations

. Contraception

. Diseases and Cures

. Errors

. Falsehoods (Old Wives Tales)

. God

Like a priest in the pulpit, she could arrange her presentation in any order, the main message, of course, coming at the end. The ladies to whom she'd be speaking were no different from any other demimondes: young–seldom older than herself–poorly educated, generally coarse and unrefined.

Big Bo, none too pleased by the Colonel's decision to allow the lecture, had told her that nine of ten girls would attend. Bernadette inquired about the tenth. Big Bo said someone had to hold herself open for congress.

Nine was better than none. She'd gained the Colonel's personal guarantee for the private use of his back room and set up two rows of chairs on one side of the big felt-covered table.

The ladies arrived promptly at two. Bernadette welcomed them, saying, "Colonel Smith has asked me to speak to you today." In the back row, Big Bo held her gaze. She didn't so much as twitch at the tiny lie. "Science has shown us that three-fourths of women of your calling will succumb to some form of venereal disease. I've been trained in the medical treatment of female hygiene and safety, and am here to impart to you knowledge about your bodies which, heretofore, you may not have known."

Stella LaStarr cut in. "Guess we know 'bout as much as we need to know to get the boys to spend their money and spend theirselves." Big Bo cracked her on the noggin with a purse of trick tokens. The other ladies tittered behind their hands.

"I assure you that this is a most serious matter. I would appreciate your strict attention." Bernadette pointed to two ladies in the back row who'd brought their stitching. Both put it up. "And it wouldn't hurt you to sit up straight." The ladies adjusted their posture. This would be a good lecture.

"First, to the *Falsehoods*." She explained how proper women naturally suppressed any sign of desire for pleasures of the body. They never encourage a man. Men needed little of that. When it came to natural urges, men were only slightly tamer than orangutans. The girls hooted at her just like men might do. She clapped her hands smartly. Big Bo rapped two of the ladies with her crozier. Excessive man-woman activity, Bernadette continued, damaged the woman's internal organs. Something to be shunned. To enjoy the process, or display any enjoyment whatsoever, was anathema. "Because of your calling," she said, "people outside your world falsely believe you have uncontrollable needs." Another round of hoots.

She moved to *Errors*. "Modern science sees the female of the species as inferior to the male. God's law is a law of male dominance. Men are superior. We must recognize the truth of scientific advancements."

Stella said, "Science never took care of no boys like us gals can." This time the ladies were subdued in their response. In the front row, Missy was especially quiet.

"It is a medical truism that, contrary to popular lore, men and women breathe differently. Hence, women suffer more respiratory ailments." Bernadette said women were not naturally as mechanically inclined as men. The woman's thought process was dominated not by factual cognition, but by their reproductive organs.

Aunt Rose, perhaps the eldest of Big Bo's flock, piped up. "How about you? You ever get a boy to spray the sheets?"

Bo swatted her.

It was not the first time Bernadette had taken the question. "I live under the Vow of Chastity. By the grace and power of that vow, I am able to overcome the natural inclinations from which most of you suffer."

"You get the poorlies?" Aunt Rose shot back.

Again, a question Bernadette had faced. Her Angel had the perfect response, one that she copied to this day. "My impure time is the same as yours."

The next subject would be *Aborticide*, although she would never use the word publicly. She spoke to the criminality of the procedure, unnatural pharmaceuticals such as Ergot and Quinine, and the use of purgatives. No quack nostrums or patent medicines here. Certainly it was not her intent to foster a sinful practice. Rather, Bernadette's aim was to give the ladies the benefit of solid medical science on the subject.

No lecture would be complete without a discussion of birth limiting and *coitus interruptus*. They were also abhorrent, truly obscene, and totally against God's natural law. True, she knew that ladies of the night utilized such practices. She would not ennoble the subject by expanding on it, except to warn the ladies utilizing such practices of the Lord's wrath in this life and the hereafter.

Aunt Rose asked, "Are you a nurse?"

"No," Bernadette replied. "I am, however, trained by medical professionals to give these lectures. It is my chosen lot in life and that of the Good Shepherd Sisters."

Missy piped up. "Maybe I shoulda learned some of this before I got seeded, although I wouldn't trade my Poteet Bleu for anyone in this room." The ladies cheered her. Another lady dangled a male sheath at Bernadette. Big Bo slapped her hand.

Thus far, the ladies had been reasonably attentive and respectful, Stella LaStarr the exception. Stella had quickly turned into one of the most popular girls in the cribs, this jealously reported by Missy herself. Big Bo switched to a chair directly behind Stella to keep her cut-ups to a minimum, an act Bernadette most appreciated for they were approaching the final two items on the list: *Diseases* and *God*.

One of the tenets of the Good Shepherd Sisters' charter centered on controlling diseases of the fallen ladies. If Bernadette were able to cure a body damaged by a sinful way of life, she'd be well forward toward convincing the young woman to rejoin society as a productive member. She often held out hope for the woman to obtain a husband and bear his children.

"I say again that fully three-fourths of you will suffer disease during your . . . careers." She paused to see which ladies looked away. Clearly, they were the guilty ones. "Did you know that the word *venereal* derived from Venus, the goddess of love in Roman times?"

The girls shared a hearty laugh.

"After the War Between the States, venereal diseases in our country advanced to the epidemic stage. No amount of internal washing, use of salves or inspection of male consorts controlled the outbreak."

Suddenly, Big Bo Peep rose. "We got a policy for that. Any boy what catches a dose from one of us gets a token for another ride free on the house."

"Don't you see," Bernadette said, "that so-called gift only perpetuates the spread of the purulence? Syphilis incubates in three weeks. Gonorrhea can incubate within two days."

Julie-Julie said, "I came down with the gleet once. Mercury and Pine Knot Bitters took care of me, but I was off my back for half a year."

"Which is why I am here today. I have brought with me the latest medicines known to science: ointment of mercuric oxide for application directly onto the contaged areas. Calomel, to be taken orally." Bernadette produced a shoebox from beneath the table. "I will give these freely to Big Bo for distribution as needed. No treatment from any doctor has proven more successful at combating the dread diseases. Clearly, nothing will wipe them out except pure abstinence."

The ladies jeered out loud. Stella reached for the box. Big Bo was surprisingly quick, beating her to it. The women flocked around her as if she held a ciborium of the Holy Eucharist.

"Please," Bernadette said, "one more moment of your time."

"We got what we come for," Bo said.

"I appreciate your time. Please use these cures as needed, but remember the sure way to avoid the perils of the evils about which I've spoken is to praise Jesus' name and—"

Before Bernadette could complete the thought, the procession was out the back door.

20. And Then . . .

Life stalemated again. The Colonel continued his embargo against Bernadette's begging. The logs for the addition–perfect lodgepole pine, twelve feet long with nine-inch tapers–lay gathering snow. No one delivered rafters or puncheon for the floor. No one made a move to drive a nail.

Poor nutrition had turned the teething babies cranky and caused sores to grow inside Bernadette's mouth. Here she was, not yet thirty years old and developing the teeth of a centenarian. Her patience boiled over. She accosted the Colonel in the middle of Broadway and stood her ground as solid as a pier piling. She saw the snickers of Syd Dixon and Two-Chew Calderone and gave them the evil eye for laughing. The Colonel dismissed them. He said to her, "Do you always make it a practice to create your little scenes in the middle of a crowd?"

"I'll do what needs to be done to protect my babies."

He combed his beard with his graceful fingers. "Can we talk quietly at the Pack Train?"

When they had steaming coffee mugs in front of them, he said, "You didn't keep our bargain."

"We had no bargain."

"You nodded your assent."

His gaze bore through Bernadette like a deadly auger. She had no idea what the man expected as a result of a simple head nod. She'd merely agreed to appear at the dedication and she had. Still, she could not hold his look. He saw into her head. She said, "May we speak of the addition?"

"I need your help first."

How this vexing man had the cheek to be asking for anything was beyond her imagination! It was he who was derelict in promises made. But, for the sake of the babies, she'd hear him out.

He said, "For reasons not clear, I've become quite taken with you. I can foresee a time in the near future when your addition will be completed *and* you'll be allowed to beg freely in Skaguay."

This astounding statement stunned her to silence. The hint of a smile on his face betrayed a certain amusement on his part. Then he digressed.

"Anger becomes you, Sister. It gives you the color of a burning sunset."

"Colonel, the orphanage? The expansion. When can I expect satisfaction?"

The Seduction of Sister Skaguay

He ignored her question. "The fund for Widow Rowan has gone poorly." He explained that time precluded him from raising the money himself–time, and the fact that he was becoming the eye of the storm, not a witness to it. The many vigilance people respected his power, but would not rally to the widow if he were making the solicitation. "If you asked," he said, "they'd be more generous and you'd learn whom to work when seeking alms."

"If you recall, Colonel," she said with an intentional edge to her tone, "you have banned me from begging."

He folded his hands around his coffee mug. "That will change. If you raise five-hundred dollars for Widow Rowan, Skaguay will be open to you on a permanent basis. And you'll get the addition built."

"Anything else?"

"Only that I will make an announcement that you have volunteered your services for this worthwhile undertaking. I will publicly applaud your Christian efforts."

Bernadette was sure there was more to his request–something devious–but she could hardly argue. Certainly she could not fault raising funds for a widow. She nodded her assent.

"Say it," he said.

"Say what?"

"Say exactly what you will do and what you expect me to do in return. No more nods."

She paused, and took note of the lesson he was teaching. "I will raise five-hundred dollars for Widow Rowan, and you will allow me to beg alms in Skaguay. You will also see to it that the orphanage addition is built."

He extended his hand and they shook. He held onto her fingers as if holding a butterfly. She felt blood rushing through her veins, the same inner pulsing she felt when he clasped the necklace around her neck. She shouldn't be having these . . . inclinations. Only moments ago, she was terrified. Now, the once-impenetrable fabric of her vows was being assaulted. *Good Lord, give me strength.*

Rising, he bowed. "You should do your nails." His were smooth and gleaming.

*

Frank Reid lay on his back in the straw rubbing bag balm on a chestnut's stomach, wondering if he should pack his kit and caboodle and

198

move on up to Dyea. The Commissioner was in Dyea. The federals were there. The town was the equal of Skaguay, complete with its own pass into Canada. Plenty of areas to stake. He was fifty-six and his days were no smoother than a barbed-wire fence. Was it time to shuck the frontier lifestyle? Settle down maybe? Take on a school job again, although he'd always felt unfit for teaching. In his waning years, it might be a comfort. He should think about bringing a woman along.

He'd long been planning a log house up on the ridge that overlooked the Skaguay harbor. Now he didn't know. The town had gone hopelessly renegade. How many accidental fires had occurred since Soapy and his henchmen appeared? Eight? Nine? With the Spanish War looming and government being slow to act, a year might pass before Marshal Rowan's replacement was named. He should make a choice. Make it fast.

He rolled from under the horse and found the nun staring down at him. He said, "A moment please, Sister." He dipped two fingers into the pot of bag balm, rubbed his hands together and waxed the curls of his moustache.

She said, "Is the chestnut doing poorly?"

"She's testy."

The nun knelt to inspect the mare, prodded her stomach. The mare danced sideways. Pack straps had cut her back to belly. "Slather her in the salve. No packing for a week. She'll be fine."

"I aim just that."

"I'm looking for my mule."

"Out back. In the pen."

"Thank you," she said. "I am also raising alms for the Widow Rowan."

"Another one of Soapy's phony deals?"

"Is that your way of avoiding a contribution?"

He pulled a paper dollar from his jeans. "Make sure the widow gets this, not Soapy Smith." Sometimes, he couldn't keep a civil tongue in his mouth. "Sister," he said, "is it true you tossed in with him?"

"I beg your pardon?"

"You met him at the church wingding. He ran off the Salvationists and gave you that fine new cabin. Sent out a load of logs to make it bigger. He and his boys cheat and steal from everyone else. Are you in with him?"

"Mister Reid, I am with the Lord. None other."

Reid gripped the chestnut's jaw. With his thumb, he rolled down her lower lip. Good teeth on this one, he thought. The nun's right. Dry up the strap lesions and she'd be aces. Just like Skaguay: tend to the sore spots and she'd be golden. "Camp's fixing to blow."

"Is there nothing to ease the tension?"

"I spoke personally with Commissioner Seibert over to Dyea. Says we can handle our own murderers and card cheats like we did with Lazlo. Though he's never said as much, I believe he doesn't fancy coming down here and getting what Deputy Rowan got."

Reid took one of the chestnut's ears and scratched. "Skaguay has a core of honest, law-abiding folks. Smith and his cronies got the whip hand right now. Maybe not always. You singing his tune don't sit too swell with honest folks."

"For a man of few words, the ones you've chosen are most insulting."

"No insult intended. Just know that people are watching you. They don't like what they see." Only partly true, he thought. *He* liked what he saw. If she was just musing about going over to Smith, then she'd already crossed her religious threshold, whether she knew it or not. And if she'd already made that move, and Soapy happened to be taken from the landscape, Reid himself would be at the head of the parade. He fingered the cylinder of his .45.

*

EIGHT FOUND DEAD
ON CHILKOOT TRAIL
By Stroller White

By now, every Skaguay denizen has heard about–if not seen–the red-clad, jodhpur-sporting Mounties visiting our camp.

By now, you've heard about–if not read about–the ghastly murders at The Scales, the weigh station on the Alaskan side of the pass.

By now, you've come to some conclusions of your own.

So sit back, and read these facts, the sources of which are the Mounties themselves, Skaguay's Sheriff Taylor, and a pair of stampeders who agreed to be interviewed for this column, but jointly refused to have their names used in fear for their safety. In other words, you'll now hear it from the horses' mouths. I choose to use their own words in this column. Taken together, they need no caulking from the Stroller.

MOUNTIE #1. It was grisly, a slaughter. A shell game turned into a murderous ambush.

MOUNTIE #2. Evidence said there were seven players and a sure-thing operator. Someone got sore and the gunplay started. The dealer went down early, eh, then the seven were gunned down where they stood from unknown highwaymen. Mon Dieux!

MOUNTIE #1. The pistoleers must have been hiding in the trees.

STAMPEDER A. We were tented at The Scales, not a quarter-mile up the trail. I got to the shooting first. There was more blood than I ever seen. One old boy was shot in the neck. Dead as skunk when I found him, but still warm as a whore's britches.

STAMPEDER B. Not a drop on the dealer's tripe and keister. I packed it up and brung it back to the tent as a souvenir. Man got to have small pleasures in this #$%$# place.

MOUNTIE #1. I didn't know that. We'll want it back for evidence.

STAMPEDER B. To hell with you, Frenchy. You make us pack a ton of goods over the pass just to get into your country. I ain't giving you @#$#. This crime happened on American soil. (Aside to Stampeder A) We still fly the American flag, right?

MOUNTIE #2. A little more respect for the maple leaf or you'll get a taste of Canadian justice here and now.

STAMPEDER B. (Rising.) Try any of your foreigner tricks here and you'll get a good old-fashioned U.S. of A. pounding.

STAMPEDER A. Hold on, pard. They're working stiffs like us. Just here to help.

MOUNTIE #2. Mon Dieux, you cheechackos can't look out for yourselves unless we make you bring supplies. For your own dumb good.

SHERIFF TAYLOR. Enough! All of you. Where's the bodies?

MOUNTIE #1. Back of a wagon. At your livery.

MOUNTIE #2. Skaguay cutthroats did it, Sheriff. Canadians would have given them a square chance. These boys were gunned down, clear and cold.

STAMPEDER A. Pockets empty as a whore's heart, guns and loads gone, not an ounce of color among them.

MOUNTIE #1. We figure they were crossing back to you.

STAMPEDER A. More blood than I ever seen.

SHERIFF TAYLOR. Any idea who done it?

MOUNTIE #2. Like I said, not Canadians. Some of that Soapy gang, eh?

SHERIFF TAYLOR. Any proof of that?

MOUNTIE #2. Eight bodies ain't proof enough?

SHERIFF TAYLOR. Eight bodies is eight bodies. That's not proof, that's the score.

So there you have it, friends and neighbors. Other details and opinions to be found elsewhere in this reportage. The Stroller just brings you the facts.

*

Soapy folded the newspaper in half. He ran his thumbnail back and forth along the crease. What could have gone so wrong? Brose, who'd been with him as far back as Denver, dead. Seven stampeders gone. The Giambalvo Brothers laying low somewhere. This would bring the law to Skaguay for certain. What in hellfire could have gone so wrong?

Soapy recalled the easy Denver days peddling soap bars or sliding the cards around his tripe and keister. A few hours' work gave him a pocket full of double eagles, more than enough for a steak and an evening at the tiger box, plenty left over to bring home for Anna and the kids. She was back east and as gone from his heart as if dead. It was the nun who held his intrigue. Why did he think of his wife and the nun inside the same circle?

*

Reid hooked the heel of his boot over the Mascotte's brass rail. He downed his third rye, the drink feeding the burn already present in his stomach. This was it. Tonight.

*

Soapy tapped his chin with the rolled up copy of the newspaper. "Sheriff, tell me what happened."

Taylor said, "I wasn't there."

Sheriff Taylor's office occupied the back half of a frame building on Cat Alley. Shotguns and rifles were pinioned to the wall, held in place by a padlocked iron bar. A handful of wanted posters–moustaches drawn on each–were strewn over a flat-top desk amid shell casings, wrist cuffs and a canvas kit bag. A spittoon sat under the desk.

Soapy reached across the desk, balled Taylor's shirt in one hand, lifted the man off his feet and pulled him halfway across the desk. "Now. All of it.

Including what you didn't say to the Mounties and the reporter. And from now on, you come to me first." He swatted Taylor with the newspaper so quickly, the sheriff had no time to react. "Savvy?"

"Yes, Sir."

Soapy let him down. "If you want to stay in this office, you won't make such a mistake again."

"I do. I will. I mean, Yes, Sir."

Soapy was satisfied with the man's fear. He'd not had to use violence often. Truth was, he didn't enjoy it. Potential ramifications. But there were times when men of Taylor's ilk understood the iron heel and nothing else. It happened less and less. "Good," he said. "The issue is settled and won't ever come up again. Now–"

"Hard to fault me, Colonel. You give me straight-up orders to keep peace in town and on the trail, but short-handed me both places. I got to beg for a deputy when we have prisoners up in the cell, and that's all the time now. Scales have been bustling what with the boys building up for the spring crossing, a lot busier than we expected."

"You need more men?"

"Damn right. I only had the Giambalvo boys and Piedmont for the whole trail. They couldn't keep an eye on the gamers, flow the whiskey and clean up loose ends. Business is too flush."

Business *is* good, Soapy thought. How often did a merchant say that? Too good, and getting better, if he could keep the winds calm and the waters smooth.

Taylor said, "The town is getting unruly, Jeff. Restless. The hoosegow stays full."

"You keeping the drunks comfortable? Good eats and blankets?"

"Just like you told me. I treat 'em like they're in the Waldorf-Astoria, for Christ sake. Toss 'em in and cover them up. In the morning, I give Widow Pullen a number and she brings over feasts. They sleep dry and eat good, better than any day on the trail or in the fields. When I collect the trays, I say just like you told me, "Compliments of Jeff Smith's Parlor.""

Soft soap. Taylor was dumb as the blunt end of a hammer, but as hard, too. And greedy. The perfect sheriff for Skaguay. "I'll send to Seattle for a few more boys."

"That'd sure help."

"Now, what didn't you tell the Mounties?"

203

Taylor said, "They asked me to look the stiffs over. Wanted me to name names. Hell, I seen a couple around town, but the only name I knew was Brose. I sure wasn't spilling that."

"And don't," Soapy said. "Anything else?"

"Naw."

"I got something for you." Soapy said he'd just received a letter, soon to be framed and posted in his saloon. He'd been given permission from the War Department to drill his volunteer corps. "You're going to be one of my officers."

"Sir?"

"If there's ever a big ruckus, you'll declare marshal law and the corps will be assembled on a moment's notice. If we'd already had these boys in place, we maybe could have prevented this latest disaster. Likely not, but maybe."

"Yes, Sir."

Soapy tossed the newspaper on the sheriff's desk. "No more of these shootings. I'll get you the men."

"Yes, Sir."

"We're in for an outcry that'll raise the dead in Seattle. We'll get visitors, the kind we don't want. You keep steady and calm. I'll let you know when the new boys get here."

"Yes, Sir." Taylor pushed the kit bag across the desk.

Soapy raised an eyebrow in question.

"Scales bounty."

*

"Incomparable disaster," Soapy said, "is one road to unparalleled success." Bowers and Big Bo knew where he was headed. The sheriff and Two-Chew merely stared at the green felt of the round table. "The Scales were that disaster." He knew he should stick with Bowers and Bo, but the loyalty of the others was unquestioned, even if their judgment was no surer than a dice roll with unshaved cubes. They loved axle grease to their egos. If he could just convince Bat Masterson to run the games and the saloons, he'd be far better off. He'd try, but Masterson was unlikely to move to Alaska, no matter what the price. The man was going the way of the bottle, settling prize fights more than gun fights.

Soapy outlined what would happen in Skaguay. New marshals might arrive. Maybe some new Washington laws would be enacted. Commissioner

Seibert might even venture to camp and commence an investigation. The vigilantes would raise the dickens. Soldiers would be sent in. "If we're smart, they won't stay. I foresee most soldiers being sent to fight the Spanish. If we lay low when the law arrives, it will leave us quickly.

"Understand this, all of you. There will be one significant confrontation. We don't know when, but it's building. After our volunteer corps is in place, we will own the territory–legally–compliments of the Spanish.

Taylor said, "I ain't doubting you, Colonel, but how can you be so sure?"

Soapy brushed his fingernails on his lapels, folded his hands as if in prayer. "Oro City."

Bowers recognized the name. The others coughed into their hands or looked at the floor.

"Know your history, friends. Oro City. Site of a big gold strike. Three million ounces! By '79, the government census of Oro City showed thirty-six women and two-thousand needy men."

Big Bo sat up. "Not if I'd a been around. I'd a had a wagon full of fluff there in a week."

"Exactly," the Colonel said. "Silver followed the gold. Two-hundred forty million ounces. Plus lead, zinc and copper. Oro City became Leadville, and by 1880, with fifteen-thousand greedy people. Remember, greed, not God, makes the world go 'round. Dozens of saloons and gambling joints. Thirty-five crib houses. Entertainers like Oscar Wilde and Buffalo Bill's Traveling Show. Notables like Doc Holliday."

Two-Chew's tongue poked through his teeth. Bowers made notes. The sheriff shook his head. The Colonel said, "Skaguay is not sunk in quicksand; she is just warming up. The coming disaster will only be a slight bog, soon to be a smooth, flat road if we handle it properly. Remember, a miner still wants food, whiskey, a fat poke, a card game and a woman. He doesn't want–or need–for more. Soapy took a sip of his beer to let the idea settle. True, he didn't believe it would be as easy as he'd laid out, but he needed the boys to believe it would. They had to know that they were on the road to riches beyond their dreams.

"If you recall, last October I asked you to think about an opera house." He laid a rolled tube of blueprints on the table. "These just arrived. Not a word to a soul. I want you to think of Denver, Leadville, Tombstone,

The Seduction of Sister Skaguay

Creede, Cripple Creek, Deadwood, any miner's town. What did they have in common?"

Blank stares. "They were all small mining towns, all at one time profitable on a small scale, and all went mammoth." He unfurled the blueprints. "These show a box house for Skaguay, an opera house. The biggest building in town. Four, five times bigger than any saloon here. Three floors high. Let your minds wander. Charlie, you'll have a plush office with a private indoor privy. A casino over half the first floor with a fine mahogany bar and dining establishment with a San Francisco chef. Big Bo, you get the entire second floor with a dozen more gals; rooms will be draped in silk chantilies and crimson sateens. A toilet set in every room. Lace curtains. A stage with genuine theater seating on the top floor. We'll call it a variety theater, stage house, music hall–it will be all of them. We'll bring in singers and dancers, actors and musicians. We'll have curtained boxes for the gals to serve the high rollers during the shows. After, they'll draw the curtains for special private showings. We'll bring in real beauties from up and down the coast. The goats can work the rooms and cribs."

Big Bo was running her fingers along a blueprint stage.

"Your take will be tenfold."

"It's a joint I've always dreamed of working. If you toss in a bounce man, I'd become a real lady."

"As good as done."

"What about me?" Two-Chew asked.

"You'll start wearing proper suits like our friend Bat Masterson. Have three or four boys under you to do the sweat work."

"Shit sakes, like a sheriff."

Soapy thought, A monkey in a morning coat was still a monkey. "You all stand up now. Look down on this drawing. Find you your niche."

They peppered him with questions. "I'll answer what I can, but don't take your thoughts from first things. One: new law coming to town. Two: the vigilantes. Then it's all ours."

*

Was the Colonel a man of his word? Bernadette vacillated like a whisp of corn silk caught in a crosswind. One minute, Yes. The next, No. She hadn't yet had time to see if she'd be welcome in the saloons to beg for Widow Rowan. To this stalemate, she added the poor condition of her teeth,

206

not an uncommon ailment for a stampeder she'd learned. She felt the need to prove her mettle, to show one and all she was up to any task put to her.

She blued the Winchester and loaded her rucksack with hunting provender: cartridges, strips of jerky, an axe, a bone saw and some hanging rope. She explained to Miss Bonteiller on her arrival that she was in charge of all three babies for the day.

"Have you jumped clean of your wits? Three babies? I only have two tits."

"Hush your shameful mouth. Their food is prepared."

"Big Bo will have my hide!"

"And the Colonel?"

"Him? I can deuce him. Bo's the one what scares me."

"Explain it to her woman to woman."

"Hardly anything womanly about that cow."

Bernadette marched out, rucksack slung over one shoulder and Winchester strapped to the other. "Do your best. God will provide." The babies needed strengthening to their diet and she surely did as well. She was a competent shooter even though her one Alaska test had failed. If she missed again, she might just keep walking to Canada.

For an hour, she followed the riverbed without seeing so much as a single track. She sat herself on a rock to gnaw on a slice of jerky. Mister Reid had said it came from an early-season moose calf. She could barely chew any more, yet the jerky was savory in her mouth. It fairly oozed sweet juices. She said a silent prayer for a moose or deer–the latter preferably because it would be far easier to dress out.

She slogged on, nary a sighting all morning and into the afternoon. She despaired–the unforgivable sin! It was mid-afternoon and she'd begun her return to town when she spotted a fine Sitka black-tail grubbing forbs. Her prayer had certainly taken its own good time to reach the Lord's ears. The buck, not more than seventy-five yards away, wore his winter brown-gray coat. If she bagged him, she'd just have time to field-dress him and cache the meat before nightfall.

She unslung the Winchester and gathered her skirts. Softly, almost in supplication, she knelt on one knee and loosened her wimple. She brought the valley of the rifle's rear sight to rest on the deer's majestic rack–a twelve pointer at least–then snugged the rifle's stock to her shoulder. She brought the forward sight to rest on his shoulder. It would be a clean shot, no brush in the way. She could hardly miss.

Sensing danger, the buck lifted his head yet he didn't run. Bernadette mouthed, *My Mother, My Confidence*, and touched the trigger.

The buck's forelegs collapsed. He rose almost as quickly as he'd gone down. Bernadette chambered a second round. The deer took two shaky steps, turned and looked directly into her eyes. If he was asking for mercy, she'd gone deaf. Her second shot found his neck. Splinters of bone exploded from the impact. He toppled as slowly as a falling tree.

As she wrestled him onto his back, she realized that her wimple was gone, nowhere in sight. She said a quick prayer to St. Anthony for its return and then three *Our Fathers* in thanks for the buck. He had to weigh over 120 pounds. It would take every minute of the remaining daylight and every ounce of her strength to get him dressed. She stuffed another strip of jerky into her mouth and set to work.

By nightfall, she had him skinned and quartered. She used the last of her strength to hoist the quarters over stout pine branches. Each hung like a ghost in the moonlit Arctic night, but at least the black-tail would not become dinner for a wolf or bear. After loading the buck's nourishing liver into her rucksack, she dragged herself along the riverbank toward the cabin, the liver growing heavier with every step, her teeth aching, her game leg pulsing in pain. And, she'd never recovered her wimple.

*

Missy could tell that Big Bo was put out to beat all. "Bo, give me a half hour, please. This hag needs help for her head." Bernadette stood in front of crib row, her head swathed in a burlap onion sack. She looked as sodden as an old shoe. Imagine, a goddamn nun skinning out a stinky deer!

Bo waved her crozier. "Make it snappy."

"Can I borrow your comb?"

"Borrow anything but get her out of sight. One of these kind ain't exactly the best way of advertising your wares."

Missy led Bernadette into the crib.

The nun buried her face in her hands. "What if someone . . . knocks?"

Missy unwrapped the burlap. "I'll tell them they get a bonus two-fer today."

"Two-fer?"

"Skip it," Missy tied a bandanna around Bernadette's head, covering her face and eyes. "Now, no one can see it's you."

"Missy, please, just help me."

"What's this?" Missy wiped the nun's lower lip. Her thumb came away bloodied. She inspected the nun's gums. "We go from here to see Lank. You got the scurvy."

"As do many. I know my teeth are frightful. Don't fret them. I need a covering that resembles my wimple. Do you have linen?"

"Sure," Missy said. "I just happen to have a dozen bolts under my bed. A barrel of silk and satin, too. Lots more from New York and Paris." She lifted a lock of the nun's hair. "When'd you last wash this mop?"

"The Union Church dedication."

"I got me an idea. You wash it in the basin. I'll run home."

She returned with two baby's poke bonnets. She cut one side panel from each and pinned the bonnets together making one floppy hat. "This'd fit a hundred pound baby, but it will cover you up for the time." She'd been saving them for Poteet Bleu.

Bernadette said, "In the convent, the novices trimmed each other's hair. If we were alone, we'd sinfully pin it up like the styles in the dream books. Of course, we never had enough for a real fashion shaping. Since my profession, I've never had mine cut by the laity."

"Don't look now." Missy draped a towel over the mirror and commenced to snip off handfuls of the wet hair. Soggy strands lay in the nun's lap and on the crib floor. Her friend would never look the same.

*

After the haircut, Bernadette asked, "Why do you have red oilcloth over the foot of the bed?"

"If you got to know, the boys come in here and they ain't allowed to shed any duds, including gum boots, moccasins, hob-nails, galoshes. Oilcloth keeps the coverlet clean. We do our own laundry. Other places . . . never mind. Red is our color. And in case your big nose is wondering, No, we don't do nothing improper like kissing. We hardly know the boys who come calling."

Miss Bonteiller turned Bernadette to the mirror. With shortened hair and no wimple, Bernadette looked to be a different woman, one not quite so severe, even though her hair seemed to stick straight out like porcupine quills. The more Miss Bonteiller toweled it, the more it pasted down. It would have to do.

Missy said, "Are you sure you can't do without a bonnet? No one up here will pigeon on you. No matter what I do to the hat, it's still going to be a baby's fashion."

"Miss Bonteiller, I have taken a solemn Vow of Obedience. One of the rules of the Good Shepherd Sisters is that my head be covered at all times in public with not only a wimple but a collar for my neck. A cape and chestpiece are also mandatory."

"Most of that stuff is gone already."

"Well–yes."

"So?"

"In time, I'll confess my sin," she said. "I've done worse."

"I want to hear about you doing anything bad. It'd be like Snow White horsing some fellow in the hay loft."

"Hush!" Bernadette tied the strings under her chin and lifted her head. "I'll stitch it together permanently at the orphanage.

Missy said, "First you shag over to see Lank about them chompers. We got no tooth-puller in town, but some of yours need to get prized out pronto."

No doubt the lack of fruits, vegetables and fresh meat was to blame for her condition. She didn't need a doctor to tell her as much. Northern hygiene and diet left much to be desired. "Thank you so much," she said. Then, as an afterthought, "Would you consider contributing to Window Rowan's fund?"

"When you set your mind to it, you're sure good at working folks. Don't ever get my job. I'd be out on the street." She dropped a trick token into Bernadette's coin purse.

"God bless you, Miss Bonteiller. If I can ever–"

"Fact there is. I got me a sore down there." She pointed below her waist. "Would you doctor it?"

Without waiting for an answer, she hiked up her dress and spread her bare legs.

*

Lank was currying Christopher, much to Bernadette's surprise. In the end stall, Mister Two-Chew Calderone was examining a mare's foreleg. Lank motioned the nun back to the rope corral. He met her with Christopher in tow, and said, "Heard you got yourself a nice buck yesterday."

"A black-tail."

"Best eating around here short of moose. Where's the meat?"

"Still down the river, hung up in a pine. I just took the liver to the Pack Train in swap."

"If you like, I'll fetch it for you tonight."

"You do and you get a hind-quarter."

"Deal," he said. "The rest?"

"Another hind-quarter goes to Widow Pullen for spelling me with the babies. I'll keep the balance in the cache at the orphanage."

"I'll see to it."

"Thank you," she said. "Can you also have a look at several loose teeth I have?"

He washed his hands in the horse trough and they headed back to the tent. Mister Calderone was on his way out. He stepped aside to let them enter. Gentlemanly, Bernadette thought, and said, "Mister Calderone, would you donate to the fund we're collecting for the Widow Rowan and her child? It has Colonel Smith's approval." She had her coin purse out before she'd finished the question. In response, he reached over and patted her most improperly. She shrieked, and Calderone howled in laugher.

Bernadette said, "I'll not tolerate that again! Not only will I report you to the Colonel, I will tell Mister Reid as well. One of them will fix your clock."

Calderone laughed. "Give me an excuse to send Reid over the big divide." He stepped onto Broadway, drew his sidearm and shot once into the air, still laughing. People paused, and then resumed their comings and goings.

Lank said, "That man is out of true." He turned over a wooden bucket and lighted an oil lamp. "Sit."

He took hold of Bernadette's chin and tipped it back. With his free hand, he reached into her mouth and prodded a tooth. Back and forth, side to side. He tested eight teeth in this fashion. "All loose, but three lowers in the front and one upper molar have to go."

"No, please."

"Been too long," he said. "Look at these." He spread the corners of his mouth with one hand and tapped on his teeth with his fingernails. "Solid as a rock. Citrus extract every day." He disappeared and returned with a jar of quinine pills and a bottle of the extract. "The loose ones got to come out.

211

Scurvy will turn your blood to water, bring on lassitude and slothfulness. You'll die of starvation. I seen it happen."

"I can't lose my teeth!"

"Ma'am, you can't save them cripples. Too far gone. Should have come to me when you first hit town."

"If you recall, I did. You hid behind Mister Reid."

"I still got to yank them four."

"No!" The molar could go, but she couldn't bear to lose three teeth in the front of her mouth. What would people say?

"Any tooth-puller'll tell you the same and charge you up the . . . plenty for the work. For you, I work for free."

"How will I look?"

"'Bout the same as you do now oncet the swelling goes down. You can get good falsies made in Seattle. Practically anywhere nowadays. George Washington himself had wood teeth."

"I don't think I can go through with it."

"Suit yourself." He slipped the extract and the pills into his apron. "I'm not wasting good medicine on a bad patient."

"Lank, am I that bad? Do all four have to go?"

"Losing four teeth ain't the end of the world."

She was trapped. She agreed to let him take the teeth. He tossed fresh straw into a stall and bade her lay down, promising all the while that because the teeth were so loose, she'd barely feel pain. She certainly knew about the looseness.

"Close your eyes. I'll yank the front ones first. Them's easy. I may have to work some on the back one." He jiggled a front tooth and it slipped out as easily as he'd said. When he had pulled the third, she opened her eyes.

"Wide this time," he said. He braced her head with his knee and forced it back even further into the straw.

She gagged when he slid his thumb and forefinger into her mouth, feeling like she would empty her stomach. He just said, "Easy," as if soothing a skittish colt. His fingers closed on the molar, jimmying it back and forth. He withdrew his fingers without the tooth.

"I need a little persuader," he said. "Don't move."

He returned with a pair of farriers' pincers.

She said, "You're not using *them!*"

The pincers were inside her mouth before she could say another word. She tried to cry out. When the tooth yielded, blood erupted. Bernadette waved frantically and pointed to her mouth. Lank tore a corner from the hem of her Iron Maiden, folded it into a tight square around a pinch of moss and positioned the pad over the crater. "Bite down gentle and kept your mouth shut for an hour. Don't take it out. Moss'll stanch up the blood. For now, lie still."

He excused himself and she lay in the straw, her tongue testing her gums like a piano tuner tested a keyboard. She must have fallen asleep as it was dusk when he awakened her. He helped her up and checked her mouth. "Looks fine." He walked her to Christopher. "Ride real slow. No bumps. I'll get the meat tonight and drop it by. Pack some of the raw venison in your mouth. It you can find some onions, soak them in vinegar and eat as many as you can stand."

She mumbled her thanks and reached inside for her coin purse.

"This visit's on the jawbone, so to speak." For the first time since she'd met him, he smiled.

She shook her head and said, "You misunderstand." She snapped open the purse. "I'm collecting for the Widow Rowan"

He dropped in the bottle of citrus extract.

21. Time Running Out

Here was the nun, the left side of her face looking like it was stuffed with a wad of chew the size of a hard-cooked egg. A line of pink saliva ran down her chin. She dabbed at it as she wordlessly held open her purse to Frank Reid. "Midow Mowan?"

"What happened?"

"Loff four teef. Lank."

"At least I don't have to shoot someone." He waved a paper dollar at the other drinkers in the Mascotte and stuffed the bill in her purse. "You got to eat better."

She produced the bottle of citrus extract.

"Better with a shot of barleycorn."

"No, no," she said.

"Let's step outside."

On the boardwalk, he said, "Get home. In your condition, you should be abed."

"Mister Calderone touched me."

Reid squeezed shut his eyes. "I'll square that in short order." He pulled the tips of his handlebar out straight until he winced. "For now, I'm going to tell you something I hope pushes you back to the true side of the fence, and I'm trusting you to keep it to yourself." He could see she wanted to say something, but her mouth couldn't form the words quickly enough. "You're not going to have to worry about Calderone or Soapy or any of that bunch pretty soon. After The Scales' killings, the vigilance boys got together. Finally decided to demand help running the crooks and killers clear out of the district. As we speak, we're waiting on word from Seattle about troops. We'll get the town under marshal law before Soapy gets his corps formed."

*

Did Reid take him for a fool? Did he really think he could get his vigilance boys together on the q.t.? Get troops into camp on the sly? Soapy was agitated, insulted and put out. Here he was, the best sure-thing man west of the Mississippi with a hank of friends that included the President of Mexico, Bat Masterson, Governor Brady–and he was spilling time over some dry-gulching surveyor. The man had best take a long look at himself. It might be his last.

Soapy slapped the big green table. "Where's Bo?" He looked from Charlie Bowers to the sheriff to Two-Chew. Shrugs. "Never mind then." He leaned forward, brought the people closer together. "The federals are coming. Get the word out . . . in town, on the wharf and the trail, at The Scales. Any place we got boys. Tell everyone to shut down. Go hunting. Get away from Skaguay. Scatter. Cappers, dealers, muscle, boosters–everyone except the girls. They can work their charms on the officers. Even Charlie and I are disappearing."

Soapy'd been given a hand-written message from Seattle. It filled in needed particulars: the soldiers were headed north on the *Udine* direct from the Vancouver Barracks in Washington State. Two full companies. Their commander was Lieutenant Colonel George Russell. The vigilantes wouldn't have those details. "Sheriff, you stay in town. Maintain a presence. Keep the folks calm. Convince the soldiers that all the scofflaws have lit out with their tails afire . . . into Canada, on the southbound steamers to Seattle . . . anywhere out of the district."

22. A Conundrum

The soldiers stormed down Moore's Wharf and onto Broadway as if in full battle charge. They posted notices that all games of chance were hereby terminated. Gambling was prohibited. A curfew was imposed on all citizens. Warrants were circulated for a dozen of the Colonel's men, two given to Sheriff Taylor to serve.

Missy said it was one matter to have business interrupted, quite another to have the ladies put in chains and shipped out of Alaska. That would be un-American and, for sure, unsoldierly. She brazenly welcomed the military men into Cat Alley. Civilians were banned. A sentry was posted at each end. The girls were placed under house arrest in the cribs. They offered the officers delicacies ranging from pickled herring to fruitcakes and crullers . . . and themselves.

Late on the third evening of the occupation, Bernadette was horrified to hear her name bellowed out. It was called rudely and loudly and, had the babies not just been fed, she was sure it would have roused them all. She folded back the duck cloth door to see at least a half dozen soldiers with torches and another dozen with rifles trained on her.

A young officer said, "I've come for the one who calls herself Sister Bernadette."

"May I ask your reason?"

"Are you her?"

"And if I am?"

"I got a warrant for her arrest and orders to bring her, and her associated women of the night, to town."

"*A warrant? Associated women of the night?*" The officer–a boy not more than twenty–read a document aloud. In short, she was accused of operating an illicit enterprise with underage young women. The stern young man had been jobbed badly. The joke may have been intended to rile Bernadette, but she couldn't take the boy's severe demeanor with any amount of seriousness. Truly it was a fine trick.

She said, "Sir, you have caught us fair and square. If your men shoulder their weapons so no one gets hurt accidentally, we will surrender peacefully."

The soldiers shifted their rifles to their sides. Bernadette raised her hands and stepped out of the cabin, walking up to the officer. "I give up."

"Where's the rest?"

"Inside."

"Armed?"

"No, Sir." She maintained a bearing befitting a Christian funeral.

The officer held one of the torches in front of her and took in her Iron Maiden. The question in his eyes showed that he realized something was amiss. At the same moment, a corporal called out from the cabin. "Captain, you best come in here."

The Captain was studying her baby-bonnet wimple. "What'd you find, Corporal?"

"Babies, Sir. Three of 'em."

The Captain peeked through the door. "It seems that someone is making light of the United States Cavalry." He fairly bubbled over in his apology.

"Young man," Bernadette said, "this is the Alaska District. It's not like your world outside. You'll have much harder pills to swallow later in life."

After a week of martial law and curtailed business hours, the saloonkeepers banded together and closed their establishments completely. Customers who had routinely been made generous by the flow of whiskey were forced to remain in a sober state. Fights broke out. The merchants whined about their financial problems. They took their case to Frank Reid. Mister Reid said they should be happy to have the military in town protecting their interests and those of innocent travelers. Sheriff Taylor brought around a trio of merchants to confront the Lieutenant Colonel, and to argue that most of the lawless element for which he had warrants had abandoned Skaguay for Dawson and Seattle. The soldiers were really no longer needed.

Officer Russell remained unconvinced. He sent his men up the trail to search for those on the warrant list, a search cut short by an emergency edict from the War Department recalling him and his men. War with Spain was imminent.

Before his departure, Russell installed Mike Quinlan, once a detective in Bernadette's novitiate town of St. Paul, to keep the peace, replacing the late Marshal Rowan. Sheriff Taylor quickly sent word up the trail that the soldiers were departing. The sure-thing games, strong-arm robberies and round-the-clock swill became the order of the day once again with renewed vitality that only a total hiatus could cause.

*

The nun waved the arrest warrant in the air. "In truth, Colonel, the soldiers were quite generous. Officer Russell himself carried my poke bag to each of his fellow officers for a contribution to Widow Rowan. I do believe he was, in a way, apologizing for the rude prank someone had played on him. He only mildly mentioned the uniforms that had been stolen from Mrs. Lowe's."

The woman was a spectacle, Soapy thought. Here she was, baby hats on her head, a red-riding hood cape, her skirts tied up in leggings, holding a rope rosary attached to a mule. But it was spring, likely to be the most profitable season of his life. The soldiers were gone and the businesses–citizen and shyster alike–had resumed as never before. Boatloads of stampeders were arriving daily at a rate triple the prior spring. And here he was, accepting money from a nun. How could he fret? The wheel of life turned on a curious axle.

He took the pouch, hefted it in his hand. "The full five-hundred dollars?"

"In paper and color, if the scale at Clancy's is in order."

Soapy thought, I should have made her goal a thousand. "The soldiers may have contributed, but they had no call to try to arrest you. I'll see to it you receive a written apology."

"None needed, Colonel. In truth, I found the trick humorous."

"Nevertheless, an apology will be forthcoming." He'd heard of good gags in his life. Sending soldiers to arrest a nun was among the best. He'd frame the warrant that claimed her to be a madam.

"More important than an apology is that you exert some control on Mister Calderone. Please discipline him for improperly touching me. It was a sin not only in the eyes of God but of man as well."

Two-Chew again, Soapy thought. The man is a genuine scoundrel. He wouldn't still be upright if he wasn't so good with a shooter. "My sincere apology, Sister. You have my word. It will not happen again. I'll deal with him personally."

"Thank you."

"To thank me, please speak to Missy. She's like the beautiful bird that fans her feathers for all to see . . . including the hunter. She has an independent streak that's been flowering of late, showing signs of unrest. Have you noticed?"

"Colonel, the child has a difficult lot. She serves many masters."

"Remind her that she's well turned out, well cared for." The nun was intelligent enough to understand his subtlety.

"I see," Bernadette said. "I will talk with her, but make no promise. May we now speak of your part of the bargain: the addition."

"First, tell me," he said, "do you nuns celebrate birthdays?"

"In a quiet, private way, we do."

"Perhaps you'd take supper with Missy and me to celebrate mine?"

"The addition, Colonel, and one more thing."

Not only was the woman persistent, her list never ended! He'd clearly set the Rowan Fund amount too low. "That is?"

"A nanny for the babies."

Good Lord in Heaven! A nanny! The nun was the nanny. Missy was the mother. How much more could she ask?

"Your silence is telling, Colonel. If you provide a nanny, I'd have more time to beg alms. That would save you money in the long run. I could continue to help Widow Rowan and defray orphanage expenses. Plus, a nanny would allow Miss Bonteiller more time in town. It would be most beneficial to all concerned."

"A nanny?"

"Yes, Sir."

"The dinner?"

The nun nodded.

"Say it. Dinner?"

"Yes."

*

Annabelle came down with the croup. Within the day, she'd passed it to Tucker Jennings and the orphanage turned into a sea of hoarse, barking seals. Having no suitable medications for babies, Bernadette treated them with warm chest compresses and a concoction made from Lank's quinine pills and citrus extract. Miss Bonteiller offered to feed them from her own milk, but then feared the ailment would spread to Poteet Bleu, which it did. The poor dears hacked for three days and nights. Bernadette never left their sides.

She seldom had more than a quarter-hour nap during the entire week. The week stretched into two. She'd had all the washing and powdering and diapering she could take. Compounding matters, she was suffering from

219

more wobbly teeth. The idea of another trip to Lank and his pincers did not sit well. She foresaw herself looking like Mister Calderone.

Miss Bonteiller insisted she ride to town, if for no other reason than to see how the federals conscripted locals to extend the streets. In Bernadette's absence, Skaguay seemed to have doubled in size. Mrs. Lowe's laundry, once at the outskirts, now stood between the foundation for a two-story hotel and a new clothier's tent. Missy said the town numbered close to seven-thousand souls. The cheechackos could not take *No* for an answer when deciding whether to try for an early crossing. Some made it, but more returned gray, haggard, broke and broken. If they had not spent their stakes, they'd lost them to the sure-thing hustlers or the demon drink at the roadhouses along the trail.

Miss Bonteiller said the Colonel's men had multiplied like loaves and fishes. He was concentrating his new efforts on the trail. His boys wouldn't cross over the pass and risk a run-in with the likes of big Sam Steele and his Mounties, but they worked right up to The Scales in ever-increasing numbers. She claimed the Colonel had two-hundred souls on his pad now, and many more citizens siding with him. Frank Reid and his vigilance committee boys, bolder since the federals' brief visit, numbered over one-hundred and had given themselves a name: the 101 Committee.

Then Miss Bonteiller dropped a shocker: she wanted to quit the Colonel and become a fulltime mother to Poteet Bleu. Maybe become a seamstress or a typewriter gal.

Bernadette's first thought was, *All good things come to those who wait.* Missy's next idea was almost as smashing. She felt she could move into the orphanage and help tend the babies fulltime. Bernadette thought about her bargain with the Colonel, and the unfinished addition. "Interesting," she said, trying to envision another adult in the tiny cabin.

Miss Bonteiller rambled on about how they'd tidy up this and add that and maybe get some more babies to tend, maybe one or two who'd come with a dowry so they could afford to finish the addition themselves. Bernadette began to think about what the Colonel had said and her agreement with him. If Bernadette allowed Missy to move in, the Colonel would, for sure, feel that she'd been put up to leaving his . . . fold. The blame would fall in only one place. That would put an end to the addition, an end to any alms, and an end to any of his promised largesse. Bernadette said, "When do you think you'll make this change?"

"I thought it best to become a pest to Soapy and Big Bo for a few days. Be like a tiny no-see-um they can't quite scratch. Then they'd both be glad to be shed of me when I upped and quit."

A few days, Bernadette thought. That wouldn't do at all. "You're on the right path, but you need more than a few days lest they suspect something fishy."

"You don't think–"

"No, no, no, child," Bernadette said. "You know more than me, but I can't believe they'd hurt the babies. The Colonel merely needs enough time to get used to the notion that he's better off without you." Bernadette was arguing for exactly what the Colonel asked . . . that her young friend continue a life of debauchery. She couldn't believe the conundrum in which she was caught. How could she have allowed this happen?

Miss Bonteiller jumped up and threw her arms around Bernadette. She gave her a smooch on the cheek. "Thank you, Sister Bernadette. You're wonderful! Can I marry you?"

A vixen once and forever, she was. With her arms still around Bernadette, Missy possessed the audacity to speak of a wager between herself and Mister Reid. The issue in question was whether Bernadette would ever go to the Colonel in the conjugal sense. Imagine!

Missy said, "You told me you thought about Frank that way, even though Soapy sometimes fetched your fancy." She sashayed around Bernadette, her hips swaying as if she were dancing. "You said–"

"I won't discuss this!" The boldness of the strumpet vexed Bernadette to no end. How could she be so presumptuous? "I don't take kindly to your banter. It's most impertinent."

Missy realized she had wounded the nun to the quick and turned contrite as a true penitent. "It was supposed to be in fun. We didn't mean nothing by it. You know we both like you."

"The subject is closed. Forever."

"If you say so."

Bernadette could not stop herself from asking, "What did you wager?"

*

NO MAN IS AN ISLAND
UNTO HIMSELF
By Stroller White

The Seduction of Sister Skaguay

Although the Stroller is a relative cheechacko enroute, ultimately, to Dawson, and has never been on a first-name basis with poet John Donne, he has seen action and heard words most dangerous to his reportorial ear. (ASIDE: As always, the Stroller will protect the identities of those who have chosen to speak in confidence to him. If factual news is the subject, no one need fear publication of his or her name when asking the Stroller for anonymity.)

And this news is factual: the future for Skaguayans is fraught with madness and mayhem.

You'd have to be snow-blind to miss the existence of an organized band of men, and a few women, who fairly-well run roughshod over the traveling miner, be it fleecing them in questionable games of chance (that are chancy only for the miner, not at all chancy for the operator), brutalizing them on the trail, peddling rotgut for brand-name spirits (to which the Stroller heartily recommends a squeeze of lemon) and otherwise flimflamming them with phony maps, land deeds, telegrams and other dazzling shenanigans.

Such chastisement wouldn't be complete without acknowledging the fact that a great many of the fleeced dollars have been used for the "common good" and the "general welfare" of Skaguay: the Union Church, the Widow's Fund, of late a fire house. From the Stroller's vantage, these most worthwhile undertakings would never exist without sincere and deep support from all facets of Skaguay society.

On the other hand, there are those who would rule our camp with a so-called 101 Committee, a throwback to the days of the untamed Wild West when legal machinations were non-existent in frontier areas. Unchecked, those old western vigilantes hung suspected evil-doers, to wit: they lynched the three Reno Brothers in Seymour, Indiana in '68; Bald Knobbers shotgunned Charles Green in Christian County, Missouri, then pole-axed James Edens; they drove away innocent immigrants from San Francisco in the fifties.

Friends and neighbors, as the old saw goes, the absolute power these ruthless men exercise corrupts absolutely. Good men and true can go to great heights—and the deepest depths—when cloaked in unchecked power.

"No man is an island . . . ." Donne penned. We exist in a multi-faceted society, designed to give square treatment to one and all. A great Civil War proved such in the most horrible terms. Have we forgotten the agonies of

Antietam, Shiloh and Gettysburg? Father against son. Brother against brother. Two sides refusing to come together, each demanding absolute power.

The Stroller, never one to be particularly quick-witted nor intellectually gifted, does, however, possess the eyes of an eagle. He calls for the sides to meet across a truce table, to agree, to make concessions, to share the olive branch of pacification. Without it, the madness and mayhem will escalate into horrors unknown in the Alaska District. The Stroller tolls the bell of conciliation and compromise.

It tolls for thee.

23. The Gauntlet Thrown

The war against Spain held sway in daily conversation. President McKinley introduced the Volunteer Bill of 1898. It called for a quarter-of-a-million volunteers from the seven western states alone. Miss Bonteiller said that the Colonel had doubled his effort at enlisting volunteers.

The SKAGUAY NEWS reported that he'd been elected captain of the recruits, Company A, 1st Regiment, Alaska Guards. Although he was clearly the man to whom they kowtowed, he installed Bryce Trisha, a former military man, as his top officer and tailored one of the stolen uniforms for him. Other men of the Colonel's circle–John Foley, a three-card monte dealer, J.T. Miller, a capper at Clancy's, and Billy Saportas–were named his aides-de-camp and also issued stolen uniforms. The Colonel personally advanced the cost of arming the men and paid them a token wage each time they led one of the thrice-weekly drills.

On the fly of a wedge tent, he'd hung a sign, **United States Army Recruiting Corps**. In the rear of the tent, the recruits were told to remove their clothing to be properly sized for a uniform. The Colonel's boys searched the clothes and helped themselves to a pocket watch or a fat poke. If a rube protested, he was tossed into the street in his longies and hooted into total embarrassment by the Colonel's men–not even his trousers remaining. Sheriff Taylor turned a blind eye to the injustice.

Bernadette and Miss Bonteiller spent one afternoon a week in the recruitment tent rolling bandages and registering what women they could find for the nursing corps. Bernadette displayed the uniform dress, allowing numerous women the chance to try it on, but vowed to die a thousands deaths before publicly showing herself in it. She was *that* true to what remained of her Iron Maiden. She went on to draft three pages of duties for the nurses and reviewed them with the Colonel. He made several suggestions that she incorporated into a final version. He quite happily signed it one night while they were dining at the Pack Train.

"You've done very well, Sister."

Much to her amazement, the Colonel poured two glasses of wine. He pushed one across the oilcloth toward her. Bernadette pushed it back just as quickly. "Not to my lips."

He said, "It's what Christ made for the wedding guests at Cana. This is not the swill of the saloons."

"Nevertheless, it is not proper."

He poured half her wine onto the floor and filled the glass with water. "Perhaps a softer variety. After all, water and wine is the priestly morning fare. It does them no harm."

In truth, he was right again. The pink liquid was hardly the brassy rust of the saloon dregs. He touched his fingertip to the top of the mixture; she did likewise. Together they tasted.

*

Soapy scanned a handbill Bowers had given him and began to shake like a rumbling volcano.

"You okay, Boss?" Two-Chew asked.

Soapy waved off the question, hitching up his braces. "Two, go on back to work. I'll find you within the hour. Charlie, you stay."

Maybe Reid and his vigilantes thought Mike Quinlan's presence would change things. Well, one man with a badge wasn't going to change the likes of Jeff Smith and his boys. Nothing was going to alter the course of that river. Not soldiers, not Mike Quinlan nor Frank Reid.

Balling up the handbill, he said, "What caused this?"

Bowers referred to his note pad. "Last night, late, a handful of argonauts brought in one of their own, Hank Bean. He was headed to camp here. Shot on the trail. His pockets held plenty of folding money. His full poke was inside his shirt."

"If he was well heeled, they can't blame us."

"They shouldn't, Boss, but they do. That handbill was all over town by sunup."

WARNING

A word to the wise should be sufficient. All confidence men, bunco, and sure thing men and all other objectionable characters are notified to leave Skaguay immediately and to remain away. Failure to comply with this warning will be followed by prompt action.

Signed,

101 Committee

"Prompt action? Do they want a war?"

"Boss, there was a peck of them at a sit down."

"I'm tempted to round up the boys and force their hand before they get any more shine to their brass. This can't go on."

"Think about that."

"It's a reaction, Charlie, not my response. I know that. We'll have our showdown, just not now. Put the word out. Call a miners meeting. Make it a whole-camp meeting. Tonight. We want everyone there."

"Even the vigilantes?"

"Everyone. I'll give a law-and-order speech that will rattle the sconces off the wall. Be sure the boys are close by in case someone gets edgy with a pistol. Now is not the time to fight. We want our corps in place first. Tonight, we merely thunder the heavens."

"You've always been able to do that."

"Maybe I'll borrow your clerical collar."

"Let's hold it at the church."

"Perfect. That should insure peacefulness. No guns allowed. Tell Taylor to stand at the front door."

"No guns for our guys, too?"

"Under their coats."

Bowers made a note.

"And while I'm speechifying, get Billy and Steve to tack up our own handbill."

"That says . . . ?"

"I'll write one up. For now, you spread the word. Have Bo to get the gals ready for a bash-out night. Send word to the orphanage for Missy. Get her here pronto. The gold-bricking little strumpet will earn her keep tonight."

WARNING

The body of men styling themselves as "101Committee" are hereby notified that any overt act committed by them will promptly be met by the law-abiding citizens of Skaguay. Each member will be held responsible for any unlawful act on their part, and the Law and Order Society, consisting of 307 citizens, will see that justice is dealt out to its fullest extent as no blackmailers or vigilantes will be tolerated in Skaguay.

The Law and Order Society of 307

*

As Missy breast-fed Poteet, she said, "Whyn't you quit them sisters of yours and become a real woman? Find a man. Get your teeth fixed up and get married and have your own babies instead of tending someone else's. You're the true orphan around here. You got no one." Missy never understood how a gal would give everything up to live from hand to mouth panhandling like a skid row bum? The nun was a good woman, sure, but had her head buried like a turtle egg. She didn't need to go out and whore; that took a special calling. All she need do is find herself a man and be a regular gal.

"Young lady, I am married. To the Lord."

"Not quite what I meant," Missy said. "You ain't any better than anybody else, you know. In fact, you got less manners than a pot rag."

The nun paced the cabin, Annabelle riding her hip. "Child–"

"I ain't no child and don't give me your *God will provide*. He don't provide here. He don't even visit. You're plenty comely of face and body. You can do it. I could show you easy how to get a boy all het up."

The nun averted her eyes.

"If I was to go to work on you with some complexion powder and rouge, you'd stop shooting stars from falling out of the sky. I got toilet cream that'll take that chafe right off your cheeks. Make your skin soft as flower petals." Missy wasn't sure why she was giving Bernadette complexion tips. Soapy's eyes favored the nun; everybody's eyes favored her. Goddamn, it made no sense! Missy's daddy, who never lied, always told her that she was the prettiest gal in all the world. Even when she messed up, he'd set her on his knee and say no more than 'Don't act up again.' Then, he'd fix her hair with fresh ribbons. Of course, she'd go right out and flaunt those ribbons, bat her eyes at the boys and get herself in trouble all over again.

"Young lady," Bernadette said, "I thank you for the concern over my personal life. However, I assure you that I am quite happy in my current situation. The Lord is my Shepherd and Savior. It is Him I must please."

With Poteet Bleu still suckling, Missy dumped the contents of a war bag into her lap: polishing brushes, chamois rubs, files and manicure scissors. "You just think about what I said."

*

The child seemed to gain a certain contentment by working on Bernadette's nails. Bernadette's belief in the Lord had not diminished, but

227

the trappings of her office, once so inviolate, had disappeared. Sinful Skaguay had stripped her of her sisterly veil, cape, rosary and wimple. She'd given up the façade of wearing the stitched-together baby bonnets as a head cover and began to let her hair flow freely. Mother Francine would find her no longer fit to be one of her charges.

Since arriving in the district, she'd allowed sins of the flesh to go unchallenged. Was she no longer to be trusted? Carnal thoughts–the very ones she prayed for people to conquer–assaulted her daily. Images of the dashing, generous and intelligent Colonel made her breath come short. Visions of the robust and rugged Mister Reid made her misspeak words. Without her Angel as a guide, Bernadette wondered if she were still on the path of righteousness.

Miss Bonteiller declared that she needed a respite. She scooped up Poteet for an outdoor stroll. Soon they'd need full-size cribs for the children. They were near walking, yet still being put down in kerosene boxes like true orphans. Miss Bonteiller's suggestion upset her more and more. The child had called *her* the orphan. Was Bernadette not a complete person?

When Miss Bonteiller returned, Bernadette gave her a scalding. "We shan't discuss that subject again! Ever!"

"What subject?" She tucked Poteet Bleu into her bed clothes.

She'd already forgotten. Bernadette was fit. "What you said about me being an orphan, leaving the sisters. Never again! Never, ever again!"

Miss Bonteiller stared at Bernadette as if she were frothing at the mouth. Her face gave up all color. Only then did Bernadette realize that she'd shouted at the child.

"Suit your own self," Missy said. "If you're too hoity-toity to talk about such stuff, then so be it." She threw her parka over her shoulder and pushed through the duck cloth door without another word. Immediately, her head reappeared. "It's okey-dokey for you to harp on me about my job, but not verse-vicey. Poop on you!" She snapped the duck cloth with a pop so loud, the babies cried out together as if led by a choir master. Bernadette rubbed her newly-shined nails against her cheek. Surely, the child realized–

Miss Bonteiller reappeared again. "You were my only friend in all of Alaska. I never wanted you to leave so I'm telling you now that I never posted that letter to your boss lady. But lately you're giving me the fantods. I don't care what you do or where you go. You'll not snap at me again. We're through!"

*

In February and March, hard snows covered the high slopes of the pass. During the first two days of April, warming winds from the south caused an early snowmelt. New, heavy spring snows fell. Sourdoughs and experienced packers retreated to camp. Greeners, in their rush, ignored the warnings.

The first slide, far above The Scales, buried twenty men. A second covered three more. Two-hundred men took hold of a rope and descended, their gear and animals abandoned. Those at the front of the line entered a ravine. Those in the rear were struck by a torrent of wind. It whipped their faces and knocked them loose from the line. Trees, rocks, sheets of ice glaciered downward on top of them.

The rumbling roar from the third slide, the big one, was heard a mile down the trail at Sheep Camp. This time, a hundred men were buried. Every miner on the trail headed for the disaster. An eyewitness stumbled into Skaguay. More rescuers were needed. Soapy rounded up an army of his boys.

*

Two-Chew celebrated the fact that Soapy had left him in charge of the town by getting sodden drunk. He ran down Cat Alley in a barefooted rollick, firing off his pistol, scaring the bejeeps out of everyone. Missy grabbed Julie-Julie and bolted for the orphanage. She didn't stop to ask Big Bo, or tell her.

*

"Sister," Frank Reid said, brushing snow from his parka, "you pray now. Harder than you ever prayed. From the reports, there's men still buried over their heads, breathing through snow holes. I was over toward Dyea on a job when I heard. I'm on my way up with a new wave of rescuers. Soapy's already up there hauling out bodies."

"*Lord have mercy*," Bernadette said. "And this being Palm Sunday." She blessed herself.

*

Missy clutched Poteet Bleu. "Who's going to take care of us?"

"You'll be fine," Reid said. "Stay here."

"I won't be fine, Frank Reid." Abruptly, she passed Poteet to Bernadette. "I'm scared to stay here, scared to go up the trail, or back to town 'cause Two-Chew's on a drunken rampage. I'm scared of just about everything now. I don't know if Soapy's going to shoot me or screw me."

The nun started to speak. Missy hushed her and said, "Frank, you take me right now. You take me and Poteet and we'll all go down to Moore's Wharf and wait for the first boat south. I'm sick of begging you. I'll be good and true to you and give you a swad of babies. Won't be no scolding fish wife neither."

"Missy, I don't–"

"Don't give me no *Don'ts*. Don't say nothing. Just take us to a boat." If the man didn't understand now, he never would. In her life, she'd never begged like this.

"Missy–"

"Just say *Yes*."

He didn't. In her heart, Missy knew he wouldn't. He'd never be tied down and Soapy was after the nun. That left her outside the barn. But Soapy couldn't just up and let her go like a free bird. She held his secrets. Maybe more than Charlie Bowers. He'd have to kill her.

Reid wrapped her in his arms. He whispered, "I can't. Men are dying."

She doubled her fist and punched at him. He caught the fist. She tore it free. If she'd saved herself like the nun, she'd have a good man like Frank Reid on his knees. As it was, not Frank Reid nor any decent fellow would look at her any way but askance. She ran from the orphanage.

Reid said, "Sister, I got to get up there and help them men. Leave Julie-Julie with the babies and go after her. Take your Winchester."

*

Soapy directed his boys like a true military officer. No one else could take command of such a situation–an opportunity!–like he could. He'd done it all his life. This would be one more example of why he was running things.

At Sheep Camp, he'd set four men to erecting rescue tents. In minutes they were ready for the bodies. He sent two men up the trail to advise the rescuers of the tents' location. In a third tent, he told Widow Pullen to keep the coffee hot and keep it coming, then pressed a double eagle into her hand. "The coffee's compliments of Jeff's Parlor."

One by one, he directed that each corpse be hauled into the receiving tent and the bearers be sent to the coffee tent. Bowers listed the name and address of each of the dead. Billy Saportas went through each pocket collecting rings, pocket watches, pokes, and pads of folding money. Moon Face and Fatty Gray hauled the bodies to the death tent.

Soapy said, "Charlie, you're to write every family. Explain the severity of their kin's injury. Say that you're happy to be able to say that any report of his death was in error, but that the kin has sustained a serious injury. The family needs to send one-hundred dollars for special medicines that can only be ordered–cash-in-advance–from Seattle. Tell them to send it to the personal notice of Reverend Charles Bowers."

Bowers raised his hand, dangling a gold pocket watch. "Say no more, Boss. It will be a letter to make strong men weep."

*

Missy had gone absent. She'd not returned to the cribs nor to her house. Even though Bernadette was beside herself with anger over the child's failure to post Reverend Mother's letter, she still went searching . . . all the way into town. When she heard Missy's scream, she forgot her pique.

At Moore's Wharf, the tide was out. By the light of a kerosene torch jabbed into the silty mud flat, Two-Chew was giving Miss Bonteiller a rawhiding. Bernadette ran toward them. Calderone turned, his parka flapping, his britches at his knees, his long johns covering his indecency. He cuffed Bernadette a blow so solid that she didn't know she'd been struck until she was face down in the gravel, her lips sucking grit. She made it to her knees and called for help. Mister Calderone backhanded Missy and came at Bernadette again. With both fists, he pummeled her head. She rolled toward the water. He caught her and put his boot on her neck, forcing her face into the tide flat. She remained perfectly still until he seemed satisfied that she would no longer interrupt his debauchery. She admitted to saying a silent prayer of thanks. He could have bashed her head with a rock, but he returned to Missy, took a long pull from a jug and knelt over her.

Bernadette located her Winchester and crawled to it. When she had it pointed at Calderone, she shouted, "Stop! For the love of God, stop! Please!"

Calderone snorted. Mucus from his nostril sprayed across the yoke of his parka. He pursed his mouth, and spat at her.

She said, "You can spit all you want Mister Two-Chew Calderone, but you let that child be."

"You going to plug me, nun? You going to?" Mockingly, he put his hands over his head and walked toward her. "Go ahead. Shoot."

"I know how."

"You don't know shit."

"Let the child be!"

"She's no child, I guarantee you that much." He closed on the nun. She clearly heard the squish of his boots. The light from the oil torch made his beard glow. She was unsure of her next move; she'd never endured a moment's fear when facing an elk or a deer. Now, however, she had a man– even this vile devil of a man–in her sights. Should she shoot him down? She couldn't!

Missy writhed in the wet sand behind him, holding her stomach, whimpering. What would the man do if Bernadette failed to stop him? She said, "Come no further."

"Oh, I'll come further." Not ten paces from her, he said, "I'll come further and I'll take that fancy rifle for my own and then I'll take you before I finish with the slut. You don't understand that I'm the new deputy sheriff. Made so by Jeff Smith hisself."

"Stop . . . please." Bernadette was imploring him now. Still, she levered a cartridge. *Jesus, Mary and Joseph, have mercy on my soul.* "Miss Bonteiller is not–what you said. Not any more. Please leave us be."

"I'll do what I choose. Fact is, I'll show you something you ain't ever seen before."

"Stop!" He was five paces from her.

At three paces, he said, "You don't point a gun at nothing you ain't going to shoot."

When he reached arm's length, she knew she had to do something. Although she never heard the explosion, she fired.

24. Revenge Is Mine

At the conclusion of Bernadette's story, the Colonel pounded the Pack Train table so hard, the salt cellar toppled over. He drew every eye in the eatery. Bernadette said, "My warning shot deterred him. He backed away, cursing me."

The Colonel was in a fit and she'd barely finished the tale. He said, "I made a mistake." With a grand wave, he swept the dishes to the floor. "Billy!"

Restaurant customers made for the door, avoiding the Colonel's table.

"Stop!" he hollered. Every customer obeyed.

Billy Saportas was at his side in an instant. "Yes, Sir?"

The Colonel pinched Billy's few chin whiskers and pulled the boy's face to his. "Billy, are you ready to fire that cannon on your hip?"

"Yes, Sir."

"No matter what I ask?"

"Yes, Sir."

"Before you leave this establishment, I want it in your hand and cocked. You find Two-Chew and put the barrel of that gun in his mouth. Relieve him of his irons and march him here straight off. I don't much care if your finger slips and you blow the back of his head to Seattle, but then I'll shoot you for being clumsy." The Colonel pushed the boy away. "Savvy?"

Billy set to shaking, looking from the Colonel to Bernadette and back. Then he scanned the circle of diners who'd been locked in their traces. "Y-y-yes, Sir."

"Then get."

He couldn't get fast enough. He'd almost made it to the door when the Colonel shouted, "Billy!" The Colonel drew a bulldog from inside his vest and inspected its loads. It was as if the Lord had raised his hand. Every soul in the room took a breath. Seeing the small gun in the Colonel's hand, Bernadette was certain the boy thought he was about to be shot. She surely did. Rather, the Colonel said, "Are you forgetting something?"

"S-s-sir?"

"Your gun is holstered."

Billy freed his pistol. All the customers except the Colonel and Bernadette dropped to the floor. The Colonel laughed. "Cock it now and see to your orders."

233

The Seduction of Sister Skaguay

They were all much relieved to be rid of Billy Saportas. Bernadette expected to hear the report of gunfire, but when the Pack Train door swung open, Frank Reid strolled in. He took one glance at the Colonel and Bernadette, and stalked out. The Colonel squeezed closed his eyes. When he opened them, he said, "Where's Missy now?"

"The orphanage."

"The orphanage?"

Now Bernadette became fearful for herself. She hadn't told the Colonel the full truth. If he found out later what had transpired, he'd be tenfold mad at her and her punishment would be that much worse. "Colonel, Missy said she was never going back to the cribs." She then acted contrary to her own counsel by failing to tell him the whole story again. She didn't mention that Missy also said she'd shoot the Colonel or Big Bo Peep or Two-Chew Calderone himself and anyone else who tried to make her go back.

"Did you try to dissuade her?"

"No. I've been trying to save that child's immortal soul since I arrived last August. It's now May; I've waited long enough."

The Colonel jumped to his feet and overturned the table, diners ducking away from flying dishes. The man glowered at Bernadette, his neck cords taut to bursting. "I'm not ready to lose her, not yet. If I do, I'll hold you more to blame than Two-Chew. Your reasoning is misplaced."

She sat trying not to cringe, her hands folded into the lap of her Iron Maiden. For certain he was going to strike her. She was spared only because Billy Saportas arrived, the barrel of his revolver buried inside Mister Calderone's mouth. Reverend Bowers trailed, fear in his eyes. True to the letter of the order, the hammer of Saportas's pistol was pulled back. Bernadette was terrified, but curious. Only her good judgment had fled the room.

Mister Calderone's eyes buggered out like a frog's. He was soaked with perspiration. His holster was empty. The Colonel felt inside his boots.

Billy waved a knife, "I got the pig sticker, too."

Mister Calderone tried to speak. The words, formed around the barrel of the pistol, came out garbled. His vitriol was aimed at young Saportas.

The Colonel righted the spilled table and said to Mister Calderone, "Spread your hands on the table." He told Saportas and Reverend Bowers to pin the man's wrists. Calderone squirmed and broke one hand free. The Colonel rapped Calderone on the temple with the bulldog, his fight quickly sapped. The Colonel said, "Pay attention, Two. I want you clear-headed for this."

He smashed the stock of the bulldog onto the back of Mister Calderone's hand. Calderone screamed. The Colonel pounded again and again. Bits of flesh flecked the Colonel's face; droplets of blood sprayed Bowers and Saportas. Before the Colonel stopped, he'd mashed the hand into a pulpy stump.

Bernadette turned away. The Colonel wasted no time starting on the second hand. When the beating ceased, Mister Calderone's head hung backward, his mouth agape, his eyes closed. He was unconscious, still standing only by the grace of Bowers and Saportas. What bits of Calderone's fingers remained were vibrating like violin strings; a bloody pool remained where his hands had been. Bernadette counted three fingers on the oilcloth.

The Colonel was spattered with blood. Shards of pink skin clung to his suit. From his mouth, a line of bloody spittle ran down into his beard. He turned to Bernadette. "Do you now believe I have your best interests at heart? Can you comprehend this?"

She was unable to reply.

*

Bernadette tried to relate the incident to Miss Bonteiller. The child merely shook her head from side to side. The ferocity of Calderone's attack on her had turned her daft; her soul was deeply troubled. Overcome with lassitude, she cradled Poteet Bleu for hours without end. To ease her burden, Bernadette fetched up the gold rocker from its cache along the river. She tore out the filtering screens and replaced them with a padding of spruce boughs and diapers. It was the perfect size for a baby, and the babies were more important than gold.

At night, Miss Bonteiller curled up on a bearskin. Nothing Bernadette could do convinced her to take the cot. The child did not seem physically ill, yet was as silent as a stone. For two days, she spoke no more than a dozen words. The orphanage had no visitors nor did either of the women have the inclination to venture back into town. The cabin, a tiny outpost in a hostile land, had become their fortress, the babies their salvation.

In the early morning of the third day, Miss Bonteiller took a seat beside Bernadette on the cot for no longer than a blink before she was up hip-hopping across the cabin like her old self, Lazarus raised from the dead with no explanation given. Bernadette surely wouldn't ask. The child stoked the stove, set up a plate of hard tack and made them a cup of tea. The babies would be rising soon.

"It came to me suddenly," Missy said. "I got to clear up a white lie I told you. Just for your own good."

She started out by saying that what she was going to say should have no bearing on their friendship or on what might happen in the future. She knew more–lots more–than she ever let on. And she wasn't as dumb as she acted.

"I'm well aware of that, child. It's not brainpower you lack, but a proper road map for your young life and the mettle to follow it."

"Okay, then, promise you won't be mad when I tell you."

"Tell me what?"

"What I'm going to tell you."

She was deliberately mixing up her words. "Child . . . what?"

Missy studied each wall of the cabin as if inspecting for lice. "I told you a little lie. A bad little one. Really not so little."

"Miss Bonteiller, now that you're speaking to me again, is it too much to ask that you make your point?"

The child sat back on her tree stump and drank her tea in a series of long gulps. "Poteet's father is not a Louisiana Cajun like I told you."

Bernadette wasn't sure that she wanted to hear what might be coming next. For sure, it could not make their plight any less complicated.

"Child, you don't mean to say–"

"Yep. Soapy put the precious little acorn in my belly."

"All this time–" Bernadette started, but couldn't finish. "That means–" Bernadette's thoughts were racing Katy-bar-the-door. If the Colonel were Poteet's father, how could he allow Miss Bonteiller to continue as a soiled dove? Wouldn't he want his child to have a real mother?

Missy read her mind again. "I ain't answering a bunch of questions. All you got to know is that I understand how you can be taken in by Soapy. I was falling down in love with him–then, not no more–and wanted to marry him. He charmed me like he's doing you. With me, it only took two days. He ain't all rotten. He just has bad sides to him that pooch out way over the good ones."

"How did you end up in Skaguay?"

"I come up the first time he did, right on his arm like a proper misses. He brought Bowers and Two-Chew along, as well as Big Bo and a handful of girls from Denver. I was the fancy piece they stuck out front as a come-on for the boys. Sort of like you've been doing with the nurses. Funny how our lives ravel out."

"How could he have the mother of his daughter . . .?"

Missy said the Colonel had not known of her condition. When she was finally forced to tell him, he sent her down to Seattle with Old Man Tripp. Tripp watched over her until she delivered. The trio returned to Skaguay. When partly weaned, Poteet was supposed to have been sent to an orphanage in San Diego. Miss Bonteiller hid her with the Salvationists. The Colonel caught onto that jape right away. That was all just before Bernadette had arrived.

"I still need to know how he could force the mother of his child into servitude."

"I wasn't no one's servant. I was a tip-top red-lantern gal. None better."

"Didn't he offer to marry you?"

"Have you got applesauce in your eyes? He couldn't do that. He has a wife and a passel of young 'uns in St. Louis."

"Outrageous!"

"Not so bad. He's a decent provider and a responsible family man. Except he's got two families."

*

Missy thought, The nun's been stashed away all her life with a gaggle of women who don't know men from mushrooms. She don't realize that they can go rotten bad quicker than a sneeze. "Me and Poteet got to get shed of the district now. Soapy's testy as hell. I can't calm him. He'll kill me if I don't scoot out."

"Where would you go?"

Again, the nun missed the barn for all the boards. She hadn't learned a thing since she'd arrived in Skaguay. Missy said, "Don't care. I'll work a plan."

"It's the proper decision for you."

"I could stay in Seattle or go on to San Francisco. Maybe learn to use those new Acme sewing-up machines. Maybe meet a fellow who'd be a proper father to Poteet."

"Missy, I'm overjoyed, notwithstanding the circumstances in which we find ourselves. You sound truly committed to giving up your life of debauchery."

The duck cloth door burst open. Two-Chew Calderone stumbled into the cabin, a revolver tied with a bloody rag to one hand. The other hand was no more than a blunt stub of clotted bandages. His clothes stank of hooch. He'd lost his last two teeth. His legs wobbled like a new calf's. He turned the gun on the nun.

"I got no fingers on this hand." He waved the stub of his left hand. "It's your fault," he said.

The nun said, "Mister Calderone, we're all responsible for our own actions."

"Two-Chew, whyn't you let me look at them hands?" Missy took tiny steps toward him.

"You gone grow 'em back for me, whore? Maybe the sister can do miracles, not you. We all know what you do."

"Two," Missy said, "I ain't God. I can't grow back your fingers, but I can clean them. Fix 'em up."

He swung the barrel of his pistol and caught the nun in her jaw, knocking her to the floor. Missy knew she was next. Big Bo always preached to the gals, Don't baby a drunk. Don't spit in his eye either. Be firm, yet pliable. Missy thought, Not with this murdering loon.

She leaped at him, her nails going directly for his eyes. Two-Chew threw her off and turned to the fallen nun. Missy jumped on his back. Calderone slammed himself against a wall. Missy dropped with a gasp and rolled across the floor.

The nun grabbed for the Winchester and levered a round.

Calderone said, "You didn't shoot me before." He snorted, and took a step toward her.

Missy figured he was crazy-mad with hooch and pain. The nun had best finish it now. No more chances. Calderone was at the cabin to kill. She spoke quietly, almost reverently, to Bernadette. "Shoot."

The nun fired.

Calderone didn't fall. In astonishment, he stared down at his chest, then up to the nun's face, as if he'd just been told a long-withheld secret. The circle of red in his shirt widened. The nun levered a second round.

"Bitch." He toppled forward and fell against the Winchester's barrel. The nun fired again, lifting Calderone's feet off the floor.

*

Bernadette stood over him as his blood pumped out onto the cabin floor. What should she do now? Who does she turn to? Surely not the Colonel. If he'd wanted Mister Calderone dead, he'd have seen to it. Nor could she go to Mister Reid. Since he saw her with the Colonel at the Pack Train, he'd have nothing to do with her.

25. Opportunities Missed and Made

Missy refused to move until she was goddamn sure Two-Chew wasn't getting up. She kept herself motionless on the floor, her arms out at whimsical angles from her body, her legs splayed. Calderone's hand reached out to her as if in a bizarre theatrical farewell. His blood darkened the dirt floor.

The nun managed to roll him onto his back. A loud croak sounded from his toothless mouth followed by a hiss of escaping air issued from one of the holes in his chest. From the second, a long spout of blood landed on her Iron Maiden.

Missy sat up and fanned herself with a diaper. "Yep," she said, "it really happened this time. You scotched him good. He's on his way to his just reward. If you'd shot like that in the turkey match, you'd have won hands down." Missy wiped her forehead with the diaper. "I know what you're thinking, gal. Don't worry about a thing. I got it puzzled out. First we'll get you out of them bloody duds–"

The natural burlap coloring of Bernadette's sackcloth was already turning rusty brown.

Missy said, "Don't go all white-faced on me. You got to be sharp or we got no hope of getting out of this. Remember Lazlo? That's what happens to people who kill Soapy's boys."

Missy pressed the diaper to Bernadette's face. When she removed it, a tooth lay in the folds in a blush of pink.

"Number seven," Bernadette said.

The nun was too worried about some old tooth, now gone and never again to be screwed in. They had bigger problems, a whole lot bigger. "Soapy'll be out here in time, sooner rather than later if Two did any drunk talk before he set out. The man never could keep his lip buttoned," she said. "Nothing else, either."

Missy checked Poteet; the nun saw to Annabelle and Tucker-Jennings. The shooting had set them screeching; they calmed quickly.

"Here's my idea," Missy said. "We strip him to his longies and drag him down to the river. Bears are always somewhere around. They'll come to the smell. Let them chomp all over this rotten piece of scat." She kicked him in the shoulder.

"Feed him to the bears?"

"Or the wolves." Missy shrugged. "Whoever's hungriest." She thought, Here comes the religion again. The nun didn't realize there ain't no religion if you ain't breathing.

Missy slapped her. "True up, Sister. No time for disquietude. You got to get thinking."

The nun said, "What . . . about . . . his . . . clothes? What . . . if . . . the . . . bears . . . only take . . . parts of him? We have to hide the body."

"How about we burn him up? Just take him outside and drag him over some brush and a couple of them building logs and fire up the whole shooting match. Like fellows working winter diggings."

"Use the expansion logs for a funeral pyre?"

"I don't know funeral pyre, but if Soapy Smith finds out and you're still hoping for that addition, you got nose-bleeds in your brain."

"We can't cremate him. That's mortally sinful. But we can give him a quiet, Christian burial while at the same time hiding him forever."

*

Bernadette stuffed the spent cartridge casings into Mister Calderone's pocket and hauled his body outside. In the snow, Miss Bonteiller helped her rig a travois and hitch it to Christopher. They loaded him onto the travois and covered him with duck cloth from the Salvationists' tent. Alone, Bernadette made for the cemetery.

Working by light skies from the June solstice, she shoveled dirt away from Angel's coffin. Mister Calderone's body slid in easily. She covered him with Missy's shawl and replaced the dirt. After a silent prayer asking Angel's forgiveness, and a longer one praying that the Colonel did not discover the plan, she lit out for home.

Missy said, "You're a mess. Blood, dirt. Yuck!"

She made Bernadette don the nurse's uniform and took her habit down to the river for a good washing. Returning with red, icy hands, she said, "I was half tempted just to let this old rag float away. You ought to be ashamed. It can't last through two more washings. The nurse uniform is not fit for so much as a plain Jane, but it's a damn sight better than your potato sack."

Her chipper way with words never ceased to make Bernadette smile; the child could make a rock laugh. Bernadette hoped, some day, to thank her. For now, she merely hung the Iron Maiden over the cook stove. The child was right about one thing: it was so worn, the fabric was beginning to dissolve. The threadbare sackcloth was her last vestige of the Good Shepherd Sisters.

*

Missy snuck into camp and back, bringing a carpetbag of clothes and food. She didn't want to frighten the nun, but she had to lay out the story shoulder-straight. It wasn't pretty. "We're in one stinking kettle of skunk cabbage. Soapy's posted a reward for anyone finding Two-Chew. If he's alive, the reward is a hundred dollars in dust. If he's dead, it's two-fifty. That's Soapy's brand of humor. For that type of dough, I might turn you in myself."

"Does anyone suspect me?"

"I do," Missy said. If the nun got the blues, she might do something dumb like make a public confession, thinking her God would provide. About all he'd provide is a noose. Missy had to keep the nun at the cabin and away from people. That meant keeping her happy. If that meant Missy needed to keep sneaking around–she knew she was also on Soapy's list–so be it. She'd always done what needed doing, always managed to come out on top. She lifted Poteet from her crib and adjusted the child to her breast. "Are you listening to me or am I yapping in the wind."

"I'm listening," the nun said. "You were wondering whether to turn me in for the reward."

Annabelle kicked up a fuss. Bernadette sat on the cot and held her tightly.

Missy said, "All sorts of new blood in town. The *Willamette*, the *Portland*, the *Al-Ki* and the *City of Kingston* all landed inside the last twenty-four hours. Dumped off over a thousand fresh sets of britches with nothing but color and cunnie on their minds. Julie-Julie said Big Bo put a price on my head, just to get me back to work. The gals all have sore–"

"Child!"

"Sorry," she said. "With all the new bulls in town pressing their affectation on any skirt, no one gets time off. Going back to work might be the only thing that would keep Soapy from dropping me off a cliff."

"Where do all the new men stay?"

"Any place they can peg a fly tent. Look at you; you lived in a privy. Wouldn't put it past a band to come exploring out here and steal our cabin."

"I'm not sure I could shoot again."

242

"What's worse for town is that the tideland is now jammed with new horses, ox, pigs, goats. Julie-Julie said it stank like toilet pits, depending on the tide. The only time a body could catch a breath was at the ebb."

"Maybe we're lucky to be here."

"That's the spirit. Look on the bright side."

Missy's bright side was to stay one jump ahead of Soapy. If his reward didn't turn up Two-Chew in short order, he'd up the price until the whole town would go on the search. Someone would be out to the cabin. No telling what a sharpie could find. Missy figured she best put her important question to the nun now. "Sister, I know you got a shitpot full–sorry–I know you got lots on your mind right now, but I got to ask a favor."

The nun shifted Annabelle from one shoulder to the other. "That is?"

"Soapy don't like it when one of his own goes off the reservation like Two-Chew done. The other cheek says he don't cotton to one of his jumping ship like I done. And the third cheek says he really don't like someone killing a pard of his."

"Yours was the right choice. The Lord forgives all transgressions."

"Soapy's the Lord in Skaguay, but he don't forgive so much as a sideways sneeze. Don't forget neither. Your God got no space on his spread for the likeness of Jeff Smith."

"Don't be blasphemous, child. The Lord's mercy is nonpareil."

"Don't make a nevermind to Soapy. Old Man Lazlo is the proof in the pudding. In Soapy's head, I'm a deserter. He's in town this day signing up new stiffs for his militia and holding training drills for the ones he already got registered. He's the general to them all. I'm a traitor who hightailed under fire. He'd as soon as shoot me as look at me. I have to scheme like a courthouse lawyer to wile my way out of this or . . . . " She made a slashing motion across her throat.

"What would you have me do?"

"Just a promise," she said. "If something happens to me, you got to see to Poteet Bleu."

"What more can I do than what I'm doing?"

"Nothing now. Just promise me you'll see to her till she's grown. I guess that's a pretty big favor." Missy'd managed to take the nun's gloom and swallow it whole and wholesome for herself. She was downward bound for sure. "Tough to tell what will happen out here now. I brought enough chow for a week. Put it by and make it last."

"Aren't *you* safe here, too?"

"'Bout as safe as a cow in the slaughter chute," she said. "Promise me about my daughter?"

"I do, child. I promise you that."

"Something else I forgot to tell you about. With so much new meat–excuse me–so many new miners in town, Soapy ordered everyone–saloonkeepers, merchants, newspapers, even Lank–to double their prices, doubling his knock down. The way he reasons, these new guys got nowhere else to go, lest they want to hoof it over to Dyea with all their gear. With spring here, the stampeders are itchy as hell to provision up and get over the pass. No detours."

"I fear I know little of mining commerce."

"No need. I do," Missy said. "Know something else? He started drinking the whiskey again. A bad sign."

*

Bernadette and Missy schemed until sun-up, finishing with a simple plan that, they agreed, should be put into play in fast time. Bernadette would cajole Frank Reid into stashing Missy, Poteet and the nurse's uniform at his cabin in camp. Once a southbound steamer sounded its three departure blasts, Missy'd pull on the uniform, lose herself in the pandemonium that attended each outset and slip aboard with Poteet Bleu.

Bernadette snuck back into town and convinced Frank Reid to join the plot. Never before had she seen so many campfires, tents and shanties. Truly, the beach above the tideline was a city unto itself. Livestock stood everywhere. Now and again, a hoot from within a tent would pierce the night, or a wrestling match would break out. Saloons were set up on nothing more than slat doors. A dozen of the Colonel's hawkers were doing a rushing business with their whiskey and sure-thing come-ons. As ever, the bleary-eyed cheechackos would hardly understand that they'd been snookered until they awoke the next morning short of their stake.

*

Tall, lean well-driller, Sam Wheat, and two of Skaguay's dry goods merchants faced Frank Reid. They didn't like Soapy's mandate. Doubling their prices would curtail their business, they felt. They'd have to cut back on their loyal clerks. It would be a hardship.

With the three men behind him, Reid caught up with Soapy on the boardwalk outside the Pack Train. Charlie Bowers and Billy Saportas stood at Soapy's side. Frank could tell they'd been drinking. Soapy's face was uncharacteristically flushed; his four-in-hand was askew. His boots didn't carry their normal gloss and his outing shirt was misbuttoned. His normally sharp gaze was foggy, detached.

Frank spelled out the beef.

Soapy said, "You're speaking for the boys behind you?"

"I am." Frank opened his duster. Folks would die fast at this close range.

From the corner of his eye, Frank saw the town stop like a daguerreotype. No one passed them on the boardwalk. Even the milling newcomers seemed to know something big was happening. They held their spots as if tied to them. Soapy loosened his own coat, the Bisley in its holster. Bowers and Saportas followed suit. The merchants exchanged fearful glances.

Soapy said, "Don't bait me, Frank."

"No baiting here. I'm speaking my piece."

"Townsmen have a chance to make a lot of money now. Right now. Steamers are off-loading stampeders by the score. Why *shouldn't* we make it?"

"Because you're cheating honest men."

"I don't take your point," Soapy said. "The price a seller sells at is the price a buyer will buy at."

"They'll turn to Dyea, sure as hell," Frank said. "'Sides, that argument don't hold piss for your sure-thing cheats."

"Stampeders can't find in Dyea what we offer here."

Soapy wasn't stumbling drunk, but he wouldn't be quick. Billy Saportas would be lightning. The merchants would be ponderous to act. Now might be the time. Saportas would shoot first. Since Calderone had gone missing, Saportas had been Soapy's guardian. Him first. Then Soapy. Bowers last.

"You've gone quiet, Frank." He angled himself toward Reid.

His position would make the shot tougher.

Soapy closed his coat, made a show of buttoning it. "Out here, in front of God and everyone in a civilized town isn't the way to settle our differences. But we *will* settle them."

Frank had no play except to stand down. Soapy knew it, too. Everyone knew it. "I expect so." Goddammit! He'd missed his chance, maybe the best one he'd ever have short of a flat-out ambush.

*

"FIRE!" At the first call, merchants and miners alike tumbled out of the saloons to man bucket lines. Soapy shouted orders. Sam's Well Drilling tent burned before the camp bell clanged. Doc Runnall's new wooden building and Armstrong's Dry Goods, were gone in minutes. Only the foundations were saved.

"Drinks are on me, boys," Soapy called out to those who battled the fire. "You fought bravely."

The disgusted men poured into his parlor. Soapy stood atop the bar. "Boys, these are tragedies, but the business will be rebuilt. We have spirit in this town that cannot be stifled. I'm appointing Charlie Bowers to handle the relief fund for the burnouts. We got us a fire house in the works and I will personally head up the effort to get what every growing town needs–an organized volunteer fire department and a decent water pumper."

The expected cheer went up. Soapy'd wait to see what happened in the morning. For now he had to decide about Frank Reid.

He jumped down from the bar, received 'atta boys until his hand ached. He whispered to Charlie Bowers, "Check with Sam and the Doc in the morning. Tell them we have the monetary wherewithal for business investments. Offer to help them for our usual cut, but free of any interest charges."

26. Three-Card Monte

Reid wondered how the woman could have figured she'd get away with such a stunt? Did she think no one would look in the cemetery? "Sheriff, do you want to hail her or should I?"

Sheriff Taylor drew rein, signaled a halt to his four deputies, and raised himself in his stirrups to get a good look at the orphanage. His horse sunk hock deep into the muddy muskeg. "Who else might be in there?"

"Three babies and Missy Bonteiller, if I had to guess."

"We gonna have a problem?"

"Not if you keep your iron in repose," Reid said. "Let me holler them out. I doubt they'll shoot me. Not so sure about you." His real fear–the reason he'd ridden with the sheriff–was that Taylor would dry-gulch the women. The man was that much of a bounder.

"You sure?"

Reid clicked his tongue. "Sister Bernadette, you in there? This is Frank Reid. I'm here with the sheriff and a handful of legally-deputized riders."

The nun showed herself, wrapped in her great cloak. "You'll have to excuse me for not inviting you in. One of the babies is poorly."

Reid said, "Missy in there?"

The nun's head drooped. "Yes, but you can't go in. She's nursing."

Reid put forward his grullo. The other horses nickered, skittered and side-stepped. The deputies turned away as if the nun had mentioned small pox. Reid said, "Sister, have you been to the cemetery lately?"

She toed a pine cone.

"Sister?"

"I visit my Angel with a prayer each and every time I pass, coming or going."

"And the last time?"

"Two–no, four–days ago."

The sheriff dismounted, a plug of chew bulging his cheek. "Enough dancing, lady. Did you shoot Two-Chew Calderone? We found him stiff as a rod in that other lady's grave. Fresh-turned dirt made him easy to find."

Reid spat, narrowly missing the sheriff's boot. He'd planned to ease her to the story, step by step. If she lied, he could wipe her from his slate. If she truthed, she was guilty. Either way, she'd be done in by her own words. The goddamn sheriff was hell bent on a quick arrest just for the reward money.

247

She said, "Why ask me?"

"Because we know–"

"Sister," Reid cut in, "you carry a Winchester. Lever action. If Missy is indisposed, could you fetch it up, please? And your loads."

The nun brought the Winchester to Reid. He passed it to the sheriff who levered the action and ejected an unspent cartridge. The sheriff said, "A handsome long gun. It'd look fine in my saddle sock." He produced an empty casing from his pocket and compared it to the load.

"A .44-40. Same stamp on both, Frank. Exact."

"Don't nobody move!" Without showing herself, Missy held a muff gun out the door of the cabin, the gun shaking as if possessed by a body with a nervous disorder. "Stand firm, all of you," she said.

Reid said, "Missy, come out here. Put that iron up. No one's going to hurt you."

"Missy's gone, Frank Reid. It's Melissa. My name is Melissa. I chose it myself. Now you say it."

"Melissa, you pretty little thing, please put the gun up."

The gun continued to quiver. The horsemen backed off.

The nun said, "Missy, come out now."

Still inside the cabin, Missy said, "She didn't mean to do it, Frank. Two-Chew was going to kill me, kill us both. He had a pistol tied onto his shooting hand. She had to do it."

Reid stuffed his hands in his back pockets. Goddamn! With the story out in front of a half-dozen witnesses, Soapy'd take less time with the nun than he did with Sven Lazlo. A lot less. Likely Missy, too. How could he keep the women safe now?

A baby wailed. Frank said, "Missy, put up the shooter. Go tend to that contrary baby. I'm coming in."

*

The sheriff said, "I hereby arrest you under the laws of Skaguay, Alaska District, for the shooting death of Two-Chew Calderone. Give me your hands."

"No need," said Mister Reid. "She'll come along fine without the hand hobbles."

"She's a damn killer!"

Reid faced the sheriff. "I said there's no need. I'll be responsible."

"Just who the hell do you think is in charge, Frank?"

Reid dropped his hand to his side. "Do you want to find out?"

Bernadette and Missy hugged. Without saying as much, they both knew Missy's escape idea was nixed for now. Someone had to tend the babies. Missy quickly promised she'd do whatever she could. If the town women balked, she'd somehow get the crib girls to help. She whispered to Bernadette that they all had agreed as to how they truly admired the nun. Even though her calling was a strange one, they liked her gumption and said she had the courage of an Indian brave.

On the way into town, Bernadette asked Mister Reid why he and the sheriff had arrived together at the orphanage. He explained that he'd been wetting his whistle at The Mascotte when the news hit that Calderone's body had been found in the other nun's grave. He knew that spelled trouble so he beat it to the sheriff and volunteered to be deputized. "With the bounty and all, I didn't want anyone getting greedy. Besides, I wasn't sure about Soapy's intentions. Safest place for you right now might just be in jail. That's where you're headed."

"Mister Reid, you have a strange notion of safe places."

"Beats a neck stretching. Soapy's so sore at you and Missy, he might let a mob string you both up. Only thing that blunts his blade is that no one gave a hoot for Calderone. Soapy included, most times."

"But I'm a member of the Good Shepherd Sisters."

Mister Reid scanned Bernadette like a wanted poster. "You don't look any more like a sister than I do. That's the plain truth. And shooting down a man who barely had any hands don't strike folks as too sisterly."

"He was out of his head drunk and crazy. Missy was right. He was going to kill us both. I just wanted him to go away."

"You shot him through the center of his chest. Twice."

"I wasn't trying to kill him."

Mister Reid looked at her and silently tightened the ends of his moustache. "Strange place to shoot a man you're not trying to kill."

"I was no more than four feet from him," she explained. "No one could have missed."

"Amen, Sister," he said. "Amen."

*

If Bernadette was beginning the end of her days in jail, she needed to set down every detail of the truth lest it be lost. Her cell was insulated with tattered editions of the JUNEAU JOURNAL dating back to February, 1897. She'd use the margins for her thoughts.

First, the cell. Five paces wide by three paces deep. As she opined before, she was not unstruck by the size similarity to Missy Bonteiller's crib. Or, for that matter, her room growing up in Iowa. One tiny window with three iron bars allowed her a narrow view of Broadway if she stood on the cot. The steel-barred door opened onto a tiny access area complete with a cobbled-together desk, a chair, and an ammunition crate on which the jailer could rest his feet. An outer door led to a stairwell down to the backdoor of Clancy's and, across the alley, of course, to the tents of the soiled doves. Bernadette was afforded a sack of dried pine boughs for a mattress. One cell wall held bare shelves from floor to ceiling, shelves scored with the circular impressions of bottles and tins. Smells of low life–fumes from pipes and cigars and the slops of beer and whiskey–wafted up through the floorboards from the saloon below.

She was fed twice daily with Widow Rowan's victuals, cold by the time they arrived, but succulent nonetheless. An hour after each feeding, she was led barefoot from the cell for nature's functions, guarded as if she were a threat to knock down the door and make good an escape. Truly, she was treated like an animal. She assured her present jailer, Mister Tripp, that she had no intention of fleeing, although if an opportunity allowed her liberation, she'd surely take it. There was little hope for the success of such an escape. The tattered sackcloth of her habit would give her away in a moment.

Below, she could hear the evening's dissipation beginning. The swill of demon rum would, as always, turn decent men into debauchers. Even though the stampeders had temporarily cast aside their wives and children, they sought nothing more than the fulfillment of an honest man's gilded bonanza. They weren't to blame. The houses of the Lord were adorned similarly. The miners' folly lived in the devil's brew that stirred their carnal desires. They drank to excess and then traded their stake or poke for a momentary stifling of the concupiscent urge. By comparison, Judas was an archangel.

In spite of their weaknesses, they held the treasure that had been stripped from her: an admixture of trust and hope in themselves. Bernadette's life had been snatched from the Lord and placed in the hands of mere mortals, specifically, into the custody of that scalawag, Colonel

Soapy Smith. She could only pray for intervention, knowing full well that her prayers held neither the luster nor the potency as those she offered nine months earlier. Then, she possessed a strength of spirit sufficient to overcome any rigor the Klondyke might place in her path.

Yes, she had been ready last year. She'd been sure of it.

And had been so wrong.

So here she sat, her face grown gaunt and sallow from the loss of teeth. Where her countenance once was smooth, it was now drawn. Her body had been battered and her soul was in doubt. She had one foot at heaven's gate and one on the threshold to hell.

A visit from Mister Reid interrupted her musings. He peered out the window, listening to hammers pounding and saws buzzing. He must have twirled his Stetson in his hands for five minutes before placing it on his head and facing her. She finally asked, "What is all the building outside?"

"The coming Fourth of July festivities." He searched for more words. "Missy sent me."

After Bernadette had been taken to town, Mister Reid returned to the orphanage to see Miss Bonteiller and discuss what might be done to help the nun. They figured that a trial would be held shortly and that Judge Van Horn would pronounce her guilty. They agreed that there was no hope for a blue-ticket to Seattle. It was the gallows.

Mister Reid said they both had done poorly by her . . . Miss Bonteiller for blurting out the truth of the Calderone incident and himself for accompanying the sheriff. But, he quickly added, that was for her own protection.

Bernadette assured him that she understood Miss Bonteiller's reaction and his reasoning. "She cannot be seen in town under any circumstances. Once she left the Colonel's side, she was in Dutch. Failing to alert him to the Calderone incident was equally bad."

"Still, she's money in the bank to Soapy . . . if he can get her back on her back. That hope is the only thing keeping her alive."

"Mister Reid, she's done with that phase of her life."

"Maybe not."

"I'll not discuss it," Bernadette said. "How are the babies?"

"Some folks from Dyea visited the orphanage. They don't have kids and heard you had some for sale."

Bernadette's hands went cold. Orphanages were meant to provide children to good families, but the idea of giving up Annabelle, or Miss Bonteiller even considering giving up Poteet Bleu, was out of the question. Never. "Mister Reid, those children are not *for sale*. An orphanage does not *sell* its babies like sacks of coal. It finds good homes with loving parents. Do you know the religion of the Dyea people? Their background? Where and how they were raised?"

He stammered that he had no answers.

"Mister Reid, did you know that Poteet Bleu is the Colonel's daughter?"

"Everybody figured that out."

How could everyone have known, yet Bernadette had to be told? Perhaps it was a matter of her late arrival into the district. "Does that fact bode well for Missy?"

"With Soapy? Hardly a lick. He'd sell them bantlings to hell if the devil traded in nuggets."

Bernadette needed to be clear. "Missy is not to adopt out those children without my permission. Given a fair chance, she, herself, will be a fine mother. You tell her that she's to run the orphanage in my absence, however long that is."

"I'll tell her," Mister Reid said. "Won't do much good if Soapy decides to go hunting."

*

Before Reid's next visit to see the nun, he stopped at The Mascotte for a bracer of courage. Two. Three. The camp was aswirl. The visit might not go well. He didn't know who might have drawn guard duty. At the stairwell, he drew his .45 and cocked it, then took the steps softly as if stalking a deer. The outer door was cracked open. He paused. No surprise that he heard Tripp's voice. His surprise came when he heard the old man teaching the nun three-card monte. Frank peeked in. The nun's arms hung through the metal bars of her cell.

Tripp was saying, " . . . so slow you can't miss it. No matter what I do or say, never take your eyes off my hands. There's one black ace, two red queens." He exposed the ace of spades, and then shifted the cards around on his tripe and keister. The nun stared intently at the old man's hands.

Tripp asked, "Still got your eyeballs focused?"

"Yes."

"Don't be careless for a second. Still got it?" His hands moved slow, steady.

"I think so."

Reid was a wagering man. He wouldn't bet against Tripp, but he would've bet a hundred dollars he'd never see the nun in a sure-thing game. Then again, she'd learned fortune-telling at the laundry.

Tripp's fingers moved as if they'd been oiled, slower than any of the sharps on a street corner. Without pausing, Tripp said, "You got an edge, being a woman and all."

"Mister Tripp," she said, looking at him, "what does that have to do with it?" She never saw the last switch.

"Not proper to say in genteel company, Ma'am. You pick now."

With her arms hanging through the iron bars, she tapped the left card. Tripp turned it face up. A red queen. Quickly, he flipped over the center card. Another queen. He flipped the third card. The ace of spades. "You took your eyes from my hands."

Reid pushed open the door. "Mind if I try, old man?"

"Goddamn, Frank, don't sneak up on me like that."

"Your boss might have you shot." He tipped his hat to the nun, then removed it altogether. "Didn't expect to see you two playing cards."

"I am *not* playing cards, Mister Reid," she said. "Mister Tripp was merely practicing his business and I asked him to explain it to me."

"Did you place a bet?"

"Not on your life!"

"Tripp," Reid said, "you heard the morning news?"

"I been here since midnight. Ain't heard a peep. Only person I seen was Widow Pullen with our breakfasts. Mighty good, too. Had a stack of hots, a side of–"

"Shut up and listen."

"Frank, you got no call to talk to me like that."

Reid slapped his hat on his leg. The old man was right. Tripp was only trying to get by. He was a decent sort who just fell on the wrong side of the law–sixty or so years back. "Believe it or not, Tripp, I got a new order for you. Direct from Soapy. The nun's trial has been set. Your pal, Van Horn, will do the judging come Monday morning.

Tripp's hand eased down toward his holster.

"Don't be a fool and get us both killed." Reid turned his back. "I'm going back down to fetch up the other news. When I come back, have the cell door opened."

"Can't do that, Frank."

"You best."

As he climbed back up the stairs, the bundle in Reid's arms squirmed. In his fifty-six years, he couldn't ever recall having held a baby. Warm. Smiley. A few might do fine to fill that house he'd get around to building. He nudged open the jail door and faced Tripp's pistol.

"What the hell?" Tripp said.

"Open that cell," Reid said. "This is on Soapy's own orders."

The nun shrieked. "My baby!"

Reid passed Annabelle to her. "There's more to the story, Sister. The Dyea folks took the boy baby. This one's to stay with you. Missy and her young 'un have gone back to Soapy."

27. Justice Bought and Paid For

"Your lodgment is up for now." Mister Tripp swung open the heavy iron door to Bernadette's cell. "The town's waiting. Trial starts in ten minutes, give or take. Get your baby ready."

"Am I to be afforded an attorney?"

Mister Tripp scratched his beard. "I dunno about lawyers. I'm just supposed to shag you to the Union Church pronto."

"May I have my gum boots?"

"Lazlo had sand bags, you get sand bags. All the killers get them."

Bernadette left for her trial bare-footed, dragging the sand bags, Annabelle in her arms. By the time they made it down the stairs with her in tow, a crowd had packed itself around the staircase so tightly that no one was able to step into the alley.

Frank Reid bore through the mass, pushed Tripp aside and took Bernadette by the arm. "I'm going to talk for you, but I'll need your help. Like I said before, folks haven't liked what they been seeing, you cozying up to Soapy and all. His boys spread the word that you went and shot down an unarmed man."

"He had a gun!"

"The sheriff will swear contrary."

"Ask Missy."

"Soapy's got her locked up as tight as a tick. She's scared to blow her nose. Hardly stopped bawling since she got to town."

"Why can't I be taken to Dyea? John Fay was. Has anyone contacted Commissioner Seibert?"

Mister Reid shook his head from side to side. Seibert claimed Skaguay played the devil with his bowels. Dyea had permanent military troops to protect him. He once said if he were to take all the cases that came up in Skaguay, he might as well move here, and that he'd rather roll up and suffocate in a vat of pig shit before doing that. As far as he was concerned, Skaguay was part and parcel of Canada.

Mister Reid removed his hat. "Sister Bernadette, you shouldn't ought to be going through this. You killed Calderone to save them kids and yourself. You say that if I ask. You were saving the babies. It's the only thing I know to try to touch Van Horn's oakum heart. Even though folks on both sides of the law hated Calderone, Soapy owns Van Horn beginning to back, so I'm not expecting the argument to prevail."

She said, "If so many people are happy to see Mister Calderone dead, why won't they come to my defense?"

"Ain't tough enough on the inside or man enough on the outside.

"That's gibberish."

"Sister, I fought in the Piute War. Been a peace officer and a hunter and trapper, a teacher and a surveyor. One thing common in the west and north for man, woman, child, dog or horse: you got to be tough. It's nice to be smart, but you *got* to be tough to make it. No disrespect meant, but your God don't pack a pistol. Lazlo was tougher than Portland Pete and Pete ended his days with a horseshoe gouged in his head. Smith was tougher than Lazlo and Lazlo swung. John Fay was tougher than Rowan and Rowan died. You were tougher than Calderone because he's dead, but you ain't tougher than Soapy Smith and his gang."

*

Judge Van Horn, his upper lip vibrating, sat behind a small square desk on the platform that once held the oom-pah band. A shot glass, Bernadette's Winchester and a handful of cartridges lay on the desk. A long table stretched from the platform to a chalk line drawn on the floor. Mister Reid and Bernadette sat side by side at the table facing Reverend Bowers and Sheriff Taylor. Behind the chalk line, Colonel Smith sat alone in the front pew, behind him a chorus of a hundred men.

Bernadette still found it impossible to believe that she'd killed a man. She'd examined her conscience time and again trying to determine if she were guilty of mortal sin. Mister Calderone was intent on doing harm, no doubt. Could she have stopped him with a warning shot–it had worked before–or a shot to the leg? Could she have refused to fire the Winchester at all? God's law and man's law might judge her differently. For certain, she now feared man's law far more.

The judge banged the whiskey glass on the desk and called for order. No one slowed talking so the sheriff pulled his pistol and shot into the ceiling. That set Annabelle to crying. The judge thanked the sheriff and went on to explain the crime for which Bernadette stood accused. He said that Reverend Bowers would speak on behalf of the good people of Skaguay and that Mister Reid would speak on Bernadette's behalf. The judge further said he'd call anyone else who might bring evidence and truth to light.

He called on Reverend Bowers first. The serpent-tongued old imposter did his best to cook Bernadette on the spot. He told of the time she happened on Mister Calderone and Miss Bonteiller "in an honest and paid-for dalliance" and how she shot at Calderone. He allowed as how she out and out lied to the sheriff regarding the last time she'd been to the cemetery. At Bowers' reference to her lie, the men in the pews stomped their boots. Bowers summarized his arguments by saying that Mister Calderone could not have possibly posed a threat to anyone. "As everyone knows, the unfortunate man had lost all his fingers days earlier. How could he pull a trigger? How could he even hold a pistol? No, your honor," Bowers said, "this is the woman who shot Two-Chew Calderone right through the very center of his heart. She is a cold killer wrapped in the cloak of the Lord . . . but a killer nonetheless."

The spectators whooped and hollered. The judge fruitlessly pounded his shot glass until the Colonel swiveled his head, bringing silence. The sheriff rose to speak, but was forced to wait until Bernadette settled down Annabelle, who rightfully was showing her own objections to the entire proceeding.

Not surprisingly, the sheriff agreed with everything Bowers had said. He wanted to add only that it was he, himself, who personally found the body in the grave and the two bullet casings in Calderone's otherwise empty pockets. He said Bernadette was not only a murderer, but a grave robber and likely a thief as well and that the town ought not to abide scofflaws, man or woman. "Hang her today!" He pulled his gun and shot up the ceiling and was joined by a host of reckless miners.

*

Soapy drew his forefinger across his throat in a quick slash. He'd not allow the affair to turn into a stampede. The gunfire stopped. Judge Van Horn said, "We're adjourned to a call of the court."

Soapy led the exodus from the church. He still didn't understand the nun. She was about to sacrifice her life for what she perceived as her virtue, not a trade that a sane person would make. Virtue? What a misnomer! Virtue was something to be shared at the right time and place in the furtherance of the good life. The nun could save herself and he could have the most dazzling woman in the Alaska District. *That* was virtue.

Tripp led the nun by the arm toward Clancy's, her sandbags caked in mud, the girl child in the crook of her arm.

"Tripp," Soapy said, "give me a moment with the sister, please." Soapy turned to the nun. "It would be in your best interest to speak with me."

Wordlessly, Tripp tipped his hat. His hand went to the pistol inside his old flap holster.

"No need for that," Soapy said. To the nun, he said, "Where are your boots?"

"Ask him." The nun jabbed Tripp in the ribs.

The woman will never lose her spunk. What made him so attracted to spicy ladies, ladies who, in the most dire circumstances, would never yield their élan? "Tripp, would you be so kind as to free Sister Bernadette from her sandbags and fetch her shoes. We'll stray no farther than the side of the church."

Frank Reid approached.

"'Morning, Frank," Soapy said.

Reid nodded.

"Mind if I have a chat with your client? She looks like she could stand with a bit of sun."

"If she wishes."

"She'll be safe."

Tripp returned with her gum boots. Reid sidled off. The clear, cloudless skies over Skaguay provided a blissful sunny day. The mountains, greened with summer's coat, were topped with pure white snow. Soapy said, "Sister Bernadette, is there anything I can do for you?"

"Colonel . . . how . . . why . . . ?"

"Your life is now in what you Catholics call limbo."

She said, "Before we speak of me, I would like to know the circumstance of Missy and her daughter."

"They're fine. Safe with Big Bo."

"Missy's word will contradict the sheriff's, as will the word of Mister Reid."

"Missy shan't appear. I further fear the judge will not believe Reid."

The nun turned on him. "Colonel, how can you have the effrontery to offer help on one hand when you have been the source of all of my travails?"

"You must learn to accept what gifts are offered. Some things are inexplicable."

"At one time in my life, I knew all things were possible with trust in the Lord. Now, I'm beginning to agree with you. There are things–situations– He chooses merely to indulge."

"Sister, start thinking clearly. Look at what you face. Look at your alternatives. I'll not enumerate. It's enough to say that Van Horn will hang you."

"Only on the order of the most powerful man in camp."

In camp? "Sister, it's unwise if you limit my influence–influence that could be working on your behalf–to Skaguay. You misunderstand badly. For example, Governor Brady will be my personal guest for the Fourth of July festivities."

"Colonel, don't you see the irony of this conversation? You are the head of a band of toughs and the unquestioned king of sure-thing sharpers and Lord knows what else. Here I am, in an apparent word contest with you, gambling with you for my life."

"Sister, I never gamble. I've learned that lesson. So should you. Gambling involves taking chances. I don't."

"But you can stop this–whatever you choose to call it–at any time."

"I can."

"You have Missy. You have a wife and children. What would you want with me?"

He said, "Is that your answer?"

She turned her back to him.

*

Although Mister Reid was always an impressive presence when among men–he was a full head taller than most–his way with words was inept when compared to the silver-tongued Bowers. He took no more than five minutes to explain the shooting as it actually occurred. When he sat down beside Bernadette, he was soaked in perspiration, shaky and pale, shriveled as if all the strength had been sucked from his countenance.

The judge said to Bernadette, "Your turn."

She handed Annabelle to Mister Reid. He received her with a frown, causing the courtroom a chuckle. She stood, held onto the table and told how Mister Calderone burst through the duck-cloth door. For sure he had a gun bound to his hand and he was menacing with it. Someone in the crowd hollered, "Who menaced who, you witch? Calderone's the one pushing up sod." For his comment, the man received a hearty round of applause.

"That's true," she said, "but I had to protect my babies. I never meant to kill him." She felt that she could say little else so she said again, "I never meant to kill him."

The judge asked if anyone else wished to address the court.

"I do, Sir," the Colonel said.

"You have the floor."

The Colonel faced the onlookers and hooked his thumbs behind his lapels. "Gentlemen, this is a most difficult day for me." Several men snickered and were immediately silenced by the Colonel's gaze. "I've known Sister Bernadette since the day she first set foot on Moore's Wharf last summer. She got herself involved in a fracas back then and hasn't stopped since, sad to say. Deep inside, I have no doubt she's a fine woman. We all know that.

"And you all know me. You know that I make money at my games. That money is yours. I bet I could unfold my tripe and keister this very moment and pop a pea under a shell and make a handsome profit right in front of the good judge."

The judge said, "No need for that, Colonel Smith."

"I understand, Your Honor. I'm not going to do any of that, but that's my livlihood. Some of you mine gold. Some of you are packers, cooks, carpenters. Mule skinners and faro dealers. Some are drummers and merchants. Some are newsies . . . and judges and sheriffs. Me? I make entertainment; I sell you entertainment like a store clerk sells you a pair of boots. Have I ever said any different to any one of you?"

The Colonel paused, then shouted. "Have I? Ever?"

Each and every head in the church shook from side to side.

"No, you ain't, Colonel."

"You own more of my money than I do, but I keep coming back."

Soapy said, "In fact, my games are educational institutions. You come in, lay down your dust and leave the poorer for it. Lesson learned. You don't have to return. Some never do and for them, I've become a benefactor, a teacher. Gambling doesn't pay. It never has; it never will."

A voice from the crowd said, "You skin me, then stand the house to drinks. I get my money's worth from your games. A few more fools like me around and you'd own the whole goddamn district." The speaker's partners clapped him on the back. The entire congregation hooted.

260

Like a preacher now, the Colonel raised his hands for quiet. They were his, and Bernadette could see that he'd be able to lead them to hell if he so chose. He began orating on behalf of law and order. He would not abide renegade justice, not from vigilantes who'd been bent on bedlam in Skaguay, not from ne'er-do-wells nor hooligans of any shape. Not from any man, or woman. Skaguay would, by God, become a place where families would be raised, where schools and churches would thrive, where the streets would be safe. But it could only happen if the irresponsible people–ones who would take the law into their own hands–were forever run out of town like the good Lord ran out the money-changers from the temple.

He paced the chalk line and appeared to collect his next thoughts. "I take kindly to Sister Bernadette. At times, she does good works. Other times, well, she seems to believe her being a lady of the cloth gives her the rights reserved for a court of law or the Almighty himself. We can't have that. Not from her–" He ceased pacing and stood directly behind Mister Reid. "–not from anyone else."

The men murmured until the judge rapped his shot glass again. The Colonel continued. "Two-Chew Calderone had done some wrong in his life. He paid the price."

The Colonel stretched out his arms like Christ about to give the Sermon on the Mount. "He didn't have to be gunned down! Confound it all, no one deserves to be gunned down!"

The Colonel hung his head, seeming almost, to be an atoning penitent. "Judge Van Horn, the matter is in your hands." He strode from the church, each clump of his boot dropping as heavily as a falling anvil.

In almost a whisper, the judge said, "Well, we heard some facts that are disputed and some that aren't. What we ain't heard is the accused saying she didn't point that Winchester at the deceased and shoot him. Maybe he had a gun, maybe not. Maybe she wanted to kill him, maybe not. The indisputable straight fact is that she shot and killed Two-Chew Calderone and for that, this court finds her guilty as charged and sentences her three days hence, July 4, 1898, to hang."

28. The Whore's Plan

As Bernadette stepped outside Union Church, half the town hooted and called her ugly names. A smaller group cheered and held up their bibles. Many of the latter, she knew for a fact, were not even Catholic. She kept her head level and dragged her sandbags through the muck, her hands locked behind her in metal cuffs as befitting a convict. Mister Tripp carried Annabelle.

In truth, she failed to understand how this came about so quickly. She was a Good Shepherd Sister, albeit not the best of the lot, her raiment as well as her immortal soul bearing only the vaguest resemblance to the holy order. Her baby had just seen her judged guilty of murder. How had this happened?

In her cell, Tripp unfastened her wrist braces and asked if she needed anything. She turned as mute as a headstone. She needed nothing from him or his kind; she'd never need from them. She refused to bend to their level, even if they stretched her on the rack.

In an hour, Big Bo appeared, a plain black muslin shift folded over her arm like a waiter's towel. Two of her crib gals carried croaker sacks. Bo dismissed Tripp and lifted the cell key from the wall. "Lady," she said, unlocking the cell, "being that this will be your home until you swing, these bags hold your belongings from the cabin." The gals emptied the sacks onto the cell floor. Everything she owned tumbled out, even the ball gown and the nurse uniform. Everything but the Winchester.

Bo shook out the muslin shift. "Strip."

"Why? What?"

"Soapy got a new rule for condemned ladies. You wear this black from now till you stretch."

"I won't."

"Thought you might feel that way," Bo said. "I say you will, or we snatch that baby right from your arms and do it for you."

Petrified, she clutched Annabelle. The three women moved toward her. *My Mother, My Confidence. Saints preserve us!*

From her sleeve, Big Bo produced an iron rod the size and girth of an unbent horseshoe. She clanged it against the bars of the cell door. Deafening, but Bernadette understood quickly the damage the weapon could do. She passed Annabelle to one of the girls.

Had her life ever reached a lower point? She almost wished for death to come instantly. She stood, shed her red cape and Iron Maiden.

"Everything."

"You don't mean it."

For answer, Big Bo clanged the iron bars again.

Bernadette removed her underthings and peeled off her stockings. Standing in front of three sets of eyes, she was as naked as the day of her birth. Her chin was set in marble; she was ready for any blow they might wish to deliver. Tears streamed down her face.

Big Bo passed her the shift. Bernadette slipped it over her head and received Annabelle in return. The women backed out of the cell. Big Bo hung the key on the wall and led the girls out. Bernadette couldn't even conjure up a prayer.

*

Soapy admitted that he'd made a tactical error. He'd not discussed the hanging schedule with Van Horn. The judge, left to his own devices, had concluded that a July Fourth hanging would be a bonus to the holiday's festivities. It would show Governor Brady first hand that Skaguay was, indeed, a law-abiding town not deserving of its scandalous reputation. His thinking had been whiskey-addled. With the parade and goings on, hundreds, if not a thousand folks would invade camp–drinking, eating, spending money. All to the good. Soapy could water the liquor down to cow piss and they'd still get drunk. In the midst of all that, would he hang a woman and put a pall on the celebration? No. He'd pick another time to gather the curious into town. Another time to sell more whiskey and women and games. Besides, he wanted the nun to mull over the portent of her death. One last chance to grasp the straw of reality.

He called on her and asked, "Have you thought about your choices?"

"It appears my life won't go on much past the holiday."

"Somehow, it seems unpatriotic to hang you on the Fourth of July."

The thunk of axes chopping on Broadway caused Annabelle to kick up a fuss. The nun lifted the baby onto her hip and set herself into a maternal sway. Even in the plain black shift and unkempt hair, the nun's beauty was unmatched.

She stepped onto her cot to peer through the bars onto Broadway. "Will the confounded pounding ever stop?"

"They're building review stands for the parade. Nothing but the finest for our governor. After, the same milling will be used to build you an equally-fine gallows. After you hang, the gallows will be dismantled and used as part of the foundation for Skaguay's first fire house. My design and my money. Unless, of course . . . "

As if she hadn't heard him, she said, "How is your daughter, Colonel?"

He couldn't fashion how the woman refused every opportunity he provided for her. "Do you really want to die?"

"How can you ask such a cruel question? *Why* would you ask it? Are you still bargaining with my life?"

"Do you believe that I can save you?"

"I do."

"Not only *can* I save you, do you believe that I am the *only* one who can save you?" This was a test. Had the woman shifted from her staunch unwavering belief in a deity to the truth of her situation?

Skillfully, she dodged the question. "Can you speak your mind straightaway, Colonel?"

Like an elusive salmon, she refused to be netted. "Come with me this minute. To my house. Live at my side. You and the baby, if you like."

"Come with you?"

"Now."

"So my trial was a sham?"

He withdrew a pack of cards from his vest and set to cutting the pack with one hand. Over and over. Not looking up. "The trial was not a sham. It was an attempt to show you the light. On that score, it appears I've succeeded. You believe I can free you, if you want your freedom badly enough. This is not deeply philosophical, Sister. It's not one of the mysteries of your faith."

"Missy is at your house."

"Can you see nothing? Missy only came back to me to save your skin. She's not the one I want. You could have been hung an hour after the trial."

"And she–?" The nun paused. A look of understanding crossed her face as if a mystery had been revealed. "–she promised herself to you in return for sparing me."

"At first, that was the agreement, yes. However, humans are ever-changing animals."

"And you think you can buy me?"

He sat quietly cutting the cards, nodding his head. "I can buy anything."

She slapped the cards. They flew from his hands like fluff from a dried dandelion.

*

"Sister Bernadette, sometimes you can't count from one to two." Missy held up the gray nurse uniform that had been the nun's pillow. "Would this look good on me?"

"It doesn't matter, Missy! You didn't have to go back to living in adulterous sin with that man. That was your worst possible option."

"Would it be better for me to be sleeping with Two-Chew?"

"Anything would be better than the choice you made."

"I talked Soapy into giving you more life to live and that's all you got to say? Now, at least, we got some time."

"He asked me if I wanted to die."

The women shared the cell cot, bouncing the babies on their knees. Poteet and Annabelle giggled and reached out to each other.

"Good question," Missy said. "I wonder that, too."

"I'm still upset with you, child. Don't make light."

"Look, you marblehead, did all your brains scatter out when you lost that bonnet of yours? It's as simple as applesauce. I go back to Soapy. Keep him—well, take his edge off. He's staring down a lot of barrels these days. If you'd take up his offer, you'd move into the house, right into the same bedroom I have now. I got it fixed up peaches and cream."

"Child!"

"Hush your mush. I'm spelling it all out. This is the way to save both our skins. I got his ear now. I can talk business to him much better when I got his business in my hand."

"Stop!"

"No more preachments." She tucked a blanket around Poteet Bleu. "Okay, I'm with Soapy. For now. In a bit, you agree to go to him."

Missy laid it out. The nun would agree to move in with Soapy. Soapy would tell Van Horn to change the sentence to house arrest. Soapy'd be content. Missy and Poteet could slip away during the Fourth of July gala.

"He'll treat you fine," Missy said. "Without stint. Ever. No steerage with Soapy Smith. Grub. Duds. He wouldn't even make you work the cribs. You'd be the highest of the high fancy pieces. Then you'd convince him it was a waste of his boys' time to chase me down when they could be out making money at their games. I'd still be alive and you'd be alive and the babies would be alive. As it stands now, if you hang, he'll axe me in no-time-Charlie. Likely take up with Stella. He's really a one-woman man. Too bad it's whichever one he's around."

"Do you realize what you're asking of me?"

"Do you realize what happens if they hang you? You're dead forever! After that, nobody asks you anything." Goddamn, Missy thought, the woman would never learn. "And when he's done with you, I'm next. He's got no use for the babies, either. It's so clear."

"To you, perhaps."

"Think on it. Just think on it. One way, we both die. All four of us die. The other way, at least we have a rube's chance. You got to admit, you killed the wrong man. Soapy's still playing all the cards."

*

Could Missy be right? Bernadette saw the irony. She'd finally lured the child from whoring, only to become one herself. She would forsake her vows and her beliefs, losing her immortal soul while saving four lives.

My God, help me.

29. Twilight's Last Gleaming

"I got Soapy where I want him." Missy opened her war bag of manicure tools. "But I still ain't letting you out of this cage looking like an urchin boy."

"You're a miracle worker." The nun submitted a hand to Missy and her nail chamois.

"No miracle. That's your angle. I just told him you might appreciate it if he showed a little mercy, that you might look a little different toward him if he did. I asked him, Where could a nun run off to? He wouldn't agree to let you out for the parade–you can see it standing on your cot–but I got us two whole hours to promenade Broadway before the Governor arrives. This camp's turned out in its finest. We'll have such fun! But I ain't taking you so far as the alley looking the way you do."

Missy set to work in earnest on the nun's fingernails. She snipped and filed, polished, kneaded and thumbed, finishing with a minty balm from fingertips to elbows.

The nun said, "In your next life, if you don't get a job as a typewriter girl, you can always become a hand groom. I am close to heaven." She sighed and slumped against the cell wall.

"Wait till you see the booths and games. None of Soapy's sure-thing games, either. He put the word out. Everything's on the square. There's even a pie-throwing contest. That rascal reporter is the rube. Widow Pullen has her own shack for her jams and jellies. The Union Church is being used to show off all manner of antimacassars, doilies and quilts. The camp will be perfect. Even a fireworks display at sundown big enough to chase away the devil. Pow! Pow! Pow!"

Tripp hollered in from the hallway. "Will you two pipe down. On holidays, a man gets to catch forty winks between drinks."

"Hush, you drunken old sot or I'll skin you alive." Missy leaned to the nun. "Did you think about what I said?"

"At length."

"And you're not going to bop me on the head for raising the question again?"

"No, child."

"You're strangely quiet."

"Can you get rid of Mister Tripp?"

267

"As good as done," she said. "Tripp, go over to Widow Pullen's and get me jam and bread."

Tripp hollered, "She's been here already this morning."

"Well, I worked a different shift from you. If I tell Soapy you got sassy with me, it won't go pleasant. In case you ain't heard, I'm back in his good graces and making him plenty of money."

The women heard him clomp down the stairs.

The nun said, "I'll go to the Colonel."

"Laws, woman! Did I hear proper? Say it again. My hearing tubes must be filled with corn cobs."

"I'll go to the Colonel only if you promise to leave this sinful town immediately. Not just quit your business, which you must also promise to do, but to get out of this town, and away from the Colonel's influence forever. Take Poteet. I'll keep Annabelle. I'll make that part of any agreement between the Colonel and me."

"Hell, yes! I mean, Yes, I will. No dickering. I'll go today . . . while everyone's busy celebrating."

The nun unclasped the gold cross around her neck. "Use this as currency."

"Keep it. I know where Soapy stashes his rainy-day poke. I'll just help myself on the way out the door. He'll be too busy with the governor to check."

"A question, child," the nun said. "Since you returned to his house, have you–have you shared his bed? You have the syphilis, you know. Have you been using the balm?"

"Hush about them things, Sister. There's more than one way to skin a cat."

"Meaning . . . ?"

The reply was one lie Missy couldn't tell. "Yes, I've been to his bed." And thought, Even with Soapy's eyes and ears everywhere, explaining this will be harder than sneaking on a boat. "What you do is you take his prod in one hand–"

*

Missy fetched Poteet Bleu and settled her on the cell cot next to Annabelle. She gave Mister Tripp sharp instructions–on the Colonel's own orders, she said–that he tend the babies like they were his own. Bernadette was to be freed from the cell without the sandbags and allowed to wander through the Fourth of July festivities. "Come on," Missy said, "your hours are ticking."

The summer's air was suffocating but it was fresh, not the fumes of slops and swills from Clancy's. Bernadette was to be back in her cell before the noon arrival of the Governor's steamer. Soapy wanted no chance for her to talk to him, or even have him get a gander of her. Bernadette hardly cared a whit. She was free!

People stared like she was a marked woman, or worse, a witch from hell. Others embraced her and said they were praying for her. A few damned the evil element in the town. Each and every one, however, took time to visit with Missy, even the women of the newly-formed Union Church Ladies Choir. The child had always been the first choice of men, but, notwithstanding the episode from the mercantile months earlier, she'd somehow managed to win over the good women of Skaguay.

They encountered a dozen wagons decked out in red, white and blue bunting. On the wharf, a band of Tlingits went through elaborate dance rituals. Sheriff Taylor was gussied up in an Uncle Sam suit. Widow Rowan, hawking her preserves, had been painted stem to stern in white barn wash. She was portraying the Goddess of Liberty herself.

The stores along Broadway–Bernadette counted no fewer than seventy wooden structures–were draped in patriotic colors and American flags. Every shop door was propped open, every tent flap folded back. The saloons were doing a rushing business and it was not yet eleven o'clock.

A fusillade of gunfire set every dog in camp howling. Miss Bonteiller scanned the handbill. "Time for the greased pole contest. Then the tug-of-war. That's about all you'll be able to see. There's a real baseball game against the men from Dyea. The girls made up twenty picnic lunches for all the players. Then comes the big parade. I think you'll be able to see it from your cell. Soapy and the Governor will be sitting in them new seats right across from Clancy's. Maybe you can wave at them."

Missy thought herself humorous; Bernadette did not.

After their stroll, she returned Bernadette to the cell. "Here," she said, and secreted with Bernadette a fat moosehide poke as heavy as a bag of agates. "I swiped this from Soapy's cache. It's some of the color he's saved out. Even Bowers don't know about this. Find it a hidey hole among the baby things. During the parade, I'll tie up loose ends and come by before the next boat sails off. I'll leave Poteet with you for now. Have the uniform ready for me. Won't be no time for a long good-bye when I come back."

"God speed you, child."

"God, and Frank Reid. He won't marry me, but he agreed to help me escape. How's that for a pickle? The man I love will help me escape his town and never see him again."

"It's for the best."

"I told him he ought to solve a lot of problems and just shoot Soapy. He allowed as how he might have to."

*

Bernadette heard the parade band, a disjointed effort of clarinet, tuba and fife, and looked out her cell window. The Colonel, straight of spine and splendid of raiment, sat aback the dapple. His cutaway was slashed with a red-velvet sash; the G.A.R. atop his head was topped with a fresh plume. Governor Brady, astride a chestnut, wore a long-tailed frock coat, ruffled shirt and freshly blacked boots. They both clearly welcomed the rousing fanfare. When the Colonel and the Governor had dismounted and taken their seats of honor, the bleachers quickly filled around them.

The Colonel rose to welcome the Governor. In his deepest pulpit voice, he noted that Skaguay was a fine, peaceable town, unlike the reputation it was gaining from its jealous neighbors in Dyea. The Colonel winked at the Governor's traveling companion, Commissioner Seibert. From the cell, Bernadette could see the Commissioner's face redden; his bushy white muttonchops seemed to stand right out from the sides of his face. She thought to shout through the bars that things were not quite so fine here, but feared the Colonel might return to the judge's original plan and hang her on the spot.

She took to her cot, snuggled the babies to her breast and tried to think of a way out of her predicament. No ideas came. In the novitiate, they'd been taught to walk and meditate when temptation assaulted, or when they needed tranquility of thought to decipher a complex problem. The novice masters could have never envisioned one of theirs walking with two babies across a jail cell that measured no more than five paces.

Every now and again, Bernadette heard a rousing cheer from the celebrants below. Another irony struck: this was the Fourth of July, the day marking the country's freedom and yet here she was, locked up in a hoosegow. In days henceforth, the cheering throng would collect again to watch her swing.

Until now, she hadn't truly visualized a thick, rough noose around her neck, her body stretched, sand bags around her ankles. As a sister, she had always prayed for the repose of the souls of the dead. Bernadette never considered how she might pray at the hour of her own death. Annabelle cooed and rubbed her tiny fists into the sockets of her eyes. This is the finest of all the Lord's creations. Could Bernadette bring her to a life of sin? If she did not, what might be her lot in life? Would she have a life at all? Bernadette was entertaining second thoughts about her commitment to the Colonel, yet saw no clear choice. She was wrong, whichever way she turned.

A thundering boom rocked the cell and startled Poteet to flailing. Bernadette tried to sooth her, but the baby swatted her on the lips and knocked loose an upper incisor. Now shy four uppers and four lowers, Bernadette felt she must look like a jack-o'-lantern. Curiously, she wondered what Mother Francine would say. Then wondered how badly Missy would tease her.

Was the Colonel for sure her sole hope? Mister Reid, by his own admission, could not save her. Only if the citizenry rose up might he be in a position to help. The Governor? Why not?

Bernadette settled the babies with bottles and waved Annabelle's blanket through the window bars. The Governor merely waved back, a wide smile on his face. Within minutes, the window was boarded over, shutting out her last hope. Now, no one but the Colonel could save her from the noose.

She would keep her word and exchange her temporal flesh for eternal damnation.

30. Not a Fair Divvy

The town quieted after the holiday hullabaloo. Missy, bless her heart, called on Bernadette the day following the festivities wearing neither her customary rouge nor face powder. She was feeling poorly. Her hair was hidden under a wide-brimmed Benwood. She wished for a full day in the soaker and had tried to convince the Colonel to allow the two gals to visit the bathhouse. When he refused, she upped and left him naked in bed.

She settled Poteet Bleu next to Annabelle and recalled the events of the Governor's visit. "We were doing a wild business in the cribs." Customers came from sun-up until well past four in the morning. The girls had been begging Big Bo to close down since midnight–they were so tired that they were ready to faint–but Big Bo had driven them on. At four, she finally gave in.

Missy waved a small poke at Bernadette. "This is all my gimmes for the time. Add it to what I give you before. Keep it safe." She passed over a moosehide pouch. "Over $100 in nuggets and dust," she said. Bernadette tucked it under the blanket in Annabelle's crib.

As Missy worked on Bernadette's fingers, the child carried on a line of patter about how charming the governor had turned out to be "for a politician." And added, "The boys drank every drop of real whiskey in Clancy's and Jeff's . . . probably a few other canteens, too." She said the baseball team that came down from Dyea beat Soapy's boys by two points, but that was because Soapy's boys were drunk before the game ever began. Soapy good-naturedly stood both teams to a round of drinks. The governor had headed south on the midnight steamer, himself a bit tipsy and sporting a face protector from the baseball contest.

Missy finished Bernadette's nails with the chamois. "That midnight steamer will be perfect for my get-away." She held up the nun's hands for an inspection. "You have lovely fingers. They'd be like satin on any man." Then jumped to her feet. "You watch the babies a spell. I don't care what Jeff Smith says, I'm going for a bath."

*

Miss Bonteiller didn't return. No matter how Bernadette badgered Mister Tripp, she received no answer as to the child's whereabouts. Of course, a string of horrors ran through Bernadette's head, from the idea of abandonment to the deadliest of endings.

On the evening of the second day of Miss Bonteiller's absence, Tripp commenced a three-card monte game. A street gamin Bernadette had met before, a boy called Jimmy Fresh, showed up with a pilgrim gent. Hours later, two more. Each time, the gent walked away with winnings in his pocket. Mister Tripp, abetted by his demijohn of devil's brew, seemed undisturbed by his losses. Of course, Bernadette didn't understand this and went so far as to inquire.

He said, "Just getting the word out that some drunken old jailer is giving away his money. Waiting for a fat lamb."

"Thank you," she said. "But won't you please tell me about Missy?"

"You say her name again and I board up the door tighter than the window."

Three days on, Jimmy Fish arrived with a drunken miner. Bernadette remembered John Stewart from the spat on the *Al-Ki* the day she'd arrived in the district. The boy made a show of introducing the raspy-voiced miner to Mister Tripp, who seemed more drunk than he'd been just moments before. Stewart's once-sharp moustache had been blended into a faceful of wooly beard, the trademark of the stampeder.

He guarded his sizeable poke closely and won slightly. Jimmy Fresh, also drunk, joined the game, lost heavily and became belligerent. To calm the brewing storm, Tripp began passing his jug to both men, cussing each time he handed it across his tripe and keister. In time, the men agreed to double the stakes. They settled down to quiet play.

Bernadette made a special effort to keep the babies hushed. Each of the three men carried pistols; Jimmy Fresh carried two. He continued to lose. Mister Tripp set to jobbing him. "Your eyes ain't sharp like this miner, son," he said. "You best pack it in."

"I beat you before, you mangy old son-of-a-bitch. My luck'll come back. Double the bet again?"

John Stewart, a fistful of folding money now in his lap, agreed. They were playing for the unheard of sum of two-hundred dollars a hand! *Jesus, Mary and Joseph.* Not in any of the saloons on Broadway had Bernadette ever seen the like.

After an hour, John Stewart's winnings had dwindled, but Mister Tripp complained that the miner was skinning him good. Tripp tipped his head back and free-poured whiskey into his mouth.

"Not as good as before, Tripp. Make it five-hundred a hand?"

Tripp cast a worried look around the hallway. He crossed Bernadette's glance with a clear, sharp eye. In that moment, she knew what was about to happen.

Jimmy Fresh said, "Too rich for me. I'll watch."

Mister Tripp's fingertips danced like water dropped on a hot oil skillet. He coughed, spit in the sawdust, drooled, talked a ceaseless line of patter–all the while sliding the cards around the felt rectangle. John Stewart lost the first two of the five-hundred dollar hands, then won three in a row. Tripp cussed him like never before.

"Deal!" cried John Stewart. "I'm coming back. You can't weasel on me now."

"Weasel nothing," Mister Tripp said, showing the ace of spades before sliding the cards in magical circles. A tear rolled from his eye into the crevice along his ruddy nose. He sniffled, and kept his hands moving. John Stewart lost. And lost.

"This is it," Stewart finally said. "Eight-hundred in folding money. All I got left. One hand. If I win, I don't go home skinned. If I lose, I'm sunk." He took a long pull from Tripp's jug.

Tripp flashed the ace and began to slide the cards.

*

Through her boarded up window, Bernadette heard the fracas on Broadway. John Stewart's throaty voice drunkenly shouted to one and all how he'd been cheated. He fired off his pistol. She covered the babies with her own body in fear that he might be shooting toward the jailer. Stewart screamed that he was going to board the *Al-Ki* that very night to spread the word from Seattle to San Francisco of crooked Skaguay.

Tripp batched up the miner's money and sent it off with Jimmy Fresh. He ripped the boards from Bernadette's cell window. Together, standing on the cot, they watched the town build itself to a major affray right at Clancy's front door.

*

Clots of men trolled the street, torches lighted. Groups huddled together, their heads almost touching in conspiratorial agreement. Soapy's boys strutted everywhere, armed and swarthy. Reid's vigilantes were also armed. They chewed their lower lips and drummed their fingers on the unfamiliar firearms riding their hips. With John Stewart in tow, Reid worked the muddy street, back slapping townsmen. Soapy appeared in the doorway

274

of his parlor, Bowers and Saportas at his flanks. He tottered on the boardwalk until Bowers ushered him inside.

Reid said to John Stewart, "We'll get your poke back. You keep talking to the miners. I'm going to gather our camp fellows at the church. Meet me there in fifteen minutes." They're ready, Reid thought. They're finally ready.

*

Union Church overflowed. Stewart made his way to the platform. He whispered to Reid, "There's another hundred outside."

Reid said, "Find Tanner and Landers. You met them earlier. Tell them to lead everyone down to the wharf. That's the only other place big enough for all of us and where we can keep Soapy's thugs at bay."

*

Charlie Bowers, Billy Saportas, Big Bo, Syd Dixon and Soapy sat at the round table. Billy said, "Boss, they got the entrance to the dock shut off. Wouldn't let me pass. I bet they got two-hundred boys out there. Fixing for a big stir."

"Well, God damn them." Soapy tossed back a shot, poured another. "What'd they say?"

"That me and my type ain't invited."

"Billy, I take unkindly to that."

"Tanner had his pistol on me. Other boys with rifles. I couldn't do a thing."

"Understandable," Soapy said. "Fetch us all fresh glasses."

Soapy poured a round of shots, lifted his glass to toast with his men. "It appears tonight is a night of history."

Bowers covered his glass. "They're riled about that miner, John Stewart. We been here lapping up the Belmont. Maybe we should wait."

"No more waiting, Charlie," Soapy said. "Billy, did you see Reid?"

"No, Sir."

"Drink, boys, then we'll stroll down to the wharf and have a looksee into their meeting," Soapy said. "Then to business. Peaceful, unless the need is otherwise."

Empty shot glasses hit the table as one.

"Billy," Soapy said, "run on back to my house and fetch the Winchester." It was time to finish the vigilante business once and forever.

275

Then he'd see to the woman and prepare for her coronation. "Charlie, what was the take from that miner who stirred this all up?"

"Twenty-eight hundred dollars."

"Henceforth, there's a twenty-eight hundred dollar bounty on the head of Frank Reid. Severed from the body. Cut the head from the snake and the snake dies."

*

Reid picked up a quart of Belmont before climbing the stairs to the cell. Old Man Tripp had been on a guzzler since the Fourth of July. Considering his age and condition, guarding a defenseless nun and two babies was the perfect job.

Tripp saw the bottle of prime whiskey. Spittle seeped from the corner of his mouth. Took the bottle gladly and wordlessly motioned Frank to the cell.

The nun asked, "Do you have word of Missy?"

Before he could answer, a steamer's whistle sounded three short blasts. "The *Al-Ki*. Headed out in a couple of hours. Right now, there's a big pow-wow brewing on the wharf."

"Miss Bonteiller?"

"Was anything untoward going on with her, Sister?"

"Untoward?"

"Guess I'll say it straightaway. Some packers saw her body at the bottom of Devil's Slide."

"My God."

"No God to it. Arms still tied. She never got a fair divvy. Was tossed over like a log."

The nun wobbled. Reid caught her, eased her down onto the cot. "Sister, nothing you can do about it now. Look to yourself. This town will light up before the night's over."

"Dead?"

Reid nodded. "One leg ripped clean off. Dead for sure."

The nun jumped up and swung a fist at Reid. He let her pummel his chest until her strength faded. Then he wrapped his arms around her. "Calm it, Sister."

"You could have stopped it. You could have taken her–"

She didn't finish the thought. Not hard for Reid to tell what it was. He said, "She knew I never had that inclination for her." He pressed Missy's

276

blue hair ribbon into Bernadette's hand. "She gave it to me when she told me of her escape plan. You take it."

"She was beloved."

"She knew too much. Always said she did. Town talk says that you're going over to Soapy for good. I'll kill him first. That's a promise you can take to your God."

*

Holding sweet Poteet to her bosom, Bernadette wondered what would become of the children? Of her?

*

Soapy carried the Winchester in one hand. In the other, a bottle of champagne. He stormed through Clancy's, the saloon as empty as a cemetery at midnight, and out the back door to the stairs. At the top, he hollered, "Tripp, open up."

*

The Colonel stumbled into Bernadette's cell. She didn't know what to make of him. His vest was mis-buttoned. His shirttail hung over two pistols jammed into his belt. He carried, *God forgive us*, her Winchester and a bottle of spirits. Outside, the shouts of men racing toward the wharf breached the dark night. Truly, something was welling up.

"This," he said, hoisting the bottle, "is a 100-year old bottle of Mont-Saint-Michel. He produced a slim pen-knife, slit the seal and gripped the cork in his smooth hand. "In the joints and whorehouses, I make my boys pop the corks. All for show." He twisted ever-so-slowly. "In the world's fine establishments, never a sound is made. Champagne is opened hush quietly. The release of the bouquet is saved for the aeration." He poured several drops onto his fingertips and touched Poteet's forehead, then Annabelle's. He sipped from the bottle and passed it to her.

"I shouldn't."

"For your daughters."

What did he mean? The champagne tickled her tongue. She was looking at Annabelle and Poteet Bleu, yet thinking of her two friends lying at the base of Devil's Slide.

"I intend to make you Queen of the Klondyke. Bigger than any woman in Creede, bigger even than Mattie Silks in Denver. Stay here tonight. You'll be out after the shooting."

277

31. Lies

In the eyes of the Lord, Bernadette had sinned mortally. She was a fallen woman, a harlot, an adulteress. No circumstance could assuage that fact. Not only had she sinned, she caused her friends' deaths. God should punish her doubly. She deserved no less. Did she make her commitment to the Colonel to save Missy's future or to save her own life? Could there be two answers?

On her toes, she peered onto Broadway. Stragglers with torches and guns moved toward the wharf until the street was empty. She crooned to the babies. The thought of going to the Colonel roiled in her stomach. The choice had been hers and she'd made the wrong one.

*

Soapy's hour was at hand. He double-checked his Bisley and the waist guns, and levered a cartridge into the Winchester. Bowers and Billy Saportas loaded pistols. As on the night they were going to hang John Fay, the townsfolk had mustered themselves into a mutiny. Soapy had faced them down then, he'd do it again. They were sheep, acting like wolves. Not for long.

He started down the boardwalk toward the wharf, crossed the street to look up at the cell window. Only days before he had gloried in the July Fourth festivities–the Governor, the parade, his proud Skaguay Militia. Now, he faced an Armageddon. Could it be, somehow, that the nun had caused it all? He raised her Winchester over his head in a mock salute.

"Colonel! Colonel!"

It was the Widow Pullen, dragging along an unfamiliar gent.

"Colonel, this is my husband."

Husband? Soapy stopped. One and all had called her *Widow* Pullen since she'd arrived.

"Widow Pullen, I–" He stumbled his words. Now was not the time for this conversation. He was closing in on the mob. He didn't need tinhorns around, but folks were watching him.

She saved him embarrassment. "I only let on to being a widow lady. I thought I'd get less trouble that way in this new land."

"Probably wise," he said. "I'm pleased to meet you, Sir."

Her husband appeared dumbstruck in the presence of Colonel Jefferson R. Smith.

278

"Colonel," Mrs. Pullen said, "he just lit from the *Al-Ki* this night. I want him to join up here with me to buy Billy Moore's homestead down by the wharf. It would be perfect for a hotel."

Another woman who wouldn't go away. "Yes?"

"Would you be interested in investing? I promise you it would be a first-class establishment to make you proud, complete with a restaurant I was thinking of calling *The Colonel's Table*."

Bowers looked around, his eyes dashing from the excited woman to the boisterous wharf. Billy Saportas handed Soapy a whiskey bottle, then put both hands on his gun butts. Soapy took a drink. "A fine idea. Perhaps we could speak tomorrow. Right now, the town awaits."

"Whatever you say, Colonel."

He shook the man's hand and watched the couple walk off. To Billy Saportas he said, "Be ready, but I get Frank Reid."

They continued toward the wharf, Soapy thinking, *Widow* Pullen. Are there no honest people left?

*

"They're coming, sure as you're a foot tall," John Stewart said to Reid and the three men at the entrance to the wharf. Behind them, stretched out along the wharf, vigilantes and citizens stood armed with rifles, shotguns, pistols, pitchforks and hoes.

The *Al-Ki*, tethered to the end of the dock, waited for her departure, her steam engines vibrating the entire wharf.

"How many?" Reid asked.

"Soapy, Billy Saportas and Bowers at the head. Them Fuller brothers and the rest of the gang behind. Maybe thirty."

"Alert the boys in the back of the pack. Us four will try to turn 'em. If it works, we'll have the meeting. If not, no telling."

Turn them? Frank figured the odds were on his side. Bunched up on the wharf, his vigilantes had nowhere to run. They'd have to fight. Soapy's cutthroats might scatter. Frank had fought Indians and killed more than one white man. If this came to a shootout, Frank would be first to the trigger. He loosened his .45 in its holster, lifted it once, twice, three times. Saw the brim of Soapy's parson's hat in the torchlight.

*

The *Al-Ki's* whistle sounded three times again. Bernadette had made up her mind–again. No time for prayer. Outside, hooting could be heard from

279

the wharf. She needed to job Mister Tripp into opening her cell door, and needed something with which to knock him on the head if he took the bait. Missy's heavy moose hide poke! She batted it into her hand for practice. In the excitement, no one would miss her if she escaped, so long as Tripp did not knell the alarm. She again smacked the pouch into her hand.

Curling into a ball, she clutched her stomach and retched loud enough so that Mister Tripp would think she was sick. She gagged and coughed until he spoke up in a drunken slur. "You hush in there."

"Please, Tripp. Please take me to the privy. I'm awful sick and soon will be spilling my innards all over the cell."

"No," was all he said. "Trouble brewing in the streets."

"Please, Sir, if I get stomach sick, you'll have to smell it all night. It'll keep the babies awake and crying." Bernadette nudged Annabelle. She responded with a wondrous wail.

Tripp's chair creaked. He slipped the key into the lock and bent to examine her. She knocked him on the head. He slumped to his knees and she hit him three times more, two solid blows on the side of his head and one to the jaw. The last one separated him from two of his teeth. Not a fair trade for her eight lost, but she took fleeting satisfaction nonetheless.

She slipped the gun belt from his waist. He tried to speak, scaring her so that she drew the revolver and pointed it at his head. He struggled to turn over. As he mouthed words to her, she thought about shooting him. No sound came from his mouth, yet his big eyes never left her. He was helpless. No shooting necessary. She stripped off the black shift, mindless of her nakedness. Tripp's eyes whitened at the vision. He reached a shaky old hand to her. She hit him with the poke of nuggets and pulled on the nurse's dress, then donned the uniform hat and lowered its brim over her eyes. She moved the babies to the hallway floor, then tore the black shift into strips, stuffing Tripp's mouth. She bound his hands and feet. When she locked the cell, she was careful to take the latchkey.

*

Reid and his men blocked the entrance to the wharf. "You'll come no further, Soapy Smith. This ain't a meeting for you."

"I go where I please," Soapy said, the rifle resting on his shoulder.

"You don't often carry a Winchester. I recognize it."

"The rifle and its rightful owner now belong to me. Stand away, Frank." Soapy lowered the rifle's barrel as if to use it as a broom to sweep

Reid aside. Reid backhanded the barrel, drew his .45. Soapy fired. Reid shot into Soapy's chest. Once. Twice. The parson's hat flew from Soapy's head; he slumped to the dock.

Reid gripped his hip and fell. "I got him, boys."

*

The *Al-Ki* steamed from the wharf. Torches still lighted the mass of men milling about. On a bench in the steamer's stern, the babies slept comfortably in Bernadette's arms, lulled by the engines steady pumping.

A well-dressed gentleman in a bowler neared. "Skaguay is a cruel town. Two men faced off in a pistol fight this very night. One died instantly."

Bernadette removed the uniform hat, but kept her face in the shadows. "Indeed." She wished not to have a dialog with anyone, yet was hungry for the news.

The man smiled and pointed toward her hair. "Fetching blue ribbons."

Bernadette said nothing.

"I see by your uniform that you're a nurse."

"Yes, Sir."

"And these are your babies?" He chucked Annabelle under the chin.

"Yes, Sir." He seemed a gentlemanly sort.

Pointing to her nugget cross, he said, "You are a woman of strong religious beliefs?"

"I . . . we . . . ." She was unsure of her answer.

"Permit my boldness," he said. "Did you lose your man?"

"Yes."

"My condolences." He doffed his bowler.

Bernadette merely nodded, then looked to his face. Yes, a kindly man.

"The Alaska District is no place for such a fine lady. Nor for me. I gave up a lucrative dental practice to venture north. The ruckus in camp this night caused me to climb right back on the boat. I'll return from whence I came and begin anew."

"New beginnings are not necessarily setbacks."

"Will you be needing a position in Seattle?"

In truth, Bernadette hadn't thought much of what she'd need after her escape. "I will," she said, keeping her lips as tightly closed as possible. She thought of Miss Bonteiller and raised her index finger just noticeably.

"May I take the seat next to you?"

281

She nodded her head. Poteet Bleu reached up to Bernadette's gold cross.

END

About the Author

Bill Miles has lived as far south as McMurdo, Antarctica, after spending 35 years in Alaska at jobs ranging from truck driver and bartender to advertising executive and legislator. Along the way, he's been a sky-diver, snowmobile racer, boxer and pilot.

His fiction has been published in numerous literary journals, and his articles have appeared in the *Anchorage Daily News, the Anchorage Times, the Chicago Tribune, and the Los Angeles Times Book Review.* Additionally, his short story, *Dancing with Mrs. Remarque* was nominated for a Pushcart Prize, and his collection of short fiction, *Alaska Unsalted* was nominated for a Hemingway/PEN Foundation Award.

Made in the USA
San Bernardino, CA
27 December 2015